Who was my mother?

Rokey, a poor orphan, has lived his entire life sheltered within the walls of the Noble Contemplative Monastery. Growing up, he never dreamt anything would haunt him more than the riddle of his parents' identity. But at seventeen, Rokey is discovering that while his roommate, Ely, can think only of girls, his own feelings draw him toward other boys instead. Soon the question of whether or not he is a "samer" is occupying his mind to the exclusion of all else. But when a tragedy results in his expulsion from the only home he has ever known, and an unknown enemy begins trying to kill him, Rokey's mind abruptly returns to the mystery of his parentage. Solving that puzzle, he determines, could mean the difference between life and death.

On the road, Rokey soon meets up with a charming elf named Flaskamper. Captivated by the handsome young exile, the elf promptly volunteers his help, as well as that of his three unlikely companions. Before long, the five become swept up in the effort to solve the riddle of Rokey's origins, finding out who is trying to kill him, and why. Along the way, Rokey endures some harsh lessons about disappointment and betrayal, but also delights in the joy and excitement of first love.

Foiled in initial attempts, Rokey's enigmatic foe escalates the attacks. As the young orphan and his new-found friends pursue the trail of clues that leads them across the land of Firma, they find themselves battling an ever-deadlier array of assassins. When they finally do uncover the truth, it is in the last place Rokey had ever expected to find it.

Book One of
The Chronicles of Firma

Orphan's Quest

Pat Nelson Childs

GLYNWORKS PUBLISHING

Copyright © 2007 by Pat Nelson Childs
Cover Design by Gregory A. Porter
Cover Art by Karen Petrasko

Published in the United States of America by Glynworks Publishing, Dixfield, Maine.

ISBN: Hardcover   978-0-9795912-0-4
        Softcover   978-0-9795912-1-1
        E-book   978-0-9795912-4-2

Library of Congress Control Number: 2007927636

To order additional copies of this book, contact:
Glynworks Publishing
orders@glynworkspublishing.com

For Vicki –

She will live forever in the hearts of her friends.

Acknowledgments

I want to extend my heartfelt thanks to all the people who helped me whip this novel into shape: Jessica Baldwin, Pete Brown, Glynda Childs, Michael Gray, Laura Maurer, Casey McCarter and Rick Reynolds. Thanks to Matt Mallon for being my cover model (he's Rokey). Very special thanks to my uncle, Louis Charity, who proofread the final galley, and to my friend Heather Phillips, who was on board with me the entire time – from the first draft to the last revision. I couldn't have done it without you, guys.

Two Quick Notes About Time on Firma

I.

Firma has no clocks, as we know them. The citizens there (those who use measuring devices at all) employ various types of candles and oil lamps that are made to burn at a constant and easily measured rate. These devices are standardized throughout most of Firma.

As far as the terminology goes, it is very simple:

> 1 mark = 1/20 of a day
>
> 1 minmark = 1/50 of a mark
>
> 1 tik = 1/50 of a minmark

In other words, there are 50 tiks (about one Earth second) in a minmark, 50 minmarks (about one Earth minute) in a mark and 20 marks (about one Earth hour) in a day. Two other terms used are quartermark (1/4 of a mark) and halfmark (1/2 a mark).

Denizens of Firma also use mark glasses and minmark glasses, which are filled with a particular amount of fine sand. When the glass is turned over, the sand inside takes a fixed amount of time (normally a minmark, quartermark, halfmark or mark) to run from top to bottom.

The lengths of days, months and years are slightly different on Firma than on Earth, but not so different as to require technical specificity.

II.

The Faerie term *moonsround*, refers to a period of approximately 29 days, or the amount of time that passes during one full phase of the moon. Unlike Earth's months, a moonsround on Firma has a fixed number of days. But Firma's months, like those on Earth, differ somewhat in the number of their days.

Pat Nelson Childs

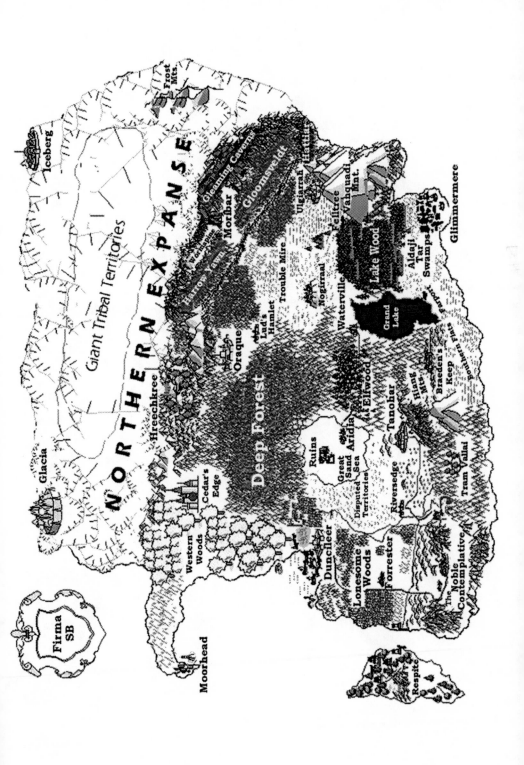

Prologue

T welve men in black robes stood in a wide circle in the large, damp chamber. It was very dark; only four torches burned in sconces at the four corners of the room, and the grey stone walls absorbed most of the light they gave off.

"Kratu hah manna
Kratu hah manna..."

They chanted their mantra softly, as they awaited the High Lord's entrance.

In the center of the room was a sarcophagus, made of the same grey stone as the walls. There was no lid; one could plainly see the bones lying inside – a large, nearly complete skeleton. Only the right femur and the skull were missing, just as they had been for centuries. Today, however, that was going to change. Today they would move one step closer to their objective, the driving ambition that was their entire reason for being.

On the east wall of the room, a door swung open, and a single figure entered. He looked just like the others, dressed in the same black robe. The one difference was that while the other men wore their cowls up, hiding their individual identities, this man, the High Lord, wore his hood down in order to accommodate his large headpiece and mask. It was a hideous thing, a large, exaggerated skull formed entirely, it was said, from black leather that had been soaked in sacrificial blood. It had been the High Lord's badge of office for centuries.

The High Lord carried an object reverently in front of him – a large femur bone, *the* femur bone. He circled the room, giving each of the twelve men a chance to lean down and kiss the precious object, then took his place on the lower right hand side of the sarcophagus, at the spot where the bone was to be placed. The room virtually hummed with excitement. It had been three centuries since the last placement ceremony. This ritual marked the high point of the life of each man in the room, including the High Lord.

The mantra changed, grew more intense – urgent. From a different door came another figure, identical to the others. In front of him walked a boy of perhaps ten. He was naked, and walked with a certain unsteadiness. The man behind him – a high priest – guided his movements. The boy's eyes were wide and glassy – one of the effects of the infusion of terrifour root he had been given to drink earlier. It also made him calm, and suggestible.

Man and boy took their place at the head of the sarcophagus. The men gathered around closer. Two of them took hold of the boy, one grasping each arm, as the high priest took a step back, and produced a scroll from the folds of his robe. The mantra stopped as he unrolled it and began to read. When he had finished, the chant started again, stronger and faster. The men began to stomp their feet to its rhythm. The boy stood silently, seemingly oblivious to all the commotion around him. The High Lord leaned forward and carefully placed the femur bone in its proper place. The foot stomping grew louder, as did the chant.

"Kratu hah manna
Kratu hah manna
Kratu hah manna..."

From the belt of his robe, the high priest produced a tiny dagger, a beautiful thing carved in some bygone era from a piece of solid obsidian. He grasped the boy by his light brown hair, pulled his head back, and with a swift motion, drew back and plunged the little blade into a precise spot on the boy's neck. The boy's eyes widened even more, and he tried to pull free, but the other two held him fast. Blood began to spray out over the sarcophagus, drenching the bones therein. The high priest carefully turned the head of the struggling youth, aiming the spurting blood carefully so that it covered the entire surface of the skeleton.

At last, the bleeding ceased, and the lad's body slumped. The priest replaced the little dagger in his belt, scooped the now lifeless boy up into his arms, and left the room the same way he had entered.

A new chant began, starting low, and building, more and more, until the pitch bordered on mania.

> "Cyure ato nuedas
> Cyure ato nuedas
> Cyure ato nuedas..."

Only one of the robed men felt a twinge of sorrow over the event they had just witnessed. As the priest disappeared through the door, he looked upon the bloody bones in the sarcophagus, and offered up a small, silent prayer – for his son.

Part One

Chapter 1:

Hunter's Moon

The cock crowed. The sun had just begun to creep above the Emerald Mountains. The autumn days still bore the sweetness of summer, but in the nighttime, cold air now swept over the peaks and high hills, leaving a crispness on the morning breeze. It wafted through the window of a dormitory room, and touched the faces of the two figures sleeping there. One of them yawned and sat up, shivering a bit as the bedcovers slid down and bared his torso. He stretched, flung back the grey woolen blanket and swung himself out of bed. Naked, and immediately chilled, he quickly headed for the basin to wash. The water, too, was ice cold, and he hurried through his ablutions so that he could dress.

This was Ely, a novice of the Brotherhood of the Noble Contemplative. He was a strapping lad of 17, with short brown hair, hazel eyes, and a wide, handsome face flawed only by a nose slightly crooked from a childhood break. Ely pulled on his muslin shorts and donned his robe, the cobalt blue color worn by all novices. Then he turned his attention to the still-sleeping figure in the other bed.

"Hey sleepy head," he said, giving the bed leg a kick. "Hey, Rokey! You're going to be late...again."

The other boy groaned and opened his eyes.

"Yes, Mother," he grumbled, and struggled out of bed. He was slightly shorter than the other boy, but similarly well-built. His shoulder-length hair was black as midnight; his eyes a deep chocolate brown. Where Ely's chest was already covered with dark, downy hair, Rokey's was completely smooth.

"I'd wait for you," Ely told him, "but it's my turn to change the candles and refill the incense before meditation starts."

"That's alright," Rokey answered, splashing himself with the icy water. "I'll be along directly."

"You'd better," Ely joked, "or you may find yourself on dung duty again."

Rokey threw a towel at him as he ducked out the door. As he combed his hair, Rokey walked over to the window. The sun was well up now, and the sky was clear except for a few wispy white clouds. It was going to be a beautiful day.

In spite of his tardiness, he took the time for his usual morning stretch, then hurriedly dressed in his own shorts and blue robe, and headed out the door.

*   *   *

The Brotherhood of the Noble Contemplative had existed in the land of Firma for over a thousand years. Perched atop the Emerald Mountain range, it was a secular monastery, open to males of all religious (or non-religious) persuasions. What bound the brothers together was the commitment to a philosophy of personal betterment, both physically and mentally. Novices coming into the Contemplative studied a variety of subjects ranging from geography to poetry to swordsmanship. At the end of the novitiate, a period of 5 to 12 years depending on one's age and prior experience, they took the Vow of Brotherhood and became full-fledged members of the Contemplative. At that point, one could choose to stay and focus on meditation, a particular field of study, or the day-to-day functions of the monastery. Alternatively, many brothers served in townships and kingdoms throughout the land as diplomats, elite guards and financial advisors. The skills and high moral character of the Brotherhood were known and respected throughout Firma. Many orphaned boys were brought to the monastery, for it offered a brighter alternative to the often squalid and always overcrowded orphanages in most kingdoms.

Rokey was one such orphan. He had been brought to the Brotherhood as a young child and raised by the brothers. He was well schooled in a wide variety of disciplines, math and geography, as well as hand-to-hand combat and swordsmanship. Now 17, he was in his final year of his novitiate. That following spring, he would start his preparatory year, a period during which he would be readied to take his final vows and choose his vocation. To the novices, very little was known about this year. Its curriculum was a closely held secret, one that had been strictly kept for centuries.

Rokey sped along the colonnade toward the academics hall. He was, indeed, late for his comparative religion class. Brother Crinshire was waiting with the door open, tapping his foot and wearing his usual scowl.

"I apologize, brother", Rokey said breathlessly, "I was –,"

"Spare me the excuse, young man," he said curtly. "I am docking you ten points on today's lesson, and if this tardiness continues, you will fail this class."

"Ten points!" Rokey protested. "Brother the bell has only just rung!"

"Do not argue with me," Crinshire snapped, "or you will find yourself in detention as well."

He hustled Rokey inside and closed the door behind them. Rokey took his seat, cursing inwardly. Brother Crinshire was never a pleasant person. Rokey often wondered why he had chosen the Brotherhood, and why the Brotherhood had accepted him. He seemed always unhappy in his work, delighting only in inflicting petty torments on his young charges. He had always enjoyed his comparative religion classes in prior years. This year he was struggling with both the personality and the teaching style of his instructor. He would consider himself fortunate if he could just finish the class with a passing score.

After morning classes, it was time for the senior novices to begin their proctorships. This month, Rokey was in charge of monitoring the younger boys at their gardening chores. He had enjoyed this proctorship, for he liked being outdoors, especially on a fine day such as this, and was somewhat sorry that the month was at an end. Today was his last day in the garden, and the day after tomorrow, new proctorships would be posted. Before that, though, came the Hunter's Moon Festival.

The first moon of autumn was known as the Hunter's Moon. Each year at that time, the Brotherhood and the villagers celebrated the approaching harvest with a festival. It was an event that all the brothers, as well as the inhabitants of the adjacent Noble Village, looked forward to with great anticipation. Casks of the monastery's finest honey ale would be tapped. The cooks at the Contemplative had been hard at work all week long, producing an impressive variety of foods, cakes and confections. Music and dancing would start early and go on late into the night.

There was little for the proctor to do in the gardens today, so Rokey found his thoughts drifting to festivals past, and to hopes of a mild autumn and winter this year. Soon the bell sounded. The boys filed past, handing in their gardening implements as they went, and made for the dining hall. When they had all gone, Rokey closed up the gardening shed. The younger boys ate earlier than the older ones, so Rokey had one more class before lunch – swordsmanship. Brother

Barrow, who was his personal mentor as well as his swordsmanship teacher, was waiting for him on the training ground. At this point in his training, the lessons were one-on-one. Brother Barrow, a brawny, barrel-chested man with a wild mop of short, red hair, was an excellent swordsman, and Rokey's own skills had improved greatly under his tutelage. Today he was holding a bastard sword, the weapon at which Rokey's skill was still the weakest. He groaned inwardly.

"Don't give me that face!" Brother Barrow chastised him. "The bastard sword's your shortcoming. You need the practice and you know it. Now choose your weapon."

"Yes Brother." He was right, of course, but Rokey was no happier for it.

He went to the weapons rack. All the swords were crafted by the Brotherhood and even the practice weapons were finely made. He chose a sword, a bastard type similar to Brother Barrow's, slipped the leather safety sheath over the blade, and returned to face his instructor. They worked for a while on his recoveries, arcs and parries. Rokey found the bastard sword difficult, not only because it was heavier than a regular longsword, but also because of the hand-and-a-half grip, which allowed one to use it with either one or two hands. While that could be a great advantage in battle, it also made it more challenging to master.

At the end of the lesson, they bowed to one another and returned the swords to the rack.

"You did well today, Rokey," Brother Barrow told him. "I'm pleased with your progress. You have the makings of a fine swordsman."

"Thank you Brother," Rokey said, flattered. Barrow was not one to bestow empty compliments.

It was now time for Rokey and the other boys his age to eat lunch. He trotted off to the bathhouse for a quick wash, his mentor's praise still ringing in his ears. After Brother Crinshire's stinging rebuke that morning, he had been in need of a boost.

* * *

Later that day, Rokey and Ely were in their room, preparing for the festival. Ely had slicked his hair back with vegetable grease and splashed himself with musk which he insisted 'drives the lasses mad with desire.' He offered some to Rokey who politely declined. He also put on regular clothing, which novices were allowed to do for such festivals. Rokey was still in his robe. He owned no regular clothing.

"Tonight is my night, Rokey," Ely said. "I've had my eye on this little milkmaid these past several months. She always makes it a point to lace her sandals just as I'm walking by. You know what that means." He nudged Rokey in the ribs.

"No, what?" Rokey asked.

"She wants me. You know...she bends over, ties the sandals, shows off her wares a bit. It's the oldest come-hither there is. Well tonight is the night. I'm going to show her what I'm made of."

He bucked his hips suggestively.

"Good luck, lover boy," Rokey said, shaking his head.

"And what of you?" Ely said with a smirk. "You never speak of lasses. You must have your eye on someone."

"Must I?"

"Well for pity's sake Rokey, you're 17, same as I," Ely observed. "You must think about getting it sometimes. Myself, I think about it *all* the time. I get so randy at times I'd do it with a goat if you put some lip rouge on it. Tonight I plan to sweep this lass straight off her feet."

"I'm sure that will come as excellent news to the goats," Rokey quipped.

Ely slugged him in the arm. When he had finished his preparations, they left the room and made their way to the main courtyard. For the festival, two long rows of booths had been set up down each side of the main courtyard. The booths were manned by brothers or villagers, who gave away, bartered or sold sweets, milk, ale and wine, tools, clothing and foods of every description. There were meatrolls and cheeses, sausages on a stick, liverpaste sandwiches and steaming hot vegetable stew. Desserts included cakes, redberry pies and candy made from the spun sap of sugar trees. Of course, the most popular booths were the ones that dispensed the ales, meads and wines. People came not only from the Noble Village, but also from kingdoms and territories as far away as Tanohar and Duncileer to take part in the festivities. Even though it was early, the musicians were already playing and several couples were dancing merrily on the large canvas square that had been staked down for that purpose.

The two boys had just grabbed honey seed cakes at the first booth when Ely spotted a pretty young blonde girl across the yard. He smacked Rokey on the bottom and headed her way. This was obviously the milkmaid he had spoken of. Rokey again wished him good luck. He wandered for a while among the booths and revelers, enjoying the jovial atmosphere. Then he stopped at the booth giving out honey ale. Brother Tomshire, a large and jolly man with a perpetually red nose, which suggested he partook regularly of his wares, was cheerfully manning the tap.

"Rokey my boy!" he bellowed happily. "Good to see ye. Here now, have a pint and enjoy." He drew off a frothy mug and handed it to Rokey, who accepted it gratefully. He lingered a while, chatting with the portly monk.

"So what are yer plans in the Brotherhood, Rokey?" he asked. "Have ye given it any thought yet?"

"I have brother," Rokey answered, "but I haven't yet made a decision. I'm partial to astronomy, but I also love illustration."

"What about the guard?" Tomshire asked. "Many young men your age are yearning to get out from behind these four walls and travel abroad. The guard makes that possible. It can also open a great many doors for a man with brains and ambition."

"I don't know, Brother," Rokey answered with a shake of his head, "I'm quite content right here at the Contemplative. I don't find it confining at all. I find it rather comforting. I think I may be destined for a quiet life of meditation and scholarly pursuits."

"That may well be," the brother agreed. "The world's too big for some, that's a fact. But there's still plenty of time, plenty of time. No hurry, no hurry. I was only days from my vows when I finally made my choice. Some of the brothers don't decide until long after they've sworn. And of course, one can always change one's mind later on. A career choice is not a millstone."

"I fancy I will have a better idea as my preparatory year progresses," Rokey said with a smile.

"P'raps ye will. P'raps ye will," he said, and then leaned closer to Rokey. His face grew hard and serious, a rarity for the normally jocund brother.

"But mark this," he said in a conspiratorial tone. "You're approaching what might well be the hardest year of your life, young son. Soon you're going to learn that there's considerable more to the Brotherhood than you know."

"Aye, such as what brother?" asked Rokey, his curiosity aroused.

"In good time, you'll find out," he said, "All I can say is what I've said, and that was probably too much." Abruptly he stood up straight and laughed. "But let's not fill this fine autumn eve with whispers and mysteries. Drink up and have another. I'll join ye!"

Later, blissfully intoxicated and full of roasted venison and new potatoes, Rokey stood over by the stables, watching the dancers twirl. He was not much of a dancer himself, but he enjoyed watching the couples strut and spin. As he stood there, swaying with the music, he was joined by a pretty young red-haired girl. Rokey knew only her name, Barrett, and the fact that her father was the village tanner.

"Enjoying the festivities, Brother?" she asked.

"Aye, very much," he answered, "but as you see miss," he indicated his blue robe, "I'm not a brother yet. My final vows are still more than a year hence. Til then I am simply a novice. My name is Rokey"

"A novice? I see. So tell me Rokey - are you a novice in every respect?" she asked with a sly grin.

It took Rokey a moment to grasp her meaning, then he blushed deeply. She had been teasing him and he had fallen right into it.

"Barrett, that is hardly a suitable topic for relative strangers," he told her.

"Ah, so you knows me already, do you." She drew her shoulders back, showing off her generous bosom.

"Well, my handsome novice, we needn't remain strangers." Her long fingernails lightly scraped the back of his neck, giving him goose bumps. "Why not come with me to the stables, and.... show me how you ride"

"I, I – ," Rokey stammered, completely at a loss for words. Barrett leaned closer and whispered in his ear.

"I see you out running some days," she cooed, "with nothin' but those little shorts on. You cut a fine figure, covered in sweat, your muscles rippling..."

Rokey's knees were trembling, his stomach fluttered with butterflies.

"Barrett, I'm...I'm -," he wasn't sure what he was.

"Nervous? No need to be, love. I'll be very... gentle." Her tongue slipped into his ear.

Rokey started violently. His half finished ale splashed over them both. Barrett squealed in surprise and annoyance.

"I'm sorry Barrett. It was an accident, really I, p-please excuse me."

Rokey sped off and merged with the folks gathered near the musicians. He was hot with embarrassment and enormously relieved when he had finally put the crowd between himself and the stables.

He avoided Barrett for the rest of the evening, and tried to have a good time, but the incident had dampened his enjoyment of the festival.

That night he lay awake, wondering about his earlier reaction. Why had he behaved that way? Barrett was a pretty enough girl. She had caught the eye, and perhaps more, of several of the other young men. And there was certainly nothing wrong with what she had suggested. Brothers had been losing their innocence in the stables since the Contemplative began. Something had just been – had just not felt right. He hoped that Barrett wouldn't spread the news of this throughout the village. He would be a laughing stock. At last, exhaustion and ale conspired to calm him into a restless sleep.

* * *

Despite a poor night's rest, Rokey was up early the next day. His mood had not much improved, so he decided to go for a morning run. The day after the festival was a day of rest, and all in the Contemplative were free to enjoy their own pursuits. Rokey saw that Ely had not returned home the previous night.

"Well," he grumbled, "at least one of us can successfully manage *that* pursuit." Then he pulled on his muslin shorts, tied his hair back into a ponytail and set out for the road.

The day was a fine one, though brisk. Rokey's sweat washed away what remained of the previous night's ales and indignities, and his mood improved. He even began to sing as he ran. Soon he approached the outskirts of the Noble Village, where homes began to dot the landscape. As he rounded a bend, a sudden, sharp sound drew his attention. He turned toward the source of the noise and stopped abruptly.

At the back of one house a few hundred yards off, a young man was chopping wood. He was shirtless; his muscular arms bulged as he hefted the heavy ax over and over. His reddish blond hair was wet with sweat, which ran in rivulets down his well-formed chest and sleek abdomen. His breeches fit like a second skin, barely containing his full thighs and –,"

"Rokey."

He snapped to and realized that he had been staring, totally engrossed, and had not heard Barrett ride up behind him.

"Barrett," said Rokey, "sorry I didn't hear you. Listen, I'm sorry about last night…"

"I forgive you," she told him, "but you might have just told me the truth up front. Here I was left all last evening wonderin' what was wrong with me."

"Told you what?" he asked.

"Well that you don't fancy girls, 'a course," she replied.

Rokey started to protest, but she cut him off.

"Don't be silly," said Barrett. "I saw you just then with yer eyes glued to me brother Jar. Cut's quite a fine figure himself, don't he? If his brain were only half the size of his willy, he'd be right dangerous."

"Barrett, really -,"

"I shouldn't bother yerself with Jar though," she explained. "He only fancies girls. The bigger the tits and the smaller the brains, the more Jar fancies 'em. 'Tis only fitting though; two-syllable words give him a bit of a hitch as well."

Once again, the tanner's daughter had rendered him utterly speechless.

Barrett shook her head.

"Humph, maybe the two of you have something in common at that," she remarked.

She pressed her horse forward and started to ride on.

"B-Barrett!" Rokey managed at last. The girl paused and turned back to him.

"Don't worry yourself, handsome," Barrett assured him. "I see no reason to keep it a secret, but if that's your wish, I'll not spill the beans. Been nice chatting with you."

She spurred the horse and galloped off toward the house. Rokey turned and sprinted back to the Contemplative as though a demon were chasing him.

* * *

Rokey awoke, sweaty and aroused. He had been dreaming about Jar. He thrashed around, untangling himself from his blanket and stumbled to the basin. He splashed some of the cold water over his face and body, until his urge began to subside. Ely stirred and sat up.

"What's wrong, Rokey?" he asked.

"Ely," said Rokey, "do I seem like a samer to you?"

"Rokey," Ely answered grumpily, "that is not a question I want to be asked by a naked man in the middle of the night."

"C'mon I'm serious," Rokey insisted. "Do I act different, talk different... like a girl?"

"Rokey all samers don't act like lasses," Ely told him. "Look at brother Neesuch. He's tough as a bear."

"Brother Neesuch is a –,"

"Certainly," Ely said. "You didn't know that? And he's not the only one. There's Brother Franklin, oh and Clive, the blacksmith's apprentice – "

"How do you know all this?" Rokey asked.

"It's no secret, for pity's sake. Have you seriously given no thought at all to sex before now?" Ely asked incredulously.

"Not really," Rokey replied, shaking his head. "I guess I'm a late bloomer."

"Well, what's bringing all this on all of a sudden?" asked Ely. "Did you have...an experience with someone?"

"No. Well, not exactly." Rokey told Ely everything, about Barrett, his run that day, and his dream about Jar.

"Well," said Ely. "Sure sounds like you're a samer to me. Not that I'm an expert," he added hastily. "But that Barrett – *whew* – she could raise the dead, if you follow my drift."

"I don't want to be a samer," Rokey said miserably. "I just want to be normal."

"As far as I understand these things," his friend explained, "you don't really get to choose. Besides, who's to judge what's normal anyways? You? Look Rokey, I'm not really the best fellow to talk to about this. I've got nothing against samers mind you, but I'm strictly a ladies' man. I've got no experience with the issue. Maybe you ought to talk to your mentor, or better yet, brother Neesuch. I'm sure he'd be much more of a help."

"Gods, I couldn't," Rokey told him. "I'd be too embarrassed."

"Why?" Ely asked. "You told me."

"That's different," Rokey replied. "You're my best friend. You still are, right?"

"Of course, stupid," Ely answered. "But I won't lie to you. I'm going to feel a bit more self-conscious running around bare-arsed in here."

"I'd never feel that way about you," said Rokey.

"And why in blazes not might I ask?" Ely demanded mischievously. "What's wrong with me exactly?"

"That would be like having the hots for my own brother," Rokey explained.

"Well, that's a relief I must say," said the other boy. "I didn't look forward to having to kick your arse out of my bed in the wee marks of the morn."

Ely fluffed up his pillow and lay back down.

Rokey got back into his own bed.

"Thanks Ely," he said.

"Don't mention it," Ely muttered. "Now shut the devil up and let me get some sleep, will ya?"

Rokey lay his head back down. The events of the past two days kept replaying in his mind, but eventually he fell into a deep and, thankfully, dreamless sleep.

Chapter 2:

Assignment

T hings began normally enough the next day. Ely said nothing about the previous night's conversation. He just slapped Rokey on the bottom as he left the room. Rokey knew this was his way of reassuring him that their relationship had not suffered. He was grateful to have such a good friend, but still felt unsettled, and adrift. Things were happening too fast. Ely was right: before two days ago, he had given little thought to sex. Now it seemed suddenly to be the only thing he could think about. He left for his daily meditation, determined to use the time of contemplation to get his thoughts straightened out.

As it turned out, this was not to be, for instead of the usual proctor, Brother Neesuch himself was there to lead the mantra. Rokey studied the brother as he rang the small triangle, signaling the beginning of meditation. He estimated him to be in his mid-forties, taller than Rokey, but more slightly built. Ely's comment about him being tough as a bear had not been a reference to his physique, but to his formidable hand-to-hand combat skills. Rokey had at first found it a strange combination of specialties – meditation and unarmed combat. As he trained and improved his skills in both, however, he began to appreciate how well the two disciplines complemented one another. Now he found himself in the uncomfortable position of wondering about the brother's sexuality, and whether he could possibly gather the courage to broach the subject to him. What if he took it wrong? What if he thought Rokey was making a pass at him?

Brother Neesuch was not a bad-looking man, for his age, but Rokey would be completely mortified if he found himself fending off the amorous attentions of one of his instructors.

"You are being silly," he chided himself. If he explained himself clearly, and asked for advice, there was no reason that he should be misinterpreted. And he had always gotten on well with Brother Neesuch.

"Was that the reason?" he wondered. "Had Neesuch seen something in him long before he had begun to see it himself?"

Before he knew it, the mark had elapsed. He had done no meditating, and had not reached a decision about approaching the brother. As it happened, Neesuch stopped *him* on his way out the door.

"Rokey," he said, "I do not know where your mind was today, but it was most certainly *not* on your mantra. Pressing matters on your mind?"

Rokey thought about spilling it all – Barrett, Jar, the dream, all the questions that had been swirling furiously around inside his head since the festival. However, when he opened his mouth, none of that would come out.

"No Brother," he answered instead. "I just didn't sleep well last night – a bit groggy today. I apologize."

"No need," said the brother. "We all have our off days now and again. Just promise me that tomorrow you will try and focus on the task at hand, hmmm?"

"I will Brother," Rokey mumbled.

"Very well," said Neesuch. "On your way, and do not forget to check the new assignment list. New proctor assignments today, remember?"

"Yes I will, Brother. Thank you." Rokey left, immediately scolding himself for his cowardice. He vowed to himself that he would see Brother Neesuch the next day and ask for his advice.

His intentions affirmed, he walked across the main road to the administrative building where the new proctorship assignment list would be posted. There was already a small group of other novices there. Some were smiling with satisfaction; others were not. As he approached, Novice Karpra, a pudgy, blond-haired boy turned to him, a look of disgust on his face.

"Horse shite," he declared.

"What is it Karpra?" Rokey asked.

"*It* is what I am going to smell for the next month, that's what," Karpra told him. "I drew stable duty."

Rokey tried to hide a smile. He remembered his stint in the stables. It was not a particularly fond recollection. He reminded the unhappy lad that at least he was a proctor now, and would not have to muck out the stalls himself.

"That doesn't make the smell any better though, does it?" he responded. "I'm going to the greenhouse for some eucalyptus leaves."

"Oh, do you have a cold?" Rokey asked.

"No, I'm going to stick them up my nose." He stalked off, still muttering to himself, and Rokey moved closer to the bulletin board. He found his name, read across to the corresponding assignment and furrowed his brow in surprise. Instead of a new proctor post, it said: "Report to Brother Dalfore." That was odd. Why would the abbot's administrative assistant want to see him? He knew of no proctorships that were connected with his office. Shaking his head, he walked past the board, up the wide stone steps and into the building through the large double doors.

The administrative building housed the offices and living quarters of the abbot, the office of his administrative assistant, and the foreign affairs offices. There was also the abbot's kitchen and a banquet room in which special guests and dignitaries were entertained. The most intriguing aspect of the building, however, stood at the very end of the long slate-floored corridor. It was a large stone door, which neither Rokey nor, as far as he knew, any of the other novices had ever seen open. He had asked one of the brothers once where the door led and was told curtly that it was no concern of a novice, which of course made him all the more curious. Rumors abounded, but no novice knew its secret, for no brother would give even a hint.

Rokey knocked on the first door on the right side of the hall, the door to Brother Dalfore's office. A voice behind the door told him to enter. Inside he found the brother sitting behind a large oak desk. There were papers piled all over it and he was obviously very busy. He was surprised when the brother motioned to one of the empty chairs. It was customary for novices to stand when addressing one of the head officers, but Rokey did as he was told. Brother Dalfore got straight to the point.

"Rokey, I'm sure that you are aware that Abbot Tomasso is quite advanced in years. In recent months, he has become more and more frail, and his eyesight has all but failed. While his mind is still keen as ever, he is no longer able to fully care for himself physically. Therefore, we have decided to assign someone to be his companion and caretaker."

Dalfore paused and peered over his desk, apparently waiting for Rokey to respond in some way.

"And... am I to assist the person assigned in some way, Brother?" Rokey asked, feeling obtuse.

"No Rokey," Dalfore explained patiently, "you are to *be* the person assigned."

Rokey was stunned. He couldn't imagine why the brothers would choose a novice for such an assignment. And him, of all the novices. He was not always the most punctual, the most responsible or, he had to be honest with himself, the brightest of all potential candidates. Haltingly, he began to try to point these things out to Brother Dalfore, but the brother was having none of it. He stood and walked over to his chair.

"You underestimate yourself," he said. "We understand that you are not at the very top of your class, but you have other qualities that make you supremely suited to this task.

"May I ask, Brother, what qualities?" Rokey inquired.

Dalfore chuckled.

"Well, humility obviously," the brother responded. "But more importantly, you are a kind, caring and patient lad. Your friends think a great deal of you and describe you in the best possible terms, as do many of the brothers. You are also honest and, we believe, trustworthy. We feel confident that you are a fine choice."

"I – I don't know what to say," said Rokey. "It's an honor."

"It is more than an honor, lad," Dalfore told him. "It is a difficult and time-consuming job. You will be expected to stay with the abbot and be at his disposal morning and night, see to his every need, help him to eat, bathe, dress, and keep him from harm. It will be a laborious assignment."

"And my lessons, brother?" Rokey asked.

"You will rise and help the abbot prepare for the day," Dalfore explained, "attend your classes while he is in his office, then come and resume your care of him afterwards. Should he need you during that time, you will be summoned and excused from class. Your normal evening activities will have to be suspended while you are on this duty, but you will lose no academic credits."

"I – will certainly do my best to prove myself worthy of your trust, Brother Dalfore," Rokey assured him.

"I know you will," said the brother. "Now run along to your next class. After your lessons are finished, go and get your things and bring them here. I have arranged to have your wardrobe chest and some sleeping cushions brought into the abbot's quarters. I'm sure you will find it quite comfortable. There is a kitchen attendant on duty from breakfast until bedtime. He is familiar with the abbot's routine and preferences, but if there is anything additional you or the abbot require, you have only to ring for him."

Dalfore nodded toward the door. Rokey stood and nearly stumbled out of the office. He was dazed as he made his way to his mathematics class. In fact, he was completely flabbergasted. As far as he knew, no novice had ever been given such a mission, and even if all the things the brother had said about him were true, and he was by no means convinced of that, he still couldn't fathom why he had been the one chosen.

He was unable to concentrate on anything else for the rest of the day (would he ever be able to focus on his studies again?), and when classes were over, he headed back to the dormitory with mixed emotions. He was deeply honored at having been chosen for such an undertaking, but he was going to miss his evening astronomy and illustration electives. Even more than that, he would miss living with Ely. They had been roommates for the past four years, and during that time Rokey had come to think of him as more of a brother than a friend. It was going to be strange sharing quarters with the old abbot, but he determined that he would adjust and make the experience a rewarding and educational one.

At first, Ely thought Rokey was playing a joke on him. When Rokey finally convinced him it was true, his friend was overjoyed for him. Rokey confided his conflicting emotions.

"Are you mad?" Ely exclaimed. "Don't you realize what a feather in your cap this will be? Success in this job will put you in solid with the administration. You'll be able to sail through your prep year. I must admit to a little confusion as to why they chose *you* –"

"Why not me?" Rokey asked. Even though he had wondered the same thing, he still felt a trifle hurt.

"Now, now," said Ely. "Don't get into a snit. I know you're a prince, but let's face it mate, you are not exactly the teacher's pet these days."

"I know, I know," said Rokey. "I asked Brother Dalfore and he gave me a perfectly reasonable explanation. At least it seemed reasonable when I was sitting in his office. But with each mark that passes it seems stranger and stranger to me."

"Listen, who cares?" said Ely. "The important thing is you were chosen. A golden opportunity has fallen into your lap. Make the most of it. Come on, I'll help you pack up."

Ely helped Rokey pack his few belongings, and they exchanged a warm hug. Rokey had tears in his eyes as he left, which he knew was silly. He'd still see Ely every day. He pondered for a moment whether his feelings about Ely may be a bit more than brotherly. However he quickly dismissed the idea. He certainly appreciated Ely's physical attributes, and loved him dearly, but it was not a romantic love. Not like the dream.

Suddenly Rokey was gripped by a terrible feeling of foreboding. He stopped in his tracks and stared up into the star-filled sky. So many things had happened in the past few days, and somehow he feared even more change was in the wind. For someone content to stay at the Contemplative and study the stars for the rest of his life, all this activity and excitement were almost too much for him to handle. He *would* handle it though, take one step at a time and, what did Ely always say, *always steer your boat downstream.* With a sigh, he continued on into the darkness.

* * *

"Abbot Tomasso, where did I come from?"

They were sitting in the abbot's spacious bath, relaxing in the hot water. For Rokey, this was an amazing luxury. Although there was a communal bathhouse at the Contemplative, on most days the water was tepid, at best. One of the privileges the abbot enjoyed was a large sunken bath, warmed continuously to his specifications. Abbot Tomasso liked to make full use of this perquisite. Each night they soaked contentedly for at least a mark, after which Rokey rang for their evening chamomile tea and honey cakes. The abbot, being an independent-minded man, had not been happy about the need for a caretaker, but he had warmed to Rokey right away and took a great interest in his life and experiences at the Contemplative. When Rokey had asked him why, the abbot had explained that it had been over three score years since he had come to the Contemplative, a gangly lad of ten, eager to embrace the life of the brotherhood. Through Rokey he was able to recapture some of that freshness and enthusiasm. Additionally, his position as abbot meant that he needed to focus on the overall running of the monastery. He rarely had the time to query his young charges about their hopes and dreams for the future.

To Rokey, the past three weeks had been a dream. Things had been a bit awkward at first, especially the more personal aspects of the older man's care. Though the abbot was upset about the need for such assistance, he was never rude or cross with the young novice. Rokey had been sensitive to his feelings of embarrassment, and had allowed the man time to adjust to his presence without being too pushy. Within a week, the two had settled into an efficient and largely enjoyable routine. Abbot Tomasso began to treat Rokey like a grandson, and Rokey relished the parental attention. It was at the end of the third week that he asked the question that had been on his mind off and on for the past 15 years. He chose their nightly soak, a time that they set aside to discuss the day's events, Rokey's plans for his future in the brotherhood, philosophy, religion and a variety of other topics. The abbot had just finished a juicy account of his days as a palace guard in the far-off land of Oraque, and a young princess whose favor he had won. It seems the abbot had been quite a ladies' man in his day, and Rokey couldn't help but think of Ely and his many assignations. Tomasso had traveled extensively as a young man, taking advantage of the high demand for guards trained by the Contemplative. In his youth, he took no fewer than fifteen separate assignments, which took him from the Sea of Laribus in the West all the way to the Great Vast, the seemingly endless ocean to the East. Rokey loved these stories, and was even beginning to consider a career that would take him outside the walls of the monastery, to all of the wonderful places described by the abbot. The tales also started him thinking again about his own origins and ancestry. After an appropriate pause, he asked the question:

"Abbot Tomasso, where did I come from?"

The abbot sat with his eyes closed and said nothing for a long time. In fact, he took so long to reply that Rokey feared he might have fallen asleep. He was just about to give him a gentle shake when he began to speak.

"Well, my boy," he said. "I promised myself that when you were older I'd tell you the truth. I suppose now is as good a time as any. I'll tell you the story as we have our tea. Go and ring for it, why don't you."

Rokey stood and pulled the bell rope, then sat back down. Tea was served at nearly the same time every night, so the attendant usually had it ready. They sat and soaked in comfortable silence for several minmarks, but no one came. He rang again, but again, several minmarks past with no response.

"That's odd," Rokey muttered. "I wonder where he's gone."

"Probably forgot the time and went out to have a pipe," said the abbot. "Why don't you run in and fetch it for us. I'll be perfectly comfortable here."

"I should not leave you here alone, abbot," said Rokey. "Brother Dalfore was most specific on this point."

"Oh, Brother Dalfore is an old woman," Tomasso sputtered. "I think I can manage on my own long enough for you to boil a pot of water."

"But –"

"Go."

Reluctantly, Rokey dried himself, slipped on his Robe and left for the kitchen.

"Fine lad, that," the abbot thought to himself as he waited. "Going to be a credit to the brotherhood." He wasn't sure if he was doing him any favors telling him the truth about himself, but the old man felt he was entitled to know at least the little bit that he knew.

He shifted a bit and winced. His hip had been bothering more and more these past few days. A change in the weather must be on the way. He hoped that winter wouldn't settle in too early this year. The cold weather always wreaked havoc on his rheumatism. Spring and summer were the best months, when the aches and pains that plagued him in old age briefly relaxed their grip. He could no longer see, but he enjoyed the sounds of the birds, and the children at play, the smell of the flowers that wafted through the air, the feel of the sun on –

"Hello?" the abbot sat up, listening. "Rokey is that you?"

Silence. Had he not just heard the door? Apparently not. Tomasso, you old fool, now your ears are playing tricks on you. The abbot settled back into the hot bathwater with a sigh, and began to think about how he was going to tell Rokey the truth about his parents.

* * *

Rokey walked first to the end of the hall and opened the front door, checking for Asmor, the attendant. He was nowhere to be seen. With a shrug, he closed the door and went to the kitchen. As he put the water on and brought the tea out of the cupboard, he wondered what the abbot would tell him about his arrival at the monastery. Had his mother brought him? Had they talked? Had she told him about his father? He had so many questions he hoped the older man could answer.

The water was boiling. Rokey put the tea into the pot and poured the hot water in. While it steeped, he placed the pot and two of the abbot's fine porcelain cups onto a tray, along with two honey seed cakes. Then he picked up the tray and headed back to the abbot's quarters.

"I couldn't find Asmor," Rokey said as he backed through the doorway carrying the tray, "so I made it myself. I hope I didn't mess it – "

He turned around and stopped dead in his tracks. The abbot lay face down in the pool, motionless. The tray crashed down; the porcelain shattered into a million tiny pieces as Rokey sprinted to the bathing pool. He had no trouble pulling the old man from the water, as his weight barely exceeded 100 pounds. There were no breath signs.

"No!" Rokey cried. "Don't die. You can't die. Not like this."

With tears streaming down his face, he attempted to breathe life into him as he had been taught; first pinching the nose and holding the head back to force a breath in, then pushing rhythmically on the chest. He kept this up for as long as he could, until his arms ached and his head swam. It was no use though. The abbot was dead. For several minmarks, Rokey sat there beside the dead man, sobbing bitterly. When he had gotten control again, he got up and went to fetch Brother Pilarus, the healer. He knew it was hopeless, but it was the required protocol. He paused for a moment at the doorway, and once again the feeling of dread stole over him. It was more than the tragedy of this sudden death. It was the certainty that all of life as he had known it was about to transform. He steeled himself as best he could and stepped out into the night air.

Chapter 3:

Judgment

R okey sat in his room, watching as the morning sun began to illuminate the Emerald Mountains. He had not slept that night, nor the night before. Would he ever sleep through another night? His face was swollen and flushed with grief, and his eyes seemed hollow and empty.

Ely woke and dressed quickly. He had tried to talk to his friend, to offer some support and solace, but it had done no good, and Ely could think of nothing more to say. Three days had passed since the death of the abbot. The Brotherhood was in an uproar. Most blamed Rokey for the disaster, including Rokey himself. The high council had gone into closed session to elect a new abbot. They had asked Rokey to confine himself to his room except when absolutely necessary. They needn't have asked, for he had no desire to face his brethren.

Before leaving, Ely stood and watched his friend for a moment, trying once more to come up with something to say that would lift his spirits. With a sigh, he walked over and put his hand on Rokey's shoulder.

"I'm going to breakfast," he said. "Let me bring you something back from the kitchens."

"I'm not hungry," Rokey answered, his voice barely rising above a whisper.

"Nevertheless, you must eat." He kneeled down next to the chair. "Rokey, I know you blame yourself."

"I and everyone else," he said.

Ely shook his head.

"No, not everyone. Not me." He turned Rokey's chair to face him. "The abbot sent you on an errand," he said. "You didn't want to go, but you did what you were told. There was no reason to think that anything bad was going to happen."

"I should have taken him out of the bath first," Rokey muttered.

"Maybe so. It seems obvious now, but at the time you had no way of knowing that such a thing could happen. The abbot seemed strong enough."

"Yes," Rokey answered. "He seemed to have no trouble getting in and out by himself. He had never stumbled, or lost his footing before. That's why I cannot understand what happened. How he came to –," His voice broke. Ely took his hands.

"What happened was an accident," Ely insisted, "just a horrible accident."

"If I had only been there," he said, more to himself than to his roommate.

"If...if...if!" his friend cried. "There's always *ifs*, Rokey. We all have regrets – places we wish we'd been; things we wish we'd said. But we just have to pick ourselves up and go on. It's a terrible thing that's happened, and yes, some do blame you for it. But they don't know you as I do. They don't see how you torture yourself over this, how you would gladly swap your life for his if you could."

"I would," Rokey said.

"I know. But you cannot," said Ely. "The rest of your life is ahead of you. Forgive yourself, and others will do the same."

"Will they Ely?" Rokey asked miserably. "Will they forgive me?"

There was a knock at that moment. Ely opened the door to find a young novice standing there. Ely didn't know his name, but he had seen him working in Brother Dalfore's office.

Rokey glanced back and saw the young man talking in a low voice to Ely, who nodded and shut the door. He walked back to the window.

"The high council commands that you present yourself before them immediately, in the abbot's office," he told Rokey, who closed his eyes and shivered.

"Now I will learn what's to become of me," he said.

"They are fair men Rokey," Ely assured him. "I'm certain that they will see this for what it was."

"I hope you're right," Rokey said. "I was so looking forward to moving into my preparatory year. To be left back would be..." a tear slid down his cheek, "well, not more than I deserve."

"It is more than you deserve," Ely insisted, "for a thing that was not your fault. Look, do you want me to come with you? I could speak to them on your behalf."

Rokey stood and shook his head.

"Thank you Ely," he said, embracing him. "You are a better friend than anyone could hope to have. But I must face this on my own." He donned his robe and stopped for a moment to look in the mirror. He still looked dreadful, and felt the same way, but it was too late now. He would have to face them as he was.

A few minmarks later, he braced himself and knocked on the door of the abbot's office. It was opened by brother Jammad, a dark, quiet young man who had just taken his vows the previous year. As Rokey entered, he took stock of the men in the room. Brother Dalfore, the abbot's personal assistant was there, and brother Marinus, who was in charge of foreign affairs, brother Levinton, head of academics, brother Sitifro, master of arms and armory, and of course, his mentor, Brother Barrow. However there was one man there that he had not expected to see, and his presence made his heart sink. Sitting behind the desk, in the bright red robe of the abbot, was Brother Crinshire. Rokey could not help but gape in astonishment. Surely this was some trick, some error. Brother Crinshire, the new Abbot? It was an unbelievable, preposterous notion. Crinshire had only come to the Brotherhood five years before. He held no place on the high council, had earned no emeritus scrolls. He was a mean, petty and vindictive man. This just couldn't be!

Jammad led him forward until he was standing directly in front of the abbot's desk. His mind was whirling. He simply couldn't believe his eyes. Then Brother Crinshire spoke.

"You are surprised to see that the council has chosen me as Abbot," he said. There was that harshness in Crinshire's voice that Rokey had always disliked. He nodded his head.

"Yes, Brother," Rokey admitted. "To be truthful, I am surprised."

Crinshire smiled, but there was no warmth in it.

"It is not the habit of the High Council of the Noble Contemplative to consult the novitiate in such matters," he said with obvious disdain. "In any case, we are not here to discuss *my* competency. We are here to discuss *yours*."

The abbot cleared his throat, and his voice took on a businesslike tone.

"You were given an assignment by Brother Dalfore," he said. "The assignment was to care for the now late Abbot Tomasso, to assist him, to keep him from harm. Is that correct?"

Rokey lowered his head.

"Yes, brother, I mean, Abbot." he answered softly.

"Brother Dalfore," Crinshire continued, "I believe you instructed this young man to stay with the abbot at all times save during daily office time, when the abbot had others to look after his welfare. Is that correct?"

"It is, abbot," Dalfore answered. "My instructions were, I thought, most clear."

Rokey could feel the harsh gaze of the brothers on his back. He wished desperately that he could crawl under the rug.

"Did you not feel that this was a rather...heavy responsibility to entrust to a novice?" He spat the word so harshly that Rokey wondered if he even remembered being a novice himself only what - two years back? How had this man been elected Abbot?

"I was concerned when it was first suggested to me abbot," Dalfore explained, "but the boy was highly recommended by several of the faculty. I trusted that he was capable of the undertaking."

"Yesss," the abbot hissed like a viper. "You trusted. The abbot also trusted." He stood and leaned forward over his desk. "It seems, however, that your trust, and his were...misplaced."

Rokey could feel hot tears running down his face. Now the new abbot addressed him directly.

"You left the abbot alone in his bathing pool," he said. "At some point during your absence, the abbot slipped under the water and, lacking the strength to pull himself back up... he drowned!" With the word *drowned*, he pounded his fist onto the desk. Rokey flinched.

"When you got back to the room and found the abbot dead," he continued, "you made some efforts to revive him, to no avail. You then fetched brother Pilarus, who came immediately, but was also, by then, unable to render any further assistance."

The abbot paused and turned his head away. There was a dreadful silence, and one of the brothers coughed uncomfortably. Finally the abbot turned his steely gaze back to Rokey.

"You will agree, will you not, that I have just accurately described the circumstances of the death of Abbot Tomasso?" said Crinshire.

"Yes, Abbot," Rokey whispered.

"We cannot hear you," said the abbot.

Yes, Abbot," Rokey repeated miserably.

"Have you particulars to add, that would in any way diminish your culpability in this matter?" Crinshire asked. "Any argument that you can put forth to defend this shameful – this, this... reprehensible act of negligence? If you have anything at all to say in mitigation of your behavior, now is your chance to speak it."

Crinshire sat down and folded his hands on his desk. Rokey stood quietly for a moment to gather his thoughts. His head was pounding and his stomach churned. He thought of his earlier conversation with Ely. Ely did not blame him for what had happened. He had only done what the abbot had told him to do. He had seen no evidence of the type of physical weakness that had caused the abbot to drown in his bathing pool. And what of Asmor, the attendant? Where had he been that night? Was it not his absence that created the need for him to leave the abbot? He had tried his best, had given everything he had to this assignment. Ely saw that, and did not fault him. Despite Ely's support though, and in spite of all these other circumstances, when it came down to it, Rokey could still find only one person to blame for the tragedy. The one person who could have insisted that the abbot get out of the pool before he left him to make the tea. The one person to whom his health and welfare had been entrusted. *Himself...*

Rokey had faltered in his duty, and a man whom he had come to respect and care deeply for was now dead. The least he could do now was take responsibility and accept his punishment. As the tears continued to flow, he raised his head, took a deep breath and said, his voice quavering, "Members of the high council, I have nothing to say in mitigation of my profound dereliction of duty. While other events may have contributed to this dire tragedy – the absence of the attendant, and the order I was given by the abbot himself – when it comes down to the sum and substance of it, the decision to leave the abbot in what we now know was a risky situation, falls on me and me alone. I will carry the guilt and shame of it with me for the remainder of my days, and grieve for a man whom I had come to hold in the highest regard. I can only promise to learn from my grave error in judgment and, in future, to comport myself in the most judicious and vigilant manner possible. I hold myself ready for whatever reprimand you see fit to impose upon me."

The abbot turned to Brother Barrow.

"Have you anything to add, Barrow?" he asked.

Barrow cleared his throat. Rokey imagined him struggling for something to say on his behalf.

"Brothers," he said, "I ask only that you consider the boy's deep contrition for his error in judgment as you consider his punishment."

His eyes met Rokey's for a moment, and Rokey could see the disappointment in them. It was clear that his mentor also held him responsible for the tragedy.

After a moment of silence, the abbot spread his hands out on the desk and stood.

"It is clear that you have a certain eloquence, master Rokey", said the abbot. It did not sound like a compliment. "It is also clear that you are sincere in your sorrow and remorse. Yet for all that, you offer us nothing further of substance to consider in the disposition of your case. We are therefore ready to pronounce judgment without further delay. For gross malfeasance, resulting in the untimely and unfortunate death of the honorable Abbot Tomasso, it is the decision of this council that you be banished forever from the Noble Contemplative, effective immediately. You will be given a severance of six hundred docats and a letter from the Brotherhood enumerating your skills, so that you may establish yourself in another profession in Forrester, or wherever you choose. Because you have no other garments, you will be permitted to continue to wear the blue robe of the novice until such time as you are able to purchase other attire, after which you are honor-bound to dispose of it with due reverence. This is the unanimous vote of the high council of the Brotherhood."

* * *

Rokey followed Brother Jammad out the door, a small purse containing six hundred docats clutched tightly in his hand. Brother Barrow walked to the door with them.

"I am sorry, Rokey," said Barrow, squeezing his shoulder lightly. Rokey did not hear him, did not feel him. He felt nothing, and could only hear the words of the abbot repeating again and again –

Banished from the Brotherhood.
Banished from the Brotherhood.
Banished, banished, banished.

Before he knew it, he found himself back in his room. Ely was not there. He had classes all day. He would not even be able to say goodbye to his best friend.

Banished.

In a matter of moments, the high council had swept away the only life he had ever known. His heart was broken, his hopes and dreams for the future all gone. The abbot had ordered him to leave by midday, giving him time to pack up his possessions. Only he had no possessions, save his robe, a blanket and a pillow. He was finished well before noon. He decided to sit down to write a good-bye note to Ely. After several tries, he decided that the simple approach was best. He didn't want to cause his friend undue suffering. He finished, and then paused to read it over:

My dear Ely,

For my offense, I have been sent out from the Brotherhood, never to return. I will always warmly remember your support and your undying friendship, and hope that we will one day meet again. Good luck in whichever path you choose. I know that you will be a credit to the Brotherhood.

Fondly,
Rokey

As he prepared to leave, there was a knock at the door. A young novice was there with a parcel of food and drink for his journey. He thanked him, and the boy went on his way. The parcel contained two loaves of bread, some dried venison and fruit, a wedge of hard cheese and a skin of wine. Rokey added the items to his pack and, with a sigh and one parting look, left his room for the last time.

As he passed through the main gate, the noonday bell rang. He turned back for a moment and watched as the flurry of brothers and young novices poured from the classrooms, heading for lunch in the dining hall. He hoped for a glimpse of Ely, but his friend was nowhere to be seen. One last time, Rokey's eyes swept over the place that had been his only home. It still seemed unreal to him that he was to leave this place forever. He could not quite wrap his mind around that notion. At some point, he knew it would sink in, and at that moment the pain, the terrible sense of loss, would overtake him. But now, still numb with shock and grief, he turned from the Noble Contemplative, and started along the road to his new future.

Chapter 4:

The Road to Forrester

It was getting close to nightfall. Rokey had been walking for many marks. Since leaving the confines of the Noble Village, he had not encountered a soul. He knew that the nearest town, Forrester, was still another day's walk away, so he would have to find someplace to camp for the night soon. He had cleared the wooded area that stretched out at the foot of the Emerald Mountains. Now he was traversing a series of low hills which, if he remembered his geography correctly, would flatten into a broad, grassy plain sometime tomorrow. At the end of that was the large evergreen forest from which the town of Forrester derived its name. From the tops of the hills he could just make out the line of trees in the distance. There were no trees in this area though. No shelter at all in fact – only a well-worn road cutting through the countryside. Rokey had no fire-making implements. He would just have to camp near the road and hope that both the weather and the wild animals remained friendly.

He had cried like a baby for several marks after he left, but with the Contemplative forever behind him now, and his future, however uncertain, stretched out before him, he at last resolved that he would grieve no more. It served no purpose and would only hinder him now. He made up his mind to approach whatever lay ahead with a positive attitude. What was done was done. There was no going back.

When the sun had finally disappeared over the horizon, Rokey stepped a few paces off the road and spread out his blanket. He ate some of the dried venison and had some wine, and then lay back on his pillow, watching the stars come out. The sky was clear and the air pleasing. Soon Rokey had fallen fast asleep.

* * *

"Where's he comin' from d'ya think, Vorn?"

"He looks like one of them blokes from the monastery. Got no weapons far as I can see."

"But there's gold on 'im. I can smell it. Give 'im a good clout, Deaver, afore he wakes up."

Rokey rolled quickly off to the side. A tik later, the star mace came crashing down on his pillow. He sprang up to face his attackers. The moon was bright overhead and he could easily make them out. Three large men; one was holding the star mace, the other two carried machetes.

"You missed, Deaver," one of them said. "He's like a rabbit. C'mere little rabbit. We doesn't wanna hurt ye. We just wants yer gold." He lunged forward. Rokey sidestepped and slammed his elbow into his assailant's back. The man yelped and cursed loudly.

"Get 'im you gits!" he yelled at the others. They both closed on him, weapons at the ready.

* * *

Flaskamper had just sat down in front of the fire when he heard the commotion.

"Anyone else hear that?" he asked.

His three companions all shook their heads.

"What have those ears of yours picked up on now?" asked the dark-skinned man sitting beside him. He sipped on a cup of hot black tea, winced and blew gently on the cup to cool it.

"I'm not sure," Flaskamper answered. "Sounds like some sort of tussle, just there over the hill."

"Well, whatever it is, it doesn't concern us. Have some tea and forget about it."

Flaskamper poured himself a cup of tea, but continued to listen. After a few minmarks, he jumped up.

"I'm going to go investigate," he said.

The dark man stood. His hooded cloak was pulled back, showing long, blue-grey braids. He had a long scar that ran the length of his face, adding to his already formidable appearance.

"No one is going anywhere," he stated flatly. "We have troubles enough without going out to look for more."

"C'mon Stamford, please?" said Flaskamper. "Let me just go have a look. My curiosity is killing me."

"Your curiosity will kill us all one day," he answered, then gave in. "Be quick and quiet," he ordered, "and be back here in a quartermark."

"Thanks Stam," said the elf.

"A quartermark, mind you!" Stamford repeated.

Flaskamper put up his hood and vanished into the darkness. Stamford sat down and continued with his tea. One of the two other figures chuckled softly.

"You spoil him like a son," she teased.

"If he were my son I would beat him senseless," Stamford grumbled. He filled his pipe and lit up, then relaxed, savoring the sweet smoke.

"If he's not back in the space of this pipe," he said, "I'm going to hang him by those pointed ears of his."

*   *   *

Rokey was tiring. The three attackers were powerful, and armed. So far he had suffered no harm except a scratch across the back of one hand, but the men were determined, and keeping clear of them was growing more and more difficult. The leader, the one called Vorn, lunged at him with his machete. Rokey dove into a half-twisted summersault, which carried him momentarily beyond their range. He took advantage of the moment to cast off his robe. While it provided a small amount of protection, it kept him from using his most powerful assets, his legs. Now clad only in his shorts, he stood in the classic combat stance, awaiting the next move. It was not long in coming. The man with the other machete charged, slashing wildly at Rokey. He ducked and fired two rapid blows at the man's kidneys, then spun into a roundhouse kick, which connected hard at the side of the man's head. He went down hard with a groan. But now the man called Deaver had circled around him. His star mace connected with Rokey's shoulder. Rokey rolled with the blow, but landed hard on the ground. His whole left side exploded in pain, and before he could recover, he felt huge arms circle under his shoulders and up around his neck. He would normally have no trouble breaking this wrestler's hold, but the mace blow had weakened his arm. The man, Vorn, went to one knee and Rokey was forced down with him.

"Check his robe," he said to Deaver. "I'll wager we'll find his purse there."

Rokey's money was indeed in his robe. Deaver held it up and shook it, grinning appreciatively as it jingled. The third man who Rokey had flattened got slowly to his feet and stood before him. His eyes burned with rage.

"Right then," he rasped, "we got the gold. Let me finish him."

Vorn got roughly to his feet, dragging Rokey up with him. He continued to struggle, but he was weak and groggy with pain.

"Please yerself," said Vorn, and heaved Rokey to the ground. Rokey rolled over on his back, but couldn't get up.

"This is goin' ta hurt," the man said, and grinned as he raised his machete over his head. Rokey closed his eyes steeled himself for the blow that would cleave his head open.

Then he heard a strange sound. A long hissing noise, followed by a thump. He opened his eyes again and saw his attacker, still poised with his machete raised, but a peculiar look had come over his face. Then, the next tik, he fell forward, directly on top of him. A huge din broke out. He could hear the other bandits shouting, and the clash of metal against metal. Rokey struggled to get out from under the now dead weight that pinned him. He managed to get his arm free and when he reached around, he discovered what had felled the man – the long shaft of an arrow protruded from the back of his head. There was more yelling, and a sharp cry of pain, followed closely by another. He tried again to free himself, but the pain shooting through his shoulder prevented him from marshalling enough strength.

It was now quiet. He could hear nothing but the wind rustling over the grass. Tiks that felt like marks went by, and then he saw a pair of hands grip the corpse that covered him. A moment later, he was free. He managed to get up on one elbow and look around. The two other assailants also lay dead, and standing over him was a tall figure in a long, hooded cloak. He held a sword, still bloody from the men he had just dispatched. Slung across his back were a short bow and a quiver of arrows, which obviously accounted for the third man's dire state. But why had this man intervened? Had he come in aid, or was he, too, after his bag of gold?

"I have not come to rob you sir," he said, as if reading his thoughts. "I seek only to help you."

"I am pleased to hear that, good sir," Rokey replied, "for I would be in no state to hinder you whatever your motives should be. I am... most... grateful." He made one last feeble attempt to rise, but fell back heavily to the ground. The stranger knelt down beside him and threw back his hood. Rokey was amazed to see what appeared to be a lad not much older than he. He had short blonde spiked hair and a lean, almost feminine face. Then he noticed the ears. They were long and tapered up to a point. Not the ears of a man at all.

"You're – an elf!" he exclaimed, and then he fainted.

* * *

When he awoke a few minmarks later; the elf was still there, kneeling over him. He was the finest looking man Rokey had ever seen. Of course, strictly speaking, he wasn't a man at all.

"Oh good," he said, "you're awake. I was beginning to worry. Where are you injured?"

"My shoulder," Rokey told him. "The mace."

"Ah, well let's sit you up and have a look." He gently helped Rokey to reach a sitting position, and then examined his shoulder.

"I don't think anything is broken," said the elf, and then he reached into a pouch that he wore at his hip and pulled something out. It looked like a wad of leaves. "Open your mouth."

Rokey looked dubious. The elf smiled.

"Trust me," he said. These will make you feel better. Just chew on them."

Well, Rokey thought, *he did save my life*. He opened his mouth and the elf popped the leaves in. They tasted bitter, but as he chewed, he felt energy returning to his body, and the sharp pain in his shoulder was reduced to a dull ache.

"What are these?" he asked, amazed.

"Rembis leaves," Flaskamper explained. "They grow in the forest where I live. Well, used to live."

"Forgive me sir," said Rokey. "You have saved my life and I have neither thanked you nor asked your name. I am Rokey. I offer you my heartfelt gratitude, for without your help I would surely be dead now. I shall repay you one day if I am able."

The elf helped Rokey stand up and then shook his hand.

"I am Flaskamper," he said. "My friends call me Flash. Your gratitude is payment enough. You're shivering. Let me fetch your robe." He went to get Rokey's robe from the ground nearby, stopping on his return to retrieve the bag of gold from one of the dead men's hands. He helped Rokey on with his robe and handed him the purse.

"There you are, my friend," said Flaskamper. "The rembis will help you heal quickly. Since nothing appears to be broken, I think in another day you will be fully restored."

Rokey held out the purse to Flaskamper.

"There isn't much here," he said, "but you are welcome to it. I wish I had more of a reward to offer you."

Flaskamper smiled and shook his head.

"As I said, no reward is necessary," the elf repeated. "My motives for acting were purely selfish. I was bored and your predicament gave me a bit of exercise. Listen, since your campsite is in no fit state for the living anymore, I would be honored if you would come and join me and my friends by our fire tonight."

"Others?" Rokey's head came up. "You are not alone then?"

"No indeed," said Flaskamper. "Three others await me just over the hill there. If you look carefully, you can barely see the light of our fire."

"Three other – elves?"

Flaskamper laughed.

"No. I'm the only elf in these parts, as far as I know," the elf told him. "I travel with a dark, frightening man, a fair, sweet maiden and gentle giant. Now if that doesn't spark your curiosity, I don't know what else will."

"It certainly sounds like an intriguing group," Rokey admitted.

"So what say you, Rokey," said the elf. "Will you accept my hospitality?"

"I will, sir" said Rokey, "with many thanks."

*   *   *

The rest of the company stood as Rokey and Flaskamper approached the campfire. Stamford came forward to greet them.

"Flaskamper," he said, his teeth clenched into something that vaguely resembled a smile. "We were beginning to wonder what had become of you. And you have brought a guest, I see. Greetings to you sir." He dipped his head slightly. His voice was light and friendly, but his eyes told Flaskamper a different story. He would get a serious dressing down, if not worse, when they were alone. He forced his apprehensions aside and introduced Rokey.

"Rokey, may I present my friends and traveling companions," said Flaskamper. "This is Stamford, our leader. The lovely lady is Fia, and that colossus over there is Lorq."

Rokey exchanged greetings with each of them: Stamford, the tall, imposing leader of the group, with his dark skin and coal black eyes; the woman, Fia, was indeed a beauty, with green sparkling eyes and fiery red hair. It was the giant, though, who made the biggest impression on the boy, for he had never before seen one. Even seated, it was clear that Lorq towered over them all. He wore his curly, reddish-brown hair cropped very short; his face and features were broad and had a look of gentleness that seemed ill-matched to his huge frame.

"Put down your things and come sit with us Master Rokey," said Fia. "You too, Flaskamper. We are eager to hear what *adventure* you managed to find for yourself."

They all sat down by the fire and Flaskamper filled them in on the earlier events.

"Roamers," said Stamford. "Lowlifes that prey on unsuspecting travelers. 'Tis well for you, sir, that our friend here has sharp ears... and a *curious* nature."

Flaskamper grimaced.

"It is indeed," Rokey replied. "I had no knowledge of such dangers. Travel is...new to me."

"If I may ask," the leader continued, "what brings a novice of the Noble Contemplative so far from his monastery. Or does the blue robe no longer mean what it has for so many years?"

"No, you are right sir," Rokey answered. "The blue robe's significance has not changed. I was, until today, a novice of the Brotherhood. I have left their service, but as I had no other clothing, I am permitted to wear it until I reach Forrester. There it will be incumbent on me to purchase more suitable attire and to burn my robe."

"My understanding is that it is most unusual for someone to leave the service of the Contemplative," said Flaskamper. "What –"

Stamford held up his hand to silence him.

"It is not our business to concern ourselves with the personal matters of others," he said reproachfully.

"Indeed," the elf said, chastened. "My apologies."

"In any case," Stamford continued, "your young friend needs rest, and it's late. Why don't you go and settle him into your tent. Then come back here. We have a few matters to discuss."

Flaskamper winced. He knew what the matters were and was not looking forward to the discussion. He got up and motioned for Rokey to follow him. Rokey gathered up his blanket and pillow and followed the elf into his tent.

"Don't be too hard on him Stamford," Fia said gently.

"He did a very brave thing, saving the boy's life," Lorq added.

Stamford growled, and said nothing. A short while later, Flaskamper emerged from the tent and sat down again by the fire. He waited for the harangue to begin, but Stamford sat in silence, smoking his pipe.

"Alright, let's have it!" the elf cried out. "I can't take all this quiet. Just tell me what a stupid, fool thing I did and get it over with. Just for the record though, I'm not sorry I saved his life. It would have been wrong for me to just leave him there. Now go on. Chew my head off."

"Flaskamper," said Stamford, "if you want to play the gallant hero, that's your privilege. But why was it necessary to bring him here?"

"He was hurt, Stamford. And scared – "

"And pretty to look at?" Stamford retorted.

Flash reddened, but said nothing.

"You don't fool me," said the dark man. "Your little sword is guiding your big sword again. Well fine, you've earned your bread, now go butter it. Give the boy a poke and send him on his way at first light."

"I can't do that." Flaskamper protested. "He's asleep, and he's fresh from a monastery for pity's sake. Besides, I don't even know if he fancies boys or not."

"What of it?" said Stamford. "You saved the lad's life. The least he can do is give you a tumble. If he's a virgin, so much the better. You know what they say, 'the fresher the milk –' "

"Yes, I know, I know," said the elf, "but I don't want to get my milk that way."

"Since when?" Stamford asked, arching an eyebrow. "Have you undergone some religious conversion in the last – how long has it been now – nearly five whole days since your last conquest?"

Flash let the provocation pass with uncharacteristic silence. A few moments later, he cleared his throat nervously.

"Um," he said, "There's something else."

Stamford sighed heavily.

"I might have guessed," he said. "Come on, out with it."

"I – uh, I promised him that he could travel with us to Forrester," he blurted out.

Fia giggled, but covered her mouth after a look from Stamford.

"Well, that's a bit of a dilemma isn't it," he growled, "since we aren't going to Forester! We're heading southeast, away from Forrester. You do remember that don't you?"

"Yes, I remember," Flaskamper told him, "but I got carried away and -,"

"He batted those big brown eyes at you, and you melted into a little pointy-eared puddle." Stamford stood and went to kneel beside Flaskamper. He reached out and grasped his chin. "Now listen to me, boy; tomorrow morning, you are going to wave good-bye to your new little friend – with or without having sullied his virtue – and we, the four of us, are taking the southwest road toward the Respite ferry. Now, as the leader of this little company, am I making myself perfectly clear?"

"Yes, Stamford," the elf said miserably.

"Good. Now go to bed," Stamford ordered. "We've a long journey tomorrow."

Flaskamper tramped off to his tent. Fia watched him go sadly. Then she turned to Stamford.

"Stamford–" she began.

"Don't start with me woman!" Stamford said.

"What would be the harm in going with him to Forrester?" she asked.

"The harm is that it's two days walk out of our way," Stamford replied, "there's little if any work to be had there, and our purses, if you haven't noticed, are considerably light of late. We have a personal recommendation from the mayor of Riversedge to the King of Respite, which should clinch us some lucrative work, for once without us having to stick our necks out too far."

Fia gave Stamford her most engaging smile.

"That's all true. You're absolutely right," she said.

"But," he said. "Come on, I know there's a *but*."

"*But* I think it would mean a lot to Flaskamper if we could," she told him. "It seems he may be taking an interest in someone that's deeper than a quick tumble and a kiss good-bye. *I* think that we should encourage it, though I know it rubs sorely against your nature.

We're not destitute yet, and we'll still have our letter from the mayor tomorrow, a week, or a month from now."

"We've barely met the lad, Fia," the dark man protested. "Why go to all that bother for a total stranger?"

"We won't," she countered. "We'll do it for Flaskamper. He's obviously smitten. Why not make him happy, for a couple of days at least? Who knows? Something meaningful may actually come of it."

Stamford sneered at Fia.

Fia smiled sweetly in return.

Lorq suddenly became fascinated by the fire.

"Obviously I shall not prevail here without being branded a troll," Stamford declared. "Very well. *You* tell him in the morning. I'm going to bed before you talk me into adopting the little bastard."

As he stomped off to his tent, Lorq looked at Fia and snickered.

"You're so clever, Fia," he said with admiration.

He's a kinder man than he'll have anybody know," she said. "I just help him to show it sometimes. She stood and stretched.

"Are you going to bed, big fellow?" she asked.

"I'm going to sleep by the fire," Lorq replied, "in case there are any more of those roamers out there."

There were no more disturbances though, and the company slept well through the rest of the night.

Chapter 5:

Companionship

By noon the next day, the company, their newest member in tow, had reached the end of the rolling hills. Now they were crossing a large grassy plain which would eventually lead them to the Lonesome Woods wherein Forrester lay. The road was flat and well traveled, but on either side the grasses were tall – waist high in some places, taller than a man in others. The air was full of the buzzing of insects, and the cries of the many varieties of birds that preyed on them. Now and then the grasses rustled as some small, anonymous creature passed by.

Rokey was glad for the companionship. Stamford didn't seem too happy to be headed in this direction, and Rokey suspected that Flaskamper had somehow persuaded the group's leader to change their original plans. Though the man was polite enough, Rokey decided to stay out of his way as much as possible until they reached Forrester. So while he, Lorq and Fia led the way with their pony, Fenton, Rokey stayed to the rear, with Flaskamper keeping him company. He had meant to keep the story of his disgrace and exile from the Contemplative to himself, but as he and the elf walked and talked, he found himself recounting the whole story. With difficulty, he managed to hold back the tears of sadness and despair that threatened to burst forth, but Flaskamper could sense his deep distress.

"I know what it's like to lose everything close to you," he said, and his eyes clouded for a moment, as though he were reliving some dark episode from his past. But then he looked back at Rokey and smiled. "I don't know what I would have done if I hadn't found this group of wandering misfits."

"It *is* a strange group," Rokey said, and quickly added, "I don't mean any offence by that."

Flaskamper laughed. "No offence taken. We *are* an odd bunch and are well aware of it. It's the thing that holds us together you might say."

"What thing?" Rokey asked.

"Well, our oddness," he explained. "When I said we were misfits, I truly meant it. Each of the four of us left, or was forced to leave our homeland because, for one reason or another, we didn't belong. So you see, you're in good company. We're all outcasts just like you."

Rokey, in fact, *did* feel that he was in good company. They stopped for a quick lunch, and Rokey passed around his skin of the Brotherhood's fine wine. The gesture immediately found favor with Stamford, who took a hearty, appreciative quaff.

"Ah, wine from the Brotherhood," he said with a sigh. "One of those things I think men have managed even better than elves." He looked pointedly at Flaskamper.

"To the uneducated palate perhaps," Flaskamper retorted, but also enjoyed a long pull at the wineskin. Rokey sensed that this was an ongoing banter between the two.

"Rokey," Fia said gently, "we couldn't help but overhear the story of how you came to leave the Contemplative. May I ask, what are your plans now?"

"I don't really have any, Lady Fia," he answered. "I have a letter from the Brotherhood listing the skills I've learned while in service there, and a little money to buy some clothes and hopefully a bed for a short while. I suppose I'll try and apprentice to someone in Forrester. Unfortunately the expertise I have gained does not serve me well for such an ambition."

"What expertise would that be?" asked Stamford.

"Literature, astronomy, illustration, mathematics, diplomacy – and swordsmanship of course," Rokey replied.

"Hmmm. You're right," said the dark man. "Not much use for those in a town like Forrester, except maybe in the town militia. But militias tend to be wary of hiring on strangers. Still with a letter from the Brotherhood..."

"Militia, " said Rokey. "That hadn't occurred to me. I thought I should probably wind up as a miller's apprentice, or perhaps a shop boy."

"Tough going in Forrester. Not much trade there," Stamford explained. "It's pretty much just a stopover between Duncileer and the roads to elsewhere. Not a place where people go to settle."

"Perhaps you should think about pushing on to Duncileer," Fia told him. "I should imagine that there would be many more opportunities for someone like you in the kingdom's capital city."

"Duncileer," said Rokey, smiling at the thought. "We get visitors from there at festival times. Have you been there? What is it like?"

"Duncileer is beautiful," offered Lorq. "Cobblestone streets and fountains and brightly painted houses. People from all over Firma live there."

"Lorq is quite right," said Fia. "A large city like Duncileer is much more accommodating to strangers looking to settle. You really should give it some serious thought."

"I will," said Rokey. "Thank you for your advice," he turned to Flaskamper, "and for saving my life. I don't know how I'll ever repay you."

Stamford coughed meaningfully; Flaskamper shot him a hateful look.

"I'm sure something will occur to you," the leader said, ignoring the look. "Meanwhile, we'd best be off."

They continued on for the rest of the afternoon, occasionally meeting travelers heading in the opposite direction. Stamford greeted them in a friendly manner, but was always on the alert for thieves and brigands. As the sun began to sink lower in the sky, they could see the Lonesome Woods looming in the distance. Stamford guessed that they could reach them by nightfall, but suggested that they make camp out in the open.

"We can't reach Forrester tonight," he said, "and it's safer not to be caught in the woods after dark."

They all agreed, and though they still had a mark or more of daylight when they reached the edge of the wood, they stopped for the night. Apparently others who had recently passed this way had also feared to camp in the woods, for just beyond the shadow of the trees was a crudely circular clearing in the grass. Lorq and Stamford ventured into the woods to gather firewood. Flaskamper took his bow and slipped off into the grass to try and shoot a rabbit or a partridge. Rokey and Fia were left to set up camp. By the time the sun had set, the tents were up. A fire was going in the center of the campsite and, on a hastily assembled spit, two fat pheasants were already roasting, courtesy of the elf's fine hunting skills. When the pheasants were ready, Rokey broke out the rest of his wine and the remaining loaf of bread. As they feasted, laughing and enjoying each other's company, Rokey felt emboldened to ask the question that had been on his mind all afternoon.

"So – now that you all know my sad story," he said, "won't somebody tell me theirs? Flaskamper says that you are a band of misfits, that you were all forced to leave your homes for one reason or another. But you all seem to me perfectly fine folk. I am curious how you came to form this unusual band."

They were quiet for a time; so long in fact that Rokey began to wonder if he had made a mistake. Then finally Flaskamper spoke up.

"Well, I guess it's only fair, tit for tat," he said. "It's only that, just as your story brings you grief and sadness, so each of our stories, though much more time has passed, still produces similar distress for us."

"Look, I didn't mean to spoil our fun," said Rokey.

"No, no you haven't," Fia reassured him. "It's perfectly natural that you should be curious. I have an idea. Why don't we each tell one another's stories? That should cut the sting a bit, don't you think?"

"That's a great idea, Fia," said Flaskamper. "Whose story shall we start with?"

"I choose to keep my affairs to myself for the time being," said Stamford, filling his pipe. "But I'll tell you Flaskamper's sad tale if you like, and how I came to save him from rack and ruin on the streets of Tanohar."

Flaskamper laughed.

"Yes, go on and tell it," he said. "I can't wait to hear *your* version of events."

Stamford lit his pipe and puffed contentedly for a moment, sitting silently with his eyes closed. At last he opened them again, leaned forward, and began the story.

* * *

"I had just finished a successful quest for King Hadropal in the Northern Expanse. Seems a frost nymph had stolen his jewels of state, and he was most eager to have them back, lest some challenge to his right of rule be assayed. Complicated business, Northern politics. Anyhow, I was fairly worn out; had an impressive reward in my purse and a few frostbitten toes in need of warming, so I decided to head to Respite for a well-earned holiday. That required a stop at Tanohar to resupply for the journey. While I waited for the trader to gather the things I would need, I stopped off in the Golden Eagle Tavern for a quick pint. That's when I first laid eyes on Flaskamper.

I noticed him because an elf is something of a strange sight outside the forest of Elfwood, and because he was playing dice with one of the local militia officers, apparently without giving him a handicap. I knew that was going to lead to trouble."

"Why a handicap? Rokey asked.

"Because," Stamford answered, "elves are lucky. I don't mean in the way some people are lucky. I mean in a way that defies the odds of random chance. For instance, if you were to flip a coin one hundred times and call it heads or tails, how often, according to the odds, would you be right?"

"Half of the time," said Rokey.

"Exactly. But what if I told you that if Flaskamper were to play the same game, flip the same coin one hundred times and call it heads or tails, he'd be right seven out of ten times, give or take."

Rokey shook his head.

"That's impossible," he declared.

Stamford smiled and nodded.

"For you or I, yes. For elves, no. Elves are magical beings. Though they look for the most part like you and me, they are possessed of earth magic, some of which alters the forces of chance in their favor. That is why, in the rare circumstance in which an elf might participate in games of chance with humans, it is customary for the elf to offer a handicap."

He looked pointedly at Flaskamper.

"I know, I know," said Flaskamper, holding up his hands, "but I needed some fast gold."

"In any case." Stamford continued, "it wasn't long before the situation I expected came to pass. The man began to suspect that Flaskamper was cheating him, and called him out. Now, I've no doubts that our friend here was expecting something of the sort, and he was more than ready to club the man senseless and abscond with his winnings, however dubiously obtained."

Flaskamper made a rude gesture. Stamford ignored him and pressed on.

"What he hadn't prepared for was the fact that four other members of the militia had come in a few moments before, and immediately stepped in to aid their fellow guardsman. Now I had been in Tanohar a number of times and I knew something of their brand of justice. It wasn't uncommon for a cheat, proven or otherwise, to have his hands summarily lopped off. For some reason, I was moved to feel sorry for this poor, unscrupulous elf and, in a fit of compassion which I have regretted ever since, I stepped into the imminent fray to help even things up.

"It was a nice gesture, but I didn't really need the help," Flaskamper interrupted. "The day I can't take on a pack of some local constabulary –"

"Here, who's telling this story?" said Stamford, gruffly. "Shut your yap. Now where was I, oh yes, we set to battling the guardsmen. Now, the Tanohar militia is somewhat more than your typical band of no-goods with swords. These men are well trained and, generally, ill tempered. We didn't either of us want to kill anyone, lest we have the entire city guard on our heels. Our foes had no such concerns. With some difficulty, we managed to vanquish them with minimal bloodshed, none of it ours, thankfully, but one of the guards fled, no doubt to summon reinforcements. Before we even knew one another's names, we were on the run together. Fortunately, the trader had finished assembling my supplies, and we sped off through the rear gate just as a company of armed guards came thundering toward the tavern. Technically, of course, a city's militia only has authority within the bounds of the kingdom, but those bastards chased us for the entire day and well into the evening. By the time they turned back, our horses were ready to collapse with exhaustion, as were we. We stopped by a small creek, left the horses to graze and drink, and set up camp. That was our very first meeting, and we've been traveling together ever since."

Stamford paused to refill his pipe.

"But how had Flaskamper come to be in Tanohar in the first place?" Rokey asked.

"Patience, lad" Stamford said. "I'm coming to that part." He lit his pipe and continued between puffs.

"Well, Flaskamper was, or course, suitably grateful to me for pulling his fat from the fire – "

Flaskamper grunted. Again, Stamford ignored him.

"So when I expressed a similar curiosity, he was more than willing to share his sad tale with me. I brewed up a pot of tea, and over a few pipes of fine kingsleaf, he told me the story of how he had come to be in a place so far from the land of his birth.

"Young Flaskamper, you should know, is no ordinary, undistinguished elf, if such a thing exists. No indeed. Your tent mate is none other than his royal highness Prince Flaskamper, younger son of Angorath and Ferriwhyl, king and queen of the forest realm of Elfwood. What do you think about that?"

Rokey was suitably impressed. Flaskamper flushed with embarrassment and motioned for Stamford to get on with the story.

"He is one of two sons born to the royal couple. His older brother is Alrontin, a prince among princes, if one is to be believed. captain of the elite army of the elf forest, known throughout Firma as the "Silver Sentinels". Husband to the fair Mellynda, father to two beautiful children, in every way, the perfect son. So perfect, in fact, as to leave little at which a younger brother may excel, and much at which he may fall short."

Rokey was beginning to grasp the essence of the story, and felt an immediate stab of sympathy for his new friend. Stamford went on.

"King Angorath doted on his oldest son, but had little affection to spare for his younger child, and though his mother loved them both equally, a young man craves the esteem of his father, and suffers greatly in its absence. Young Flaskamper tried everything to gain Angorath's notice. He excelled in his studies, in horsemanship and swordsmanship, in music and poetry, but however formidable his skills, Alrontin was always first, and always a little bit better. A melancholy settled on him that, at last, became too much to bear. Flaskamper decided to leave his homeland and venture out into the broader world of men. He hoped that there he might find a means to prove his unique worth to his father, and thus win his respect. But the world of men can be cruel, especially for one unaccustomed to its workings. It wasn't long before he found himself stranded in the city of Tanohar, with no money or means by which to acquire it. To try and obtain the funds with which to buy travel supplies, he resorted to gambling, a sure, if somewhat nefarious way to gain a fast cache of gold. It was that decision which ultimately brought us together."

"Wow, how long ago was that?" Rokey asked.

"It's been nearly five years now," Flaskamper answered. "Lorq and Fia joined us along the way, each suffering their own anguish and looking for someplace to belong. We've had some grand adventures together."

"And have you been back to Elfwood?" Rokey inquired. Flash put his head down.

"No," he said quietly. "I have had no pressing business in my homeland as yet."

Rokey let the subject drop. It was obviously distressing to him. Rokey nearly regretted having asked for the story, though he now felt a bit less like an outsider and more a part of the group. He said as much to the company. Fia smiled at him.

"Well, you certainly meet the eligibility requirements," she quipped.

This broke the gloom in the air and they all laughed before heading off to their separate tents. As Rokey and Flaskamper readied themselves for sleep, Rokey asked Flaskamper to tell him more about elf magic.

"Oh it's not such a grand thing really," said Flaskamper. "It's just, well, hard to describe, really. It's like a little push that makes us able to run a bit faster, jump a bit higher. And as you heard, luck favors us a little more than ordinary men. That's the everyday elf magic."

He lay back on his pillow, with his hands behind his head.

"Then there are other sorts of magic," he told Rokey, "more powerful ones that involve complex spell-weaving and charms..

"And do you have those skills as well?" Rokey asked excitedly.

"No. Well, nothing big or fancy," the elf replied. "Just parlor tricks mostly. The higher elf magics are usually not studied until one is quite a lot older, and then only if one is to become a mage or a healer. I never had such ambitions, though I may have come to less grief at home if I had. It's one skill that Alrontin possesses only in small measure."

"So you and your brother don't get on together?" Rokey asked.

"Oh no, that's not it at all," Flaskamper explained. "We love one another dearly. It was never Alrontin's desire to show me up or make me look bad. He was simply older and, at most things, better than I.

He hated the way things were between my father and I, but there was little he could do about it. Sometimes, when we were both little, he would let me beat him at things in an attempt to make me feel better. But it was always obvious that he was not trying his best and, in the end, it wound up making me feel worse. I tried not to resent him for it, but sometimes my envy got the best of me. That was one of the reasons I left. In Elfwood, there is nothing to which I endeavor that would not be compared, unfavorably, to my brother. In all things save women, our interests have always been very similar."

"You have different taste in women?" Rokey asked.

Flaskamper turned over with his back to Rokey.

"Not exactly," Flaskamper answered carefully. "What I mean is that he prefers women; I prefer men."

Rokey was suddenly flooded with a number of emotions, all of which conspired to tie his tongue in knots.

"Oh," was all he could finally manage.

"I hope that doesn't make you too uncomfortable," said Flaskamper, his heart beginning to sink. "I know some men find it...awkward. Especially sharing a tent and all. If you'd rather –"

"No, no. Not at all." Rokey broke in, finding his voice at last. "In fact, well...as it happens... that is to say I'm pretty sure, as far as I know, that I am – that I also prefer, you know, men."

Idiot, Rokey chided himself. *You sound like a blithering simpleton.*

Flaskamper turned back to face Rokey, the darkness hiding his broad grin.

"Well then," the elf responded, "there's something else we have in common." His voice was matter-of-fact, but inside, his spirits soared.

They said goodnight and settled down to sleep. Rokey, feeling foolish yet strangely relieved, fell asleep at once, but Flaskamper remained wide-awake well into the night. He felt a wild sense of excitement that went well beyond physical desire. For reasons he was not yet fully ready to explore, life suddenly seemed a great deal brighter.

Chapter 6:

Attack

Because of his excitement, Flaskamper was still awake and heard their approach. His sensitive ears picked up the gentle rustle of bodies in the grass. He couldn't identify what they were, but knew they were coming in some number. He jumped up, pulled on his breeches, grabbed his sword and bolted from the tent. It was the night of the new moon, and cloudy, so the sky was pitch black. The fire had died down to embers. Even with his keen elven eyesight, he could see nothing. He sensed them there however, slipping stealthily through the tall weeds. How many were they? What were they?

Fenton whinnied nervously, startling the daylights out of the elf. He backed slowly toward Stamford and Lorq's tent. He didn't want to alert whatever they were that he was awake. He was hoping to quietly rouse the others and surprise them when they arrived. In the pitch-blackness, though, he stumbled over a stone and, with an involuntary grunt, fell hard onto his backside.

It started then, a loud, high-pitched squeaking that set his teeth on edge. He felt them surge ahead, no longer trying to sneak in unheard. A rush of panic washed over him. He was blind and outnumbered. He could call out to his friends, but they would be in no better shape. They needed light, or the darkness would eat them alive.

Parlor tricks.

There was a spell. He had learned it as a child, but he hadn't used it in so long. How did it go? The things were closer now. He heard Stamford cry out in surprise, and fumble for his things. The shrieks had awakened him, but he, too, was blind. How did that blasted spell go? The first of them had just crashed into the circle of their campsite when it came to him. He cried out into the darkness, a string of Elvish words from the far recesses of his memory.

> *"Al an te fatch*
> *To miney duros*
> *Al fieras mor*
> *Nya pos na toros."*

A brilliant white orb suddenly materialized overhead, illuminating the entire campsite. When Flaskamper's eyes adjusted a moment later, he was horrified by what he saw advancing towards him.

Rats. But no, not rats exactly. Some kind of amalgam, creatures with bodies like deformed gnomes and oversized rat heads. They were naked, but covered with thick brown fur that was matted and slick with grime. They smelled of rotten meat and mold, like the inside of a tomb. The light caught their eyes, causing them to glow bright red. Each one carried a small, gleaming scythe. They shrieked horribly as the orb's radiance hit them, but rapidly grew accustomed to the light and rushed headlong into the campsite, directly at Flaskamper. He stood up quickly and, without pausing to think, raised his sword in defense. There was a clang as it blocked the stroke of the first ratman's scythe. He wished to blazes he had grabbed his shield as well. He swung quickly to parry another blow from behind. They were all around him.

Stamford and Lorq burst from their tent, Stamford with his longsword and shield, Lorq with his iron-tipped quarterstaff. They stopped short for a moment, aghast at the scene in front of them, but quickly recovered and sprang into battle. Fia, armed with her shortsword, joined them a moment later. Flaskamper dipped back to a feint as the first ratman's scythe swung toward his chest; he countered and drove his blade straight into its eye. He pulled it out quickly and, as it died screaming, turned to face the one behind him again. He heard other shrieks and the grunts of his comrades as they fought.

"How many are there?" Stamford shouted.

"I don't know!", Flaskamper yelled in reply. "A whole horde from what I could hear."

"Remind me never to curse your ears again," he shouted back.

They kept coming. After a few minmarks, Flaskamper saw the flap of his tent rustle.

"Rokey, go back!" he cried. If he came out unarmed, they would chop him to pieces before Flaskamper could help him.

However, his concern was misplaced. Rokey emerged fully dressed in his robe, armed with the elf's shield and spare blade – a bastard sword, as it happened. His eyes grew large as he surveyed the enemy, but then he set his jaw and charged into the melee. Suddenly the attention of the ratmen turned. The ones engaged in battle with the rest of the company continued, but those still emerging from the grass all made directly for Rokey. Flaskamper dispatched his adversary and rushed to the young man's aid. He tried to engage one of the rushing creatures, but it barely acknowledged him in its fervor to reach Rokey. Only when the elf's sword ripped a gaping wound in its back did it turn to fight him. The others seemed to be finding it equally difficult to take on the enemy. There was no doubt that killing Rokey was their sole intention. Flaskamper couldn't imagine why, but it was clearly the case.

Fortunately, Rokey's recent lessons with Brother Barrow had greatly improved his skills with the bastard sword and shield. While the others strove to impose themselves between him and the ratmen, he swung the sword in a high confident arc, cleaving one foe in two, blocking another's blow with the shield and with a backhanded swipe, chopping its legs from under it. Even amidst all the chaos, Flaskamper could not help but be impressed at his new friend's bravery and fighting skill.

Finally, just as Rokey was beginning to tire, his companions managed to fight their way through the pack and form a ring around him. The bodies of dead ratmen were piling up, but a dozen or so remained, rabidly single-minded in their purpose. One made it through their perimeter and flew at Rokey, shrieking and foaming at the mouth. It swung its scythe furiously. Rokey blocked it with the shield but the shock of the blow knocked him off his feet. The ratman threw its weight onto Rokey's shield arm, pinning it to the ground, and again raised its scythe to strike. With speed only an elf could have managed, Flaskamper kicked the legs out from under his own opponent and, in an instant, hurled his sword at the ratman poised to strike Rokey. It flew true and buried itself in the creature's back. Rokey freed his arm and rolled away just as the thing fell dead.

Flaskamper, now unarmed, faced his own foe, which had righted itself and stood slavering before him. He dove as it struck at him, but as he turned to regain his footing, he felt the scythe slice deep into his calf. He fell back to the ground in agony, certain that he was finished. Instead, to his surprise, the beast's head fell with a thud next to him. He rolled over on his back and saw Rokey standing above him smiling, bastard sword in hand, as the creature's decapitated body joined its head in the grass. Rokey's smile quickly faded when he saw the blood pouring from Flaskamper's wounded leg. He looked quickly around to make sure there were no other charging ratmen, then dropped to the ground to attend to the injury. He tore one strip from his robe and tied it tightly above the wound, then tore another, broader one to use as a bandage.

"Lie still," he said, then stood, grabbed the sword and charged off again. Flaskamper was in no mood to argue. His leg was on fire and chills gripped his body. He listened to the sounds of clashing weapons, and tried to sit up to see what was happening, but his stomach turned over and he vomited onto the ground.

Poisoned.

The ratmen's blades were poisoned. He was sure of it. He could feel it now, coursing through his veins, ravaging his body. He had to warn the others. He struggled, but everything began to spin uncontrollably. Then the orb above him seemed to dim, and a moment later, he was swallowed by the darkness.

*   *   *

Rokey swung the bastard sword with all his remaining strength. It sliced through the last remaining ratman, leaving it in two blood-soaked halves on the ground. The four of them stood still for a moment, listening for the sounds of more creatures tramping through the grassy darkness. There were none. They lowered their weapons and heaved a collective sigh. Rokey started back to attend to Flaskamper, but before he had gone a step, the magical light suddenly died, plunging them into utter blackness.

"Lorq, fetch the goblin torches from Fenton's pack," Stamford ordered. "Everybody else stay put."

Fenton was hitched to a tree behind Fia's tent. Rokey heard Lorq fumble his way to the pony and start rustling through the saddlebags. In a few moments there was a sharp crack, like a stick breaking. A bright greenish glow appeared behind the tent and Lorq emerged holding three torches, one of which was alight with an eerie green fire. He handed the two unlit torches to Stamford and Fia, who held them in both hands and snapped off the topmost portion. Instantly they both lit up with the same green flame. It wasn't nearly as bright as the elven orb that Flaskamper had invoked, but it was sufficient for them to find their way around the campsite.

Rokey went and knelt next to Flaskamper. The elf was unconscious and barely breathing. He felt his wrist for a pulse and was rewarded with a faint, but steady beat. The others gathered around him.

"Something's wrong," he said. "He lost a fair amount of blood, but not enough to have put him in this state. He's soaked to the skin in sweat, and cold to touch."

"The things' blades must have been poisoned," Fia exclaimed breathlessly. "Is anyone else wounded?"

No one was. Fia knelt on the other side of the elf and unwrapped the bandage on his leg to examine the wound. Even in the torch's poor green glow, they could see that it looked angry and infected.

"Rokey, Flaskamper keeps Rembis leaves in his pack. They look like –"

"I know," said Rokey. "He gave me some before. I'll fetch them."

Lorq handed him a torch and Rokey ran to their tent. It took him only a moment to find the pouch full of dark, soft leaves. He clutched it to his chest and ran back to where Fia was waiting. She quickly took a bunch from the pouch and put them in her mouth. After chewing them for a bit, she spit them out into her hand and pressed them into Flaskamper's gash. He woke briefly with a scream, then fell lifeless again. Fia wrapped the wound again with Rokey's bandage, then looked up at the three men standing above her.

"We need to get him help, fast," she said. "The rembis leaves will slow the spread of the poison, but they will not cure him. He needs a skilled healer."

"In Forrester?" Stamford snorted. "Fat chance."

"We have to break camp and leave now," she said, standing. "Lorq, bring him to his tent. We'll break that down last."

"Maybe one of you should take him on ahead with Fenton," Rokey suggested. Stamford considered this briefly, but then shook his head.

"It wouldn't matter," he said. "The forest trail is too narrow and uneven for a pony to run through, even if Fenton were up to the task. We should reach the town in three, maybe four marks at our best pace. I think that's the most we can hope for. It's nearly dawn. Let us hope these torches will last until daybreak."

They broke camp quickly and, with caution, entered the woods. They tried to tie Flaskamper on Fenton, but with the uneven surface of the trail, he was in constant danger of falling. Finally Lorq took him and carried him in his arms like a baby. For the giant, the elf was no burden.

Rokey stuck by Lorq, keeping an eye out for any signs of consciousness from Flaskamper. His friend had disarmed himself to save his life, and he felt responsible. Not only that, those creatures had been after him. He had no idea why, but he knew that, because of him, the whole company had nearly died. If it wasn't for Flaskamper's keen hearing –

He stopped himself. The company was alive and they were going to reach Forrester and get help for Flash. He had to keep believing that. They would reach help in time to reverse the creature's poison.

Those creatures had been after him.

But why? Who could possibly wish him harmed, dead? He hadn't left the Contemplative since his arrival there fifteen years earlier. It had to be some kind of mistake. And what a mistake! Those creatures had been evil, the product of dark magic. Whoever the real target was certainly had a powerful enemy. He shivered at the memory, that smell and those horrible squeals.

As they neared Forrester, the sun began to rise. This was fortunate, for the goblin torches were starting to burn low. In the light of the morning, hopes lifted. They would reach the city in about another mark, Stamford declared, and he was right. Before the mark had passed, they had reached the edge of town.

"There's a healer named Manchion who lives just outside the center of town," Fia told Rokey. "It is so early, we should find him at home."

"Let's hope so," Rokey replied.

Manchion was not only in, he was asleep, but when he saw Flaskamper, he hustled them inside. Fia explained to him what had transpired at the campsite, omitting those details that were not relevant to Flaskamper's situation.

"No point in telling the whole town our business," Stamford whispered to Rokey. "We may be safe in Forrester, but then again, we may not."

Manchion, a frail little man with thinning white hair and a well-wizened face, studied Flaskamper's injured leg for a few moments, then excused himself to his apothecary. He returned a bit later with two bowls and a clean cloth. The first bowl contained hot water, with which he used the cloth to thoroughly clean the wound. Next he took the second bowl full of a warm, gooey concoction and smeared it liberally onto the gash. Flaskamper did not stir throughout the process. Finally the healer fetched a clean bandage and rewrapped the injury. Then, apparently satisfied with his work, he turned to address the rest of the worried group.

"We should see him regain consciousness in a mark or two, but don't expect miracles. I'm a natural healer, not a magician. If what you say is true, and there's a component of dark magic to this poison, he'll get better, but not well. Magical harm requires magical healing and I have no such skills."

"Is there anyone in Forrester who practices magical healing?" Rokey asked

"Nope," he answered, "not a witch nor a sorcerer to be found here. But as I said, he'll recover somewhat, enough to reach Duncileer alive at least. There'll be help enough for him there I should imagine. I'd let him rest for a full day, until he's strong enough to walk by himself, then move on to the city with as much haste as you can manage. I've no way of telling what type of magic is coursing around inside him, or how it will affect him later on. The sooner he's cleansed of it, the better."

They thanked the old healer, paid his fee and headed out to find lodging. Forrester was a hub for transients, so there was no shortage of inns and boarding houses.

"We'll go to the Blue Dragon," Stamford told Rokey. "I know the innkeeper. He'll keep his mouth shut, for a few extra docats."

* * *

Flaskamper didn't wake until well after noon. His body was racked with searing pain. His stomach continued to lurch violently, as it had before he passed out, and his head felt as if it might split in two at any moment. He tried to sit up, but was unable to move. Turning his head slightly, he saw Rokey resting in the bed next to his. Relief flooded through him. He tried to call to him. Only a faint whisper emerged, but it was enough. Rokey jumped up and came to sit by him. He felt Rokey take his hand.

"It's alright, Flash," Rokey told him. "You're going to be alright. The healer fixed up your wound and you should start to feel better soon. Just lie still for a while."

"The others. Poison..." he croaked.

"Everyone is fine," Rokey assured him. "The others are in their rooms resting. No one else was wounded. Do you want me to go and get them?"

Flash managed a small shake of his head. He preferred to wait until he felt better, though he was glad to have Rokey there with him, holding his hand.

"Flash –," Rokey began haltingly. "Flash, I'm so sorry. I don't know how, or why, but this is all my fault. If I'd known this was going to happen, I'd never have let you all take me in. You've been so kind to me, and now –"

Flaskamper held up his other hand to quiet him.

"It's alright," the elf whispered, and squeezed Rokey's hand. "Don't...beat yourself...up...over it. It's...not your...fault."

"It's all so...unreal," said Rokey, as much to himself as to Flaskamper, "those things, those horrible creatures...the way they came right for me..."

He shuddered again at the thought. Despite the weakness he felt, Flaskamper offered him a reassuring smile.

"We'll...figure it out," he rasped. Rokey snapped out of his reverie and smiled back at his stricken companion.

"First, we'll get you well," Rokey told him. "That's the first priority now."

After a while, the elf was able to speak normally again and, with help, to sit up in bed. Rokey fetched some soup and, as he fed him, explained what the healer had said about the dark magic.

"It's true," Flaskamper said. "Physically, I'm getting better, but I can still feel the poison's spell inside me, feeding on my soul."

"We'll leave first thing in the morning," Rokey said, "provided you're well enough to travel."

"I will be," the elf responded. "I have to be."

He could already feel the icy grip of shadows growing stronger within him. Sinister whispers echoed in his head, enticing him to embrace the darkness, to surrender. Tomorrow he would force himself to undertake the journey to Duncileer, regardless of how his body felt. He knew exactly who he needed to see for help, and there was no time whatsoever to lose.

Chapter 7:

Trek to Duncileer

A lmost as quickly as they had arrived in Forrester, the companions prepared to depart for Duncileer. Stamford and Lorq took Fenton to the blacksmith, while Fia and Rokey went to the trading post. Flaskamper stayed behind at the inn, conserving his strength for the trip. With Fia's help, Rokey picked out a suitable pair of breeches, a handsome tunic of soft yellow cotton that laced in the front and a reddish-brown sash for his waist. Then he added a plain brown woolen cloak, similar to those the rest of the company wore. He found the purchase of his new clothes exciting, another step towards his new life, but now he was duty-bound to destroy his blue robe. At the last moment though, he couldn't bear to go through with it. Feeling guilty, he tucked the robe into the bottom of his pack.

Earlier, Rokey had volunteered to pool his funds with those of the company, minus the price of a suit of clothes, so that they could resupply for the trip to Duncileer. Now Fia gave the shop's proprietor the list of the food and other things that they would need, and he scurried off to fill the order. There was enough money to cover the cost, but little left over. When they reached the city, they would have to find some way to earn some more. This worried Rokey, but Fia seemed unconcerned.

"We always manage," she told him cheerfully.

They all met back at the Blue Dragon and prepared for departure. Rokey was relieved to see that Flaskamper's complexion had returned to its normal pale-yellow color, and he seemed to have perked up considerably.

"Physically I'm on the mend," he told Rokey, "but I can feel the dark magic still, rumbling around in my head, trying to get hold of my thoughts. Do me a favor Rokey, and keep watch over me. It's nearly two days journey to Duncileer, and I can't be certain what will happen to me, how I might behave. If I should betray the group in some way –"

"You won't, Flash," Rokey broke in.

"I can't be sure of that," the elf insisted. "I can try my best, but you must promise that you won't allow me to harm the rest of you. You must do whatever is necessary to stop me should I...turn on you."

"Flash –"

"Promise me, Rokey!" Flash said, placing his hands on his friend's shoulders. "Please."

"I promise," Rokey said.

Flaskamper relaxed and smiled sweetly. Rokey realized that he was growing very fond of that smile.

"Alright, let's get ready to go before Stamford starts barking at us," said the elf.

The group left at mid-morning. They disliked going in broad daylight, given their recent troubles, but felt that they had little choice. It was imperative that they get their friend the help that he needed with all possible haste. At first, Stamford and Fia had insisted that Flaskamper let the pony, Fenton, carry him, but he was finally able to convince them that he was fit to walk, albeit with a slight limp. No one that they encountered took any interest in the group's departure, or so it seemed.

Their hope was to reach the end of the woods before nightfall, but Flaskamper's condition required them to rest more frequently, and as a result, they were forced to make camp that night under the canopy of trees. Though the forest was particularly thick in that area, they found a clearing, small but suitable, while there was still enough light to pitch the tents and dig a fire pit.

Flaskamper insisted on helping, though Stamford put his foot down on allowing him to hunt. They had plenty of food, he told him. In reality, he was more than a little nervous about letting the elf out of his sight with all that foul magic running through him. Best to keep a close eye on him until they reached Duncileer.

Lorq returned from gathering firewood with a little blue and yellow frog that he had found and decided to make a pet of.

"He just hopped onto my arm as I bent down to pick up a log," he said. "I'm going to call him Pico. That means *jump* in my language."

Later they sat by the fire, Stamford and Flaskamper smoking their pipes, Lorq playing with Pico, Rokey and Fia chatting and drinking tea. Fia suggested that they continue telling Rokey one another's stories.

"If you don't mind hearing them out of order, I could tell Lorq's story. It's a fitting story since he's just found a new pet. You wouldn't mind if I told our new friend your story would you, dear?" she asked him gently.

"No Fia," Lorq answered. "It would be an honor to have a gifted bard like you tell it."

"I hate to have to have to leave the party," Flaskamper interjected, "but I think I'd better head for bed. It's been a long day."

"Is everything all right Flash?" Rokey asked.

Yes, everything is fine," he answered with a wave of his hand. "I'm just worn out."

They said their goodnights and Flaskamper went off to their tent. Rokey felt a twinge of concern leaving him alone, but he was still wakeful and eager to hear Lorq's tale.

"I didn't know you were a bard, Fia," he said to her.

"Sometimes, when the occasion warrants," she replied. "Of course normally, one would tell the tale in poetry or song. You'll forgive me if I extemporize, given the lack of preparation."

Fia sipped her tea, took a deep breath and began her oration.

"Far to the north of here, in the part of Firma known as the Northern expanse, there was a tribe of nomadic giants known as the Traggs. They were a warlike people, living in an unforgiving climate, in constant competition with rival tribes for food, skins and women. A man's worth was measured in large part by the battles he had won and the enemies he had slain. They knew little and cared less about the rest of Firma and, except for an occasional raid on a minnow village ('minnows' was their name for us, the smaller inhabitants of the land), they sought few contacts outside of their own domain.

"Among the Traggs, there was a tribesman named Gart, massive and powerful even for a giant, with a great unruly tuft of reddish brown hair and a thick wiry beard. He was well respected among his fellow Traggs, for he had led many successful war parties for the glory of his people, and could beat any man of the tribe in single combat.

"Gart and his wife, a raven-haired beauty named Theta, had only one child, a son they named Lorq –"

Lorq made a noise that, in a small boy, would have sounded like a giggle.

"He was a robust lad, strong and sturdy, the type of boy who would grow up to be a fine warrior, as his father was; at least, this was their hope in the beginning. But as time passed, and Lorq grew older – four, then five, then six – they began to notice something that disturbed them. Most boys his age were already playing war games. It was something that boys in all the tribes eagerly began as soon as they started to walk. Lorq, in contrast, had no interest in war, no interest in fighting whatsoever. Young Lorq loved caring for animals, and was always bringing home some sick or injured creature, much to the embarrassment of his father and mother. When it became clear that his father would quickly dispatch the unfortunate creatures, he began to care for them secretly. For years he kept this, and many other secrets from his mother and father. He learned combat skills, but would only use them to defend himself. He abhorred violence, and for that, he was ostracized not only by his peers, but also by the entire tribe. They called him *Rak Taad*, precious lamb. Not a term of endearment, but of scorn, for to the battle-hardened giant tribes, a meek and gentle nature was a source of shame.

"To try and please his father, Lorq attempted to nurture a ferocious temperament. As he grew into adolescence, he grew better at hiding his kind disposition, and his parents began to hold out hope that their son may yet become the warrior for which they had prayed.

"Before they knew it, Lorq had reached his fifteenth year, the first year in which he was to participate in the *Tokpak*, a tournament in which men and boys battle to determine their place in the tribal order. The clashes are brutal, and men are often scarred or maimed, sometimes even killed. Gart was a *Tokpak* master, having achieved the top spot in his age class every year since he himself was fifteen. He fully expected his son to do the same, and spent endless marks with him, preparing for the competition. Though Lorq still hated violence, he trained hard, relishing his father's attention. He hoped to be able to win his class without causing anyone permanent harm, though he kept this wish to himself, lest he once again lose Gart's respect.

"At last the day of the tourney came. To win his age group, Lorq needed to prevail in four contests. He won the first two with ease, just as he wished, without any serious harm to his adversaries. The third contest was more difficult. Lorq prevailed, but the other boy was hurt. It was only a broken wrist, but Lorq was demoralized. He had no wish to proceed to the final event, but could not humiliate himself and his family by quitting. He steeled himself for the final contest, hoping against hope that he would need cause no further injury.

"What he did not know was that his opponent, a cruel and clever young man named Bock, had been studying his potential competitors for weeks. One night he had followed Lorq and discovered his most closely guarded secret, the cave where he kept his beloved pets. Bock had said nothing to anyone of what he had found, but his mind had hatched a plan, one that he hoped would give him the advantage in the contest. A few moments before the two combatants were to take their stands on the battleground, Bock produced a burlap sack and threw it across the yard at Lorq.

"*A little gift Lorq*, he called, *for your table tonight.*

"When Lorq opened the bag, he was horrified to see the headless corpse of his favorite white rabbit. Bock had sneaked into the cave the previous night and killed it, hoping that the sight of it would unnerve

Lorq, and cause him to fight poorly. The plan worked better than he could have hoped. Lorq fell to his knees, the dead rabbit clutched in his arms, and wept uncontrollably. The other members of his tribe turned from him in disgust. Only upon the death of a king were men permitted to weep openly. In all other circumstances it was highly improper, and at the tournament, unforgivable. To maintain their status within the Traggs, Gart and Theta were forced to immediately disown their son. Lorq left the contest grounds, still holding his dead friend, and went home to pack his things. He knew that his life with the tribes was at an end."

Rokey looked up and saw tears in the giant's eyes. Fia noticed as well, and paused.

"Shall I stop, sweetie?" she asked him. "I have no wish to cause you unnecessary pain."

"No, go on Fia." He sniffed. "I like the way you tell it."

Fia grasped his enormous hand, and held it as she continued.

"So Lorq left the domain of the giants to live among the minnows. In many places, especially those in the high northern regions, he was unwelcome because for many years the giants had raided and pillaged those settlements. So he went to the middle of Firma, where a giant was considered more of a curiosity than a menace. Work for a person of his strength was plentiful in the area. Friendships, however, were not. Some were intimidated by his size. Others cruelly sought to take advantage of his kind and trusting nature. For several years, Lorq traveled from town to town, well fed, but lonely and disheartened.

"But all that changed one winter, nearly two years ago now, can you believe it Lorq?"

Lorq shook his head, once again grinning happily.

"The three of us, Stamford, Flash and myself, were spending some time at the palace of the regent of Moorhead..."

"Here, let us not leave out the juicy details," Stamford broke in. "In truth, we had to stay because Flaskamper had gotten into a spot of trouble..."

"Stamford..." Fia said.

"Seems the local magistrate was a tad upset with our boy. His daughter was to marry a local lad the following day..."

"Stamford, really..." she tried again.

"Unfortunately Flaskamper was discovered that evening, deflowering the future groom in the livery stable, by the bride's mother no less, who screamed and promptly fell into a dead faint. As you can imagine..."

"Stamford, that's enough!" Fia cried, a rare edge in her voice. She stood and faced Stamford angrily. "It is not fitting to tell such stories now, with Flash ill and unable to defend himself."

"Aw, Fia..."

"There's a proper time for bawdy tales," she said, more gently. "This is simply not one of them."

She cocked her head slightly toward Rokey and gave the group leader a meaningful look. Stamford realized his mistake and held up his hands.

"You're right," said Stamford. "I apologize. Flaskamper is a good lad, and doesn't deserve to be gossiped about, especially by the likes of me." He turned to Rokey. "Don't pay me any mind boy. Flash is a bit high-spirited at times, but his heart is solid gold. Go on Fia. Tell the rest of the story."

Fia sat down and closed her eyes, recovering the rhythm of her tale. Then she continued.

"Well, now that *that* cat is out of the bag...the magistrate had Flaskamper arrested, and was insisting that the regent order his execution. It seems that there was still an old law in existence, which called for the penalty of death in cases of...well, in such cases. No one had ever bothered to expunge the law. They merely stopped enforcing it. But the magistrate was furious, and insisted that the punishment be carried out. The regent had no such intention. In fact, he found the whole thing rather amusing. However, to keep peace in the kingdom, he ordered Flash locked up for an indeterminate period of time so that tempers would cool and more reasonable heads could prevail. I accepted a position as bard of the court, they hadn't had one in some time, and Stamford made himself useful to Moorhead's men-at-arms, helping the guard captain to train up new recruits. All in all it was a pleasant stay. Flaskamper went a bit stir crazy in the dungeon, but the regent saw to it that he was well treated, considering the circumstances.

"The mid-winter snows began, and Moorhead, being at the tip of a peninsula, was especially prone to harsh weather, bitter winds and thick wet snows. During one seemingly interminable snowfall, I had gone to the trading post, bundled from head to toe. The nature of the errand escapes me at the moment, but I remember that, as I plodded through the wind and snow on my way back, something made me turn back the way I had come, and in the distance, I saw a figure. For a moment I thought it a mirage. It's not only in the desert they happen you know. I've often heard of people seeing things that aren't there while traveling in a bitter storm. But I rubbed my eyes clear and looked again, and the figure was still there, trudging steadily through this raging blizzard. I forgot for the moment about my own discomfort and stood there, watching his approach. As he grew closer and closer, I became aware of his immense size. He was wrapped, as was I, from head to toe in fur, and one could almost have mistaken him for a large deep-forest bear. Of course the prudent thing would have been to hurry in the opposite direction, for I was completely unarmed. But the sight of him fascinated me, the way he had seemed just to appear from nowhere. I stood my ground until he reached me. It became obvious then that I was but half his size, and I began to grow a bit fearful. The entire scene seemed so...surreal. I half expected him to announce himself as Bal-hapsat, the stealer of souls, come to claim mine for his collection. That's what made it all the more funny when he –" Fia began to giggle. "When he –"

"When he what?" Rokey asked, catching her infectious laughter.

"When he threw off his hood and said, in perfect Common Firmish –" she lowered her voice in imitation of Lorq, " 'Pardon me miss, could you please direct me to the palace?'." Fia collapsed with mirth. After a few moments she recovered.

"I'm sorry," she said. "No one else ever finds that as amusing as I do. You had to be there to appreciate the peculiarity of it. Such an innocent question from such a formidable figure, and after such dire musings had just gone through my head.

"In any case, that was my first encounter with Lorq. The moment I looked into his big, violet eyes I knew that he meant me no harm. I invited him to walk with me back to the palace and we talked, as much as the howling wind would allow. It seems Lorq had heard tales about the fine menagerie kept by the regent, and had traveled to Moorhead hoping to see it and, if at all possible, obtain a position. The dear boy hadn't had any pets since he was forced to set his own little zoo free just before leaving the tribal lands. Since human friends had not come easily, he hoped that working with animals would help him to ease his feelings of loneliness.

"As it happened, Lorq was in luck. The zookeeper had injured himself in a fall some days earlier and was desperate for someone to help him while he recuperated. The regent was reluctant at first. He had heard the tales of the tribal giants and their barbarous ways, but I convinced him to give Lorq a chance."

"Fia could sell snow to a frost nymph," Stamford interjected. Fia smiled and continued.

"Once Lorq had started his work, it was immediately apparent that there was no need for concern. His love of the animals and the tenderness with which he cared for them immediately won him the respect of the zookeeper. He said once that he had never seen gryphon stalls mucked out with such enthusiasm. The regent was so pleased that he gave Lorq the full privileges of the palace, which meant that when his work was finished, he would often come and spend time with Stamford or me in our quarters, or in the dungeon playing cards with Flaskamper. We all took a great liking to our new friend, whom we took to calling our gentle giant.

"At last, when winter had eased its icy grip, and spring began to get a foothold on the land, the regent was finally able to convince the affronted magistrate that, in fact, Flaskamper had done them all a favor by helping them to avoid a disastrous mistake, from which they all would have suffered far greater embarrassment later on. He was freed on condition that henceforth he attend no weddings within the city limits. The zookeeper recovered, and told Lorq that, though he would have liked to keep him on, there was simply not enough work anymore to keep him busy. He wrote him a glowing recommendation and the regent gave him a handsome bonus for a job well done.

"It made Lorq sad to have to leave the animals he had grown to love, though the regent made it clear that he would be a welcome visitor anytime. The three of us convinced him that, rather than continue his nomadic life alone, he should join with us, his fellow misfits. It took little persuasion really, as we had all grown quite close over the long winter months. We left Moorhead together, and have been together ever since. And that, dear friends, is where I end my story."

They all applauded Fia for her fine account, then decided it was time to turn in for the night. So as not to be caught unawares again, they chose this time to keep the fire going and to keep watch.

Rokey volunteered for the first shift and, after the others had retired, sat watching the flames as they danced over the crackling wood. He tried to relax, but the woods were full of ominous sounds. With each twig snap he became more convinced that the ratmen were closing in once again, their glowing red eyes fixed only on him.

The thought chilled him. He was certain now that he must have been the victim of mistaken identity, but that didn't change the fact that they were all nearly killed. He hoped that, having failed, whoever had orchestrated the attack had come to realize that an error had occurred. But what if he (or she) hadn't? Could there be more horrible creatures, lurking just beyond the firelight, waiting for him to doze off?

His hand went to the bastard sword on his hip. Since he could not afford to buy his own, Flaskamper had insisted that he wear it at least until they got to Duncileer. The cold steel on his hip made him feel more secure. He thought back on his battle with the ratmen. His mentor, Brother Barrow would have been proud of his performance with the tricky sword, he thought. However, these thoughts brought on other memories of the Brotherhood, and his moment of pride was soon awash in grief and shame. He had no reason to be proud of anything. He was a failure. His eyes stung with tears, but he fought them away. He had said that he was going to look to the future, not dwell in the past. At times like this though, when it was quiet and he was alone, his mind was inexorably drawn backwards, back to the abbot, lying face down in the bathing pool...

An owl's screech snapped him out of his unhappy reverie. Was there something there? He stood to stretch his legs and walked over to where Fenton stood.

"What do you think, Fenton?" he asked the horse. "All clear out there?"

Fenton snorted and tossed his head.

"I'll take that as a 'yes'," Rokey said with a smile. He patted the pony on the neck, then headed back to his seat by the fire. Before long, Stamford came out to relieve him. He headed back to the tent, where Flaskamper was muttering something in his sleep. Rokey contemplated waking him, but decided against it. Instead, he lay down on his own bedroll and, in minmarks, also fell deeply asleep.

*   *   *

Sometime later, Rokey awoke to the sound of a sharp cry. He sat bolt upright and listened. Next to him, Flaskamper was moaning and thrashing in his sleep. Rokey was fairly certain that the cry had come from him. It was still dark outside. He crawled over and shook the elf gently.

"Flash," he said. "Flash wake up." He did not wake up though. He continued to moan and cry out. Rokey shook him harder and called his name again. Finally, Flaskamper woke with a violent start.

"NOOO!" he screamed, then gasped for air.

"Flash, it's alright. It's me, Rokey. You were having a nightmare."

"Rokey," Flaskamper said breathlessly. He sat up and threw his arms around him. "It wasn't a mistake. It *was* you they wanted."

"Who wanted me?" Rokey asked, holding onto Flaskamper. "What do you mean, Flash?"

"My nightmare. It wasn't just a nightmare. It was a vision... side effect from this... poison inside me. It's already starting to fade, but I saw the ratmen, and something else. Something hidden by the darkness, summoning them, directing them...to you."

"Flash, that's crazy. Who could possibly want to kill me? The only people I know are the brothers and some of the villagers. I know they're not very happy with me, but even if they did wish me harm, I don't know of anybody there who uses magic of any kind. It has to be a mistake. It *has* to be."

Flaskamper disengaged from his embrace, but held onto Rokey's arms. He could just make out the silhouette of his friend in the darkness.

"I know. It makes no sense. But you have to believe me. I heard your name. It was in the minds of those...those things that attacked us. Your name. Your face. I know it seems crazy, but you have to believe me."

"Flash..."

"Rokey, somehow, for some reason, somebody wants you dead. Somebody evil...and powerful. They failed once, but they'll try again...and again. You'll never be safe unless we're able to find out who's behind it and stop them."

Rokey took a deep breath. He still wasn't entirely convinced, but a cold fear was beginning to grip him. If it really was him the ratmen were after, what would be coming for him next? Suddenly the whole world seemed to close in around him.

"What can I do?" he whispered. "How can I fight against someone I don't even know? Someone with that much power?"

"We need to make it to Duncileer." Flaskamper told him. "The sorceress may be able to help both of us. If I can keep my sanity...if we can all stay alive. Something else is coming our way Rokey. Something deeper, and darker. We all have to be careful and watch out for one another, or none of us will live to see the city gates."

"We will, Flash." Rokey answered. "We will all make it to Duncileer, alive. Then we'll get you well and get to the bottom of this mystery."

They both lay back down, but neither slept. Rokey had meant what he said about them all living to see Duncileer. However, as he lay there in the darkness, listening to the eerie forest noises and his own uneasy heartbeat, he began to wonder.

*   *   *

The next day dawned grey and overcast. They ate a quick, cold breakfast and hurriedly broke camp. Flaskamper spoke to no one, answering questions with a grunt. Rokey was afraid for him, for all of them really, but especially for Flaskamper. His eyes had a hollow, distant look. His shoulders hunched forward; his feet scuffed along the ground as he walked. He looked like someone who had been defeated. The sight of it made Rokey's heart ache.

By midday they had emerged from the woods. A light rain began to fall, adding more gloom to their already dampened spirits. They broke for lunch, but no one was hungry, so they sat on their packs by the side of the road and rested, each lost in their own thoughts. Rokey looked up once and caught Flaskamper studying him. The elf quickly looked away and Rokey wondered how deeply the darkness had already leached into his mind, into his soul. If...no, *when* they reached the sorceress in Duncileer, would she be able to free him from the magic poison, or would it already be too late? Rokey knew nothing of black magic and its long-term effects. And what of elf magic? Would Flaskamper's intrinsic magic help him to withstand permanent damage longer? He fervently wished that he had some answers. Even bad news would be preferable to these lingering apprehensions.

The light rain turned into a downpour. The trail through the meadowland became muddy and their progress slowed even more. The sky was full of thick, black clouds, extinguishing the daylight. Rokey walked up to join Stamford, who was leading Fenton at the front of the group.

"Will we reach Duncileer today?" he asked the leader. "I'm worried about Flaskamper. I'm afraid of the damage he may sustain if we're forced to camp for another night."

"Under normal conditions I'd say we had a good chance to get there before nightfall," Stamford told him. "But with this foul weather slowing us down, I'd say it's unlikely. We needn't camp though. By the time true darkness falls, we should be able to see the city's perimeter lights. They will guide us. We also have one more goblin torch. I am loath to use it, but I'm afraid that if we don't, Fenton, or even one of us, may step in a hole on the trail and break an ankle. With all that we have to contend with already, we can't risk another injury."

Rokey agreed.

"Where is Flaskamper?" Stamford asked. "What is his condition?"

"He's at the back. Lorq is watching him." He told Stamford about the previous night, and about his uncomfortable feelings at lunch.

"You're right," he responded. "We can't risk any more breaks. We must reach the city with all haste, at least, what haste we can muster."

"Do you know where we need to go, Stamford? Who Flaskamper said we should see?"

"Yes," the dark man answered. "He brought me there once before. I remember where she lives."

Rokey dropped back next to Flaskamper. He shot a look back at Lorq, who was walking just a pace or two behind. The giant merely shrugged his shoulders. Rokey tried talking to the elf, but he was unresponsive. His eyes were glassy. He seemed to be in a trance of some kind.

They continued on as the day drew to a close. The sky turned from dark grey to black. As the last of the light slipped away, Stamford fetched the remaining goblin torch and snapped off the top. Its ghostly green flame sprang up. It was little help in the drenching rain, but it lit up the trail immediately ahead, and that was sufficient for their needs.

"Look!" Stamford pointed ahead. They could just see the lights of Duncileer shining in the distance. The rain made it difficult to judge the distance, but they were all heartened to have their destination in sight.

Suddenly Flaskamper clapped his hands to his head and fell to his knees, screaming. Fia ran over and kneeled on the muddy ground in front of him. She called his name over and over, but received no response. As she reached out to him, he suddenly grabbed her arms tightly and raised his head. There was a wild, feverish look in his eyes.

"Fia" he said. "I'm so tired. I can't fight with it anymore. It's beating me." His grip grew tighter, and his eyes turned menacing.

"Stamford," she called, "tie him! Quickly! Lorq, carry him. We can't trust him anymore. The poison is taking him."

Flaskamper threw his head back and laughed, a cold, unsettling sound. Stamford grabbed a length of the lightweight elf-made rope that they always carried. Flaskamper fought wildly as his hands and arms were bound. As Lorq picked him up, he closed his eyes and his body grew limp. Rokey suspected that Flash was still in there, using all his resources to keep the darkness at bay a little longer.

For the next few marks, they trudged along, the blackness broken only by the small green flame of the goblin torch. Flaskamper slept most of the way, but now and then would pipe up with a fiendish laugh or a disquieting fit of screams. The lights of Duncileer gradually grew broader and brighter, until Stamford declared the city to be less than a mark ahead of them.

At last they could see the walls of Duncileer looming in the distance. They would be there in minmarks. However, as they drew close enough to see clearly, they were horrified to see that the city gates were shut fast.

"I don't understand it," Stamford called to Rokey. "Duncileer has never closed its gates."

"Well," Rokey responded, "let's hope there's someone there to let us in." They reached the gate and began to shout and pound on the wide wooden doors. For a few tense moments there was no response, then a voice called down from the left-hand gate tower.

"Who goes there?"

"We are a party of travelers from Forrester," Stamford answered, quelling his panic. "Open the gate and let us in."

"You'll have to camp til morning," the gatekeeper answered. "Gates are closed to all between sunset and sunrise by order of the king."

"Sir, we are weary and soaked to the skin," Stamford said. "We have friends in the city with whom we can stay tonight. Please let us in."

"I can't disobey the king," the gatekeeper responded. "It would be worth my head if I disobeyed the king."

"Fia," Stamford whispered, "you give it a go. See if you can charm him."

Rokey watched as she stepped forward and threw her hood back. Even soaking wet and covered in road dust, she still looked radiant. He wondered what her story was, what qualified her as one of their misfit bunch.

"Please sir," Fia called up to him. "My brother is...is injured and needs a healer. I'm afraid that he will grow much worse before morning. I beg you to make an exception and let us in." Her voice lowered to a conspiratorial tone. "We promise not to tell anyone. We'll keep it just between us." She cast her most endearing smile up towards the tower.

For a few moments, there was silence, and they began to think that she, too, had failed. Then they heard the groan of the crossbeam being lifted, and the gate swung slowly open. The party hurried through and the gatekeeper, a chubby young man with a large nose and pocked face, quickly closed and barred it behind them. He gave Fia a shy grin.

"Now not a word to anyone now," he said to her. "Worth my life you know, disobeying the king."

Fia put her finger to her lips, then bent over and kissed him on the cheek. The young man flushed happily and all but floated back to his watchtower. Stamford shook his head.

"I don't know how you do that," he said. "Oh drek, of course I do. You do it to me all the time."

Just then Flaskamper began to struggle again in Lorq's arms.

"We'd better go quickly," Stamford said, "He may not be able to hold out much longer."

Rokey looked over at his friend. The elf was writhing in obvious discomfort; his eyes were closed, and he was muttering something in a language Rokey didn't recognize. As the party hastened into the city, toward the home of the sorceress, he prayed to any gods who might be listening that they had gotten there in time.

Chapter 8:

Battista

She was not asleep when they arrived. Stamford wondered if she ever slept. She stood in the doorway studying them. Her long, grey curls were in need of a comb, and a cigar dangled from her right hand. Her wide mouth was set into a frown of disdain. Stamford suspected the expression was permanent. She wore a long, brown housedress and housecoat that had seen better days. She took a puff of her cigar and slowly blew the smoke into the air.

"Alright", she said to Stamford in a low, raspy voice. "what do you want?"

Stamford, to Rokey's surprise, seemed somewhat intimidated by the woman. For a moment he seemed at a loss for words; then he recovered himself. He stood aside so that she could see Flaskamper lying in Lorq's arms.

"A friend of yours in is trouble, Battista," he said. "He needs your help."

It may have been Rokey's imagination, but he thought the frown on her face softened ever so slightly when she saw Flaskamper. Soundlessly, she stood aside and motioned them all inside. She directed Lorq to carry the elf into a bedroom and lay him down on the bed. Flaskamper seemed now to be in some kind of stupor. He was completely limp and unresponsive. Battista studied him closely for a few minmarks, then looked up at Stamford.

"Give me the story," she said curtly.

Stamford told her all about the ratman attack, the advice of the healer in Forrester and Flaskamper's behavior since his injury. She shook her head, looking disgusted. Without a word, she brushed past them and disappeared into another room. For a few minmarks, they stood where they were, not certain what to do.

"Sit down!" she ordered from the other room. They seated themselves around the large table in her kitchen and waited.

It seemed like ages, but she finally emerged, one arm encircling a basket filled with an assortment of items. On her way past, she pointed to Rokey.

"You," she said. "come with me."

Rokey hurried with her into the room where Flash lay, still out cold. Battista moved a small table and chair near the bed and sat down. From the basket she pulled a small pouch, a dark red glass bottle, a round, silver tray, a strangely shaped wooden spoon and a large white candle. One by one, she placed all the items on the table except for the candle, which she handed to Rokey.

"Light this from the fireplace," she told him.

Rokey looked over at the fireplace. There was wood in it, but it had not been lit.

"Um..." he said. "Ah, it's not..."

Battista waved a hand towards the fireplace and spoke a single word.

"Conflagrum"

The logs in the cold fireplace abruptly burst into flames. Rokey jumped back in amazement. Slowly he crept toward the now blazing wood and held out the candle til the wick caught. Then he returned it to the sorceress.

"How come – how come you didn't just..." she shot him a glance and he stopped abruptly. She shook her head.

"Can't use magic to light a magic candle," she muttered. "You'll taint it."

She poured what looked like a mixture of dried herbs into the silver tray. Then she poured some of the liquid from the bottle over them and stirred them with the stick until it formed a thick paste. She scooped the paste up with the wooden spoon and held it out to Rokey.

"Take this, then go sit on him," she said, tilting her head towards Flaskamper. "When I tell you to, open his mouth and feed it to him. He'll thrash around like we're killing him and try to spit it out. Whatever you do, don't let him. We might not have time to try this again."

Rokey took the spoon and went over to the bed. Flaskamper was still bound. Rokey straddled him, using his body to hold him down, and waited for Battista to give the word. He heard her get up from the chair and begin to chant.

> *"No ras pa tom billa*
> *Fadra haar son hatha mira*
> *Ecta yentro totorum ent kathal..."*

As soon as she began her chant, Flaskamper's eyes flew open. The pupils were wide, and seemed to stare out at nothing. He began to moan and scream, and tried to wriggle free, but Rokey had him securely pinned.

> *"Allenda pa forras ent regnum...*

"Feed him the herbs, now!

> *Sarantum no tom hattava sinte"*

Flaskamper opened his mouth to scream. Rokey quickly spooned the herb paste into his mouth and gripping the top of his head and his jaw, forced his mouth closed. He hated being so rough, but he knew it was for his own good.

Battista continued her mantra. Now she was over by the table, waving her hands over the burning candle. The flame grew higher and stronger, and turned from its normal yellow color to a deep blood red.

Rokey continued to struggle with Flaskamper. The elf's eyes had rolled back in his head and he began to sweat profusely. Rokey was finding it more and more difficult to keep him from spitting out the herbs, but he continued to put all of what remained of his strength into the struggle. So far, he was still winning. Suddenly Battista stopped her chant and raised her voice.

"Flaskamper!" she yelled. "Fight it boy. I've drained most of its power, but you must cast the rest out. FIGHT IT! FIGHT IT!"

"Fight it Flash," Rokey whispered to his friend. "You can do it. I know you can."

The sorceress came to stand beside the bed.

"You can let go now," she told him after a few minmarks. "The rest is up to him."

Rokey let go of Flaskamper's head.

"Swallow them," she told the elf. To Rokey's surprise, he swallowed. As they watched, his eyes slowly returned to normal, then closed. He stopped thrashing and moaning, and sweat stopped pouring from his face.

"Get up. Untie him," Battista ordered. Rokey gladly complied.

"We have one more thing to do," she told him, and led him to the table. The candle was still burning; its dark red flame raged like an open wound.

"Grab the candle," she instructed. "You'll need both hands."

He wrapped his hands around the candle and lifted. To his surprise, he could barely lift it. Battista walked over to the window and opened it.

"Bring it over and hold it out the window," she told him.

It was a struggle, but Rokey was finally able to haul the flaming candle over to the window. He stuck it out through, and Battista leaned over and blew it out. Abruptly the top of the candle exploded. A putrid greenish liquid squirted out, covering the ground outside. The foul smell of it nearly knocked him over.

"Battista," Rokey said, choking, "what is this stuff?"

"The poison," she answered. "I drew most of it from him and stored it in the candle. Go ahead and throw the rest of it into the fire."

Again, Rokey obeyed. The sorceress closed the window behind him. The remains of the candle popped and hissed in the fire like animal fat. Rokey felt his stomach turn.

"The rain will wash the rest of it away," she said matter-of-factly. "Let's see how our friend is coming along." She walked over to the bed. Rokey joined her. Flaskamper was laying quietly, his eyes closed. Abruptly she reached down and slapped him on the cheek. His eyes flew open in surprise.

"Get up!" she yelled at him. "You're all better now, and you owe me an explanation." Flash sat up quickly.

"Battista, thank you," he said.

"Don't thank me, for the gods' sakes," she wailed. "Just do me a favor and once, just once come to visit without a life or death crisis hanging over your head. I don't know why I ever let you through my door in the first place. You're nothing but a six foot, spike-eared pain in the arse!"

"Sorry," Flaskamper said, hanging his head. Battista turned to Rokey.

"You're not so bad," she informed him. "Now get out. I need to talk to your sweetheart in private."

Rokey was going to object to her choice of words, but then thought better of it and left the room, closing the door behind him. The others all stood as he came into the kitchen.

"Well?" Stamford asked.

"He's well again," Rokey told him, and filled them in on the details.

"Amazing," said Fia. She went and put her arms around Rokey. "You did a wonderful job, Rokey. You should be proud."

Rokey flushed with pleasure, but quickly shook his head.

"I'm the one that got Flash into this mess," he said. "I owe him whatever it takes to get him out of it."

"So you're a man of honor, too," Lorq told him. "I'm glad you're with us now. Right Stamford?"

To Stamford's credit, he only hesitated a moment before nodding his head. Rokey laughed. He felt an immense calm wash over him. They had made it, all of them, and Flash was going to be alright. His nemesis, whoever or whatever it was, was still out there, but Rokey was too relieved and exhausted to think any more about it tonight. Now, more than anything, he just wanted to crawl into bed with Flash and... that is, next to Flash, with the others, and go to sleep. He hoped that they could do that soon, for he knew each of them was completely done in.

Still, it was more than a mark before the door opened and Battista and Flash joined them. Rokey thought Flash still looked a little shaky, but he was certainly much improved, and had his wonderful smile back. He introduced the sorceress to Rokey officially, as well as to Fia, Lorq and Stamford. She nodded curtly to all but Rokey. To him she held out her hand. Rokey cautiously reached out and took it. She turned his hand over, and studied his palm for a minmark. A puzzled look came over her briefly, but then it was gone. She let go of Rokey's hand and looked back at Flaskamper.

"This one has some character, Junior, she said. "You ought to hang onto him for a while." Flaskamper grew flustered.

"I- I...I mean we – we're just friends, Battista."

The woman snorted.

"If you say so," she said. "Nevertheless, you two should stick together."

"We plan to," Flaskamper told her. "We need to get to the bottom of who's out to harm Rokey."

"All in good time," she answered. "Tonight you'll get some rest. Tomorrow's the King's Fair. It seems you've been relatively safe during the daytime. Go celebrate, unwind some. After that, we'll see what we can see."

"Why have they started locking the gates at night?" Stamford asked her.

"We've had a sharp increase in violent crime this past year," Battista answered. "The militia captain suspected that brigands were sneaking into the city by night to pray on the citizenry, so he ordered that the gates be shut from sundown to sunup. It has helped to keep some of the crime under control, but not all. Dark things lurk in the alleyways at night, looking for unwary prey. Slowly, but steadily, the city is changing"

She led them into another room. This one was larger and, except for a half dozen chairs, was completely devoid of furnishings. With a word, she lit the fire.

"You can all camp in here tonight," she said. "Hang your clothes on the chairs by the fire. They'll dry overnight. The privy is just through that door. If there's anything you need before tomorrow, too bad. I'm going to bed."

Flaskamper gave her a hug, and her mouth turned into what might have been construed as a smile. Then she turned and shuffled from the room. Fia walked over and put her arms around Flaskamper.

"Are you alright, sweetie?" she asked. "All better now?"

"Yes Fia. It's all gone," he said. "I feel like myself again."

"Glad to hear it," said Stamford, who was in the process of stripping off his wet clothes. Now let's get some sleep. I don't know about the rest of you, but I'm worn out."

As he stood in his shorts, unpacking his bedroll, Rokey saw that Stamford's entire body was covered with scars. The man had obviously seen a great deal of battle. He wondered what sort of life the man had led before forming this band of misfits. He would ask Flash when there was time. He didn't quite dare ask Stamford. He liked the man, but still felt a little intimidated by him.

Their outer clothes drying by the fire, the group climbed under their blankets and soon fell fast asleep. For the first time in days, each of them felt completely safe.

Chapter 9:

King's Fair

R okey woke the next morning to the sound of trumpets in the distance. It was well past dawn and the sun was streaming through the window. He could hear the sound of Battista clattering around in the kitchen, but none of his friends were awake yet. He looked over at Flaskamper, asleep next to him. The elf had thrown his blankets off and was lying on his back wearing only his underwear, a tight elven knit that hid very little. Rokey couldn't help but indulge in a lingering look at his friend's lean, strong body. He suppressed the urge to reach out and caress his soft, pale-yellow skin. His eyes skimmed over Flaskamper's face, studying his features. His eyes, when they were open, were wide and bright. His nose was straight and slender, his lips, red and full. Rokey wondered what it would be like to kiss them, and the thought began to stir him physically. He got up quickly and headed for the privy to wash up, lest he wind up caught in an embarrassing situation. He would have given almost anything for a soak in a hot, sunken bath, like the one the abbot had (the thought brought a sudden stab of memory), but he had to make do with a pitcher and basin. There was a bottle of liquid soap here, something he had never seen before. He used it to wash his hair and body, and felt much better afterwards. By the time he emerged, still toweling his hair, Flaskamper and the others were awake.

"Ah, he emerges at last," said the elf with a smile. "I was about to break in and make sure you hadn't gotten stuck in the loo."

"I was enjoying getting clean," Rokey answered. He fished in his pack and found his comb and began running it through his hair.

For some reason, Flaskamper found this incredibly sexy.

One by one they took turns washing up, then they emerged into Battista's big kitchen. The sorceress had been busy. She fed them hot oatmeal, biscuits with honey and fresh goat's milk. When the company had eaten its fill, she took Rokey into her private chamber.

"I need a snip of your hair and a drop of your blood," she told him. "I'll have the privacy I need while you're all gone to consult my spirit patrons, and try to determine what's going on here."

Rokey was happy to oblige and she trimmed a small lock of hair and pricked his finger with a tiny obsidian knife, letting the blood fall onto a small muslin square. They rejoined the others and she sent them all off to the King's Fair. When they had all gone, she studied the small square of cloth, stained with Rokey's blood, and wondered what mysteries it might unlock for them.

*   *   *

They were all excited about attending the King's fair. Among them, only Flaskamper had been before, and he knew exactly what *he* was going to do.

"This year I'm going to win the archery contest," he declared. "Last time I got beat by some woodsman, but not this time. I've been practicing."

"Is your leg well enough for that, do you think?" Rokey asked.

"Oh sure," Flaskamper replied. "The physical wound is mending quickly. That's another handy bit of elf magic – fast healing. Now that the poison is all gone, I'm fit and frisky."

The elf winked mischievously at Rokey, and was rewarded with a shy smile and flush of pink in his friend's cheeks.

"This will be nothing like the festival at the Noble Contemplative," Flaskamper told him. "It's *huge*. Rows and rows of food and games of chance and acrobats and artisans. And there will be thousands of people there. Everyone comes to the King's fair. He's very generous. He's been known to give away parcels of land as contest prizes. First prize for the archery contest is one hundred gold sovereigns. If I win, we won't have to work for a year."

They arrived at the king's palace. The gates had been thrown wide and already there was a huge throng of revelers about. Rokey gazed around in astonishment at all the booths and wagons. Hunter's Moon really paled in comparison to this. One could easily become lost in all this commotion.

Flaskamper stopped at the guard's booth to sign up for the archery contest, which was to take place later that afternoon at the king's tournament grounds.

"Now don't let me drink too much," he said to Rokey. "I need to stay sharp if I'm to win. Some of the best archers in Firma come to compete in this contest. I'll be up against some stiff competition."

Stamford was immediately drawn to the many weaponry exhibits and Fia wanted to look at the instrument makers' booths.

"We should set a meeting place in case we lose one another," Fia suggested.

"Good idea," said Flaskamper. "The Lazy Peasant Tavern has a tent right over there. We can all meet back there for lunch. Nothing is ever very expensive at the Fair, so we can afford a good meal."

They all agreed.

"Don't let Rokey go off by himself," Stamford reminded the elf. "He should be safe in the daylight with all these people about, but you never know."

"Don't worry," Flaskamper said. "I'll keep him close by." He grabbed Rokey by the arm.

"I thought as much," Stamford remarked. "Don't know why I mentioned it."

They went their separate ways. Stamford alone, Lorq with Fia, Rokey with Flaskamper. Rokey could hardly take it all in. He could never have imagined such a massive assembly of people when he was still living at the monastery.

Flaskamper led him toward the performance tents. The inside of the tents were arranged in a circular fashion, with the performers' platforms forming a ring around the center. Rokey and Flaskamper slowly walked around, enjoying all the different acts. One man was eating fire. Next to him, a woman swallowed swords, and beyond her was a man called a contortionist. Rokey gaped as he bent his body into impossible shapes, and then scrunched himself into a tiny box barely large enough for a small dog. Flaskamper enjoyed watching Rokey's reactions. He found his friend's innocence tremendously endearing.

When they had finished watching the performers, Rokey spied a vendor selling imported Elfwood wine.

"Come on," he told Flash. "I want to try this nectar of the gods."

The price of the wine was high, due to its rarity, but when the man saw that Flaskamper was an elf, he gave them a considerable discount.

They sipped the wine. It was light and fruity, with hints of some kind of spice that Rokey couldn't identify. For Flaskamper, it brought back memories of home, both good and bad.

"Well, which is better," Flaskamper asked Rokey, "ours or the Brotherhood's?"

"I don't think you can compare the two," Rokey answered diplomatically. "They're both excellent in their own way."

"That was a skillful dodge," the elf said with a grin. Rokey smiled back and said nothing.

Before they knew it, it was time to head back to the Lazy Peasant's tent to meet the others for lunch. The rest of the company was already there when they arrived and they sat down to enjoy a sumptuous meal. Fia showed them the small stuffed animal that Lorq had won at one of the game booths and given to her. It was a little lamb, whose body was covered with soft, white, carded wool. Stamford talked of the enormous variety of weapons for sale there. He was glad to have so little money, he said, or he would have bought more than he could travel with.

After lunch they walked through the artisan section, looking at pottery, jewelry and other crafts from throughout the land. They were admiring a booth filled with fine imported fabrics when the first trumpet sounded to summon the contestants to the archery contest. They made their way to the king's tournament grounds. There they separated, Flaskamper heading to the contestants' area, the others to the spectator seating. The final trumpet sounded to gather any stragglers. A few minmarks later, the master of ceremonies for the contest came out and introduced the contestants. The company cheered when Flaskamper's name was announced. He beamed and waved to them.

There were over sixty contestants in the tournament, which consisted of several elimination rounds. Each round cut the number of contenders in half. Eventually, only two would be left to shoot it out for the grand prize. Flaskamper made it through the first several rounds with ease, shooting with confidence and grace, as well as keen accuracy. The woodsman who had beaten him at his previous attempt was not there this year, but there was a young soldier from the far-off northern city of Iceberg participating this year who also possessed incredible skills. The elf seemed unfazed, but his friends were on pins and needles. Through round after round, Flaskamper made the cut, until at last he was one of the two finalists left in the competition. No one was surprised to see that his opponent was the young soldier from Iceberg.

The finals were a kind of biathlon. The two finalists first rode around a target range on horseback, shooting three arrows into each target. It was not a race, but one was penalized for taking more than one minmark. After that they would dismount, and proceed to a standing range, where they would have thirty tiks to fire five arrows into each of two swinging targets. Points were awarded based on distance from the center and grouping. The contestant with the most points would win the match. Only in the event of a tie would it matter who finished first. In such a case, the first one to finish was declared the winner. An ornate little minmark glass was brought out to time the event. Rokey sat on his hands to keep from wringing them with anxiety. He would never have guessed that a simple sporting event could be so exciting.

Flaskamper and the soldier mounted up, and a moment later, when the queen dropped her handkerchief, they sped off. This portion of the event required not only skill with a bow, but with a horse as well. Both men seemed to be shooting well, but the northerner's skill on horseback was slightly superior to Flaskamper's, so the young man completed that section first by several tiks. At the standing range, the elf caught up, aiming and firing his ten arrows at lightning speed, quicker than his opponent, but not quite fast enough to make up his lead. The soldier finished firing and held his hands in the air a split tik before Flaskamper. This meant that in the event of a tie, Flaskamper would lose. His four friends sat anxiously as the scores were tallied up. Flaskamper looked over at Rokey and winked, but Rokey was sure he was nervous. He wanted this win badly. It seemed like forever, but the Master of Ceremonies finally stepped to the middle of the field, a slip of paper in one hand, and his bullhorn in another. Flaskamper and the soldier came and stood on either side of him. He raised the bullhorn and addressed the audience.

"Ladies and gentlemen," he began, "the results of His Majesty's archery finals have been tabulated. First to complete the course, Lieutenant Erich, of the city of Iceberg. Out of a possible one hundred points, Erich scores..." there was a rolling of drums..."ninety-seven".

The crowd roared. It was a very impressive score. Nearly perfect shooting. Rokey's forehead broke into a nervous sweat.

"Second to complete the course, Flaskamper, of Elfwood. Out of a possible one hundred points, Flaskamper scores..." the drums rolled again... "ninety-*eight* points. I hereby declare Flaskamper the new King's Champion Archer." He held up Flaskamper's hand. The crowd cheered loudly, his friends loudest of all. The elf offered his hand to the soldier, who pumped it firmly and clapped Flaskamper on the shoulder. The Master of Ceremonies then led Flash to the king's box, where the queen placed a gold medallion around his neck and the king handed him his prize purse...one hundred gold sovereigns. He bowed deeply to each of them, then turned and saluted the crowd, who roared their appreciation.

After stopping to accept congratulations from other competitors and audience members, Flaskamper rejoined his companions. They were all overjoyed for him, and the elf was flushed with pride and pleasure. Rokey gave him a hug. Flash was still sweaty from the competition, and the feel of his hot, wet skin against him filled Rokey again with an almost overwhelming urge to plant a kiss on those full, red lips. He held back though, squeezing the King's Archery Champion all the harder instead.

"My friend," said Stamford, thumping Flaskamper on the back, "it is time for us to celebrate!"

They all heartily agreed.

"And I know just the tavern to celebrate in," he added.

They made their way from the tournament grounds, through the still crowded fairgrounds toward the gates of the palace. The gate guards, who always closely followed the outcome of the tournaments, shouted congratulations at Flaskamper. Flash waved back at them, and the company continued out into the city.

A few marks later, well fed and drunk on fine Duncileer ale, they spilled out of the Drunken Sailor, one of the city's oldest and finest establishments. They had spent nearly two of Flaskamper's hard-won sovereigns, but it had been well worth the expense. For the first time in days they all felt relaxed and happy. Stamford and Flaskamper were loudly singing a bawdy song involving a farm girl and a well-endowed field hand. Rokey, Fia and Lorq stayed a short distance behind, prepared to deny knowing them should anyone ask. It had grown dark outside, but not terribly late, and the streets of the city still bustled with people. Rokey took in all the comings and goings with great enthusiasm. He liked the idea of potentially settling down in a city like this, after his troubles were put to an end. He certainly hoped that would be soon.

Battista did not meet them at the door. She was in her private chamber with the door shut fast. Rather than disturb her, they retired to their room, where the fire had already been lit. They removed their cloaks and moved the chairs away from the fireplace. Then they spread their blankets out there and sat down to enjoy the warm blaze.

"I should be sleepy," said Flaskamper, "but I'm not."

"Nor am I," Stamford agreed.

"We're all still energized by our Flaskamper's stunning victory today," said Fia. The elf blushed and smiled appreciatively.

"I tell you what," she said, "let's give Rokey another story. Lorq, I bestow on you the task of recounting my tale of woe for the newest member of our group. She smiled at Rokey, who grinned back at her. She was obviously a little tipsy, but then, he was a little more than tipsy. He was not sleepy either though, and he wanted to hear Lorq tell Fia's story. Lorq, however, was reluctant.

"I'm not a very good story teller, Fia," he protested.

"Nonsense, you've told us some marvelous stories," she argued. "Go ahead, sweetie, don't be shy."

Lorq gave in and agreed to give it a try. Stamford and Flash filled their pipes, and when they had finished lighting them with a stick from the fire, Lorq began his narrative.

"Once upon a time," he began, and smiled at Fia, who smiled back encouragingly, "Fia was born in a town called Cedar's Edge. That's a town right next to the Western Woods, where the huge cedar trees grow. Her father and her mother worked with the cedar wood, making beautiful handmade furnishings that they sold to merchants from all over Firma.

They had two beautiful daughters, called Liesha and Carmandie. Then, a few years later, Fia was born. At first it looked like she was perfect, just like her two sisters, but when she turned two years old, things started to change. Her skin turned hard and rough, and her face wasn't pretty anymore. Her parents took her to every healer in the area to try and find a cure, but none of them could do anything for her.

Time passed and Fia grew up. She had a beautiful voice and was funny and had a kind heart, but her looks made things hard for her. Her family still loved her, but the rest of the people of the town started to think it was some kind of curse, and they avoided her. She studied at home by herself. Her mother taught her to play music and her father taught her how to defend herself from people who might want to hurt her. As she got older, things got worse. People gradually began to shun not just her, but the whole family. Finally, when Fia was sixteen, she ran away from home, because she didn't want the rest of her family to continue to suffer because of her.

She traveled around a lot, because no place would accept her. Sometimes a healer or sorcerer would take pity on her and let her stay and study with them for a while, but she never stayed long in any one place because she couldn't find enough work to support herself. Finally she took a job in a traveling carnival, as *The Dragon Lady*. She hated it, but at least it gave her money to feed and clothe herself. She traveled with the show as The Dragon Lady for a few years, but then the show broke up, and she was all alone again. With no place to go, she ended up on the streets of Oraque, begging to live. It was embarrassing and dangerous too. In fact, the dangerous part was how she came to meet Stamford and Flaskamper. Right Fia?"

Fia smiled and nodded at Lorq. He continued on.

"Stamford and Flash were in Oraque. They had both taken jobs as private guards for a wealthy merchant there. One day, when they were off duty, they were heading into an inn and saw Fia fighting with some men who were trying to steal the little bit of money she had. She didn't have her sword back then, just her little dagger, and there were three of them. Stamford and Flaskamper felt sorry for her, because they're both nice fellows, and they helped her fight off the bad men. Then they even brought her in with them and bought her a meal and a room. The more they got to know her, the more they liked her. They didn't care about the way she looked. They knew she was a good person. When they found out she could fight, they even got her a job with them as a guard, and when it was time for them to move on, they asked her to come and travel with them. And that was how Fia got to be part of the group."

Fia clapped her hands.

"Very good Lorq," she said to the smiling giant. "You told it very well."

Rokey shook his head.

"But that can't be all," he said. "I mean, look at you. You're beautiful. There's not a thing wrong with your skin."

Fia smiled at him.

"Well," she said, "that's a different story. It was about a year after I had joined Stamford and Flash. We had done a service for an old sorcerer in Oraque. He had been very successful once, but had fallen on difficult times. The old man had amassed many magical trinkets over the years. Most he had already been forced to sell, but he had some treasured items left, and he paid us for our service with a couple of them. One of them was this –"

Fia picked up the blue pendant she always wore and held it out for Rokey to see.

"What is it?" he asked.

"It's a glamour pendant," she replied. "The man claims to have gotten it directly from the Faerie, though I suspect that the item had been floating around Firma for some centuries before he came to possess it. Its function is simple: it makes its wearer beautiful."

"You mean – " Rokey began. Fia nodded.

"My beauty is not my own," she admitted. "It is the magic of the pendant which creates it. Without it, I would once again be...*The Dragon Lady*. Watch, I'll show you."

"Fia you don't have to," Rokey said, not wanting to cause her any distress. But she waved her hand at him.

"I'm among friends," she said. She removed the pendant and placed it on the floor in front of her. In tiks, her beauty faded, revealing the rough, scaly skin that covered her body, and the misshapen features of her face.

Rokey had no words. He felt such pity for her, for the life she must have had, but he was careful not to show it. After a moment, she put the pendant back around her neck. Almost instantly, her beauty returned. Rokey asked her if she were ever tempted to return to her home.

"I *have*," she answered. "I like to see my family from time to time, to let them know I'm alright. Besides, our travels take us to Cedar's Edge now and then. But I'm happiest here, among friends who love me with or without my magical glamour. I'm sure I would be bored to tears if I tried to settle down in one place. I've been spoiled by my life as a traveling adventurer."

"Ha!" Stamford barked. "That's a nice way of putting it. Most would call us shiftless vagabonds."

Fia laughed.

"Well," she declared, "I wouldn't trade my shiftless vagabondery for anything."

They continued to laugh and joke, until Battista appeared in the doorway. Her face looked even more grave than usual.

"What is it Battista?" asked Flaskamper. "What's wrong?"

"I don't know," she answered, "not for sure. I've been trying all day to get a clear picture, but something keeps mucking it up. We're going to need to consult a specialist."

"A specialist?" said Rokey. "For me? What kind of specialist?"

"A specialist in black magic," she answered. "Someone who can help me identify what it is that's being hidden. It won't be cheap."

"Fortunately," said Flaskamper, "that's no longer a problem. When and where?"

"When is now," said the sorceress. "Where....the Underside."

Flaskamper's eyes grew wide.

"The Underside? At night?"

Battista nodded.

The elf swallowed hard. The Underside was what they called the easternmost section of the city. It was a run-down, dangerous place, separated from the rest of the city by a high stone wall. There was only one way in; at least, that's what most people thought. He explained this to Rokey.

"You can't all go," she told the group. "It should be just myself and the boy, but since I know you're just going to follow us anyway, Flaskamper, you may as well come along. That way I don't have to worry about you."

Flaskamper didn't need to ask Battista if the trip was really necessary. No one went into the Underside at night without good reason. And because he trusted Battista, Rokey trusted her too. Stamford, though, did not.

"Flash, are you sure about this?" he asked the elf when the sorceress went to fetch her cloak. "Are you sure you can trust this woman?"

"Yes, Stamford, I'm sure. Don't get me wrong; I'm not looking forward to running around in the Underside in the middle of the night. But if she says it's important, it's important."

"We're not going to like just sitting here waiting," Stamford told him.

"I know, I know," Flaskamper said, putting up his hands. "If I were you I'd feel the same way. But you've got to promise you won't follow us. It may scare off whoever we're going to see."

"Alright," said Stamford. "We'll do it her way. But if anything happens to either of you –"

"We'll be alright." Flaskamper sounded far more certain of that than he felt.

Battista returned. Rokey and Flaskamper donned their cloaks, and the three of them headed out into the cold night.

Chapter 10:

The Underside

Battista led Rokey and Flaskamper through the dark streets of Duncileer. It was a residential section of the city, so there was no one about at that time. Though Flaskamper had been to Duncileer before, he wasn't sure which way they were going until they reached King's Road, the main street that ran from the palace all the way to the city's rear gates. Battista turned and started west towards the temple, which further confused him.

"Battista, why are we going this way? Isn't the gate to The Underside southeast of here?"

"Yes," she answered, "but there are other ways in besides the gate, ways that won't call undue attention to us."

They walked past the grounds of the huge temple of Endis, the principal deity worshipped in Duncileer and the surrounding villages. Across the road ran the wall separating the Underside from the rest of the city. Just before the point where they would have been visible from the rear guard towers, Battista led them across to a portion of the wall that was overgrown with a thick cover of shrubs and vines. She thrust her hand through the vines and felt around for a moment. Then there was a click, and a small section of the wall swung inward.

"Come on," she said softly, and disappeared through the opening. Rokey and Flaskamper followed, swinging the wall opening closed behind them.

To Rokey, The Underside looked like a whole different city. The streets were narrow and untended. The buildings were squalid and dilapidated. There were no streetlights. Only the stars and the crescent moon lit their way as they wound through the streets and alleyways, around buildings and shacks. Occasionally Rokey thought he could feel eyes upon them, and once they heard a blood-curdling scream come from somewhere nearby. Battista paid it no mind. Then, at one corner, a menacing pair of thugs emerged from the shadows. Flaskamper pulled his cloak aside, revealing his sword, and the men vanished back into the darkness.

At last they reached a large, nondescript house with wattled walls and a thatched roof that looked as though a strong wind would tear it to pieces. Battista turned back to the boys.

"The man we're going to see doesn't look it," she said, "but he's dangerous. Watch yourselves, and try not to get on his bad side."

She knocked so quietly on the door that Rokey couldn't imagine that anyone inside could have heard, but a moment later the door was opened by a tall, impossibly thin man dressed from head to toe in black. His thinning black hair was slicked back on his skull-like head. Were he not moving, Rokey thought, one could easily mistake him for a corpse. Battista greeted him with a single word.

"Jamba."

The tall man stood aside so they could enter, then led them down a narrow hallway. He opened a door to their left and gestured for them to go in. They walked in and Rokey and Flaskamper were amazed by what they saw. Far from being sparse and dingy, as they had expected, it was warm, bright and elaborately decorated. The windows were covered in heavy silk draperies. A large plush carpet covered the floors. Two of the walls were lined with shelves containing hundreds of books of every subject matter, and on the others hung several exquisite tapestries from the far corners of Firma. A cheerful fire was lit in the hearth, around which several pieces of well-crafted furniture were artfully arranged. An elaborately adorned mahogany desk stood on the far end of the room, behind which sat, Rokey assumed, the man they had come to see. He stood when he saw them and approached, smiling, his arms held out in a welcoming gesture.

"Battista," he said warmly. "What a pleasant surprise."

"Hello, Jamba," said Battista, with not nearly as much warmth.

"Please, come and sit, all of you. Marrow, take their cloaks." He gestured toward the large sofa and overstuffed chair by the fire. The thin man took their cloaks and they sat, the three visitors on the sofa, their host in the chair. Marrow served them all brandy, a variety which Flaskamper immediately recognized.

"This is my father's label," he said in astonishment. "How in blazes were you able to get hold of Angorath brandy? It's illegal to export. It's not even supposed to leave the palace."

Jamba smiled and nodded.

"It is indeed difficult to secure," he admitted. "How did I come by it? Well, I have my ways. But rest assured elf prince, it does not go unappreciated. I delight in every drop." He raised his glass. "Your excellent health."

They drank in silence for a moment, savoring the rich, buttery flavor of the fine elf liquor. It made Flaskamper somewhat uncomfortable, partaking of something that had been illegally obtained from his own father's house, but he couldn't help himself. He suspected that Jamba had served it to them for a reason. Perhaps it was his way of communicating to them just how far his reach could span. It was a subtle, clever display of power, and it had produced the desired effect.

As he sipped the brandy, Rokey studied their host. He was much younger than he had expected, no more than thirty-five, he guessed, but that could be a ruse. He was completely bald, with small, slanted eyes, a straight nose and thin, cruel lips. He wore bright purple lounging pajamas of fine silk, with a fit that flattered his muscular frame. His slippers matched the pajamas' pale grey piping. Each of his ears sported a gold hoop earring. Rokey found him seductive and frightening.

"So," said Jamba, after a few moments, "what brings you to my home in the small marks of the night?"

"Someone means to harm this boy," she said succinctly. "I tried to do a reading, but something, or someone is blocking me."

"Hair and blood?" he asked. The sorceress nodded.

"And I tried every reveal spell I know," she said. "The source of the menace is cloaked in shadow, and his blood... his blood wouldn't talk. It's locked up tight."

"Did you push?" Again she nodded. "And?"

Battista held up her hand, revealing a fresh, angry burn on her palm. Flaskamper and Rokey gasped, but Jamba just nodded, then turned to stare fixedly at Rokey. After a moment, Rokey felt a strange sensation, a kind of tingling deep inside his head. He assumed the man was trying to probe his memories. It was a disturbing feeling.

"Bad business recently," Jamba said, confirming Rokey's suspicion. "I see snatches of memory from early on, but not enough to form a picture. Doesn't appear sinister though."

"So you can't help us then?" Flaskamper asked. Jamba snorted.

"That was just the overture," he said. "The concert has yet to begin. But...it is not a free concert." He turned to Battista. "I trust you've made them aware of my fees?"

"I have," she responded.

"And the fact that results are not guaranteed?"

"I told them," she said.

"Very well," he said. "I take my fee in advance. Then we can proceed."

Flaskamper fished five gold sovereigns out of his breeches and dropped them into Jamba's outstretched hand. He had already been warned not to try to haggle. He certainly hoped the man's services were worth this exorbitant cost.

Jamba stood and placed his empty glass on the table.

"Come with me," he said, and headed for the door. Rokey and Flaskamper also put down their glasses and stood to follow him. Battista stayed seated.

"Sorcerers – Necromancers in his case – don't watch one another work," she offered when they turned back. The boys nervously followed Jamba back into the hallway. There, he opened a door and led them into another corridor. This one seemed to lead nowhere at all, but when they reached the end, the necromancer gestured with his hand and a door suddenly appeared in what a moment ago had been a solid wall. They passed through this door into another room. This one was dark except for the glowing coals of a fireplace.

"Flamma."

At Jamba's magic word, torches all around the room sprang to life. This room looked more like a dungeon. The walls and the floor were all of grey stone. Just inside the doorway was what appeared to be a worktable. On it were magic books, bottles, candles, several clay pots which held an assortment of colored paints, brushes, a small ornate wooden box, a long dagger and a mask woven of some strange material. A large urn, a chair, a brazier, a length of rope, a basket and several sacks were situated in various other parts of the room. On the walls hung many shields, emblazoned with the coats of arms from kings both past and present. However, the largest and most commanding of the room's features covered the floor on its far side. It was a huge white ring, around which many mysterious symbols had been drawn in red. The center of the ring was also painted red, and sitting atop that was a stone altar, large enough for a man to lie on. Though the room was extremely warm, the sight of this strange platform made Rokey shiver. Instinctively, he placed his hand on the small of Flaskamper's back. The elf offered him a reassuring smile, but neither of them was very reassured.

Jamba stood at his worktable and thumbed through one of the books until he had found the page he wanted, then lay the book open on the table. Next, he went to the basket and removed a small rug, which he unrolled and placed on the floor just in front of the altar. From there he returned to the table, donned the mask and turned to the boys.

"You," he said, pointing to Flaskamper, "sit." Flash pulled over the only chair and sat down. Then the necromancer pointed to Rokey.

"You," he said, "strip."

Rokey's eyes widened.

"You mean...?"

"Naked. The ritual requires it."

"Um, now wait..." Flash began.

Jamba turned on him. Behind the mask his eyes flashed angrily.

"You will both do as I instruct, now... or else get out. I have no time to waste on bashful children." He turned back to Rokey. "Well?"

Rokey glanced at Flaskamper, who shrugged in resignation. The elf then watched with guilty anticipation as Rokey peeled off each article of clothing. He knew the polite thing to do would be to turn his head, but in the end, lust won an easy victory over courtesy. When Rokey had finished, Jamba pointed to the stone altar.

"Lie there," he instructed.

Rokey started for the altar, then stopped and turned nervously back to the necromancer.

"This isn't going to hurt... is it?" he asked.

"Physically, no" Jamba answered "But up here...." He tapped his finger on his head ominously. "Don't worry though, you won't remember it, and the ritual causes no permanent damage...usually."

"Usually? ... great ..." said Rokey, far from reassured. He walked to the altar, and climbed up onto it. The stone felt cold and rough on his naked body. He watched as the necromancer took a handful of grey powder from the box on the table and threw it into the brazier. There was a small explosion and the air was instantly thick with pungent smoke. Rokey started to choke, but after a minmark, his lungs grew accustomed to it, and his coughing stopped. The lights grew dimmer, and the altar beneath him seemed to rock and sway. His eyes couldn't seem to focus on anything and he could hear a loud ringing, or was it singing? He couldn't be sure. Then, over the sound of the ringing...

or was it singing?

he heard chanting, loud, rhythmic chanting in an unfamiliar language. It must be Jamba, he thought, the ritual has begun. He wondered what was going to happen next. He felt so weird, heavy, as though he were part of the stone altar. Part of him just wanted to sleep, but another part was frightened, and determined to stay wakeful. His head swam despite his efforts though. Then a shadowy figure approached him. As it drew closer he could see that it was... a man, a naked man... but something was wrong. His face was all... twisted. He shook his head to try and clear it. It was the mask. The necromancer *what was his name?*

was wearing a mask. Now he was holding something up. What was it? What else had been on the table? He couldn't think. Candles, books, bottles and

a dagger.

The man raised his arm, and then the thing in his hand swung down in an arc towards him.

a dagger.

Rokey threw his head back and screamed.

*   *   *

A moment after the acrid smoke filled the room, Flaskamper felt things start to spin, and a loud hum began in his ears. He held onto the chair for support while he tried to get his bearings. Eventually the spinning slowed, then stopped, but the objects in the room still swam in front of him. Some of it he could make out. He saw Jamba strip naked and pick up something from the table, something he couldn't quite identify. The necromancer began to chant then turned and started toward Rokey, who appeared to be writhing on the stone altar. He couldn't trust his eyes though. Perhaps Rokey was lying still and it was *he* that was moving. They should never have come here, should never have come to this horrible place. If anything should happen to Rokey...
    What was that in the necromancer's hand? Flaskamper watched fearfully as the man raised his arm
    What was that in his hand?
and brought it down toward Rokey, then...
    Rokey threw his head back and screamed.
    Flaskamper screamed Rokey's name and tried to run to him, but his legs wouldn't move. He watched, horrified as something red began to spill out over the altar onto the floor. With all his might, he willed himself to move. With one step, then another... he drew closer. The fog in his head was starting to clear a little. He could see the necromancer – lean, powerful, naked – standing over Rokey. And Rokey was lying there, trembling...his body covered in blood...

covered in blood?

No...it wasn't blood. It was paint. Red paint. The thing in the necromancer's hand was a paintbrush. He was painting symbols on

Rokey's body, but the pot had spilled, and red paint had run all down the altar and dripped onto the floor.

Flaskamper felt his knees give way and he fell down, nearly sobbing with relief. He was alright. Rokey was alright. It was just the damned magic smoke, mucking up their minds. He got back to his feet and stumbled back to the chair. His – his *friend* was in safe enough hands. He could sit and relax. A few minmarks later, exhaustion from the long day caught up with him, and he slept.

*   *   *

"Rokey."

He heard his name, all thick and garbled, as if someone had spoken it underwater. He listened carefully, and heard it again. Was he underwater? He felt wet, and cool. But no. He was breathing. One couldn't breathe underwater...unless one was a fish. Only then did it occur to him to open his eyes.

Flaskamper was standing over him. He smiled...that beautiful smile.

Where was he? What was happening?

He was wet, and naked. Flash was washing him. Had he been ill? He sat up and a searing pain shot through his head.

"Easy," Flash told him. "Jamba says it'll be a mark or so yet before you're fully recovered."

Jamba. Ritual. Altar. Dagger.

No, not a dagger...a paintbrush. Jamba had painted things, all over his body. He was still up on the altar, and Flash was washing him clean. A rush of affection swept over him, followed by a rush of embarrassment at being in so vulnerable a position. He swung his legs around and got to his feet. Flaskamper wrapped a big towel around him.

"Clothes?," Rokey mumbled.

"Right here." The elf disappeared for a moment and returned with his things. He helped Rokey dress, then helped him back to Jamba's study, where the necromancer and Battista awaited them. They sat down on the sofa again, and Jamba handed Rokey a cup of some hot liquid.

"Drink it down," he said. "It will speed your recovery."

It did. Within minmarks Rokey's headache was gone and he felt some of his energy returning.

"How do you feel?" Jamba asked, taking the empty cup from him.

"How does he feel?" Flaskamper asked, his temper rising. "How *should* he feel? Brutalized? Despoiled?"

"Flaskamper – " Battista attempted to quiet him, but he jumped to his feet.

"I hope to blazes we learned something of value from that...that *violation!*" he cried. "If not, *sir*, I should be sorely tempted to part your head from your shoulders!"

"Flash!" Rokey stood and grabbed the elf by the shoulders. "Calm down," he told him urgently. "Calm down. It's all right. I'm alright." He turned to Jamba.

"He doesn't mean it," Rokey told him. "He's just tired...and overwrought. Please... don't hurt him."

The necromancer regarded them severely for a minmark, then smiled and shook his head.

"Ah, Battista, do you remember young love?" he asked.

"Not when I can help it," she answered.

Rokey and Flaskamper sat down, crimson with embarrassment.

"I'd best tell you what I've learned, though it may cost me my head," he joked. "It's less than even I had hoped for, and I have no interest in the matter except personal pride."

He leaned forward and addressed Rokey.

"You, young man, are quite an enigma. Without getting into the arcana of my magic, the ritual I performed is meant to strip a man bare, literally *and* metaphorically. In essence, I should have been able to glean the details of your life from that very moment back to the beginning, including your parentage, your friends and more importantly, your *enemies*. To a certain extent, the ritual was successful. The story from the point that you were brought to the Noble Contemplative until now was clear as day...with one exception. As Battista has said, whoever is behind the attempts on your life remains in shadow. I could garner no clue as to his or her identity. But I was able to push somewhat harder than Battista, and discovered some things that may be useful. First, the person who is arranging the attacks is not acting alone. There are others involved. Perhaps many others. Second, the reason for the attacks has nothing to do with your life at the monastery. The reasons go back further, before the monastery, perhaps back to your birth itself.

"But you weren't able to find anything out about my birth, my parents?" Rokey asked.

"I didn't say that," Jamba answered. "While I wasn't able to get a clear picture of anything before the monastery, I was able to garner one important fact. Something about your birth is significant. I don't mean just in the sense that every person's life is significant. I mean in a way that one day may well, for better or worse, affect all of Firma."

Rokey looked incredulous.

"You don't believe it," said Jamba. "I don't blame you. Were I in your position, I too would be dubious. But I assure you there's a very high probability that the information is correct, so I advise you to keep it in mind."

"But what could possibly be so important about me?" Rokey asked.

The necromancer shook his head.

"I know not," he said. "Without any clue to your parentage, I dare not even speculate. But think of it. Why would a sinister and powerful force be working so hard to kill you? If there's nothing more to you than meets the eye, no reason at all. But if my information is correct, and I'm quite sure that it is, well... it makes more sense doesn't it? Listen lad, it has been my experience that only powerful people have powerful enemies. Now, some person or persons, with even more skill than I, has gone to enormous pains to cover up your lineage. Yet another commanding entity is striving equally hard to snuff you out. These things simply don't happen to ordinary folk, no indeed. My belief, for what's it's worth, is that you will have some instrumental role to play in some monumental occurrence, but unless you accept that, and act quickly to unravel the truth, your enemies will prevail."

"But how?" Rokey cried. "I mean, look, let's say I believe you; I'm some important cog in some crucial, momentous event. Fine. But you've... you've nearly dissected me already trying to get the answers and, no offence meant, there's precious little to show for it. What is there left for me to do? What oracle do I consult now?"

Jamba cleared his throat.

"Funny you should mention oracles..." he shot Battista a look.

"Glimmermere?" she asked, arching one eyebrow. He nodded.

"I can think of no other," he said.

Flaskamper looked at them, first to one, then the other, as though they had each just sprouted a second head.

"Glimmermere?" he exclaimed in amazement. "Have you both gone mad? That's a two-week journey from here. More! Desert, lakes, swamps - " he ticked off the impediments with his fingers.

"Excuse me," Rokey interjected. "Should I know what you all are talking about? What, and where, is Glimmermere?"

"Glimmermere," Flaskamper explained, "is an auger... an oracle, hundreds of miles to the east, guarded by a ghost, surrounded by a swamp..."

"There's no denying it's an arduous journey," Jamba broke in. "But the options are limited. There are many other sorcerers, necromancers, clairvoyants...all within a few days journey of Duncileer. But they'll be no help to you. I know them all and, meaning no conceit, I'm the best. I've given you as much as ordinary magic, white or black, can tender. Aside from those who orchestrated this mystery, Glimmermere is the only other source that I know of which may offer you more. Battista will agree."

She did. They sat silently for a moment, pondering the situation, and then Jamba stood.

"Well," he said, "I hate to be a poor host, but there are other matters which require my attention, so I must bid you goodnight. Please feel free to stay until the lad is fit to travel. Marrow will bring you your cloaks."

He stood without another word, and left the room. Rokey, though still drained from the ordeal, was eager to go, so they took their cloaks from Marrow, who showed them to the door, and they departed.

The three made it to the secret entrance, observed but unmolested this time, and emerged back onto King's Road. They had walked a short ways toward home when, Battista stopped.

"Flaskamper," she said, "can you find your way back on your own? I have an errand I need to run."

"Uh - yes, of course. We'll be fine. Right Rokey?" Rokey nodded.

"I'll see you back at the house," she said, and disappeared around the corner.

Rokey and Flaskamper made their way back toward Battista's house. In contrast to the Underside, the streets of the city proper were broad and well lit, so they had no trouble finding their way. They didn't speak at all, feeling too fatigued even to talk. Flaskamper wanted nothing more than a few marks of sleep, but he knew that the others would still be awake, keen to hear what had happened. He hoped they would accept an abbreviated explanation until the next morning, when he would be more up to a full recounting of the night's events.

As they neared the street where the house was located, the streetlights were suddenly extinguished. Flaskamper immediately drew his sword, and Rokey followed suit. For a few moments nothing happened.

"Coincidence?" Rokey whispered to Flash.

"No," he answered. "Look at the sky."

Rokey looked up. Where stars had filled the sky moments before, there was now only utter blackness.

"Flash, should we run?," asked Rokey, a note of panic creeping in his voice.

But it was too late. The darkness fell in on them like a heavy blanket, forcing them to the ground. High, menacing whispers filled their ears, and biting cold bit their skin. Then they felt an odd sensation inside...the feeling of being drained.

"Flash, what are these things," Rokey gasped.

"I don't know," the elf answered, "but they mean to do us serious harm, that's for certain."

They struggled, but they'd had little strength left to begin with. The things held them fast, like flies caught in a spider's web. Rokey reached for Flash's hand, but in the darkness, he was unable to find it. He tried to speak, to scream, but nothing came. He felt his consciousness slipping away. After all they had been through, was this to be their end?

Flaskamper couldn't breath. The formless creatures had filled his mouth, his throat, choking off his air. He was drowning, suffocating in shadow. Even in the midst of his panic, he cursed himself. He had failed. He had sworn to himself that he would protect Rokey, keep him safe from the dark forces trying to take his life. In the end though, he hadn't been strong enough, or clever enough to meet the challenge. The draining sensation and the lack of air were pulling him under. Silver sparks of light began to dance in front of his eyes.

Then suddenly the sky was filled with blazing white light. Rokey and Flash both wondered whether they had died. However, a moment later, they discovered that they were able to move their arms, and promptly lifted them to shield their eyes. The creatures were disappearing, drying up like puddles in the sun. To Rokey their demise was silent, but Flaskamper's highly attuned ears picked up the sound of their shrill, agonized shrieks. He smiled with grim satisfaction.

"Take that, you bastards," he said to himself.

When the last of the shadowy creatures had vanished, the intense light dimmed, then also disappeared. It was night still, but the streetlights were functioning again. All was quiet except for the distant barking of a dog. When their eyes adjusted, they saw Battista standing before them, bent over with fatigue. They stood and went to her.

"Damn," she wheezed. "Those muckers... are hard... to kill. Help me back... to the house...boys. I'm...done in."

They stood on either side, and supported her, moving forward slowly.

"Battista," what were those things?" Flaskamper asked.

"Bleaks," she answered. "One of the things I told you about that have been lurking lately in the shadows of the city. In this case, they *are* the shadows. When they first began cropping up, they were more of a nuisance than a danger, pilfering small amounts of life force. Lately, though, they've been taking more, sometimes all. People have begun to die.

"You knew they were going to hit us," Flaskamper said to her.

"That's why you left to run an *errand*," Rokey added.

The sorceress nodded.

"I sensed them in the darkness just outside the wall," she told them. "I knew they'd come after us, so I left, hoping they'd follow you and give me time to call up enough lumen orbs."

"Lumen orbs?" Rokey asked.

"Light Spirits," Flaskamper explained, "like the one I called up the other night when the ratmen attacked."

"Yes," said Battista, "only to kill bleaks, you need a lot of them. That's why –"

"You used us as bait!" Flash exclaimed.

He pondered this for a moment, then began to laugh. Rokey joined him. Exhaustion and shock set them giggling like children the rest of the way home, holding one another up. As Battista watched them, a rare smile crept onto her face.

Just friends, my arse, she thought to herself.

Chapter 11:

Into the Sunrise

C onvincing Stamford that they should undertake the long and dangerous journey to Glimmermere had been surprisingly painless. In fact, he seemed more amenable to the idea than Flaskamper. Rokey had wondered about his friend's hesitancy, until Fia explained that the easiest route to the oracle would lead them straight through Elfwood, Flaskamper's home. The elf hadn't been home in more than five years, and it was understandable that he would have some apprehensions, given the circumstances under which he had left. However, the only alternative was to skirt the forest entirely, which would add several days to their journey. They offered to make the detour, but Flaskamper wouldn't hear of it.

"Absolutely not," he insisted. "Elfwood will provide us with at least one safe haven on the trip. I'll manage my personal issues on my own."

"You'll do no such thing," said Fia. "We'll all be there to manage them with you."

"That's right, Flash," Lorq added. "We're a team, remember?"

"I know that," the elf said, touched. "Thank you, all of you."

"I hate to break up this love-fest," said Stamford, "but we've got preparations to make."

They were sitting around the large kitchen table. Stamford had one of Battista's maps spread out and was trying to work out the easiest route to Glimmermere. The beginning portion of the trip they knew well enough. From Duncileer, they would head due east, braving a four-day trek through the desert known as the Great Sand Sea. After that they would continue on to the Elfwood forest. Beyond that, their experience was limited, for none of them had ever been east of Elfwood except Lorq, and his travels had occurred far up in the Northern Expanse.

"As I see it," Stamford said, "our best bet beyond Elfwood is to head for Waterville. It looks like the largest settlement on the west side of Grand Lake, so I imagine we should have no trouble chartering a boat to ferry us across."

"What are we going to do about Fenton?" asked Fia. "He won't be able to make this journey with us."

"I asked Battista about facilities in the city," said Flaskamper. "There's a stable where we can board him for a not-too-ridiculous fee. He'll be well cared-for until we return. And Battista has promised to check on him for us."

"Where is the old girl?" asked Stamford. "I wanted to ask her about these ports along the eastern side of the lake."

"She's out on a house call," Flaskamper answered. "She should be back soon."

It was well past midday. They had all been up until nearly dawn the previous night discussing Rokey and Flaskamper's visit to The Underside, and the necromancer Jamba. As a result, it was near midmorning before they finally roused themselves. Stamford had immediately begun to plot out their course and made a list of the things that they would need for the trip. Fia and Lorq had promptly gone off to purchase the necessary items. Flaskamper had taken Rokey to a clothier to buy him some more clothes.

"A man can't have just one suit of clothes," he explained when Rokey protested. "It's not... well, it's just not right, that's all. Listen, don't argue with a fellow who's prepared to spend money on you. As long as that fellow is me," he added hastily.

When they had all returned, Rokey modeled his new outfit for them – a fine white linen shirt with buttons down the front and a pair of dark umber woolen trousers that flattered him so well the others were sure that Flaskamper had chosen them. His lightweight and well-worn shoes from the monastery had been replaced with a fine pair of hand-tooled, leather boots. They had quarreled over this purchase. Rokey insisted it was much too extravagant, but Flaskamper had eventually worn him down. Now with his feet comfortably nestled in the soft, warm lining, Rokey was glad that he had lost the argument.

Battista returned with a chicken and some potatoes for their supper. Fia and Flaskamper insisted on cooking so that the sorceress could rest. It was almost unheard of for the older woman to surrender her kitchen to anyone, but once again Fia's charm prevailed. As Battista sat by the fire, Stamford quizzed her about the best port to head for when they crossed Grand Lake.

"Well, the choices are bad and worse," she told them. "The towns on the west side of the lake are fine, but the ones to the east – well let's just say that there are safer and more pleasant places to tarry for a night. And I hate to tell you, but the one you want to head for is Farport, the worst of the lot."

"Why Farport?" Flaskamper asked, peeling potatoes.

"Because that's where pilgrims heading for Glimmermere always wound up, so it'll be a better place than most to gather what information there is. Not that there's likely to be much. There's little known about either Glimmermere or Aldaji anymore."

"What's Aldaji?" Rokey asked, biting into the slice of raw potato he had just swiped.

"The Aldaji tar swamps," Flash answered. "They surround Glimmermere on three sides. The Great Vast is on the fourth, so you have to cross the tar swamps to get there. The problem is finding a safe route through. Many pilgrims have tried to reach Glimmermere and never returned. It's easy to get on the wrong path and wind up sinking in the tar."

"Why not just sail around on the Great Vast?" Rokey had studied the enormous sea called the Great Vast at the Contemplative, and had read about men who had sailed her.

"Because it's surrounded by a treacherous, rocky reef," said the elf. "Apparently it's even more dangerous than the tar swamps. I've never heard of anyone who's managed it."

"No one has," said Battista. "The waters near Glimmermere are littered with the husks of vessels that have made the attempt. Legend has it that the reef is made partly from the bones of the sailors who manned those vessels. They say on a clear, dark night, you can see their ghosts wafting atop the waters just offshore. It may be just a tall tale, but I have seen enough not to dismiss anything out of hand."

"What do you know about Glimmermere itself, Battista?" asked Fia. She had just basted the chicken and was putting the potatoes on to boil.

"As I said, precious little," the sorceress replied. "Myths and old folktales mostly. It is an ancient place, one of the oldest known to Firma. But no one visits there anymore. When times were more desperate, many were prepared to risk life and limb in the tar swamps to seek the advice of the oracle. Now – "

"Now we're the only ones desperate enough to try," Flash interjected.

"Or foolish enough," Rokey added.

"Indeed," said Stamford. "Well it won't be our first foolish pursuit, nor will it be our last... we hope."

"Maybe it's not there anymore," Lorq put in. He was feeding his little frog Pico with a few flies he had caught.

"Lorq, must you do that at the dinner table?" Stamford chided.

"Well, it *is* dinner – for *him*," Lorq answered.

Stamford frowned in disgust, but gave up the fight.

"Well, it is always possible that the place has collapsed," Battista said. "But I am inclined to doubt it. True, Glimmermere is beginning to fade into the realm of folklore, but it is not so long abandoned that it's likely to have fallen to ruin. It is a magical place after all, one that goes back a millennium or more in our history. No, I suspect that the oracle remains, awaiting the return of darker days, when kings and clerics are once again drawn to seek its counsel." She shook her head. "The way this city has changed these past few months, there are those who believe that those days are already upon us."

"Yourself among them?" Flaskamper inquired, thinking of Jamba's cryptic words the previous night.

"Perhaps," she answered soberly. "Perhaps."

*   *   *

They set out before dawn the next morning. Battista had arranged for them to be let out through the city's seldom-used rear gates. She handed the guard a small bottle and he ran to raise the wooden portcullis.

"What was that you gave him?" asked Rokey.

"Something to bolster a sagging libido, " she told him. "Worth its weight in gold, to those who need it. One of my most useful bribes."

The gate groaned and began to rise.

"Go on." She waved them on. "He will only keep it open for a minmark or so."

Flaskamper gave the sorceress a hug.

"Thank you, Battista," he said, "for everything."

"I don't want to see you again unless you're healthy," she told him, "and trouble-free."

"If I follow that restriction, I'm afraid we shall never meet again," he said with a smile.

Battista smiled back, but her heart was heavy, for she feared that his words, though spoken in jest, might just carry the weight of prophecy.

They cleared the gate and, a moment later, it clattered shut behind them. To Rokey it was a sorrowful sound. He was passing once more from the familiar to the unknown, armed with only a borrowed sword, a vague quest and a head full of doubts.

He looked about him, studying his companions as the first purple light of dawn crept into the sky. He was glad of these new friends. They had saved his life, but more than that, they had given him a new place to belong, and a new reason to go on. Yes, he was glad of them, but regretful, too – regretful of the perils he had already brought them, and all of the risks and hazards still to come.

Flaskamper left Rokey deep in thought and caught up to Stamford, walking a few paces ahead. Stamford glanced over at him, but said nothing. They walked silently, side by side as the sun began to rise over the distant hills. Finally the elf couldn't contain himself any longer.

"Alright," he said, "spill it. Come clean. I can't take it."

"Flaskamper, I have no idea what you're babbling about," said Stamford.

"Why you agreed to this trip..." he snapped his fingers, "just like that. No arguments. No *are you out of that pointy-eared head of yours?*. No nothing. Shite, you were on board with this thing before I was."

He paused. Stamford said nothing.

"Damn it, talk to me!" the elf said through clenched teeth. "I'm not crazy. There's something weird going on with you and I want to know what it is!"

Stamford's silence continued, until Flaskamper thought sure he would have to strike the man to get his attention. But then the dark man spoke, choosing his words with care.

"Flaskamper," he said, "you know my story. You know where I've come from, and what the mission of my life is now."

Flash nodded.

"Yes, but what does that – "

"Shut up and listen. I think that the necromancer was right. I think something big is getting ready to happen, and I think our friend back there has some major part to play. I don't know how it's going to unfold exactly, but I suspect that a time is approaching when all of Firma is going to have to choose a side. Now I've seen Rokey, and I've seen what's been sent out to stop him. If a time of choosing is near, I already know which side I want to be on. There was a time when the choice would not have been so clear to me, but now it is. Do you understand what I'm saying?"

"I think so," said Flaskamper. "You've found the quest you need, or... you think you have."

"Precisely. No way to be sure, but it's what my instincts tell me. As usual, yours were sharper than mine. When you wouldn't bed him that first night, I should have known. You've never been one to pass up a free bowl of cherries and cream."

Flash laughed and slugged Stamford's shoulder.

"Dirty bastard," the elf said. Stamford nodded.

"I am indeed," he murmured to himself, "but one day...one day soon...I may be clean again."

Part Two

Chapter 12:

Across the Sands

F laskamper wiped the sweat and grit from his face with the sleeve of his robe, but the sun's heat was merciless, and in moments beads of perspiration were once again running down his forehead and into his eyes. The elf had climbed one of the massive sand dunes in the area to see if his sharp eyes could pick out the distant settlement of Aridia. By their calculations, it was still a full day's walk, so he wasn't particularly surprised to see only miles and miles of burning sand ahead of him. He half trotted, half slid down the hill and rejoined the rest of the company.

"Ballocks!" Stamford exclaimed after Flaskamper's report, "I was hoping Aridia would at least be in view by now."

"I'm not surprised," Flaskamper responded. "This whole area is nothing but rolling sand hills. Even if a settlement were just half a mile distant, I wouldn't be able to see it. Good thing we've got the compass."

Rokey wiped his sweaty hands on his robes, grabbed his water skin, removed the stopper and took a short drink. The water was unpleasantly warm, but it served its purpose... to a point. With only two large skins of water each, they were always parched, but it was important to resist the temptation to drink too much. To run out before reaching Aridia would be disastrous. He replaced the top and let the skin drop back to his side.

"It's approaching midday," remarked Stamford. "I don't know about the rest of you, but I'm ready for a rest."

The others agreed. They were in a small valley amid several large dunes. They unpacked the lean-to, and set it up to block the roasting midday sun. They had a light meal of dates and dried beef, washing it down with as little of their water as possible. Lorq doused Pico with a bit of the precious liquid, prompting Stamford to peevishly declare that it was alright if one of them should die of thirst, just so long as the damned frog got its bath. Lorq made no response, but quietly tucked the little object of contention back into his pocket. They then all lay back under the shelter for a nap. The sun was so hot that it was wisest to relax in the middle part of the day and travel only in the early morning and late afternoon. It made the going slower, but helped to conserve vital body fluids, an important consideration when traversing the desert.

As Rokey rested, he thought back on the previous two days. This was the third day of their trek across the Great Sand Sea. They had stopped in a small hamlet on the outskirts of the wasteland and suited up in functional desert attire, which consisted of light muslin robes, head wraps which also covered their noses and mouths, and woven reed sandals. They had also purchased several large skins of water with shoulder straps, a cream that helped protect their skin from the sun, and the lean-to, which was easy to set up and break down for their noontime respites. The man at the trading post had been very helpful. Having been in business on the rim of the desert for many years, he had known exactly what they would need, what they should look for and what they should avoid.

"Above all, beware the ruins," he had told them soberly. "There's evil afoot there. Curious scholars and unwary travelers both have ventured in to explore them, only to disappear, never to be seen again."

"And no one knows what caused them to vanish?" Fia had enquired.

"None that's still living, miss," had been the answer.

Their journey to this point, though grueling, had been mostly uneventful. Thus far they had encountered no ruins, nothing more dangerous than a few desert lizards. But the heat – Rokey had never felt such unrelenting, intense heat. But for the protective cover of the muslin head-wrap, his head and face would have burned to a crisp. And the sand was everywhere. Flaskamper had complained that the grit had reached places that seldom saw the light of day. Rokey had laughed, but knew exactly what he meant. He couldn't wait for a cool bath and a thorough scrub.

When the sun had passed its zenith and begun to descend westward, they broke camp and continued on. As they were traveling east, they found this time of day to be the least unpleasant, as the sun was behind them. No one spoke much. Their mouths were too dry to do much talking, so they trudged on in silence. The only sounds around them were the gentle sweep of the wind as it brushed over the barren sand, and the occasional cry of some desert-dwelling bird. Rokey suspected that they were deathbirds, discussing the prospect of a hearty meal in the foreseeable future. He sincerely hoped that they would be disappointed.

Marks passed. The pale blue sky above their heads began to turn pink. Another mile or two and it would be time to pitch their tents for the night. But then, during a quick rest stop, they noticed another sound – a distant rumbling, as though a large herd of beasts were approaching from a great distance. Surprisingly, it was Lorq, not Flaskamper who first brought it to everyone's attention.

"Listen," said the giant. "Can you all hear that noise?"

They all paused to listen.

"It can't be a storm," said Flaskamper. "It never rains here."

"No, not rain," Stamford said, "but something."

They turned their attention westward, where the sun was now low in the sky. Too low, it seemed to Stamford.

"There's something wrong with the horizon," he said. "See there how high it looks... and how it blurs the sun."

As they watched and listened, the horizon seemed to draw closer, the booming noise grew steadily louder.

"Sand," said Fia. "A sandstorm is coming."

"Yes," Stamford agreed. "Coming straight for us – and fast."

"What are we going to do?" Lorq asked.

"Flash," Stamford ordered, "Run up that hill and see if there's any kind of cover that we can reach."

The elf sprinted up the dune and peered out all around. After a few moments, he gave a cry and pointed off to the north. Stamford beckoned to him and he came running back down.

"I see...buildings...to the north," he panted. "Looks like they're all...falling down. But I think... we could catch some cover there."

"Must be the ruins we were warned against," Stamford mused. "Perfect. Our choices are, take refuge in the haunted ruins, or be buried by the sand storm. Typical. Well, what's it to be people?"

"Well, we know the sand will bury us alive, once it's finished blasting the flesh from our bones," Flaskamper pointed out grimly. "As to the ruins, the only evidence we have that those are dangerous is some tall tales."

"I agree," said Fia.

"I don't know," said Rokey. "I'd agree too if I hadn't so recently been up to my neck in ratmen. Now I'm slow to doubt most anything."

"Good point," Stamford agreed, "but our options at this juncture are rather limited. I think potential death sounds better than certain death, don't you?"

They all concurred and started running north, toward the ruins. By the time they got there, the wind was already shrieking around them. Dust and sand filled the air, burning their eyes and choking them, in spite of their protective head-wraps.

The ruins were extensive. Obviously this had once been a flourishing city, but now very little remained. They searched and searched for shelter. Then, just when it had begun to look like the old city would be of little help after all, they came across a large building that, though half buried in the sand, still seemed to be intact. The huge wooden door still hung on one hinge, held in place by years of drifting sand. They dug furiously to free it, and finally were able to heave it open and hurry inside. Lorq gripped the door handle firmly and battled the blustering wind in an attempt to get it closed. At last it gave way and slammed shut with a bang that echoed throughout the cavernous structure. They found themselves standing in a large entryway. Huge stone steps led down into a massive, but nearly empty room. The only light came from several small skylights in the ceiling. Battered and broken sconces covered the walls, but there were no torches in them to light. They decided that the first thing to be done was to start a fire, as the sandstorm would soon block out what little light was there. Flaskamper and Lorq went to work on that project, gathering wood and other debris to light with the help of their flint and tinderbox. The rest of them put the packs down on the floor nearby and walked around examining the room.

"What was this place?" Rokey asked. "Who built it?"

"No idea," Stamford answered, picking up what looked like a piece of a wooden chair leg. It crumbled to dust in his hand. "It's old though, really old."

"I think it must have been a temple for whoever the people were who lived in this area. See over there? It looks like the remains of some kind of altar, and behind it...a large marble throne. This was probably their principle place of worship."

"So strange," Rokey observed, "to think that a whole city stood here once, long, long ago. They probably expected that their culture and existence would go on forever. That's how all people tend to feel I guess. But now they're gone, and no one knows how they came to be, or how they came to an end."

Fia nodded in agreement.

"Sad," she said simply.

Flaskamper got the fire going. Lorq piled scrap wood around it to build it up. The storm outside was blowing at full force now. The building groaned like some injured monster, as billions of grains of sand were hurled against it by the fierce wind. The groans, along with the storm's hiss and howl echoing through the hollow chamber produced a nearly deafening din. There was no question that they had made the right decision seeking refuge here. Still, everyone was tense, wondering what dreadful beast might be lurking in the shadows, waiting for the right moment to spring. They ate a light supper and sat around the fire, certain that none of them would sleep a wink in this uncanny atmosphere. However, before they had even begun to ponder ways to entertain themselves, a strong and relentless drowsiness came over them. Even Stamford, who had volunteered for the night's first watch, was having difficulty keeping his eyes open. After only a few minmarks, the five of them had all fallen into a deep sleep.

*   *   *

Rokey awoke to bright sunlight streaming in through the skylights. For a moment, he felt relief that the storm had apparently passed. Soon, however, his relief turned to shock as he sat up and looked around. They had fallen asleep in the ruins of a temple. Now the entire structure looked fresh and restored. The floors were covered in polished pink granite. The smashed alabaster altar was whole again, as was the pink marble throne behind it, and all the rubble was gone. Along the walls, dozens of sconces held burning torches, which filled the chamber with soft, golden light. Astounded, he walked over to examine the walls. The sections beneath the sconces were covered with carvings. Rokey assumed that they depicted scenes from the lives of the people who had built this magnificent temple. As he stood in awe, studying the carvings, he heard a gasp behind him.

"What in blazes –"

Flaskamper and the others were awake, and equally stunned at the change in their surroundings. They also started to examine the room, searching for clues as to what had transpired as they slept. However, when they turned back towards the area where they had camped, they received another shock. All of their things were gone; as were all traces of the fire they had started.

"All right everyone," Stamford said slowly. "Time to figure out what's happening here. Ideas?"

"A spell," Flaskamper mused. "We must be under some kind of enchantment."

"Sounds reasonable," said Stamford. "Now, if we can figure out the nature of –"

He was interrupted by the sound of the temple door opening. There was no time nor any place to conceal themselves. Two figures hustled through the door and closed it quickly behind them. As they came from the doorway into the foyer, Rokey saw that it was a young man and woman. The man wore a garment, which wrapped at the waist like a skirt. It was elaborately embroidered with multi-colored designs and adorned with a variety of beautiful stones. The girl's garment wrapped similarly, but covered her whole body. It had none of the elaborate designs present on the man's attire. She appeared frightened, and clung to his arm as they descended the stairs. The group stood tensely, waiting for the pair to notice them. To their surprise, the two seemed completely oblivious to their presence, in spite of the fact that they were standing only a few feet apart. The girl spoke in a hushed voice.

"My Lord," she said, "we should not be here. What if we are discovered?"

"What if we are?" the young man replied brashly. "I am a Prince of Haddam. I may do as I please."

"*You*, yes. There would be no punishment for you. But *me*...they would stone me to death."

"Do not be afraid," he said soothingly. "I would not let anyone harm you. Come."

He led her by the hand to the altar, where he began to kiss her passionately. Stamford cleared his throat loudly. The couple took no notice. Though reluctant at first, the girl began to respond to his kisses; that is until he tried to maneuver her onto the altar. At that point she resisted.

"No!" she cried. "It is wrong for us to be here...like this."

"It is *not* wrong," he snapped, "and your disobedience begins to vex me. If *you* will not do as I wish, there are others who will."

"Arrogant little toad, isn't he?" Stamford muttered to Flaskamper.

"Indeed," the elf concurred. "Stamford, what's going on here? Why can't they see us? And how is it that we can understand them? How can they be speaking Common Firmish?."

"Not sure," he said. "We may be seeing ghosts. Or perhaps we've traveled in time, and we ourselves are the ghosts. I can't answer the language question either, except to surmise that it's somehow part of the spell."

"I think you're right, Stamford," said Fia. "I've been watching their lips. Although it *sounds* like Common Firmish to us, the movements of their lips do not correspond with the words we're hearing. I suspect translation *is* a part of this spell."

Stamford nodded.

"Well, whatever the case," he said, "I think we're about to be treated to a show."

He was right. The girl had relented and they were now in the process of shedding their garments. Fia reddened and turned her back to them, as did Lorq and, after some hesitation, Rokey.

"Tell me when it's over," she said to Stamford.

"Here now, what makes you so sure I'm going to stay and watch," he objected.

She shot him a glance and rolled her eyes. The dark man laughed.

"You know me far too well," he said. "Damned right I'm going to watch."

"Me too," said Flaskamper. "I mean come on, who hasn't dreamed occasionally of being an invisible voyeur."

"Dreamed," Fia repeated, pondering the possibility. "Maybe that's what's happening here. Perhaps they're not ghosts, but part of a dream, one which we're all sharing."

"How is that possible?" asked Rokey.

"I don't know," Fia admitted. "I assume that it is also part of the nature of the temple's enchantment. It causes visitors to fall asleep and share dreams of the distant past. It's only a conjecture, but it fits the facts as we know them so far."

"True," said Stamford, momentarily distracted from the entertainment. "If that's the case though, if we're all dreaming, it begs the question...will we ever wake up again? Or will we remain here as phantoms, while our sleeping bodies wither and die?"

"That's a creepy thought," Lorq said with a shiver.

"What can we do about it?" Rokey asked. "There must be a way we can wake ourselves up."

"There must be more to see here than – this," Fia surmised, gesturing to the undulating couple. "Perhaps the events that take place will give us some clue as to the nature of the enchantment, and possibly how to break it."

"Well, there, you see?" said Stamford. "It is incumbent on us to pay close attention to everything that happens here." With that, he turned back to the scene on the altar, which seemed to be approaching its climax.

"Oh for pity's sake," Fia said with disgust. "I feel as though I'm the mother of two giggling children at times. Rokey, Lorq...while those two enjoy their spectacle, let us see what, if anything, can be gleaned from the carvings on the walls."

The numerous carvings seemed to depict a number of different religious ceremonies. The altar was featured in many of them. Depending on the occasion, piles of fruits, vegetables or grains were burned there as the priests performed some kind of ceremonial rites.

"What are those things they're holding?" Lorq asked.

In each ceremony, the priest held an object, roughly oval in shape and either green, yellow or blue in color.

"It looks like a rock of some kind," said Rokey. Fia nodded.

"They obviously held some sort of religious significance." She said.

Before they had a chance to study them further, Stamford called to them from across the room.

"Hey, show's over!" he called. The trio rejoined Stamford and Flaskamper near the altar. The woman was still seated there. The man stood behind her. She was still naked, but he had put his garment back around his waist.

"I feel so guilty," said the girl. "The Gods are bound to punish us for this. Why was it so important that we – that we do it here?"

"Because I need your help," he said, stroking her long, black hair. "I've discovered a way by which I may become King of Haddam, but I can't do it without you." He reached for something behind the altar.

"Me?" she said, surprised and flattered. "I'm only a peasant girl. How can I help you become king? How can anyone? Aren't there three brothers in line ahead of you?"

"Indeed there are, but I've been studying with a man who has found a way for me. All I need is some patience, a ritual... and you, my sweet."

He kissed the top of her head, and then made a swift movement behind her. Her eyes grew wide and she uttered a cry. He wrapped his other arm around her and held her fast. Her hands grasped at his arm, but only for a moment. After that, they fell limp. She gasped, then her head slumped forward. Behind her, the prince pulled a long dagger from her back and tossed it to the floor.

"Of course, I don't mean you specifically," he told her corpse as he laid it on the altar. "Any girl would do, or boy for that matter, provided they were young and fresh. You happened to be the one at hand. How fortunate for you."

He reached down behind the altar and pulled out a small, green velvet sack. From the sack he withdrew a beautiful red, polished stone.

"Look Fia," Lorq gasped. "It's a stone like the ones from the pictures!"

"Yes," she concurred, "only this one is red. There were no red stones depicted in the carvings. This seems to be an entirely different sort of ritual."

The prince laid the stone on the dead girl's chest and reached into the sack again. This time he brought out a scroll, which he immediately unrolled and studied for a few minmarks.

"This doesn't look good," Stamford remarked. "Blood sacrifice rituals are powerful things. Not the kind of things to be undertaken by some rapacious youngster. From what little I know, even with expert tutelage, there are many elements that can go wrong."

The prince began to chant the spell written on the scroll.

> "I call upon you, Barrad-karr, to share with me
> The secret of life for all eternity,
> The secret of power over life and death,
> For this, one gasp of your immortal breath
> I offer you this youthful blood,
> This most tender flesh.
> Grant me this boon, Barrad-karr.
> Reward the servant who pleases you..."

As he read, his voice grew louder and more strident, and the red stone began to glow brightly. Before the startled group's eyes, the body of the girl began to disappear. It seemed to them as though the stone were soaking her up, as a sponge soaks up liquid. The prince finished the invocation and immediately began reading it again. He looked sweaty and feverish now, as though the brightly shining stone were pouring vast amounts of heat into the room. The company felt nothing, but that was not surprising. After all, they were only specters here.

The girl was gone now. The stone had consumed even the blood that had soaked into the alabaster. Fia felt sorry for her, but reminded herself that, if their notion was correct, this had all happened centuries ago. Then the red stone began to hum. It started at a very low pitch, so low that they felt the sound rumbling through their bodies before they actually heard it. The prince had finished his second reading and was now sitting in the throne, watching the stone intently. His lips were curled into a frenzied grin, his eyes wide and eager. Gradually the pitch grew higher...and louder. The prince's initial glee began to fade somewhat as the noise grew more difficult to bear. As with the heat from the stone, Rokey and the others could hear the noise, and see its effect on the prince, but it caused them no discomfort.

"What do you think's happening?" Rokey asked Stamford.

"Looks to me like our charming prince has maybe summoned something that he can't control," he answered.

The prince clasped his hands to his ears, screaming in agony. Blood trickled down between his fingers and dripped onto the floor's polished granite. Just then, an intense beam of white light shot from the glowing stone straight at the suffering prince. For a moment after it struck him, his body seemed to turn translucent, making his entire skeleton visible. His young, supple skin turned sallow and his eyes bulged in their sockets. His black, bowl-cut hair abruptly fell to the floor around him, leaving him totally bald. More beams then exploded from the stone, pouring steady streams of light and energy through the small skylights in the ceiling. The temple thundered and shook violently. Then, as they watched in fascination, the stone seemed to suddenly cave in on itself. For a moment, there was a black circle of nothingness where it had once been. Rokey saw a red, glowing eye peer through the black hole. He felt its evil gaze sweep over him, leaving him sick and shivering. Then, with a pop, the hole closed, leaving only a puff of smoke where it had once been. The prince slumped forward on the throne, and the room became silent once again. The sun shining through the skylights vanished, and the many torches around the room were suddenly extinguished, leaving them in total darkness.

"What now?" came Flaskamper's voice.

"Beats me," Stamford replied. "Fia, any ideas?"

"I'm afraid I'm as baffled as the rest of you," she said. "I think all we can do is wait, either until something else happens or we wake up. That is, if this really is a dream."

Then, out of the darkness came a thin, raspy voice, so flat and funereal that it made the hairs on the backs of their necks stand up.

"Yes," the voice hissed, "and no. Not a dream...a nightmare. For me, for my lands, my people..."

Suddenly the roof and the walls of the temple were gone and they could see the broader area that surrounded them. It was a large, magnificent city, centered in a lush, fertile river valley. Something seemed to have gone wrong with the sky though. The sun overhead appeared larger, and hotter than normal. They watched as it set, then rose again and again, faster and faster each time. They realized that they were witnessing the swift passage of time. Days – then weeks passed in minmarks. Each day the sun poured down its merciless heat on the land below. There was no rain, not even the wisp of a cloud streaked across the sky. The land changed rapidly from green and fertile to parched and barren. Scenes of a starving populace flashed before them. Riots and revolts that were put down by the king's army, until the army itself revolted. It was a terrible sight, the death of a once thriving civilization. Finally, there were no more starving citizens, no more violent clashes. The streets were deserted, and already being swallowed by the rapidly growing desert. As the buildings began to crumble, the walls and ceiling around them returned, and they were back within the dark temple

"All that from one failed ritual," Fia whispered, awestruck.

"What in blazes are we going to do now?" Flaskamper asked urgently. "We can't just stay in this crazy dream forever."

"I agree," said Stamford. "Unfortunately, I haven't quite worked out what to do about it yet."

"I have an idea," Fia said softly. "Flaskamper, I think you should try and conjure us some light, like you did before. If it works, we'll at least be able to see where we are, and there's the chance that the spell may work outside of the dream and wake us."

"If it works at all," said Flaskamper.

"The only way to know is to try," Fia said.

"She's right Flash," Rokey put in. "Go on. Give it a try."

"Alright, here goes," said the elf, and spoke the spell to summon the light spirit –the lumen. Somewhat to his surprise, it worked. Bright light from the hovering orb immediately filled the room. They caught a momentary glimpse of their surroundings; the temple in its ruined state; their belongings still absent. They turned toward the altar and gasped in shock. In the throne behind it, there sat a skeleton, the prince they assumed, his yellow skin missing from large sections of his body. His lifeless eyes had shriveled in their sockets, and stared blankly ahead. Then, to their horror, the partially decomposed head turned toward them.

"Ahhhhh," said the prince, in the same dead rasp they had heard before, "now you see. Now... you... see."

*   *   *

They all awoke together and immediately leapt to their feet. Their packs, their water jugs and the fire were all there, and the throne was empty.

"Let's get out of this foul place," Stamford exclaimed.

Before the others could respond, large, black, scuttling insects began to pour from every hole and crevice in the room.

"By the gods!" Flaskamper cried, his voice on the edge of panic. "Those are raveners, flesh eating beetles! I've heard that they can strip a pony to its bare bones in minmarks. We've got to get out of here – fast!"

They grabbed their belongings and headed for the door, stomping and crunching the insects as fast as they could. But the door wouldn't budge. Even Lorq, with all his strength couldn't force it open.

"Shite!" Flash yelled, stomping wildly on beetles. "Shite! Shite! Shite! What now?"

Stamford cried out in pain as several raveners began devouring his toes. He shook them off and crushed them, but hundreds more were close behind.

"There! Just next to the throne!" cried Fia, pointing across the room. "There's a door!"

Without pausing for discussion they sprinted for the door, leaving footprints of bug guts in their wake. Lorq hit the door hard. It resisted, blocked by something on the other side, but on his second try it gave way. They piled inside the other room and slammed the door behind them For a moment they were in pitch blackness again, but then Flaskamper's orb reappeared, passing straight through the wall, and they found themselves facing yet another revolting sight. The room was filled with human skeletons, dozens and dozens, piled and scattered every which way. This was apparently where all the previous explorers and wayward travelers had wound up. The raveners had obviously gotten them. There was not a trace of flesh on any of the corpses.

That is... except for one.

In a chair at the far corner of the room sat the Haddam Prince, his skeletal, half-fleshed body just as it had appeared in their communal dream. He fixed them with his permanent toothy grin.

"Welcome," he said, "to the end of the road."

Chapter 13:

Oasis

The raveners hadn't given up on their meal. Rokey could hear them gnawing at the door and the wall. He was certain that they would gain access soon. As he tried to devise some means of escape, Stamford strode over to the skeleton prince, drawing his sword.

"Well, prince," said Stamford, "it looks as though at least one part of your ritual went as planned. Tell us, how is eternal life working out for you so far?"

"Insolent cur," the prince hissed. "I'll grind your bones to dust, once the raveners have finished cleaning them for me."

"Is there some other way out of this room?" Stamford demanded, brandishing his sword. "Tell us, or you'll spend the next millennium carrying your head under your arm."

The prince seemed unimpressed; nevertheless, he shook what remained of his head.

"There is no way out save the way you came in," he said. "And soon *they* will be in as well."

As if in response to his words, a small hole appeared in the wall next to Fia and one of the ugly, black insects dropped to the floor. She promptly squashed it, and quickly stopped up the hole with a piece of old sackcloth. Other holes were already forming though. In a few more minmarks they would be overrun again.

"It was not my intention that you should suffer," the prince offered. "Usually those who visit are devoured as they sleep. I then bring them here to my chamber...to keep me company. You are the first that have ever awakened."

"But why?" Fia demanded. "Why kill all of the people who visit here? Of what benefit is that to you?"

"It is not entirely my doing," the prince answered. "The ruins themselves lull visitors to sleep. An after-effect of the red stone's magic. I merely share my story, a kind of cautionary tale. Sadly, the raveners have always prevented it from ever leaving this room."

"Why don't you just awaken them," Rokey asked, "so that they can escape?"

The prince seemed to ponder this for a moment, and then he let out a hoarse laugh.

"Clever boy," he answered. "Caught me being disingenuous. The fact is I rather enjoy the show. And should my story get out, there'd be no stopping the hordes of intruders that would descend upon my kingdom. Surprise is my only way of preventing it."

More and more of the hungry creatures were now coming through the walls. Rokey and the others would kill them as quickly as they could, but the situation was rapidly becoming hopeless. He forced himself to turn and study the room again. This time he noticed two small windows high up on the far wall. To his surprise, he could see that the sky was now not only visible, but clear. The windows were both too high and too small to fit through, but it gave him an idea."

"Stamford," he yelled, "look!" He pointed to the windows.

"Great," Stamford said shortly, "the storm is over. You'll pardon me though if the weather isn't uppermost on my mind at the moment."

"No, no...the wall. An outside wall. One that isn't buried in the sand. If the bugs can break through one wall, surely we can break through the other."

"Of course!" the dark man shouted and quickly scanned the room. After a minmark, he gave a cry of elation.

"Lorq!" he called. Lorq, who was preoccupied with crunching raveners under his huge feet, didn't respond. Stamford walked over and grasped his arm.

"Lorq. Come here. It's time for you to save our arses again."

Rokey watched as he led Lorq to a pile of stone chunks. It looked like the remains of a large granite table. He saw Stamford point to the rubble, then to the wall. Lorq nodded in comprehension. Time was running out though. The beetles were coming through a myriad of holes now, faster than they could be crushed. Lorq picked up one of the stone chunks and hurled it at the wall. It made a sizeable gouge, but failed to break through. He tried again, hefting an even bigger hunk. As before, it did damage, but failed to punch through. The raveners were having more success. A large piece of the inner wall abruptly gave way. Hordes of the ugly creatures poured in.

"It's now or never, Lorq!" Flaskamper shouted.

Lorq turned and took hold of another piece of stone, this one so large that even he had to struggle to lift it. His arms bulged and his face reddened with exertion. Then, with all his might, he heaved the stone at the rear wall. It struck hard, but fell to the floor with a thud. For a moment it looked as though this attempt had also failed, but then there was a deep rumbling sound, and a large section of the wall, as well as the rear part of the ceiling came crashing down. They all whooped with joy, and sprinted for the opening. The prince leapt to his feet. Flaskamper paused and addressed him.

"Sorry to ruin your party, Your Majesty," he said, "but we really must be going now."

The prince let out a howl and charged toward the elf, but Flaskamper quickly sprang through the hole in the wall after the others.

Outside the sun was just beginning to rise. The prince continued to rage at them from inside the building, but did not attempt to follow, nor did the raveners. Apparently neither was able to tolerate the daylight. At last, the company was safe. The desert landscape, which the day before had seemed so harsh and unforgiving, today looked like paradise. Stamford slapped Rokey on the shoulder.

"Smart thinking, Son," he said. "You certainly saved all of our hides that time."

"Not me," Rokey responded. "It was Lorq who saved us." He smiled at Lorq, who grinned back at him.

"It was both of us," said the giant.

They stood and strapped on their packs. Flaskamper dug out the compass and pointed them in the proper direction, and then they set off across the sand toward their destination. Rokey couldn't help but feel a bit sorry for the wretched prince, despite his murderous obsession. He wondered if there was anyone in Aridia that would be able to free him from his eternal curse. He shook his head, thinking about how many people would jump at the chance to live forever. Twenty marks ago, he might have been one of them. Amazing, he thought, the things that one can learn in the space of a single day.

*   *   *

Several marks later, an Aridian scout met them and told them that they were nearing the perimeter of the city. He was utterly astounded to learn that they had come from the ruins. He bid them welcome and offered to show them to The Lion's Head, Aridia's only public house. They gladly accepted.

The settlement consisted mostly of tents, variously sized and shaped, although some permanent structures had been built in more recent years. The most impressive of these was the magnificent palace of the pasha, Aridia's ruler. Equal in size (though dull compared to the opulent palace) was the glass works. Aridia's principal export was its fine glass, which wasn't surprising given the endless supply of glass's primary component – sand. In response to Rokey's query, the scout, a bright young man named Jiri, explained that the permanent structures were all made of mud bricks, as there was no wood indigenous to the Great Sand Sea. Though the Elfwood Forest, an abundant source of timber, was not far off, trade negotiations between the elves and the Aridians had never resulted in a mutually satisfactory agreement. So the mud bricks, made from a mixture of sand, water, imported straw and the dung of desert donkeys were used instead. The ingredients were formed in molds, dried and then baked in the hot sun.

Even the bricks were an expensive luxury that few in Aridia could afford. As most of the wealth in the territory was controlled by the pasha, the aspirations of ordinary people normally reached only as high as to own one of the large, multiple-partitioned tents that allowed a measure of privacy to the various members of a household. Most, however, were forced to settle for the smaller, one-room models, which, Jiri told them, was the reason that so many Aridians spent most of their waking marks outside.

The Lion's Head was another of the rare permanent buildings, located squarely in the center of town. The scout introduced them to the innkeeper, a short, generously proportioned fellow with an enormous black moustache. He greeted them jovially, and when he spied the size of the gratuity that Flaskamper handed to Jiri, he became positively obsequious. He served them all cool water in some of Aridia's fine glasses, and then showed them to what he assured them were the most excellent rooms in the inn. This was a suite, consisting of a main sitting room with three large bedrooms connected to it. To Rokey, they seemed excellent indeed, though after his experiences these past three days, he would have been content with a straw mat in a stable. Their host explained that the chamber pots were changed daily, more frequently upon request (for an additional fee of course), and that the town had a lovely spring-fed pond, the only one in the Great Sand Sea, for bathing. After arranging for lunch to be sent to their room in a few marks, Flaskamper sent the man off with a gratuity which, he was certain, would assure their continued prompt service. They all dropped their things in their selected rooms, pushed off their sandals and flopped onto their beds. In minmarks, they were sound asleep.

Three marks later, they were awakened by a knock on the door. Flaskamper staggered to the door and opened it for a young, dark-skinned lad carrying a large and beautifully crafted glass tray piled high with food. He set it down on the table and, after Flaskamper had flipped him a coin, bowed his head and left the room. The elf's stomach growled as he examined the tray. It was laden with meats, dried fruit, and a variety of cheeses, many of which he had never seen before. There were also two large loaves of bread, one white and long, the other dark and round. In the center of the tray were several glasses and a tall, glass pitcher filled with a white liquid that Flaskamper didn't recognize. No doubt Stamford would know what it was.

Tempted though he was by the fare, he held off long enough to rouse the others to join him. They weren't eager at first, but once they laid eyes on the heavily burdened tray, they realized how famished they were, and tore in with gusto. When Stamford reached for the pitcher, Flaskamper asked him about the drink.

"It's called *Dokkas*," Stamford answered, pouring some into one of the glasses. It's essentially fermented spiced goat's milk. Takes some getting used to, but it's very refreshing. I once worked for a man who imported it regularly from here. He swore by it, said it was an aphrodisiac."

"Well, can't say no to that." The elf poured himself a cup, and then handed the pitcher to Rokey with a smile and a wink. Rokey returned the smile and poured some for himself. It had an odd flavor, both sweet and sour at once. It was, as Stamford had described, very refreshing. As to its other purported quality, Rokey had his doubts.

When they had all stuffed themselves, Flaskamper suggested that they all make a visit to the bathing spring.

"I don't know about the rest of you," he said, "but I've got enough sand covering my arse to start my own beach."

The companions headed for the public pool. There were few other people there. The attendant told them that most Aridians did their bathing in the early morning marks or after their evening meal. He went on to explain that most locals bathed naked, but there was bathing attire available to accommodate more modest visitors. Flaskamper elected to go native and promptly stripped naked and made for the pool. Rokey tried not to watch him, but was entirely unsuccessful. The rest of them opted for modesty, though adapting something to fit Lorq required some creativity on the part of the attendant.

The water was a perfect temperature, warmed by the sun, but also cooled by the springs. The pond was large enough to fit at least three score people and had been sculpted to be shallow at one end, much deeper at the other. Along the far end of the shallow section was a long stone bench. Stamford sank down onto it with a groan. Fia joined him there while Lorq, Rokey and Flaskamper splashed around in the deeper end. The attendant came around and handed them each a scrubbing cloth, rough on one side and smoother on the other, and then left them to enjoy themselves.

After he and the elf had finished dunking each other underwater, Rokey lay back and floated quietly for a while. He could feel the fresh water bringing his whole body back to life. It was a truly magnificent sensation. Here in the cool springs, ringed by the tall, broad-leafed sway trees, his problems all seemed far away. He knew, of course, that this was an illusion. There was no telling when or where trouble would strike them again. For now though, he was content just to enjoy the moment.

When the whole group was clean and relaxed, they returned to their rooms at the Lion's Head. There they were surprised, and somewhat apprehensive, when the innkeeper handed them a message. When asked where it came from, he told them that a boy had delivered it just after they'd left for the pool. Back in their bedroom suite, Stamford opened the sealed envelope and read the contents.

"Well I'll be damned," he muttered.

"What is it Stamford?" asked Fia nervously.

"It's from the pasha's chief minister," he said. "Word of our escape from the ruins has reached his master, thanks to our helpful scout, I'm certain. We are invited to dine with the pasha and his entourage tonight at the palace, *'where we will be asked to give an account of our most fascinating tale'*."

"Hmmm," Fia examined the invitation. "My guess is the pasha wouldn't take kindly to a polite, 'no thanks'."

Stamford nodded.

"My guess is that your guess is right, my dear. Does everybody have clean clothes to wear?"

"Depends on your definition of clean," Flash quipped, "but I think I can manage not to set the dogs to howling."

They got as well polished as they could, considering the state of their things. Since they had worn desert garb for the past three days, their regular clothes, though somewhat rumpled, were at least presentable. Fia, of course, looked stunning, thanks to her glamour pendant. The rest...faired as well as they could.

At the appointed time they arrived at the pasha's palace. The gate guard was expecting them and an escort was summoned to take them in and announce them. The escort was a friendly young woman named Pilan, who took all of their names, and then instructed them that the pasha was to be addressed as 'Your Excellency'. She also warned them that 'His Excellency' had a clubfoot, about which he was quite sensitive.

"He is unlikely to stand, but if he should, just try not to take any notice of it," she advised. "He'll appreciate that."

They had just finished walking down a long corridor and now stood in front of a large set of double doors that, being made of wood, had obviously cost a fortune. Pilan turned to them.

"Ready?" she asked.

They all nodded. She straightened up, threw open the doors and stepped in.

"Special guests of his Excellency, the Pasha B'el Thazal of Aridia..."
she announced to the room, and introduced them each by name.

Rokey's jaw dropped at the sights that spread out before him. The
room they entered was vast and lavish. Silk draperies of every color
covered the walls. A long table stood in the center of the room, on
which all manner of food and drink had been laid out. There were
massive hams, platters full of fowl and venison steaks, bowls of yams
and assorted vegetables, plates of fruit and cheese, pitchers filled with
water, wine, beer and dokkas. Immense, overstuffed lounges
upholstered with the same brightly colored silks were located all
throughout the room. Elaborately dressed individuals, both male and
female, occupied most of these; eating, drinking and chatting merrily
as a flock of bustling servants waited on them. In the front left corner,
a band of musicians were playing. The instruments themselves were
not familiar to Rokey, but he saw that some had strings like a lyre;
others had holes into which one blew like a flute. Then his attention
was drawn to the far end of the room where, up on a raised platform,
he saw the largest lounge of all, strewn with literally hundreds of
pillows of all shapes and colors. In the center of that lay a man decked
out from head to toe in bright yellow silk. He was short and corpulent,
with small, beady eyes, chubby red cheeks and a slightly turned up
nose, all of which combined to give him a distinctly piggish
appearance. Rokey decided that this must be the pasha. Reclining all
around the man was a bevy of beautiful young women, scantily
costumed in translucent lavender gauze. They immediately captured
Stamford's attention, and when their escort explained that they were
to be guests of honor and share the pasha's lounge, or *takrah* as they
were called, he was happy to lead the way.

Pasha B'el Thazal turned out to be a gracious and genial man.
When it became obvious that Lorq could not fit comfortably on the
takrah, he had several enormous pillows brought and placed on the
floor just in front of them for the giant to sit on. He didn't so much as
mention their escape from the ruins until they were all well fed and
sated with wine. In fact, they consumed so much food and drink that
Rokey, reclining comfortably among the soft pillows, began to fear that
he might fall asleep. He shared his concern with Flaskamper.

"Me too," said the elf, his eyes a bit hazy from the wine. "Tell you
what, we'll keep an eye on one another. If you fall asleep, I'll pinch
you. You do the same to me."

The bargain made, they turned their attention back to their host,
who had now decided it was time to hear their story. He was
interested not only in the ruins, but in the eclectic company itself, and
the reasons for their journey across the Great Sand Sea. As Stamford
was their leader, he was elected to be that evening's raconteur, with
Fia adding a bit of feminine charm. This went over well with the
pasha, who obviously had an eye for the ladies. Rokey was happy to

leave them in charge of the storytelling. Stamford and Fia were much more worldly than he was, and would know how to judiciously edit the tale. He sat and listened; paying as much attention as he could in his somewhat inebriated state. Stamford was laying it on a bit thick for the benefit of the ladies, occasionally causing Fia to roll her eyes. They had reached the point of giving an abbreviated account of Lorq's history in the Northern Expanse. The next thing Rokey knew, something was pinching his arm. He started awake and Flaskamper gave him a wink. He had fallen asleep after all. He hoped that no one but the elf had noticed.

When Stamford and Fia reached their adventure in the ruins, the pasha became even more attentive. He was astonished that a sand storm had driven them there, as this was not the time of year for sand storms. Upon hearing this, Rokey was certain that the unusual weather phenomenon had been sent deliberately by his unknown nemesis to force them into the ruins. It was only by the barest of margins that the plan had not successfully resulted in their deaths. Stamford made no mention of this, for he had omitted the part about their being pursued from the story entirely. As far as the pasha or anyone else in the room knew, they were traveling to Waterford on some personal business for their employer in Duncileer. However, when His Excellency made the comment about the unseasonable storm, Stamford gave Rokey a look that told him he too had made the connection. The pasha quizzed them about every detail of their stay in the ruins. He wanted to know all about the way the restored temple had looked, the details of the wall carvings and even the clothing the prince and the woman had worn.

When the story was finished, the pasha and all the other listeners enthusiastically applauded. Everyone had thoroughly enjoyed the tale, especially the insights into the ruined city.

"The reason for our intense curiosity," B'el Thazal explained, "is that we Aridians believe ourselves to be descended from the people who had once occupied the city, but every attempt to gain further knowledge about it thus far has resulted in the mysterious disappearance of our explorers. Now that you have given us some idea of the nature of the enemy that lurks there, it may be possible for us to devise a means of thwarting it."

As he said this, Rokey thought of the prince's comments about hordes of visitors descending on his kingdom. He felt just the slightest pang of pity for the skeleton prince.

"Do you suppose you might discover a way to free the prince from his curse, Your Excellency?" Rokey asked. The pasha reflected on this for a moment.

"Well, magic is not our strong suit here in Aridia," he said, "but because we export our fine glass to the farthest reaches of Firma, we have a great many connections in the land abroad. I shall put out a call and see if some way can't be found. It would be in everyone's best interests, I think, if the ruins were freed of this dangerous enchantment."

It grew late. Many of the remaining revelers had fallen fast asleep on their takrahs when the group bid the pasha and his entourage goodnight. His Excellency promised that they were welcome to visit again any time. As they walked back to the inn through the darkened and deserted streets, Stamford's mood became sober.

"So," he remarked, "the evil pursues us even through the Great Sand Sea."

"I noted that as well," said Fia. "What I wonder is how? By what means does our enemy track our movements?"

"Maybe word of our destination has leaked from Duncileer," Rokey suggested.

Flaskamper shook his head.

"Battista would never have told anyone," he said. "As to that Jamba fellow, *I* don't trust him a whit, but Battista must, or she would never have brought us there.. So I have to believe in his integrity too...at least in that regard."

"We'll have to leave here early tomorrow," Stamford told them. "I know our heads will be heavy from tonight's revelry, but we must try to reach the safety of Elfwood before the next impediment is hurled at us. Each obstacle seems more powerful than the last. It would be well for us if we could rest up a bit before our next battle."

'Our' next battle.

Rokey was touched by Stamford's remark. It was not just Rokey's dilemma now, but also the entire company's. They were committed to aid him in this, whatever strife may befall them. For the moment at least, it filled him with a feeling of warmth and security. Suddenly Flaskamper put his arm around Rokey's shoulder, and another feeling was added to the mix, one far too complicated for him to fathom. He placed his hand on the small of the elf's back and they walked together in companionable silence. Behind them were Stamford and Fia, with Lorq bringing up the rear. Fia tapped Stamford's arm and inclined her head toward the boys in front of them. Stamford saw that she was giving him *that look*, the one that said, *'See? What did I tell you?'*. But she needn't have bothered. He already knew that he had made the right decision, not just for Flaskamper's sake, but for his own. He didn't know the reasons just yet, but had the feeling that, soon enough, things were all going to become clear.

Chapter 14:

Elfwood

T hough he felt miserable when he awoke that next morning, Rokey was nevertheless pleased to finally be leaving the desert. Fortunately for the weary band, Aridia was located on the far eastern side of the Great Sand Sea, so within half a day, the bare sand had already become sparsely dotted with thornwhistle and a few ragged shrubs. They were also relieved to see clouds skittering across the sky once again. Rokey wondered how any efforts to free the ruins from their disastrous enchantment might affect the desert's weather. He mentioned this to Flaskamper at one point as they walked along together.

"Good question," he responded. "Magic is a complicated business. The prince found that out the hard way. No telling what could happen if they try tampering with it now."

Rokey tried to coax him into further conversation, but the elf was subdued today, and not in the mood for discourse. Rokey knew that he was nervous about their imminent visit to Elfwood, but wasn't sure what he could say that would be of any help. He opted to simply walk along with him, in case he should feel like talking to someone.

Flaskamper's stomach had been flip-flopping all morning. He had tried to convince himself that it was because of all the wine he had drunk the previous night, but in his heart, he knew what the problem really was. He dreaded seeing his father again. He could just picture the scowl on his face, that look of reproach that he had seen so many times while growing up.

Why had he not agreed to go around Elfwood? The others had offered him the option. He should have jumped at the chance. Well, it wasn't too late. It would be a mark or two before they reached the Elfwood Forest. They could turn south, head down past the elven territories. It would only take them two or three days out of their way – four at the outside. Right, days of walking through the unprotected southern woodlands; no chance to rest in the safety of Elfwood; jeopardize everyone's life because he was too great a coward to look his own father in the eye. No. It was time for him to stop running and face his demons, even if one of them *was* his father.

He glanced over at Rokey, walking quietly beside him. The boy looked back and smiled. Flaskamper knew that Rokey had sensed his mood, and was leaving him to his own thoughts. Yet his friend still remained by his side, comforting him with his presence. It boggled his mind to think of the things that they had been through together during the past few days. Only a few short days, yet he felt that he had already known Rokey for so much longer.

The sun was now directly overhead, but much less intense than it had been in the desert. White, puffy clouds dotted the azure sky, and a gentle wind blew up from the south. They had put on their regular clothing that morning, choosing only to wear the reed sandals, as they were much better in the sand. Now that they were leaving the desert, they stopped briefly for a bite to eat and changed back to their regular footwear. The sand had given way to a short expanse of hard, rocky ground, which not long afterwards became a grassy meadow. They could see the woods beyond and, a short time later, they were entering Elfwood Forest.

Having grown accustomed to the desert heat, they found the woods uncomfortably chilly, and donned their cloaks. In spite of his trepidation, Flaskamper was reassured by the familiar smells of Elfwood Forest; the pungent, earthy smell of henniger moss and the evergreen trees; the sweetness of the bright red fireflowers, which were among the last of the season's blooming flora. Memories came rushing back to him – some good, some bitter – as though he had left home only yesterday. It was just as it had always been...or was it?

"What is it Flash?" Rokey asked, noticing the curious look that passed over his face.

The elf stopped short, and stood quietly with his eyes closed. He held up his hand for silence, and stood listening for a few moments. At last, he opened his eyes and shook his head, perplexed.

"Something's amiss here," he said. "I don't know how to explain it. There's something – something doesn't sound quite right."

"Don't get cryptic on us," growled Stamford. "What have your little pointy ears picked up on now?"

"It's not something I can put into words," said Flaskamper. "Elves are – we're in tune with our forest. Like musicians are in tune with their instruments."

"You're saying the forest is out of tune?" Stamford jibed.

"Yes, that's it," the elf answered distractedly, unmindful of the sarcasm. "That's it exactly."

They continued on through the wood. Flaskamper continued to pause periodically and listen, but he said nothing further about his strange impressions. They had traveled nearly a half-mile when the elf at last heard a familiar and comforting sound – a blue forest owl.

"It's about time," he muttered.

"Now what?" Stamford asked. "Is the owl out of tune?"

The leader let out a yelp as Fia smacked him on the arm.

"It's not an owl," the elf answered. "It's a sentry. We've been spotted, but it came later than it should have. Something is definitely going on. I'll be glad when the sentinels arrive. They should be able to tell me what's happening."

They didn't have to wait long. In a few minmarks, the companions found themselves surrounded by a company of green-uniformed elf guards, shortbows drawn and pointed directly at them. The company commander, a tall, thin fellow, moved forward and curtly challenged them to identify themselves. None of them recognized Flaskamper until he stepped up and threw back the hood of his cloak. The commander immediately flushed, and he and all of the other elves bowed low.

"Forgive me, My Prince," the commander said. "I did not know you thus attired."

Rokey could see that Flaskamper was embarrassed by the display.

"For pity's sake, get up," he told them. "Save the formalities for my father, Limeron. Just shake my hand."

The commander smiled and took Flaskamper's outstretched hand.

"It is good to see you again, Flaskamper," Limeron said warmly. "You have been too long away from us."

"Says you," Flaskamper retorted. "My friends and I are just passing through on our way to Waterville. I thought I'd show them what elven hospitality is like, though it seems to have diminished a trifle in my absence. Why the display of arms at the ready?"

"Grim happenings, Highness," Limeron told him with a shake of his head. "There's evil afoot in the forest. But I'd best leave that for your brother to tell you. The elder prince was summoned as soon as we spotted your party and will be waiting at West Fork for news."

"Impatiently, no doubt," said Flaskamper.

"You know your brother," was the answer.

The elf soldiers escorted them to a command center known as the West Fork, named for its location at a split in one of the westerly forest trails. It took only a matter of minmarks to reach the small cluster of treetop buildings.

"I'd better go see him alone first," Flaskamper told the others.

"Do you want me to go first and announce you?" Limeron asked.

"*Announce* me?" Flaskamper said with a laugh. "I think you're right, Limeron. I *have* been too long away."

Flaskamper climbed the steep, narrow staircase that led to the walkway connecting the several small huts. He looked a question down at Limeron, who pointed to the one on the far end. Flaskamper made his way there and entered. His brother stood as he walked in the door. Alrontin was taller than Flaskamper, and slightly more muscular. He was decked out in his full silver dress uniform complete with lavender trimmings, breastplate, helm with mail hood, knee-length loincloth with military apron and high, steel-covered boots and greaves. Instead of his bow and arrows, he was armed with his long, ceremonial rapier, with the ornate matching shield and forearm guards. Flaskamper was a bit taken aback by his brother's regalia, but quickly recovered himself.

"Wow!" Flaskamper exclaimed. "Did you run and put that on just for me?"

If Alrontin felt any surprise at seeing his brother standing there, he hid it well.

"I thought it might be someone of importance," he retorted. "My mistake."

The brothers each broke into a broad grin and hugged each other warmly.

"In truth, I was presiding over the guard detail for a state luncheon when I was informed of your party's arrival." Alrontin informed him. "I was glad for the excuse to leave. Dull as dirt these diplomatic affairs. Flaskamper, what in the world are you doing here?"

"I have a long story to tell you, Ronti," Flaskamper answered, using his childhood name for his brother. "Suffice it to say for the moment that my companions and I are on a quest, and Elfwood was on our way."

"Well, I'm glad for whatever circumstances bring you home again, Soaker. Come and introduce me to these companions of yours, then I will see to your comforts."

"If only everyone here could be so happy to see me," Flaskamper said sardonically.

"Aye, I'm sorry to say that you'll not find father much changed," replied his brother, "but you must try not to take him to heart. Remember that he loves you, Flaskamper, though it pains him to express it."

"I'll say it does," Flaskamper muttered.

The two descended to the forest floor, and Flaskamper made introductions. Alrontin did not miss the sparkle in his brother's eye when he presented Rokey to him, and hoped that it meant that Flaskamper had at last found someone special. That would certainly please their mother to no end.

Alrontin relieved Limeron of his charges and sent him and the other guards back to their posts. He then linked arms with his brother and instructed the rest to follow them. On the way, Flaskamper asked him about the changes that he had felt in the forest, and the reference that Limeron had made to dark happenings of late.

"A grisly and mysterious business," Alrontin explained. "It started some months back. Fowl, livestock, even beloved pets began to mysteriously disappear, only to be discovered dead and nearly devoured a day or more later, sometimes miles from their last known location. The occurrences were infrequent at first, but as time has passed, they've begun to happen almost daily."

"Any clues to who was responsible," Flaskamper asked, "or what?"

Alrontin shook his head.

"No solid evidence," he answered, "only the mangled bodies, and some vague reports of strange creatures seen skulking in the shadows. We have set traps, hoping to lure whatever it was into the open, but so far we have had no success. And things have grown worse. Two days ago, two of our remote sentries vanished. We searched the area surrounding their tower for miles. We found no trace of them, not so much as a hat feather. We have temporarily ceased patrolling those remote stations."

"I noticed that," said Flaskamper.

"Instead we're sending full squads to patrol our perimeter. It's not as effective, but it provides the soldiers with the safety of numbers."

Alrontin leaned closer to his brother.

"The citizens are fearful," he said, his voice filled with urgency, "and who can blame them? Mothers are afraid to let their children play outdoors...here, in *our* forest."

Alrontin was clearly angry and frustrated, and Flaskamper could understand why. The Elfwood Forest had always been a safe place for elves of any age to roam. Because they were magical beings, they were treated with respect by even the wildest predators in the wood. The residents had never had any reason to be frightened here, for themselves or their livestock. Whatever was responsible for these atrocities was clearly something from the outside – something unnatural.

"My men are all on edge, as you no doubt observed," Alrontin was saying, "and father – well, even his famous dispassion is beginning to crack a bit. I fear that you will find him even more dour than usual."

"Great," Flaskamper said. "He can only just abide me when he's in an *easy* frame of mind."

"I fear that in addition to his current troubles, he may also be somewhat resentful of your lengthy absence," Alrontin informed him.

"I tell you this only to prepare you for what might be a somewhat strained reunion, at first anyway."

Flaskamper gave a sharp laugh.

"Oh Ronti, when have things been anything *but* strained between Father and I," he said. "I assumed he'd be overjoyed to have me out of his hair these past few years. Wrong again, Flaskamper – surprise, surprise. I appreciate the warning, brother, and given recent events, I shall endeavor to keep the peace, however humiliating that may prove."

"You two have always been like dueling rams, continually smashing your heads together. I must admit I've never fully understood the reasons for the conflict, but for my part, I shall do my best to make your stay a pleasant one," Alrontin said. "I really have missed you, Soaker."

"And I you," said Flaskamper, squeezing his brother's arm affectionately, "now quit calling me *Soaker*."

Rokey could barely tell when they had entered Elfwood proper because the dwellings blended so seamlessly with the natural forest. Most of the homes were in the treetops, accessible only by rope ladders or small, impossibly steep, winding staircases. Looking up, he would occasionally spot the town's inhabitants going about their business. They seemed to show little interest in the procession, though the sudden presence of a giant in their midst did draw a few second glances.

The King's Compound was located in a small clearing, and consisted of numerous buildings, both ground level and treetop, all connected by enclosed walkways. Alrontin took them through the main entrance hall on the ground level, past the King's Court and up a long, meandering staircase, into a hallway that ran just below the kitchens.

"Father and Mother will be tied-up with the delegation from Tanohar for some time yet," Alrontin said to Flaskamper. "I'll let them know that you're here, though. If you want to show your friends to the guest wing, I'll speak to Periquiel about getting the rooms prepared and have some food sent up to the guest dining room. Then I'm afraid I must rejoin the meeting, else our father will have my head."

Alrontin embraced his brother again, bid the rest of the companions farewell and went off in search of Periquiel, the steward. Flaskamper led them through another door, across one of the suspended walkways and into the wing of the complex reserved for guests. There were eight bedrooms and two large sitting rooms here, which meant that each member of the group could have their own private space. This was a luxury that none of them had enjoyed for some time. For Rokey, in fact, it would be a first.

"Normally, I would stay in my suite in the Princes' Wing," he explained to them, "but even though we're perfectly safe here, I think

I'd still feel more comfortable staying in one of these rooms, just so we're all close to one another."

"Good idea," said Stamford. "We'd never be able to find you in this labyrinth."

They had only just gotten to their rooms, when a team of servants arrived to prepare them. They quickly and efficiently dusted the furniture and made up the beds. They had even brought extra mattresses to fasten together to accommodate Lorq.

"I'm not sure I'll be able to sleep," he exclaimed giddily. "I'm so used to my legs and feet sticking out onto the floor."

"Don't get too used to it, big fellow" cautioned Flaskamper. "We won't be here all that long."

Just as the maids departed, a pair of servants arrived from the kitchen with food and drink, which, at Flaskamper's request, they set up in one of the sitting rooms. The fare consisted of cold roasted forest hen, rolls and redberry jam, a wheel of Elfwood's own fine cheese and a jug of sweet, white wine. They had stopped only a few moments for lunch earlier in the day, so they were all ravenous, and enthusiastically attacked the meal.

"If we continue eating like this," Fia remarked, smearing a roll with jam, "we shall all grow too fat to remain soldiers of fortune."

When they had finished eating, Flaskamper took them on a tour of the palace compound. He showed them his rooms in the section known as the Princes' Wing, the bathhouse, domed in frosted glass, the family's abundantly stocked library and the queen's gardens in the rear. Though Flaskamper had dreaded coming here, to Rokey he seemed eager and pleased to be able to share his home with them. Perhaps relations with his father would improve with this visit, and his friend would no longer feel anxious about returning home. For Flash's sake, he certainly hoped so.

As day turned slowly into evening the Tanohari delegates finally departed, and King Angorath sent Alrontin to summon his younger son and his companions. Rokey knew that his friend was nervous, but the elf masqued it well, shooting them his most reassuring smile.

"Don't worry," he told them. "He would never be anything but gracious to houseguests. He reserves the red hot pokers for me."

They made their way back down to the King's Court. Angorath and Ferriwhyl stood up from their finely crafted wooden thrones. Rokey immediately saw where the sons had gotten their looks. The two of them were both striking in appearance, each tall and sleek with long, flowing, white hair. While the king's features were strong and angular, the queen's were fine and delicate. He was dressed in a tunic of bright forest green with matching leggings, and a long, green cape, elaborately embroidered with fine silver thread. She wore a stunning full-length gown of violet silk, which was cut to accentuate the curves of her body, and piped with a lavender trim that matched the translucent wrap she wore loosely about her shoulders. The crowns they wore were of white gold, crafted in a simple, yet elegant style. This couple embodied royalty as Rokey had always pictured it, and he was immediately both charmed and intimidated by them.

The group made its way to the front of the room, with Flaskamper leading the way. He embraced his mother, who greeted him warmly and kissed him on the cheek. Then he moved to stand before his father, extending his hand cautiously, as though something might lash out and bite it. His father took it and favored him with a smile, which to Rokey appeared somewhat cold and ceremonious. His heart sank a bit. For Flaskamper's sake, he had hoped for more.

"Flaskamper, you honor us at last with a visit," said the king. The sarcasm was subtle, but it stung. His son smiled and feigned ignorance.

"Thank you father," he said. "It is good to see you too. May I present my friends..."

He introduced Stamford, Fia and Lorq, and then he took Rokey by the arm and guided him forward to stand next to him.

"...and this – this is Rokey."

Rokey followed the example of the others and bowed to the king and queen.

"It is a pleasure to meet you, Rokey..." the queen said sweetly, then looked up at the others, "...and all of you. You are most welcome in our kingdom, and in our home."

"Indeed," the king agreed, "most welcome. I trust our elder son has seen to your comforts. Should you require anything else during your stay, please do not hesitate to ask any one of the servants, or Flaskamper, if he has not forgotten his way about."

Another subtle jibe, Rokey thought, glancing at Flaskamper. He was still smiling, apparently oblivious to the criticism. Rokey knew better though.

"I hope that none of you will think us poor hosts if we retire early this evening," said the king. "State business has made for a very long and wearisome day, and we were not properly prepared for your arrival. Tomorrow I promise that we shall all dine together, in a manner more befitting guests of the royal household."

"Of course, father," said Flaskamper. "The day has been long for us as well."

"Then by all means," said Angorath, "let us each take some much-needed rest. First, however, your mother and I would appreciate a few moments of your time... alone."

The company took their cue and departed, closing the large, double doors behind them. Rokey felt guilty, as though he had just left Flaskamper to face a hungry firecat unaided. There was nothing to be done about it though. This was a trial that Flash would have to endure alone.

"Don't worry, Rokey," Fia said, reading his long face. "Flaskamper has a tough skin. He'll be just fine."

"You're right," he said. "I know – you're right."

He smiled and nodded at her as they continued toward their rooms, but inside, he still had his doubts.

*   *   *

Flaskamper watched his friends depart. He had steeled himself for the onslaught as the big double doors closed, but then decided to take the offensive instead.

"I already know what you're going to say," he said, "and I'm sorry. I'm sorry that I stayed away for five years without sending word. There's no excuse for it. I was wrong; I know it. There's nothing I can do, though, but apologize and ask you to forgive me."

The first volley fired, he lowered his head and bit his lip, waiting for the response.

"All very well, as far as it goes," his father answered calmly. "Parents can always forgive their children, no matter how selfish and thoughtless their behavior."

"Thank you father – "

"However, the reason that you left, so you told us, was so that you could make something of yourself in the world. You needed an opportunity to thrive, you said, outside of the shadow of your older brother, and the constant withering scrutiny of your overbearing father. Yet, five years later, you suddenly return, unheralded, with this – this rabble in tow – "

"They are NOT rabble!" Flash felt the color rising in his face. "They are the finest people I've ever known. I would gladly give my life for any one of them. How can you be so judgmental about people you've just met?"

"Flaskamper, you forget yourself," the king admonished him.

"No, I do not," Flaskamper responded. "You are the king and my father. You may berate and insult *me* as it pleases you, but I will not stand quietly by and let my friends be abused." Their son calmed his voice and held his hands out pleadingly. "If you would just...just give them a chance, instead of assuming the worst about me – about them."

Tears came unbidden to his eyes. He fought furiously to hold them back. He was *not* going to weep in front of his father. He would not grant him the satisfaction of having broken him down. Now Ferriwhyl spoke for the first time.

"Flaskamper, you must forgive us for being a bit taken aback," she said softly. "I am sure that your friends are all fine people, but the group does give one something of a turn. And to arrive so suddenly, after five years of silence – "

"I...I know mother. I *am* sorry, truly I am. I didn't mean to hurt you – either of you. I just needed – I needed the time."

"And what have you done with all this time?" his father asked. "What have you made of yourself, out there in the broader world of men?"

"Nothing I suppose, by your standards, father," Flaskamper said in exasperation. "Stamford, Fia, Lorq and I have been traveling all over Firma, offering our services as bodyguards, entertainers, whatever a potential employer may require. We're usually short of money, and we never stay put for very long, but I've loved it – every minmark of it."

"And what of Rokey?" the queen asked. "Where does he fit in?"

"That's...a long story," said Flaskamper. "As we are all tired, I should probably save that for tomorrow."

"Mercenaries," his father scoffed. "My son the mercenary. Is this revelation supposed to fill me with pride?"

Flaskamper lowered his head.

"No, father," he answered quietly. "I don't expect you to be proud of me. I'd hardly know what to do if you were. I don't even expect you to understand. I suppose all that I can hope for is that you respect my decisions, however odious they are to you, and try to give my friends at least a fair chance."

"Respect your decision to squander your life away?" said Angorath. "You are not a parent, so you realize not what you ask of us. It may be more than we are capable of. As to your friends..."

Flaskamper looked up at his father, prepared to defend his companions again.

"... a king must endeavor to be fair in all things, including the characterization of his son's friends. I shall mark them more closely tomorrow."

It was the closest thing to an apology that Flaskamper had ever received from his father. He decided to call it a win and beat a tactical retreat.

"Tomorrow we shall recount some of our adventures," he told them, "and fill you in on the quest that brings us here. It may be that our journey relates in some way to the troubles plaguing Elfwood Forest, though at this point that is mere speculation."

"We shall be most eager to hear all about it," said Ferriwhyl. "Now go and get a good night's sleep, dear. It has been a trying day for us all."

Ferriwhyl took her son in her arms and gave him another kiss, then sent him on his way. When he got to his room, he found Rokey waiting up for him.

"I just wanted to make sure – you know, that everything was all right.," Rokey said, worry apparent on his face.

Flaskamper embraced Rokey affectionately.

"Everything is fine," he said with a smile. "Either father has grown softer, or my hide has thickened. Either way, it wasn't as bad as I'd feared it would be."

"I'm glad," Rokey said, with a sigh of relief. "Now I'll be able to sleep tonight."

"As will I," Flaskamper replied with weary satisfaction. "As will I.

*　　*　　*

The entire company slept in late the next morning. The beds were so comfortable, it had seemed to Rokey as though he'd crawled into a cloud. He had never felt anything so soft and inviting in all his life. Over the traditional elven breakfast of sweetcakes with honey and cream, poached trill (a local fish) and goat's milk, Flaskamper explained that nothing vexed his mother more than an uncomfortable bed. As she had grown up in a rather poor household with many children, she had spent the years prior to her marriage to the king sleeping on a simple straw mat. When it became her duty to manage the palace, she swore that no one would ever have a poor night's rest under her roof. The pillows were hand made in the far-off northern city of Iceberg and generously stuffed with the soft, thick down of their snow geese, as were the featherbeds atop each mattress. The sheets were woven of the finest Respitean silk, the quality of which was guaranteed by royal edict. Once a year, Flaskamper explained, a silk merchant would travel all the way to Elfwood from Respite just to visit the palace. His mother insisted on meeting with him and doing all of the buying personally. She did the same with the merchant from Iceberg, who only made the journey every three years. The queen, being very generous, would often send one of these fine bedding sets to young newlyweds as a wedding gift. The fortunate couples prized these gifts more than gold.

It was clear to Rokey that Flaskamper was very close with his mother. He wondered what it must be like to grow up in such a home, with a loving mother to care for you. This naturally brought his thoughts back to their journey, and the question of his own parentage. What, if anything, he wondered, would he learn about them by visiting this ancient and mysterious place known as Glimmermere? And what if he were to learn that his parents had been ordinary shopkeepers from Cedar Glen? How would that revelation fit into the events now taking place? Hard to believe, he pondered, that a mere month ago he had been happily cloistered in the Noble Contemplative, with few ambitions beyond the walls of the Brotherhood.

"Hey Rokey," said Flaskamper, waving a hand in front of him.

"Huh?" Rokey realized that he had been daydreaming.

"You're a thousand miles away," said the elf. "What's going on it that handsome head of yours?"

"Sorry," Rokey said. "I was just thinking of how different life has turned out from what I had expected. If you had told me a month ago that today I would be sitting in the palace of Elfwood, a guest of the royal family – "

"Quite a change from what you had intended, I'm sure," said Fia, "though I think that, to a greater or lesser degree, everyone's life turns out differently from what they plan or imagine. I suppose one's best course of action is to roll with the tide and make the best one can of things."

"*Always steer your boat downstream,*" Rokey murmured.

"What was that?" Fia asked.

"Nothing," Rokey replied. "Just thinking of something another friend of mine used to say."

He wondered what Ely was doing right now, and sorrow fluttered briefly across his heart.

While the king and queen held court, Flaskamper brought his friends for a soak in the palace's well-appointed bathhouse, after which they went for a stroll through the town. There wasn't a great deal to see – a market, a bakery, a clothier – nothing unusual except for the fact that so much of it was nestled high in the treetops. For Lorq, this presented something of a problem, and he chose to wait on the ground on some occasions rather than attempt to squeeze himself into some of the prohibitively tight spaces. But he had lived among the 'minnows' for many years now, and was quite accustomed to these occasional quandaries.

Later, they all joined the king, queen and Prince Alrontin for dinner in the king's private dining room. There, Flaskamper filled the family in on some of the details of his five years away, judiciously editing the parts that one normally withholds from one's parents. His brother later demanded the unexpurgated version, which Flaskamper promised to deliver in private before they departed. When Flaskamper came to the point of recounting his first encounter with Rokey, and the events which had brought them all to Elfwood, he became more serious. This time, he left nothing out. His friends added details here and there, especially to fill in portions of the trip during which Flaskamper had been under the spell of the poison. His mother grew quite concerned at this part of the tale, and was greatly relieved to hear that all traces of the evil substance had been removed by Battista. All three of the elf's family members broke in with questions from time to time, but for the greatest part, they listened without interruption. Flaskamper finished by relating the feelings of both Stamford and the necromancer Jamba that something big was underway, and wondered aloud whether the dark events reported of late in both Elfwood and Duncileer might somehow be related to the multiple attempts on Rokey's life. After careful consideration, Flaskamper had chosen not to mention the fact that someone was sneaking Angorath brandy out of Elfwood. It did no one any harm, as far as he could see, and there was no point in making an enemy of Jamba.

When he had finished, his family sat in silence for a few moments, ruminating on all that they had been told. Flaskamper could tell by the way his father was stroking his chin that he was giving the matter serious consideration. He could not help but fear that the king would ultimately dismiss his fears as foolish and irrational, the product of his childish imagination. However, when Angorath spoke at last, there was no derision in his voice, only deep concern.

"I have been in this world a long time," he began, "long enough to remember times less harmonious than these – times of greater peril, where evil's footprints were clearly visible in the land. Recently, when these animals began to mysteriously vanish, only to reappear later half-devoured, I tried, against my better judgment, to convince myself that it was only some forest predator run amok. But when my two guards also disappeared, I feared that the instincts I had tried so hard to ignore were likely correct. Then yesterday, the emissaries from Tanohar shared with me the fact that, only a few weeks before, an attempt was made on the life of King Edvar. The effort failed, though a bodyguard was killed, and the perpetrator escaped. But disturbing though any attempt on a head of state may be, the truly unnerving part was that, according to those who witnessed the attack, the would be assassin was...a wraith."

There was a collective gasp. Rokey remembered reading about wraiths in a book once. They were made by preserving a dead body with a combination of salts and herbs, until only a shriveled husk remained. Then, by means of dark, powerful magic, new life was breathed into it. The soulless creature then became the slave of whatever witch or sorcerer had reanimated it. Just thinking about it made Rokey shiver.

"Now that you have told me your story," the king continued, "I am more certain than ever – certain that the tide of good and evil in Firma is again experiencing a shift. The signs are all there, and only a fool ignores what is right under his nose."

He looked over at the queen, who nodded solemnly in agreement.

"Rokey," she said, "it certainly appears that you, through no fault of your own, are likely an integral component in some dark construct. Whether taking your life is meant to bring about some crucial event, or whether your enemies fear that, alive, you possess the means to thwart them, seems impossible at this point to conjecture. However, I think you are fortunate to be in the company of my son and his intrepid friends as you undertake this perilous journey."

"I do indeed consider myself most fortunate, Your Majesty," Rokey replied, looking affectionately at Flaskamper, "fortunate and grateful."

Across the table, Ferriwhyl and Alrontin shared a meaningful glance, to which the king was completely oblivious.

"I am now more eager than ever," Angorath said, "to get to the bottom of these baffling occurrences in Elfwood Forest. Alrontin, I think that as soon as your brother and his companions have departed, we must put our heads together and see if we cannot devise some way to capture, or at the very least identify the culprit, or culprits."

"Yes, father," Alrontin agreed.

"As for you, Flaskamper, and your company – "

Flaskamper cleared his throat.

"Actually father," he said, "Stamford is the leader of our group. I don't mean to interrupt you, but it would be disrespectful of me to allow the misperception to persist."

"Quite right, son," the king agreed. "I appreciate the clarification."

Angorath turned to Stamford.

"Forgive me, sir," said the king. "As I was saying, as far as you and your company are concerned, I cannot see any means by which we can readily assist you at this moment, except to offer you such safety and hospitality as is presently ours to give. Of course, if you have any other notions..."

"Nothing else comes to mind at the moment, Your Majesty," said Stamford, "but, we are grateful for your patronage, and will keep in mind your generous offer should anything else occur to us."

*　　*　　*

They decided to stay for just one more day before moving on to Waterville. While it felt good to be contented and safe, they were all eager to reach the oracle at Glimmermere, to find out what counsel it could give them. Flaskamper spent part of that last day alone with Alrontin, filling his brother in, as promised, on some of his more sordid adventures. The two of them then collected the rest of the troop and went to see Alrontin's wife, Mellynda, and Flaskamper's niece and nephew, Liesyll and Jontrin. The youngsters were fascinated by Lorq, and though happy to see their long, lost uncle, spent most of the visit riding astride the giant's great arms. Mellynda was a bit apprehensive at first, but when she observed how gentle and kind Lorq was, she soon relaxed and laughed along with her children.

That evening they dined again with Flaskamper's family, this time attempting to focus their conversation on less weighty matters. While it was clear to Flaskamper that his father was still not pleased with his choice of professions, the king was less harsh than he had once been; at least it seemed that way to him. As they all lingered over sweet white wine and redberry tarts, Ferriwhyl stood quietly and motioned for her younger son to follow her. She led him through the sitting room and up the stairs to the royal couple's private observation tower. Here, on the circular walkway above the treetops, they had a beautiful view of the clear, evening sky. The night air was chilly, but still more refreshing than unpleasant at this point in the season. Mother and son stood side by side, watching the stars twinkle brightly overhead. Flaskamper wasn't sure why she had brought him up here, but he knew that she would come round to it in her own time. At last, she turned and faced him, placing her hands upon his shoulders.

"You have grown even taller since you left," she said. "I can scarcely look you in the eye without straining my neck."

"Sorry," said Flaskamper with a grin. "I'll try to stop, but it may be out of my hands."

She smiled back and pinched his ear, her standard punishment for his cheeky sass. Then her expression sobered.

"Are you happy, darling?" she asked him. "Have you found what you were looking for?"

"Some of it, yes" Flaskamper replied honestly. "There's more for me to discover yet, but I don't regret the choices I've made so far."

"And what about Rokey?"

Flaskamper met her gaze and abruptly, tears began to spill down his cheeks. She pulled him closer and he cried on her shoulder for a moment.

"Does he know how you feel about him?" she asked.

He said nothing, just shook his head.

"Do you not think that it is something he might like to hear?"

Flaskamper picked his head up and wiped his eyes.

"I'm afraid," he told her. "If I tell him, and he doesn't feel the same way – "

"What do your instincts tell you?"

I know that he likes me, a lot even. But I just can't tell if he – if he…"

"If he loves you as much as you love him?" she asked. He nodded.

"I've never felt like this about anyone before," he told her. "I'm mortally afraid that he might not feel the same way. There have been a few times – I've come so close to telling him…but then I freeze up with fear, and the moment passes. It's killing me, mother…keeping things all light and breezy. I don't want to hide my feelings anymore, but I'm just so scared. I've always been – forgive me, I don't mean to sound conceited – but I've always been the one to break the hearts. Having things the other way round is…"

"Terrifying?" the queen asked. When he nodded, she smiled sweetly at him.

Has it ever occurred to you," she asked, "how much this fear may have cost you already?"

Flaskamper gave her a puzzled look.

"I don't understand," he said.

"Did you never consider that, perhaps, some of those hearts in the past were broken because of this fear," she asserted, "because you were too afraid to share yourself with another in any deep or meaningful way?"

Flaskamper lowered his head, pondering this idea. It made perfect sense, of course. It had been so much simpler to cut a lover loose and find another when things grew serious, rather than open himself up to any possible hurt. For the first time, he wondered at what he had missed, for better or worse, by always taking the easy way out.

"You're right mother," he said softly. "I had never considered it in that light before...but you're right. I've always been afraid, just as I am now. Only this time it's different. I can't imagine saying goodbye to Rokey, and yet, that just makes the fear so much greater."

"Falling in love is a danger," she told him, lifting his eyes to hers. "Sharing yourself – your true self – is a tremendous risk. But the greatest risks, my son, are those whose rewards are so precious. To be in love entails...the willingness to lay yourself open, to trust someone with that deepest part of you, that portion of your soul that no one else in the world is allowed to see. And that is a genuinely fearsome prospect for anyone, especially one who is contemplating it for the first time.

"You shall see," she continued, turning to stare out over the tower rail, "sooner or later will come a moment in time when the notion of letting your feelings be known will simply seem...right, and it will all come pouring out, like water past a broken dam. Then, depending on his response, you will be either terribly happy or else terribly hurt. As I said, it means taking a risk, but darling, what truly worthwhile thing in this life does not?"

She stood quietly for a moment, allowing her words to sink in, then reached into a small pocket in her pale green gown and pulled something out. After that, she turned to him and placed the object in his hand. Flaskamper looked down and studied it. It was some kind of glass or possibly crystal sphere, a beautiful smoky brown in color. In its center was a much smaller sphere, this one of deepest gold. Flaskamper had never seen anything like it before, and he knew instinctively that the object was magical.

"What is it?" he asked his mother.

"It is called an owl's eye," Ferriwhyl told him. "As you have no doubt guessed, it has magical properties. I want you to have it, to keep it with you for the rest of your journey. It will help to protect you from harm, and it has other uses. Now, listen to me carefully..."

*   *   *

They rejoined the rest of the gathering a short while later. To his delight, his father, Alrontin and his friends were all talking and laughing easily with one another. Flaskamper had the owl's eye in his pocket, which was both reassuring and a tad unnerving. For a magical being, he had little actual use for magic. He had never felt comfortable with it. Even casting simple spells like summoning the lumen orb made him uneasy. He wasn't sure exactly why. It had just always been that way. Nevertheless, he was glad for any and all help, given the forces they were up against.

When it was time for them to retire, the king and queen bade them all goodnight and Alrontin and the rest of the group went off to bed. Flaskamper lingered a moment with his parents.

"I just wanted to – to thank you both," he said. "For your help, and your support."

He turned to leave, but Angorath stopped him.

"Flaskamper," said the king. Somewhat anxiously, Flaskamper turned back to face him.

"Yes father," he said.

The king came and stood before him. Even though Flaskamper had grown taller these past five years, his father still towered above him. The king put a hand on his son's shoulder, a gesture that surprised Flaskamper.

"I will not pretend to be happy with your choice of vocations," Angorath told his son. "I find the idea that a prince of the realm of Elfwood should choose to live the life of a mercenary...abhorrent."

"Father –" Flaskamper began, but the king raised his other hand to silence him.

"Nevertheless," he continued, "I find, having given it further consideration, that I *am*, in fact, impressed by your choice of friends, as well as with the courage that you have shown in undertaking this quest. I shall continue to hope that you will one day come to your senses, and choose a more suitable profession. Meanwhile – meanwhile, you have...many qualities...of which a father can be proud."

Flaskamper gazed up at his father with unconcealed astonishment. The king's austere expression had not changed, but his words, and the hand on his shoulder –

"Thank you, father," he said, his voice hoarse with emotion, "and goodnight. Goodnight mother," he added, and quickly turned and hurried for the door. He had to get out of that room before he started to bawl like an infant.

When Flaskamper had left the room, Angorath reached for his wife's hand.

"Well," he asked, without looking at her, "have I repaired the damage?"

"You have done your best, *chatka*," the queen said quietly, resting her head affectionately against her husband's arm, "Perhaps it was enough, but if not...it was most certainly a marvelous beginning."

Chapter 15:

Waterville

T he next morning, the company started off toward the east again. Alrontin and his personal squad went along to escort them as far as the edge of the forest. Today Flaskamper's brother was dressed in his regular green uniform tunic and leggings which, with the exception of the insignia of rank on his right shoulder, matched those worn by the rest of the Elfwood guard.

Contrary to his expectations, Flaskamper was not eager to leave. Though he had stoically bid his parents farewell, promising to return for another visit as soon as their quest was over, inside he felt torn. He was leaving his home in crisis, and that did not sit well with him. Had he not felt that their own mission was equally vital, and in some way related, he probably could not have brought himself to leave, despite his feelings for Rokey. The past three days had fundamentally changed his outlook about his home and his family, especially his father. Unlike his previous departure five years before, this time he was certain that their love and support went with him. With that knowledge, however, came an additional sense of responsibility. He welcomed these changes, but it made life even more complicated.

It was colder today, and gloomy, with the sharp scent of rain permeating the air. The party's movement through the forest was cautious, but steady, and they made good progress throughout the day. That night, they camped overnight in a clearing. It was too small for the entire party, but that didn't matter, as the guards slept in the trees, on hammocks woven out of the elves' slender, sturdy rope. As they all prepared to retire for the night, the rain came, a hard, soaking deluge. Though the companions felt sorry for their elf escorts, they were privately relieved not to have to stand watch that night.

The torrent stopped just after sunrise, and by mid-afternoon the troop had reached the eastern edge of Elfwood Forest. There had been no trouble the entire way. Flaskamper again felt pangs of guilt at having to leave his brother in a time of turmoil, but Alrontin assured him that he was doing the right thing.

"If this turns out to be as big a thing as we believe," he told Flaskamper, "your actions will impact all of Firma, Elfwood included. So it is vital that you go. Just remember what father said, all of our resources are behind you. And I'm glad you and he had a nice visit...Soaker," he added, shooting his brother a broad grin. Flaskamper punched his arm.

They embraced, and Alrontin bade farewell to his brother and his companions. Then he and his squad vanished back into the forest the way they had come, and the company moved on towards Grand Lake, and the town of Waterville. Stamford estimated that they should arrive somewhere around nightfall, so there should be no need to camp again outside in the open. This came as a great relief to Rokey. The fact that there had been no trouble during their journey through the forest did little to reassure him. It seemed that whatever force was after him had always known exactly when the best times to strike would be. Clearly, to attack them in the Elfwood territories would have been a waste of time and effort. Now they were exposed again, with nothing but their swords and their wits to protect them. Fortunately, his companions were highly skilled with both these weapons.

Beyond the forest was a stretch of rocky scrubland, covered with short, stubbly grass and dotted with a few small clumps of trees. Though the rain had ceased some marks ago, the ground was still wet and soggy, slowing their progress and dampening their mood. The air was frigid again that day, and a sharp wind cut across the landscape, chilling them straight through their wool cloaks. Already the comforts of Elfwood seemed far behind, and unknown perils loomed before them.

Their journey however, though unpleasant, was also thankfully uneventful. Apart from a few deathbirds circling high above, they encountered nothing and no one. They were so eager to reach their destination that they did not even stop to eat lunch. They simply divided a small loaf of bread among them and sullenly chewed on it as they walked.

The sun had nearly set when they entered the town of Waterville. It seemed a pleasant enough place, despite its slightly battered and washed-out look, which Flaskamper explained was typical of settlements located close to the water. There were no walls or towers surrounding the town. If the inhabitants had ever had any concerns about being invaded, there was no evidence of it now. They found Waterville's only inn, a large, rambling place called Haven's Light, with little difficulty. It was located at the end of the wide main street, and directly overlooked the lake. Before going in, they took advantage of the few remaining moments of daylight to stand on the deck and look out over the water. Rokey was awed by the beauty of it. Grand Lake was a massive freshwater body, surrounded by verdant evergreen woods. Down a short incline, over a sandy shore, a large, multi-sectioned wooden pier shot out thirty yards or more. A variety of boats were moored there, most of them fishing boats of various sizes, but there were also a few pleasure craft, and some others that looked like they were designed for transporting passengers. Rokey wondered what it would be like traversing a lake this size. He had never been in a boat before, but had heard that the experience could make one very ill. He would be sure to ask whether there was some way of combating this before they set out. He didn't relish the thought of spending the bulk of his first boat trip retching over its side.

There were few visitors to Waterville at that time of year, so they had no trouble securing three rooms together. They dropped their things off, and then went downstairs for supper. Rokey declined to join them, deciding instead to have a small cold supper in the room, curled up by the fire. Flaskamper expressed some concern about his health, but Rokey assured him that he felt fine, only tired. While the four of them ate, Stamford called to the innkeeper, a tall, lanky fellow named Heelbor, and asked him about the price for chartering a boat.

"Depends on whether you want it for a lake tour, or fishin', or transport," the innkeeper said in a heavy eastern accent.

"Transport," Stamford answered.

"Well, there's reg'lar ferries what go to the surroundin' towns. They'll be runnin' reg'lar for a few more weeks yet."

"What if we want to go further, say to... Farport?" asked Fia, keeping her voice low.

The innkeeper's expression soured.

"Not many people goin' there these days," said Heelbor, and eyed them warily, "least ways not those what aren't lookin' for trouble."

Fia laughed.

"Well, we're not looking for trouble," she assured him, "but we do have important business there, and would appreciate whatever assistance you could give us."

She offered him her best, most charming smile, but the innkeeper was having none of it. He did not return the smile. Nevertheless, he did reluctantly provide them with the name of a man who would most likely be willing to make the long trip.

"For the right price, 'a course," he said. "You'll find 'im on the docks tomorrow mornin'."

When supper was over, Flaskamper ordered two goblets of mulled wine, then paid the innkeeper for the meal. Heelbor looked at the gold sovereign suspiciously, and Flaskamper half expected that he would sink his teeth into it to make sure it wasn't counterfeit. But he only dropped it into his moneybox and fished out the change. Flaskamper thought the man might call a magistrate on them if he dared overtip him, so he carefully counted out the standard gratuity, said goodnight to the others, who were still finishing their drinks, and made for the room with the two goblets of wine.

He opened the door to find Rokey sitting on their blankets in front of the fire. He paused for a moment to watch him. The fire made his lush, black hair turn almost midnight blue, and gave his face a deep golden hue. He had washed up and dressed in fresh clothing, and was staring into the flames humming a little tune, which the elf thought sounded strangely familiar. Flaskamper walked over and sat down beside him.

"Thought you might like some mulled wine," he said, handing Rokey one of the goblets, "to help you get a good night's sleep."

"Thanks. I'm not sure I'll ever get a good night's sleep again," Rokey said. " I've been spoiled by your mother's wonderful beds. But I'll give it a try. What shall we drink to?"

"To our hearts' desires," Flaskamper answered without thinking.

Rokey smiled.

"Alright, to our hearts' desires," he said, and they tapped the goblets together.

For a few moments they sat together in companionable silence, sipping their wine and watching the fire.

"That song you were humming," Flaskamper said finally, "where did you learn it?"

"It's something I remember from when I was a child," Rokey replied. "Just that little part of it. It just floats through my head sometimes. Why?"

"It's strange. I'm sure I know it. And I seem to remember it being something unusual. Damned if I can remember what it is now though."

"You mean it's Elvish?" Rokey asked.

"I don't think so," said the elf. "I'm sure the harder I try to remember, the less successful I'll be. That's always the way of it."

Somewhere in the back of Rokey's mind a little light came on. He closed his eyes for a moment, concentrating.

"How – ,"

"Shh," Rokey held up a hand. "I'm remembering something"

Flaskamper sat quietly as Rokey turned something over in his mind, trying to grasp at thin strands of memory.

"A dance," Rokey said at last. "I seem to remember a dance. In a clearing. A circle of dancing figures. And I'm in someone's....I'm in my, my mother's arms. Flash, I've never had this memory before!" He frowned. "But what in the world could it mean?"

The elf shook his head.

"I don't know," he said. "When I think of where I've heard the blasted tune before, maybe we can make some sense of it. Keep in mind though, distant memories are tricky things. This new bit that just came to you, it could mean nothing at all."

"Killjoy," said Rokey, pouting.

"I'm not saying that's the case. I just don't want you to build your hopes needlessly."

"And I appreciate that...I guess."

They let the subject drop, and turned back to the fire.

"So, what's yours?" Rokey asked, after a while.

"What's my what? Flaskamper asked.

"Your heart's desire. We toasted to our hearts' desires. I was just wondering, you know, what yours was."

Flaskamper's throat was suddenly very dry. He took a large gulp of the wine.

Well, Mother, Flaskamper thought to himself, *you said the moment would come. I suppose it might as well be now.*

"I'm sorry," Rokey began. "If that's too personal –"

"No –" Flaskamper squeaked, then cleared his throat and took another slug of fortification. "No, not at all."

He paused again for a moment.

"Rokey, you see, there's been...well, there have been...a lot of people in my life, men I mean. Some of them for a week or, on rare occasions, a little bit longer, but mostly for just a night. I liked all of them, even imagined that I loved one or two –"

"Flash, you don't have to – "

Flaskamper held up his hand to stop him, but noticed that it was shaking, and quickly tucked it under his leg.

"But I was wrong," he continued after a moment. "Truth is, I've never been in love before. I knew that – ," he took a deep breath and looked deep into Rokey's brown eyes. "I knew it as soon as I first saw you."

Inside, his heart was racing in terror, but he swallowed hard and forged on.

"From the minmark I laid eyes on you, I knew that I felt something different for you – different than anything I'd ever felt before. And as these days have passed, any lingering doubts I may have had have tumbled away. I tried – tried to fight it, but I can't." Tears were welling up in his eyes, but he ignored them. "You're my heart's desire, Rokey. I'm totally and completely in love, and if you don't love me back ... I don't know but – but I just can't keep it inside anymore. I – ,"

His voice broke, but then Rokey's arms were around him, comforting him.

"It's alright Flash," Rokey whispered soothingly. "I do. I do love you. I do."

Flaskamper trembled as he lay in Rokey's arms, letting the words sink in. Then his lips found Rokey's. They kissed, softly and tenderly at first – but then the energy began to rise, building steadily, until a nearly furious passion gripped them. The elf's trembling hands slid under Rokey's shirt. The boy's skin was so warm and smooth beneath his fingertips... and so soft. Then he grabbed the shirt, resisting the urge just to tear the fabric apart, and Rokey leaned forward so it would slip off. Then he took Flaskamper's off as well, and they held each other for a while, savoring the feel of one another's bare flesh.

Flaskamper began kissing his neck, and Rokey felt himself being guided backwards, lowered down to the blankets on the floor. Flash lay down on top of him, and as the elf's long fingers began to unbuckle his breeches, Rokey was gripped by a sudden surge of panic.

"Flash," he cried, his body tensing, "I'm afraid."

Flash stopped abruptly and pulled back.

"Alright," he said breathlessly. "It's alright. I'm sorry. I didn't mean to push you so fast. I got – I got carried away. We can stop –"

"No!" Rokey said. "No, I don't want to stop. That's not what I meant. What I'm afraid of is, well – I'm just afraid that I'll disappoint you."

They were silent for a moment, then Flaskamper threw his head back and laughed.

"Why are you laughing at me?" asked Rokey, his eyes widening in hurt surprise.

"Oh, Rokey," Flaskamper said gently. "I'm sorry, honey. I'm not laughing at you, just at the idea that you could possibly disappoint me."

"Well – well, I'm just worried because – you're the first, and...."

"I know, and because of that, it's *I* who should be worried about disappointing *you*. It's *my* job to make *your* first time special." Flash ran his fingers through Rokey's thick, dark hair. "But, *chatka*, there's never in my life been a job that I was so eager to do."

"*Chatka* is an elvish word," he explained, in response to Rokey's quizzical look. "Literally, it means *treasure*, but it's also used to mean the one you love."

He smiled down at Rokey.

"If you trust me," said the elf, "and love me as much as I love you, then neither of us is going to be disappointed. I promise."

"I do trust you," Rokey said, "and I love you so much it hurts."

Flaskamper lay down again on top of him and resumed kissing his neck. A moment later, Rokey gasped as he felt the elf's slender hand slip down into his breeches.

"Hurts, huh?" Flaskamper whispered playfully, "In that case, let me kiss it and make it better."

*   *   *

The fire had burned low. Flaskamper sat on the floor, his eyes fixed adoringly on Rokey. The light of the moon shone through the window, casting a pale blue glow over the boy's naked body as he slept. Flaskamper ran a hand lightly over Rokey's back, causing him to moan and shift slightly.

The elf could never remember a time in his life when he had been so contented. In a way, lovemaking had been just as new to him as it had to Rokey, and he realized now what he had been missing in his many previous sexual encounters. All those other experiences, once the fun was over, had left him feeling empty inside. With Rokey, it was just the opposite; he felt whole, and fulfilled, and quite honestly amazed at his good fortune. He simply couldn't fathom how something so wonderful could happen to him. It was this bemusement that caused a few fine threads of worry to run through his otherwise blissful mood. He had gained so much; yet it meant that he now had so much to lose.

He stood and went to the window. The moon was full and bright, nested in an abundance of twinkling stars. It reminded Flaskamper of a little prayer to Secta, the moon goddess, that he had learned as a child. Though he was not generally a religious elf, he decided that it couldn't hurt. He closed his eyes and murmured it quietly –

"Heavenly Goddess,
Guard us tonight.
Keep us til morning
Cradled in your light."

Having thus hedged his bet, he went and lay back down beside Rokey. The sleeping boy rolled over and put his arm around him. Flash sighed with satisfaction and closed his eyes.

"It's going to be alright," he assured himself. "Whatever else happens to us – in the end, we're going to be alright."

Chapter 16:

The Grand Lady

T hey were all in high spirits the next morning. Before Rokey came down to Breakfast, Stamford teased Flaskamper about the sounds he had overheard the previous night. Flaskamper turned bright red.

"You keep your trap shut about that," said Flaskamper. "I'm not going to let you embarrass him."

"*Him?*" Stamford asked, returning to the table where the breakfast food had been laid out. "Look at you! I've never seen you color so over a bit of boisterous sex."

"Stamford," Flaskamper said, smiling in spite of himself, "I swear I'm going to..."

"The lad is really quite talkative isn't he?" Stamford pressed on. "I mean, once you've – ah – *penetrated* that shyness of his."

A biscuit flew toward his head. Stamford ducked.

"Stamford, I'm warning you," said the elf, "you'd better not –"

"Better not what?" asked Rokey, who had just rounded the corner.

"Nothing," Stamford replied, chuckling. "Your friend here is just giving me a hard time today for reasons that, frankly, I am at a loss to explain."

Flaskamper rolled his eyes, then quietly resumed his breakfast. Rokey shook his head in bewilderment, and leaned down to give Flaskamper a kiss before visiting the food table. Stamford gave Flaskamper a knowing wink, and the elf shot him a final warning glare.

When they had finished eating, the company went down to the pier in search of the man the innkeeper had recommended to them. As the docks were not busy this time of year, they had little trouble finding him. The lad they stopped for directions pointed them towards the last mooring on the left hand side of the pier, to a mid-sized vessel called *The Grand Lady*. Even to Rokey's untrained eyes, he thought the ship had seen better days. Still, it was afloat, a good early sign.

Captain Baltimel was a stocky man in his late thirties, with his long, dark-blonde hair tied back tightly behind his head. He wore a dark blue, wool knit cap with a matching diamond knit sweater, and heavy grey wool breeches that were tucked into a pair of sturdy leather boots. His handsome face was as weathered as his torn leather jacket, but Rokey was relieved to see that the man had a ready smile and an easy manner about him. When they told him their destination, however, his smile faltered somewhat.

"Rough place, Farport," he said with that same heavy eastern drawl. "Dangerous, 'specially for visitors."

"Yes, we were warned already," Stamford told him. "Nevertheless we have business there. We were told you were the man to talk to."

"Oh yah, I got the ship to get you there. Provided 'a course, that the price is right."

They haggled for a while, finally settling on a figure that was little less than what Baltimel had originally asked for. Sensing their strong need, he wasn't about to give much ground, especially given their destination.

"I'll need a mark or two to get things ready for the trip," he told them. "My ship can make it in just about three days, sooner if the wind's with us."

Rokey asked the captain about seasickness, and whether there was a remedy for it.

"Yah, there's a remedy," he said. "They sell it in the tradin' post. You can head over there while I get ready. Careena will fix you up. You all should get yourselves some raincloaks as well. Otherwise you're likely to spend the next few days soaked to the skin."

They departed from the pier to run the recommended errands. Lorq stayed behind on the sandy beach. He needed to collect some more insects for his frog, Pico. The rest of them found the trading post, which was right in the middle of Waterville's single main street. Careena was a bubbly, oversized woman with sparkling blue eyes and hair the color of corn silk. They relayed their needs to her and she bustled off to fill the order, after taking note of their sizes. She was a bit doubtful as to whether she would be able to find something to fit Lorq, but promised to do her best. She returned a short time later with the supplies. There were seasickness tablets which, she told them, were made by the local healer from plants that grew on the lakeshore. When asked if they really worked, she said with some pride that she had been selling them for years, and that locals as well as visitors swore by them. She also had several wax-treated light wool raincloaks, along with a rope and a large tent cloth, which had been similarly waterproofed.

"This is the best I could do for your giant friend", she said, indicating the tent cloth. "Truth be told, it's the same material as the cloaks. Only difference besides the size is the fact that the rope hasn't been sewn in to form the hood. If you have a mark, I'd be happy to do that for you for a small extra charge."

In fact, they did have the time, so Careena headed off to the rear of the store to construct the oversized cloak. While they waited, the four of them rejoined Lorq for a walk along the beach. It was a beautiful day, and the fresh air off the water was cool and invigorating. When a mark had passed, Flaskamper and Fia returned for the merchandise.

"I think I'd like to meet the owner of this garment," Careena told them, and her corpulent frame shook with mirth. "He looks like a man after me own heart."

When the items were all paid for, the two of them met the others on the boat. The cloak fit perfectly, which surprised the giant.

"I was sure at least half of me would spend the trip wet," he said.

"Now Lorq," Fia teased, "would we let that happen to you?"

Lorq smiled and shook his head.

In their absence, Captain Baltimel had assembled his crew – a dozen heavily armed men. In addition, Stamford noticed several boxes containing bows, arrows, axes, swords, shields and other assorted instruments of violence.

"Are we expecting a war?" he asked, arching his eyebrows.

"On the eastern side of the lake, you never know what you're goin' to run into," he replied. "Besides, there's been known to be a pirate ship or two off the Farport shores. If they see you're heavily armed, they tend to leave you be. That's why we always take this little beauty along."

He pulled the canvas cover off the large object beside him, revealing a huge mounted crossbow. The open box beside it contained a variety of different bolts, from simple sharpened points to complicated grappling hooks attached to long lengths of elf rope. Both Stamford and Flaskamper oohed and ahhed with appreciation as Baltimel covered it again and went off to see to the rest of the provisions.

It was late morning when they set sail. The weather was fine and the winds favorable. Rokey dutifully swallowed his seasickness tablets as directed and, just as promised, he had no problems with the rolling ship. Flaskamper was not so fortunate. He had refused Rokey's earlier offer to share his pills. Now, several marks into the voyage, he was deeply regretting his decision. His normal pale yellow color was now decidedly greener, and he had spent most of the past mark with his head hung over the side. Unable to stand the pitiful sight any longer, Rokey approached the captain again to ask if there was some other way to cure the seasickness.

"Don't you have any more a Careena's tablets?" he asked, raising his voice to be heard over the pounding waves.

Rokey explained that Flaskamper was already too sick to keep anything down.

"That's alright," Baltimel shouted, "they work just as well in the other end!"

"You mean..."

"Yah. Just shove em – "

Rokey turned crimson when the captain finished his sentence, but nevertheless went to collect Flaskamper and administer the suggested remedy. After their previous night together, it wasn't nearly as embarrassing as discussing it with the captain had been. In another mark, the elf was back to his old self and thoroughly enjoying their journey, though he made Rokey swear never to tell Stamford how they had gotten the pills into him. Rokey raised his hand and solemnly swore, and Flaskamper wrapped his arms around him.

"Have I told you today how much I adore you?" said Flash.

"Yes, but I'm willing to hear it again," Rokey replied.

Flash kissed him, and was just going to suggest that they go below for more when Lorq called to them from the other side.

"Come and see the lake otters!" he yelled.

Flaskamper groaned.

"That wasn't what I had in mind," he said with a mischievous grin.

"I know what you had in mind," Rokey replied. "There'll be plenty of time for *that* later. Let's go and see the otters with Lorq."

Rokey and Flaskamper spent the rest of the day enjoying the scenery, then most of the night enjoying each other. They woke late the next morning to find the captain giving Fia a sailing lesson. Lorq was also there, watching with rapt attention. Stamford, who they found standing a short ways off, seemed out of sorts.

"If I didn't know you better," said Flaskamper, shaking his head, "I'd swear you were jealous."

"Don't be a fool," Stamford growled. "I am merely vexed that such scenes are all built upon a lie. Were Fia not wearing that pendant, the captain would not be within ten feet of her, and she knows it. Now she appears quite happy to stand there, basking in his shallow fawning. Later she will think back on the falseness of it, and be all the more miserable for having encouraged it."

"Maybe," Flaskamper responded, "but maybe not. Perhaps she no longer sees the pendant as just a lie."

"Then she deludes herself," said the dark man.

"A little maybe. But really, how different is the pendant than lip rouge, or powder, or wigs, or any of the other things people wear to enhance their natural beauty?"

"It *is* different," Stamford insisted. "As you said, they enhance natural beauty. They do not produce it out of thin air. Fia's beauty is a lie in its entirety."

Flaskamper found that he had no response to this.

"What do you think about it, Rokey?" the elf asked.

Rokey thought about it for a few moments.

"Well, this may sound silly," he began, "but I think the lie is in the way she looks *without* the pendant on."

His companions both looked at him quizzically.

"I mean, think about it," he continued, "Fia is such a beautiful person inside. Yet this horrible thing happened, and she was left looking like a *Dragon Lady*. But that isn't who Fia is at all. *That's* the lie. To me all the pendant does is put things as they should be. It brings to the outside what we all know is already on the inside."

Flaskamper slipped an arm around Rokey's waist and drew him close.

"All this and a brain too," the elf announced proudly.

Stamford wrinkled his nose in disgust.

"If you continue to behave this way," he told Flaskamper, "I shall have no choice but to chuck you overboard."

"Interesting point of view," the dark man said to Rokey. "And now, if you two rabbits will excuse me, I have some further contemplating to do."

Stamford strode away, leaving the two entwined boys on the foredeck. Rokey shook his head as he watched him go.

"I never know how to take anything he says," Rokey remarked.

"Shite, you're not the only one," said Flaskamper.

"How do you know whether or not he likes you?"

"Well, if he refrains from killing you," the elf replied, "then you're probably on his good side."

"That's comforting," said Rokey.

"Look don't worry," said Flaskamper. "If he hasn't killed *me* yet, *you've* got nothing to worry about. Gods above, I remember one time in Riversedge..."

Rokey tried to listen to the story, but he soon became distracted by something in the sky. Several somethings, in fact, circling high up the clouds. He watched as three became four, then five, then six... They were still too high up to make out in any detail. He wondered if they were water fowl of some –"

"Hey, am I talking to myself here?" Flaskamper said, putting his hand on his hip.

"Flash," Rokey said, pointing to the sky, "what do you think those are?"

Flaskamper looked up at the spot Rokey was indicating. There were now eight of the flying specks up there. The elf's thin brows furrowed.

"I don't know," he said, "but it wouldn't hurt to ask the captain. No point in taking any chances. Wait here."

By the time he had reached the end of the ship, the specks – a dozen now – had begun to grow steadily larger, though not yet large enough even for Flaskamper's keen eyes to make out. The captain was initially dismissive when they pointed them out to him, but as the creatures spiraled steadily lower, he too grew concerned.

"They're not behaving like any water birds I've seen," he said, and pulled what looked like a long cylinder from his pocket. He pulled at both ends, and the tube extended, until it looked something like a fat magic wand.

"What is that thing?" the elf asked him.

"It's a spyglass," Baltimel replied. "It makes things far away look closer up."

He aimed the larger end of the spyglass at the sky and peered through the smaller end.

"Great Gods! To your battle posts everyone!" he yelled. "Arms up, now!"

"What is it?" Flaskamper asked.

"Look for yourself!" he thrust the instrument into Flaskamper's hand and ran to open the weapons boxes. Flaskamper held up the spyglass and peered through. Immediately the hairs on the back of his neck stood up, and he broke out into a cold sweat. He snapped the tube shut just as Stamford joined him.

"What in blazes is going on here?" the dark man demanded.

Flaskamper pointed to the sky. He looked up again and saw that the spy tool was no longer necessary. He could now make out the distinct shape of the creatures descending on them . The long, snake-like hair, the tattered wings and scaly legs that ended in razor sharp talons –

"Harpies!" he heard Fia exclaim. Now they were close enough for ordinary human eyes to make out: a dozen of the vile bird-women, coming in very fast. Flaskamper needed his bow, but was armed only with his sword. He nearly dove toward the weapons box to retrieve a bow and some arrows. It was cheap, low-quality equipment, but he didn't have time to go below and get his own. Shite! Why hadn't he anticipated an attack from the air? He should have been armed for any situation. He sited one of the creatures and followed it. It was still out of range, but they had gotten close enough now to start launching–

thump!   thump!   thump!

their droppings, small wet clumps of them began to strike the deck, hissing where they landed. One of the men screamed as a wad of the corrosive waste landed on his arm and began to burn through the flesh. The man stumbled to a bucket of mop water and began furiously scrubbing it off. Now the crew was panicking, wildly dodging the caustic bombs instead of readying their weapons. Flaskamper hauled back on his bow and let fly, three times in rapid succession. The harpy he had aimed for successfully dodged the first arrow, but Flash had anticipated its direction, and the other two penetrated its chest and belly. It gave a hideous shriek as it fell to its death in the water. This impelled the others to take up the cry, and soon the air was filled with their foul squawks and screams.

Flaskamper observed with dismay that all the others had drawn their swords, even those with bows and arrows. There was no time to point out their mistake to them. Had they readied the proper arms, they might have felled most of them before their talons could do any harm. Now he would be lucky to sink another two before they reached the men. He let fly another rapid triad of arrows. His target took one of the shafts directly in the eye, and was dead before it reached the water. They were close now; he had one more chance... three more arrows zinged through the air. The wind sent two of them wide, and the third only struck his target in the leg. Fortunately, it threw its balance off, and the creature tumbled screeching into the water. Flash ran to the edge to try and finish it, but it had already sunk below the waves. Apparently harpies could not swim. Tough luck for them.

Another group of four was coming in low now, swooping in a fast U shape, then abruptly dropping like dead weight on their targets. Men screamed as talons sank deep into their chests, arms and necks. Those not completely frozen in terror were blocking with their swords, but the heavy scales covering the creatures' legs made them difficult to fight in this manner. Spiked weapons, like arrows and spears, were more effective.

Flaskamper loosed another arrow that buried itself in the neck of a fourth creature, sadly too late to save the man already impaled on its talons. Abruptly, one of the harpies flew in behind the elf, knocking him off his feet. He rocked aside quickly to avoid being skewered by the extended talons, but the thing caught his bicep with the sharp claws on its fingers. He quickly drew his sword and flipped onto his back, rolling away from the darting talons and thrusting his sword straight up, aiming for the weaker spots in the creases of its groin. This was the closest that Flaskamper had ever been to a harpy. It looked vaguely female from the waist up, but only in the way of some grotesque caricature. Its long hair was actually a collection of writhing, snake-like appendages. Its coal-black eyes, burning with hate, were bulging and bloodshot, and its bare breasts were leathery and misshapen. For several moments they were at a stalemate, and he feared that he would be the one to tire first. Then a huge metal club swung into view, and came crashing down, splitting the harpy's head open. Flaskamper dodged once more to keep from being pinned under the dead creature, then giant hands helped him to his feet. Flash gave Lorq a smack of thanks on the arm, then turned to assess where everyone was. Lorq was beside him, watching the midship below. Stamford and Fia were down there along with most of the men and four more harpies, Rokey...where was Rokey? He froze in fear for a moment, but then spotted him through a gap between the two front sails. He was still on the foredeck. Baltimel was with him. The captain had also thought to grab a spear and had just thrust it through one of the creatures there, bringing them both tumbling to the deck. It looked to Flash as though his side was actually winning the fight, but – but something was not right. He had counted a dozen harpies. He had shot and killed or wounded three initially, then four had swooped in, then four more. Between the dead and those that still stood, there were only eleven.

Then he felt the shadow pass over his head.

Flaskamper watched in slow motion as the twelfth harpy swept in over him. It could easily have surprised either him or Lorq, taking one of their heads clean off, but they were not its target. Its target was –

"ROKEY!!!" he screamed. "ROKEY, LOOK OUT!!!"

Rokey had been watching Baltimel dispatch his foe, but looked up just in time to see the huge screeching bird-woman drop out of the sky toward him. It did not land though, as all the others did. That would have put it within the range of the captain's spear, or the elf's arrows. Instead, it sunk its talons into Rokey's shoulders and swung aloft again. It was a heavy burden, heavier prey than a harpy would normally attempt to carry. However, this had been no ordinary hunting party. There had been only one target of this raid. The rest had merely been a distraction.

Using every ounce of speed he could muster, Flaskamper sprinted toward the bow of the ship, struggling the entire way to quell his blinding panic and think. The harpy was struggling with its quarry, finding it difficult – thank the gods – to gain altitude. He couldn't just shoot it dead. He might either hit Rokey, or else the thing might drag him to the bottom before anyone could rescue him. He needed to catch it somehow, to cast a line – Yes! That's it! – He knew what he had to try, but he was only going to get one shot at it.

He slipped in the blood that covered the steps leading to the foredeck, cracking his elbow hard on the wooden rail. Fiery pain and tingling shot up his arm. He jumped up quickly, cursing himself, and hoping that his clumsiness would not throw his aim off too badly. The harpy was already a good thirty feet away. One chance. He would only have one chance.

On the foredeck, he threw the canvas cover off of the huge crossbow, quickly swung open the box of assorted bolts and rummaged around for the one he wanted. Tiks seemed like marks, but at last he located the bolt with the small metal grappling star on one end, and the rope attached to the other. He grabbed it and set it into place, then pulled back and locked the bow mechanism. Now he would have to aim carefully. It wasn't enough to hit the target. He had to hit it just right. Sweat stung his eyes. He swiped at them fiercely, then cautiously lined up his shot.

"If you're there, Secta," he whispered to the moon goddess, "I could certainly use your help right now."

Then he held his breath, and pulled the lever.

The kick from the recoiling weapon knocked him backwards. He leapt back to his feet just in time to see the thin, silver-barbed star punch through the upper part of the creature's left wing. There it lodged fast, as a hook would lodge in the mouth of a fish. The harpy screamed and thrashed wildly, trying to both remain in the air and hold tight to its precious cargo. It was a vain attempt, however. Still clutching Rokey in its talons, the beast plunged into the water, dragging the rope behind it.

Flaskamper, seeing that the coil of attached rope was rapidly vanishing, quickly grabbed the end and tied it fast to the crossbow base. Tiks later, he had shed his weapons and clothes and plunged into the icy water. The shock was like scores of knives piercing his skin, and his head immediately began to pound. It took him a few moments to orient himself, and a few more still to find the rope. He then took a deep breath, and dove under the water, following the rope. Down and down it went, until it seemed to Flaskamper that he would never reach the end of it. Then at last his hands came upon feathers in the darkness. It was only then that he realized that he had brought no weapon with him. If the harpy was not yet dead – but no, the creature was not moving. Clearly it was either dead or nearly so. As for Rokey...he felt along down the harpy's legs, praying that the creature hadn't let go. He got to the end or one leg and found – nothing.

Flaskamper was near panic. He searched frantically for the creature's other leg. To his immense relief, he found Rokey on the other end, held only by a single talon. He grabbed the unconscious boy around the chest, wrested him free from the claw and began to kick furiously toward the surface. Now his chest was starting to burn and his mind was reeling from the lack of air. The urge to inhale was becoming overwhelming. In addition to that, his legs were tiring. If he had let go of Rokey, he could have easily reached the surface, but the thought never entered his mind. Finally, at the last possible tik, he broke the surface, gasping and coughing, then struggled to quickly get Rokey's head above water as well.

By now the others had finished off the rest of the attackers and those who were able had gathered along the front rail of the ship. By the time the two boys bobbed to the surface, Stamford and Lorq had both shed their clothes and were ready to go. They leapt into the freezing water, each holding the end of a coil of rope. They swam over to Rokey and Flaskamper and tied one of the ropes around each of them, then signaled for the others to pull them up. The man and the giant then swam around to the ladder on the opposite side of the ship and clamored aboard. Shivering, they immediately donned their woolen cloaks to warm up while they hurried to check on Rokey and Flash.

Flaskamper, now wrapped in a blanket, was also shivering, and choking on the water he had swallowed. Rokey, however, was ominously quiet. Captain Baltimel began breathing into him, and pumping his chest. For five minmarks... nothing... then ten. The captain shook his head. Even Flaskamper was beginning to think the worst... but then he remembered his mother's gift. It was in his breeches. He lunged forward, grabbed his breeches and dug into his pocket for the owl's eye. Then, with the precious object clutched in his hand, he crawled over to Rokey.

Please oh please oh please let this thing work.

He told everyone to give them some room. A space was cleared around them. Flaskamper held the owl's eye pressed to Rokey's forehead and closed his eyes, remembering what his mother had said when she gave it to him. One didn't work its magic by casting a spell, but by offering a gift. He concentrated on the one thing that he could now give which would benefit Rokey. He felt a warm surge travel through his hand and into Rokey's lifeless form. The small gold orb inside the larger glass sphere glowed brightly for only a few tiks, before going dark again. Flaskamper slumped backwards onto the deck next to Rokey, and their three friends began to worry that something had gone terribly wrong. Then abruptly, Rokey's chest heaved, and a flood of water gushed from his nose and mouth. They quickly rolled him over so that all the water could escape. When his lungs had cleared, he sat up to look around and saw Flaskamper lying next to him. Rokey's heart leapt to his throat.

"Is he – ?" He glanced frantically at his companions, who had no answer to give him.

"Flash!" he cried hoarsely. "Flash, wake up!"

Rokey grabbed the elf and shook him. His lips looked so pale, and blue.

"Flash, dammit, you have to wake up now!" He felt hot tears stinging his frigidly cold face.

The elf's eyelids fluttered open. Rokey collapsed onto him, weeping with joy and exhaustion. Flaskamper brought his arms up weakly, trying to put them around Rokey, but then fatigue took them, and they both passed into unconsciousness.

Lorq picked the couple up together and carried them gingerly to their cabin below. Pulling his clothes on again, Stamford looked at Fia and shook his head.

Our boy there is quite the hero," he marveled. "It must be something to love somebody that much."

Fia suddenly turned her head away; Stamford never saw the tears that filled her eyes.

"Yes", she said, when she could trust her voice again, "Yes... it certainly must."

Chapter 17:

The Farther Shore

Flaskamper sat in the ship's hold with Lorq, drinking some hot beef broth. Being in the hold was not a punishment. It was the only place below decks that was roomy enough for the giant to sleep in. Though Rokey was fast asleep in the cabin they shared, Flaskamper, though he still felt horrible, was unable to rest. He had gone in search of another wakeful companion and found that Lorq, too, was restless that night. So Flaskamper went to the galley, heated some meat broth for himself and swiped a loaf of bread to share with Lorq.

The battle with the harpies had left four of Captain Baltimel's crew dead, and one other not expected to live through the night. Fortunately, the ship could be sailed with as few as four crewmen, so they would be able to make it home without having to recruit anyone new. However, the captain's manner had grown grave now, and he was eager to reach their destination and be rid of his passengers. The rest of the crew had been all for throwing the five of them overboard and turning back immediately, but the captain, aside from being a compassionate man, was also a practical one. He convinced what was left of the crew that it was unlikely they could manage such a task, as their passengers were all highly skilled fighters. Best to get to where they were headed and be done with them that way. They reluctantly agreed, but only because it was not scheduled to be a round trip.

Flaskamper noticed that Lorq was eyeing him nervously as he drank his broth. The giant clearly had something on his mind.

"Lorq," the elf said finally, "what is it? Something's rattling around in that big head of yours. Why don't you spill it?"

"I was just wondering ... " Lorq's voice trailed off.

"Alright, that's a start," Flaskamper joked. "Now what is it that you were just wondering?"

"Well," replied the giant, "you said that the owl's eye was like a gift-giving charm."

"Yes," Flash explained. "It allows you to give something you have to someone else who lacks it. It even lets you, to a certain extent, swap circumstances with another, just so long as the eye is touching both individuals when it is invoked."

"And you gave Rokey..."

"Some of my life force. He needed a jolt to get going again, that's all. No harm done to me. I've got life force by the bushel."

He smiled at Lorq. For once, the giant did not smile back, but continued to look somber.

"But you didn't know that," he said, "did you?"

"Know what?" Flaskamper asked, puzzled.

"You didn't know that all Rokey needed was a *jolt*. You thought he was dead, didn't you, just like the rest of us did?"

"Where are we going with this, Lorq?" Flash said uneasily.

"You thought that Rokey was dead," the giant persisted, "and you thought that you were swapping with him. You thought that you were giving him your whole life, not just a little piece of it. You were going to leave us...just like that."

Flaskamper put his hand on Lorq's. It looked like the hand of an infant compared to the giant's.

"You're right," he said, after a moment of silence. "That's exactly what I thought. I'm sorry I didn't take time to consider how it would affect the rest of you. But...there was no time. The idea of having to live without Rokey – well, it just wasn't an option I could consider, not when I had the means to prevent it. Fortunately, it worked out well for all of us."

The two of them sat quietly for a moment, then the elf continued.

"Listen Lorq," he said, "so far you're the only one that's been clever enough to figure this out. I know you're upset with me, but I'd appreciate it very much if you would do me a huge favor, all right big fellow?"

"Sure Flash," Lorq replied. "What is it?"

"Well, I'd just as soon no one else knew about this, especially Rokey. With a little luck, time will pass, the thought won't occur to anybody else, and we can all put the whole thing behind us. So let's just keep it between the two of us, alright old friend? Will you do that for me?"

"I will Flash, I promise," the giant said solemnly.

"Thanks, Lorq," said the elf, "I knew I could count on you."

"Always," said Lorq.

*   *   *

They experienced no further misfortunes before reaching Farport. In fact, the winds were sufficiently strong to put them at their destination early that next afternoon, well ahead of schedule. The docks there were too shallow for a ship of that size to sail into, so the captain brought his party in on the ship's large rowboat. Rokey and Flaskamper were both feeling considerably better, though the wounds that Rokey had received from the harpy's talons were painful, and it would be some time yet before they healed fully. When Baltimel had moored the boat and unloaded their possessions, Fia thanked the captain, and apologized profusely for all the trouble that had occurred. The captain nodded, but the ready smile from before was absent.

"I won't say I've enjoyed the trip, nor that I hope we meet again, because we'd both know it was a lie," he said. "But I wish you luck with...whatever your business be."

With that, he returned to his boat, cast off and headed back to The Grand Lady. No one from the ship waved good-bye. They weren't surprised. Though Flaskamper had added a hefty sum to the negotiated price by way of compensation, no amount of money could bring back the crew's lost shipmates.

The companions picked up their gear and headed into town. Farport looked very similar to Waterville, though dirtier and more run down. The faces of the people walking the streets looked hardened, and there were beggars, not an uncommon site in the larger kingdoms, but rare in small settlements like this one. They made a modest contribution to one such unfortunate, and asked him for directions to an inn.

"Just round the corner there," said the blind man, gesturing in the general direction with a trembling hand. "Port's Pride. Only one in town." They thanked him and continued on.

The Port's Pride was ironically named, for there was precious little about it of which one could be proud. It was creaky and dilapidated, and stank of old beer and...other things of an odious nature. The innkeeper, who introduced himself as Pock, was a fat, balding middle-aged man with two missing teeth in the front and permanent sweat stains under his arms. He leered shamelessly at Fia, and let her know that a room could be had free of charge if one were a *special friend*. Stamford stepped forward and grabbed the man by the shirtfront, nearly lifting him off the ground.

"Tempted though I'm sure she is by your generous offer," he said through clenched teeth, "we really have no time for fun and games.

Now kindly fetch us the keys to two adjoining rooms, preferably ones without too much of an accumulation of filth." He released the man with a shove that nearly knocked him to the floor.

"Right away, sir," said the frightened innkeeper, and hurried off to fetch the keys.

"We shall have to be on our guard tonight," Fia observed.

"Most definitely," Stamford agreed. "That is why I asked for only two rooms. With apologies to our love birds, it's best not to spread ourselves too thin."

"Why must he always be so damned sensible?" Flaskamper muttered.

None of the group particularly wanted to visit the tavern that night, but determined that any information they could garner about Glimmermere and the Aldaji tar swamps would be helpful. They decided that only Stamford and Flaskamper would go. They were no strangers to rough crowds. The pair waited until raucous laughter could be heard from the tavern downstairs, then donned their cloaks. Rokey gave Flash a kiss that made the elf wish they had a bit more privacy and a lot more time.

"Good luck, boys," said Fia. "Do try not to kill or be killed, alright?"

"Don't worry Fia," Flaskamper assured her, "we're old pros at this."

"That's what worries me," she retorted.

Stamford and Flaskamper went down the back stairs and out into the night. They had decided not to advertise the fact that they were staying upstairs. Though the innkeeper was likely to blab, they decided to be cautious anyway. They re-entered the tavern through the front door. Some heads turned their way, but most people simply ignored them.

"Alright," Stamford said under his breath to Flash, "you know the type we're looking for – likes to drink, likes to talk, doesn't like to pay."

"Gotcha," said Flash.

The two made their way to an empty table, and a beleaguered but pretty young girl came to take their orders. This was Flaskamper's department. Young girls tended to find Stamford a trifle frightening. The elf beamed her his best, non-threatening smile and asked her what the best ale in the house was.

"Ooh, that'd be the Tanohar Gold," she said, then lowered her voice, "a damn sight better than the local swill, but too pricey for most. Pock drinks most of it hisself, truth be told."

"That sounds fine," said Flaskamper. "We'll have two pints, and do us a favor, beautiful – order it loudly enough to be overheard."

She gave him a quizzical look, but he just smiled broadly. They watched the room carefully as she ordered the expensive ales, loudly enough to be clearly heard, to see who might take an interest. As it turned out several did, which worried them a bit.

"What do you suppose the chances are that we *won't* be held up when we leave here?" Stamford asked

"Between slim and none," replied Flaskamper, "and Slim just left town."

"I see possibilities, said Stamford, "too many really. This may take us some time."

"Maybe I can create us a shortcut," said the elf.

When the girl returned with their ales, Flaskamper gave her a handsome gratuity, for which she smiled and thanked him very much.

"How would you like to add fifty more ducats to that?" he asked her.

Her smile disappeared.

"I am a tavern girl, sir," she informed him stiffly. "The girls *you* want are just down the street." She turned to walk away.

"Wait!" he said, kicking himself for his clumsiness. "That isn't what I meant."

Reluctantly, the girl turned back to face him.

"I apologize for giving you the wrong impression, miss...?"

"Shade, sir," she replied.

"Well, Shade, I'm truly sorry. I only wanted your help in finding a little information." He tried his best to look disarming. Apparently it worked, because her smile returned.

"Well, I shall do my best to help you if I can, sir," she said.

"Call me Flash." Under the hood of his cloak, Stamford rolled his eyes.

"Alright...Flash. What is it you need to know?"

The elf made a show of looking all around, then crooked his finger for her to lean in closer.

"I'm looking for someone," he told her, "who may have some information about the Aldaji tar swamps and Glimmermere. I thought you might be able to introduce us to someone who might be willing to talk to us for a while in exchange for a few pints of this very tasty Tanohar Gold."

Shade chuckled.

"There's plenty who'd be willing to talk to you for that," she said, "but not so many as would tell you anything truthful. But I think I know of a fellow here who might be of some help. Name's Braymon. Shall I fetch him over for you?"

Flaskamper nodded, then placed fifty ducats into her hand.

"Please tell him to be discreet," he added, "and I wouldn't mention the fifty ducats if I were you, for you own safety if nothing else."

"Don't worry, sir... Flash." Shade said in a whisper. "I weren't born yesterday, nor the day before neither."

When she had gone, Stamford chuckled.

"I like her," he said. "If I were only ten years younger –"

"If you were *only* ten years younger," Flaskamper jibed, "you'd still need to be ten years younger.

"Why in the world did I ever fish you out of that water?" growled Stamford.

A few minmarks later, a man approached their table. He was a nondescript fellow, of average height and weight, with some grey starting to creep into his tousled brown hair and several days' growth on his chin. He smiled and spoke to them in a low, measured voice.

"Pardon my intrusion, gentlemen. Allow me to introduce myself. My name is Braymon. Shade was kind enough to tell me of your desire for some information, and your kind offer of a tankard or two in exchange. If I may join you, I shall be happy to tell you what I know. In the spirit of fairness, however, I must warn you that my knowledge is neither extensive, nor necessarily reliable, being as so much of it was acquired second hand."

"We shall keep that in mind," said Stamford. "Please, sir, do join us. My name is Stamford. This is Flaskamper." He motioned for Shade to bring them three more ales.

Shade was there in a trice with the tankards. With 50 ducats jingling in her apron, Flaskamper doubted that they would have to wait long for anything that evening. Braymon took a healthy pull on the Tanohar Gold and smacked his lips appreciatively.

"I thank you, gentlemen," he said. "A man of my...limited means cannot often indulge in such a fine brew as this. I hope that what I have to tell you will be sufficient payment for the privilege. Now then, what is it specifically that you wish to know?"

"Well," Flaskamper began, "our primary concern is getting through the Aldaji swamps alive. The rumor is that there is no fixed path due to the constant shifting of the ground. If that is the truth, how has anyone ever managed it?"

Braymon had already downed half of his pint. Stamford suspected that this information was going to be more expensive than they had originally thought.

"The rumor is true," Braymon told them, "as far as I know. I have never assayed the swamps myself, but a few pilgrims still come through from time to time, though you are the first in a good many years."

"But *how* do they get through?" Flaskamper pressed. "Is there a secret path, or some spell that must be cast?"

Braymon shook his head.

"Some never return," he said. "Others turn back. But those that have made it..." Braymon looked about, then lowered his voice, "those who have made it credit the *Alahgeerie*."

"The what?" said Stamford.

"The Alahgeerie," the man repeated. "They are a breed of deer who make their home in the Aldaji swamps. The story is that the

Alahgeerie are shape shifters who, when sufficiently charmed, will assume human form and lead pilgrims safely through the swamps. You doubt me I see. I doubted as well when I first heard the tale, but since then I have heard the same story from a number of different sources. That does not necessarily bestow upon it the mantle of truth, but it *is* the most consistent of the stories to come out of Aldaji so, in my opinion, it cannot be discounted out of hand."

"Alright, so to get through the swamps you have to flirt with a deer," Stamford said, "After what we've been through this past month, it really doesn't sound that far-fetched. Now, as to Glimmermere itself–"

Braymon cast a forlorn look at his empty tankard. Stamford signaled the girl for another. When it had been delivered, Braymon continued.

"Glimmermere is a different story. There are no consistent accounts about that place. There are very few accounts of *any* sort about it, except for the one thing that everybody repeats – about the fearsome ghost that stands guard there. Even though that tidbit has now graduated from a rumor to a legend, I think most people, even those around here, would think twice before calling it a fact. The truth is that nobody knows what the truth is. Glimmermere has been too long asleep. It is no longer part of the lore of the land. It has faded with time."

Stamford and Flaskamper quizzed Braymon through two more pints of Tanohar ale, more to ensure that the man felt sufficiently rewarded to keep quiet than to extract any more useful information. Afterwards, they bid him and Shade goodnight and headed back to their rooms.

After discussing what the two had learned on their fishing expedition, they all went to bed. Given the interest that some of the patrons had taken in their choice of ales, they all took turns keeping watch in their respective rooms. Some time in the middle of the night, just as he had anticipated, Stamford heard a scraping sound. Someone was trying to pick the lock on the door. The would-be thief soon gained entry, only to be confronted with the point of the dark man's sword at his throat.

"A thousand pardons, sir," the shabby little man whined. "I thought this was my room. I am," he gulped, "extremely sorry to have disturbed you."

"Mistakes happen to the best of us," growled Stamford. "You will no doubt be grateful to me if I tell you that the room next door is not yours either, and *its* occupants are also light sleepers."

"I thank you, good sir," the man squeaked. "for that useful information. I assure you that I shall trouble you no further."

"See that you do not."

They rose early the next morning, none of them having slept much, and departed, afraid that to tarry longer would result in an infestation of fleas...or worse. The weather was cold and dreary. Thick, grey clouds filled the sky, threatening rain. They were traveling across a flat, barren expanse. To the north was forest, but in the direction they were going, southeast, there was only hard, flat plain. They had estimated that it would take them only a little more than a day to reach the outskirts of the Aldaji swamps. After a few marks of traipsing across the rough ground, Rokey was actually beginning to look forward to the tar swamps. When he mentioned this to Flaskamper, the elf opined that this feeling would probably disappear soon after they had actually reached them.

"Trust me. I've been in a swamp or two in my time," he told Rokey. "The smell alone will have you wishing you were back on this grim little patch of Firma soon enough."

The day seemed to go on forever, the monotony of their progress broken up only by an occasional shower of cold, soaking rain. Late in the afternoon, the ground finally began to grow softer, as though one were walking on a carpet. The grass here was long and green. Ahead they could see that the trees grew progressively thicker and the ground even wetter. Though sunset was still a little ways off, Stamford suggested that they camp where they were, lest the ground ahead grow too soggy to sleep on. The tired group eagerly agreed. They chose a spot under a group of gnarled sinnafor trees. Their rough, serrated leaves had already turned from green to yellow and were beginning to fall, but enough remained on the branches to provide some additional shelter from the intermittent rain. They gathered wood and started a fire. Flaskamper dug out their one cooking pot, dumped some water from his skin into it and set it over the flames. When the water began to boil, he took two small leaf-wrapped packets from his pack and tossed them into the water. The others watched him curiously.

"Flash what are those?" Rokey finally asked.

"Stew bricks," Flaskamper answered. "Part of every traveling elf soldier's rations. I don't know how they make them, because frankly, I never cared enough to ask. The end result is pretty good though. A nice change from plain dried meat."

The result was, in fact, a very filling meal that tasted a great deal like the lamb stew they had eaten in Elfwood a few days before. Fia marveled at the elves and their ingenuity.

"Yes, we have all kinds of tricks up our sleeves," said Flaskamper, giving Rokey a wink. Rokey smiled and reddened, thinking of all the tricks *he* had learned in the past several nights. After their long miserable day of hiking, he could hardly wait to crawl in to bed, and into his lover's arms. Flaskamper spoiled his plan though by volunteering for the first watch. Rokey quickly volunteered for the second. That would at least get them over and done with, though he feared they would be too tired to do much more than sleep afterwards. *Oh well, one has to sleep sometime*, he supposed.

The next day dawned bright and sunny again. As the company broke camp, Stamford called the others over to where he stood, examining a particular patch of ground.

"Look here," he said, pointing down. On the muddy ground, they could clearly see a track – two long distorted teardrops atop two small ovals. He had seen enough of them to recognize them immediately – deer tracks.

"Do you think they're the Alahgeerie?" asked Rokey.

"We won't know until we see them in the flesh, but I'd say it won't be long until we know one way or the other. This track can't be more than a few marks old, which means they managed to observe us last night without being observed themselves – clever bastards."

"Speaking of seeing them face to face," Flaskamper remarked, "we ought to give some thought as to how we're going to win them over."

"True," Stamford agreed. "Well, Lorq is good with animals."

"Once they get used to him," Flash replied. "But they do tend to find him a bit threatening at first.

"There is that," said Stamford. "Well...do animals like music? Maybe Fia could sing to them."

"Animals do like music," Lorq offered.

"What do you think Fia?" Flash asked her. "Your charm works with regular people, why not deer people?"

"Well, I suppose it's worth a try," Fia answered somewhat skeptically.

"We should look for more tracks," Stamford suggested. "Find a place where they tend to congregate. There's a good square mile of good grazing area here, but we should be able to find a spot they prefer without too much trouble, especially with this wet ground."

They finished packing up and began hunting for more deer tracks. As the dark man had predicted, they were *not* difficult to find, and within a mark, Rokey followed a set that led to many others, along with numerous piles of droppings. He alerted his companions, who hurried to join him.

"Yes," said Stamford, "this is what we're looking for. They've gathered here recently. My guess is that they stay as near to the trees as possible when they come out to graze, and stick together for safety."

"Do you suppose they're nocturnal?" Fia asked.

"The species of deer that I'm familiar with are, but there are many types roaming the forests of Firma, so we can't be sure. I suggest we plant ourselves here and keep our eyes open. I'd have your lyre and some deer charming songs at the ready. Since we don't know whether or not they *are* nocturnal, we don't know at what time they're most likely to be roaming about."

"Deer charming songs. Of course," quipped Fia, "I've dozens at the ready. Deer are forever piping up in the royal courts demanding to be charmed."

They unpacked their blankets and spread them out onto the ground, then sat, watching and waiting. After a mark or so, Flaskamper went off to climb one of the nearby trees to have a look around.

"I'll give you a blue forest owl cry if I see anything headed your way," he told them, and hurried off.

For the rest of the day, they saw nothing except birds, insects and a few small rodents. Flaskamper came back at lunchtime, stiff and sore from having sat in the tree all morning. As the day wore on, they became very discouraged. If the deer did not come out, their only option was to venture into the swamps by themselves, which was not a prospect that any of them relished. At last, as the sun was getting low in the sky, a pair of deer suddenly walked out from the nearby trees, no more than one hundred yards from where they all sat. Though the group was in plain sight, the deer merely looked in their direction for a moment, then proceeded to graze. A few moments later, another emerged, then another. Soon nearly a dozen of them stood grazing in the meadow. Rokey had seen the small dwarf deer that roamed the woods up in the Emerald Mountains, but they were nothing like these beautiful creatures. These were tall and sleek, brown in color, with white ears and tails, and a ring of heavy brown fur around their necks. The males had small, delicate racks of antlers, while the females had only two tiny nubs on their foreheads. They all sat in awe, just watching the animals for several minmarks, but time was growing short.

"Fia," Stamford said softly, "you'd better give it a try. We haven't got much time before the sun sets."

Rokey watched as Fia stood slowly and, taking up her lyre, stepped gingerly toward the grazing deer. Their heads went up, and they sniffed the air for a moment. After deciding that Fia posed no threat, they went back to their dinner. Fia rested the lyre on her arm and began to play. Rokey didn't recognize the song. It was a lovely and rather haunting ballad about a doomed love affair. Her voice and the music from the lyre blended so beautifully, it almost made him want to weep. He had had no idea how talented a musician Fia was. How his friends continued to amaze him...

Every few stanzas, Fia moved another slow step closer to the deer, until she was in the center of the group. There she stayed still. The other deer had resumed eating, but one of them, a small male, had stopped. His large brown eyes studied her intently. As Fia continued to sing and play, the male took a step toward her, then another, until he was only about a foot away from her. She quit playing the lyre, but continued to sing, as she stretched her hand out towards it. Just as she was about to stroke its head, it shied away and pawed at the ground. It came forward again and again, but always retreated, pawing the ground as she reached out to touch it. Fia paused.

"It's not working," she called back to her companions. "He doesn't trust me."

"Your singing is clearly affecting him," Stamford called back. "but something seems to be putting him off at the last moment."

She was about to give it another try when a thought struck Rokey.

"Fia," he called to her, "take your pendant off."

"What?" she answered. "Do you want me to scare the poor thing to death?"

"I just have a feeling – look, just trust me, won't you? Give it a try," he said.

"Alright," she said with a wry grin, "but if he bolts for the woods, I'm holding you responsible."

Fia removed the pendant and set it down on the grass. Her beauty immediately vanished, and she stood there in her true, misshapened form. The deer seemed startled at the change, but stayed where it was.

"Now sing," said Rokey.

Fia shook her head doubtfully, but began to sing once again, and once again the deer drew closer, and closer – and then her hand was stroking its face and neck. As she sang and petted the creature, it leaned forward and nuzzled her neck. She laughed, then began another song, a happy, upbeat Elvish tune that Flaskamper immediately recognized. As she continued, the deer stepped back and suddenly seemed to shimmer, like a reflection on a pond. The next moment, a young man stood before her – that is, a man in most respects. His naked body was hairless except for his legs, which were still covered with the soft brown fur. The brown mane remained on his neck as well. His eyes were wide and brown, with no white showing around the sides, and his nose was more round and button-like than a normal man's. In all other respects, he looked quite human. The man pawed the ground with one foot and stared wide-eyed at Fia. She stopped singing and smiled at him. He sniffed back at her.

"Can you speak?" she asked.

He shook his head.

"But you can understand me?"

This time a nod.

"My name is Fia. I have come a very long way," she began, "with my friends."

She gestured to Rokey and the others. The deerman looked over to them, and his eyes grew nervous. He took a step backward and abruptly became a deer again.

"It's all right," she told him in a soft, lilting voice. "They are my friends. They will not harm you."

In another blink of an eye, the young man was back, looking slightly more reassured. Fia sang to him some more, and he relaxed visibly.

"We are on a journey to Glimmermere," she told him when she thought he was sufficiently calm. "We wish to consult the oracle there. But we have been warned of the dangers of the Aldaji tar swamps."

The deerman snorted, apparently in complete agreement with the warnings.

"We have been looking for a strong, sure-footed guide to show us the way safely to Glimmermere," Fia continued. "Do you happen to know where we might find such a brave creature to guide us?"

The deerman puffed up the fur around his neck and pawed the ground several times. Then he ran around Fia and struck himself on the chest.

"Oh, would you?" she exclaimed. "That would be wonderful. We would be very grateful to you."

He smiled and pawed the ground some more.

"I wish I knew your name." Fia said.

The deerman made a sound, like half of a donkey's bray. Fia assumed that that was his name. She laughed, then shook her head.

"That's a very nice name, but I'm afraid it's not one we humans can easily pronounce. Would it be alright if I gave you a name, just for the time being?"

Another enthusiastic nod.

"Well, it's a bit trite, but how about if we call you Buck?"

Buck apparently didn't think it at all trite, and nodded his head vigorously again.

"Alright, Buck it is. Well, Buck, won't you come and meet my friends?"

Buck was less enthusiastic about this prospect, but Fia finally convinced him that it would be all right. She led him over and introduced him to the rest of the company. Buck was nervous and turned back into a deer several times during the introductions, but eventually settled down. Having attained their objective, however, they were faced with another obstacle – the growing darkness. Buck clearly had no trouble traveling through the swamps at night, but they had no torches, and were hesitant to use Flaskamper's magical light for fear of drawing undue attention to themselves. Fia explained to Buck that their journey would have to wait until morning, and asked him if he could return and take them then. The young deer was hesitant at first, apparently it was not usual for them to be up and about at that time, but when Fia promised to sing to him some more that evening, he agreed to return and guide them through the swamps at first light.

They set up camp and ate a cold supper, not wanting to alarm the deer with the smell of cooking meat. Then Fia sang to Buck for the rest of the evening. The other deer gathered around to listen, staying just outside the ring of the firelight. Some of them changed into human form, others remained as they were. At the evening's end, when Fia tired, the deer all pawed the ground in a kind of applause, then disbursed. Fia reminded Buck, who had changed back to animal form, that he had promised to return at first light. He tossed his antlers up and down, a signal that he remembered his promise and would be there as agreed.

It wasn't until they were on their way to their tents that Fia remembered that she was not wearing her pendant. Flaskamper volunteered to go and look for it. He returned a few minmarks later and handed her the precious object. To his surprise, Fia placed it carefully in her pack.

"I'd best put it away until we reach Glimmermere," she told him. I don't want to frighten Buck."

They all laughed as the irony of that struck them. It reminded Flaskamper to ask Rokey about it when they had crawled into bed together.

"How did you know that...about the pendant?" Flash asked between kisses.

"I don't know," Rokey answered. "It just struck me that maybe an animal like that would find deceptive magic....you know – off-putting."

"It certainly had quite an effect in Fia," said Flash. "She hasn't had that pendant off for more than a minmark since the old sorcerer gave it to her – until tonight that is."

"Well," said Rokey, "it's probably good for her to realize that somebody can appreciate her for her inner beauty; someone besides us I mean. I just hope... Buck shows up again... tomorrow... ahhhhh... ooohhh."

Flaskamper had started massaging Rokey's shoulders and was now working his way slowly down his back. The elf's strong fingers kneaded the tightness from the boy's tired muscles. Then, a few minmarks later, the elf dove under the blankets, and all of Rokey's worries from a moment ago were promptly forgotten.

*   *   *

Flaskamper had been right about the swamp. It was one of the worst smells Rokey had ever encountered. They had started the long, meticulous slog through Aldaji at dawn, and had now been going for several marks. Through a painstaking series of yes or no questions, Fia had learned from Buck that they should reach Glimmermere before the end of the day. However, the going was so sluggish and arduous, Rokey was beginning to wonder. He couldn't imagine what they would do if the sun went down on them in the middle of this horrible place. There was very little dry land, only huge quagmires of mud and tar riddled with gnarled tree roots. Rokey pictured the entire place as the slowly rotting corpse of some long-dead colossus. The thought gave him the shivers.

At midday, they made a quick stop at the base of an old bizen tree. Its huge base of intertwined roots formed a dry place where they could all fit, albeit snugly, and nibble on some dry rations. None of them wanted to linger, though. The smell did nothing to bolster their appetites, and in the back of all their minds was the same thought that haunted Rokey – the thought of being caught here after dark.

As they picked their way through the muck and mire, Stamford wondered aloud how the deer could live in these conditions.

"I suspect that they don't venture this far into the swamps too often," Fia speculated, "and when they do it is undoubtedly in their human form."

From the head of the line, Buck turned and nodded to confirm her suspicion. A moment later, he stopped. When they had all caught up to him, they saw that he had reached a wide expanse of bubbling tar, with no apparent means of getting across. A little ways out they could see the skeleton of some massive animal that had apparently tried to wade across days, weeks, or perhaps centuries ago. For a few moments, they feared that Buck had gotten lost, and a moment of panic rippled through them. Then the deerman pointed out two trees on opposite sides that had each grown outward over the tar expanse. High in the air, the branches had knitted together to form a crude bridge.

"You must be kidding," said Stamford, eyeing the bridge doubtfully. Buck shook his head. He was not kidding.

"Buck, is there no other way?" Fia asked. "Even if the rest of us could manage, I can't imagine that holding up under someone Lorq's size."

Buck looked chagrined. Clearly he had not considered the giant.

"Well," Flaskamper said with a sigh, "I suppose we'd better take a look up top and see what can be done."

The elf took his pack off and handed it to Rokey, then scampered nimbly up the tree. He stepped out onto the bridge formed by the intertwined branches, and Rokey's heart skipped a beat when Flash jumped up and down to test it.

"This will hold the rest of us just fine," he called down. "It's stronger than it looks. I think we could reinforce it enough for Lorq to cross. It's a fairly short distance here at the top."

He scurried down and directed the others to help him find three or four stout tree branches five to six feet long. When that was done, Flaskamper, with Buck's help, worked on hauling the branches up into the tree. Then he tied them off to the existing structure with the elf rope they always carried. It took the better part of two marks, but when it was finished, the elf declared that he though it would safely hold the giant, at least for this one crossing. At this point, no one had given much thought as to how they were going to get out of Glimmermere when the time came. With the bridge finished, Flaskamper crossed and climbed down on the other side.

"Alright everyone," he yelled, "Your turn!"

One by one they climbed up the tree. The height was dizzying, but Flash's project had made the bridge on top remarkably strong. Lorq went last. He was not much of a climber, but managed to get to the treetop with little trouble. He stepped gingerly out onto the bridge, which groaned and buckled a bit under his weight, but ultimately held. When the giant had joined them on the other side of the tar pond, they all paused to offer Flash some well-deserved praise, then quickly moved on to try and make up the lost time.

Another mark passed. The sun was sinking lower and lower in the sky. When asked how much further they had to go, Buck merely pointed straight ahead. There was little visibility in the swamps because of the prevalence of hanging moss and vines, so it wasn't until they were nearly on top of it that they noticed what looked like a curtain of golden light cutting straight across the swamp in front of them. Behind it they could see only more of the same.

"What is it Buck?" Fia asked. "Is it dangerous?"

Buck shook his head and, to their surprise, stepped through the curtain and abruptly disappeared. A moment later, he came back through and motioned them to follow him. Nervously, they followed him, one by one, through the strange golden light and were amazed to find themselves in an entirely different place. There was no sign of the swamp here. The ground was covered with thick, green grass. The trees here were tall and lush, a sharp contrast to the gnarled and bent congestion that grew in the swamp. To Rokey, it looked like the well-manicured grounds they had seen in Duncileer at the King's Fair. Buck pointed off into the distance, where they could just make out what looked like a small thatched house. They started in that direction, but stopped when the deer stayed behind.

"What's wrong, Buck?" Fia asked. "Should we not go this way?"

Buck shook his head, then made a number of gestures; which they finally took to mean that they were to go on, but it was time for him to return home. They all thanked the deerman and said good-bye. Fia embraced him and gave him a kiss on the cheek. Buck smiled shyly, then waved and disappeared back through the golden curtain. The companions continued on toward the little house, wondering what lay ahead of them in Glimmermere.

Chapter 18:

Metamorphosis

"What a perfectly beautiful place!" exclaimed Fia.

She had once again donned her pendant, and with the magical object back around her neck, the glamour had returned. She wandered happily with the others, enjoying the pastoral landscape of Glimmermere. It had been several marks since Buck had left them there, and they had taken time to explore, after determining that no one else was about. Aside from the thick, green grass and tall trees, wildflowers grew everywhere, splashing the entire landscape with vivid color. Just past the thatch house, over a little hill was a lovely clear pond fed by a small stream, the origin of which they could not determine. Everything here was different than the dank, fetid area that surrounded it, even the temperature. Outside this enchanted area, late autumn's chill had settled over the land. Here in Glimmermere, though, it felt like a balmy spring day, and the company quickly shed their heavy wool cloaks. And the sun...the sun still shone directly overhead, though outside, in the swamps, it had set long before.

They supped on some of the fresh fruit from the various fruit trees, washed down with the last of their skin of Elfwood wine, and had just begun to seriously consider their circumstances, when suddenly they heard a voice behind them. They spun abruptly and came face to face with Glimmermere's fearsome guardian ghost; only she wasn't fearsome at all. She was, or had in life been, a beautiful woman. Now only a specter, she was partially transparent, though one could still see her pretty green eyes, her flowing, violet curls, and her long, shimmering blue dress. A pale golden aura surrounded her, and she hovered just above the ground.

"Good day, gentle folk," said the ghost. "Welcome to Glimmermere. I apologize for not greeting you at once. No one has been here for many years, and I'm afraid that I have taken to woolgathering. My name is Glaelie. I am the guardian of this realm."

Stamford stepped forward. "We are pleased to see you, my Lady. I am Stamford, and these are my companions."

He introduced the rest of the company. Glaelie smiled and nodded at each of them in turn, but focused immediately on Rokey.

"*You* are the one who has need of the oracles," she said. It was not a question.

"Yes," said Rokey. "How did you know?"

"It is apparent to me," she answered, then frowned. "But there is deceit in your midst, deceit which must be banished before the oracles will welcome you."

Glaelie closed her eyes and spread her hands out over the heads of the company. She then began an incantation.

> *"Am hommus credosa mon*
> *Skree anjus ley dias praun*
> *Venius topila banistat."*

As soon as she finished her chant, Fia's pendant ceased to function, and she reverted to her true looks. A moment later, there was a screech from inside Lorq's pocket.

"Pico?" he said, and reached in to remove the little frog from his pocket. What came out however was not a frog, but a hideous black creature with red, bulging eyes, and leathery wings. As soon as it was free of the pocket, it bit Lorq's finger and attempted to fly away. Glaelie pointed to it, and a beam of bright, red light shot from her finger, striking the creature in mid air. It shrieked and exploded into dust.

"What was that thing?" Flaskamper sputtered when the shock had worn off a bit.

"A *bolu*," Glaelie replied. "They are shape shifting creatures with the power to transmit images of their surroundings to their masters. They are often used as spies."

"So that was how our enemies always knew when to attack us," said Fia.

"So it's all my fault," said Lorq, shaken, as tears filled his eyes.

"It is *not* your fault," Stamford insisted.

"Certainly not," said Flaskamper. "None of us had any inkling that it was anything but an ordinary frog, right Rokey?"

Flaskamper turned to find that Rokey had collapsed to the ground, and was apparently unconscious. In all the excitement, none of them had seen him fall. The elf immediately dropped down beside him.

"Rokey?" he said, lightly tapping his cheeks. "Rokey, love, are you alright? Wake up." He looked up at Glaelie, anger flashing in his eyes.

"What have you done to him?" he demanded.

"I know not," she replied. "My spell was merely to expose deceptions. It should not have caused anyone harm."

Flaskamper jumped up and faced the ghost.

"Well, clearly it *has* caused harm, to my friend," he said. "I should be grateful if you would kindly find some way to reverse it."

Glaelie gestured towards the house.

"If you will bring him inside and lay him down," she said, "I shall attempt to discover the nature of what has occurred."

Flaskamper carried Rokey inside and put him on the bed. The rest of the companions waited outside. Glaelie floated in and stood at the foot of the bed, her eyes closed. She held her hand out over him and began to chant softly to herself. This continued for well over a halfmark. Flaskamper didn't dare interrupt her, but was growing more and more impatient. At last, the chanting stopped and she opened her eyes.

"Well?" he asked.

"Your friend is apparently under the influence of a concealment spell, the like of which I have never seen before," she said. "My spell has eroded it somewhat, but I am unable to banish it completely."

"But why is he unconscious?" asked Flaskamper. "What's the matter with him?"

"The spell is not an ordinary enchantment," Glaelie explained. "It is a part of him. I suspect he was probably born with it, or else it was placed on him very shortly afterwards. The shock of part of it suddenly vanishing overwhelmed him, but the effects are temporary. He needs some rest, and in time he should be fine. He may, however, have undergone some changes."

"What sort of changes?" the elf demanded.

"It is impossible to say until he wakes up," she responded. "The differences may be so subtle as to escape notice, or they may be considerable. It depends on what was being concealed by the spell and how much of the spell has actually been eroded. This is a novel occurrence for me. I have no experience from which to draw. Your friend is a most extraordinary young man."

"Yes," Flaskamper agreed, taking Rokey's hand, "he most certainly is that."

* * *

Time had no meaning in Glimmermere. Because the sun never set, never moved at all, the party had no way of knowing how long it took for Rokey to wake up. The closest they could come was to count their meals, which they ate when they all grew hungry. So far they were up to six, except for Flaskamper, who stayed by Rokey the entire time, and did not feel like eating. Fia finally brought him a silver pear and refused to leave until he had eaten it.

"You're going to make yourself sick," she said, "and that won't do Rokey any good."

Flaskamper relented and ate the pear which, he had to admit, was delicious.

"Why are you so worried, Flash," she asked the elf. "Glaelie says he's going to be fine."

"Sure," he answered, "but she also said there would be changes."

"But those changes are part of who he really is. That's one of the big reasons we're on this quest – to find that out."

"I know," Flash replied, "but – but what if, when he wakes up – what if he doesn't know me or – or love me anymore?"

"Flaskamper, that's ridiculous," she said. "Of course he'll remember you."

"How can you be so sure," Flash said miserably. "Glaelie admitted that this has never happened to her before. She has no idea what sort of spell is on him, or how her magic will have affected it. For all we know, he could be an entirely different person."

Fia came over to the elf and held him close to her.

"Well, my darling," she said gently, "if that *is* the case, if Rokey has no memory of you, or the things you have shared...you shall simply have to make him fall in love with you all over again. For a loveable fellow like you, it should be no challenge at all."

She stood back and held his face in her hands. Her heart ached at seeing the pain in his eyes, but she tried her best not to let it show. Instead she gave him her most encouraging smile.

"But I do not think that will be necessary," she told him. "It is just an instinct. I have nothing whatsoever to support it. I just have the feeling that when he wakes up, he will know you *and* love you, just as before."

Fia left her friend to his vigil, she hoped slightly less despondent than before. She prayed that her instincts were correct, and that their friend's memories were all intact, for Flaskamper's sake even more than Rokey's.

Flaskamper had dozed off in the chair when Rokey finally regained consciousness. His groan woke the elf, who stood and cautiously approached the bed. There were no windows in this room, so it was too dark to see much, even with Flaskamper's sensitive eyes, but it was clear that Rokey was awake and moving.

"Rokey," said Flash, "are you alright?"

"Yes, I think so," Rokey answered. "What happened?"

"You were struck by Glaelie's reveal spell," Flaskamper explained. "It knocked you out for – well, for a long time."

"I feel like I've been run over by an ox cart," he complained.

"Rokey, do you – do you know me?" Flash asked nervously.

"Of course I know you, Flash," said Rokey.

"Do you – do you still – " Flaskamper swallowed hard.

"Do I still what?" Rokey asked.

"Do you love me?"

"Flash, what kind of a ridiculous question is that?"

The elf held his breath.

"I love you with all my heart," Rokey said. "Did you think I would not?"

Flaskamper gave a huge sigh of relief, then explained to Rokey what Glaelie had said about the reveal charm and the possibility of changes. Rokey sat up and took Flash's hand.

"Believe me, love," Rokey assured him, "my memories are all still here, as are my feelings for you. I *do* feel different though. I can't really explain in what way. I just feel,...lighter somehow. It's strange."

He stood up and took Flash in his arms.

"I'm sorry that you had to worry," he said, giving the elf a passionate kiss. "I'll make it up to you, I promise."

"Well, there's really nothing to make up to me," Flash told him. "On the other hand, who am I to argue? Come on, I've had enough of this dark room for the time being."

"Dark?" said Rokey. "It's bright as day in here."

"Hmmm," said Flaskamper. "I think we'd better go out and have a look at you. The others will be happy to see you as well."

When they emerged into the bright sunlight, Rokey had to immediately shield his eyes. His other companions, and Glaelie, gathered around to welcome him back to the land of the living. When his eyes had finally adjusted to the sun, Rokey took his hands away. They all gasped in shock at what they saw.

"What is it?" Rokey asked. "What's wrong?"

"It's your eyes, Rokey," said Fia. "They're...different now."

"How?" he demanded. "How are they different?"

Not only had the pupils of Rokey's eyes grown larger, but the color had changed from dark brown to a glittering gold. Fia explained all this to Rokey as gently as she could. Nevertheless, he grew increasingly alarmed.

"But why?" he asked. "What does it mean?"

Flaskamper turned to Glaelie.

"Glaelie, can you explain the change?" he asked the ghost.

"Yes, I can tell you about the eyes," she answered, "but as to how he comes to have them – well, that's another mystery, for these eyes do not belong to the race of men at all. They are the eyes of the sidhe.

I assume you've heard of them. They are otherwise known as the Faerie."

"But Glaelie," said Fia, "How is that possible? I was under the impression that the sidhe had long since vanished from Firma."

"That is what most people think," Glaelie answered, "But in truth, the race lives on, in small numbers, in the woodlands to the west of here. They stay in hiding, neither seeking nor welcoming contact with the other races of Firma. So you see, the possibility *does* exist. As to how it ever came to pass, I cannot even begin to speculate. Perhaps the oracles will be of some help."

"As will, perhaps, a visit to the domain of the remaining sidhe," said Stamford.

"Aye," Glaelie agreed, "if you can manage it. As I said, the sidhe spurn the company of others, and when they choose to stay hidden, only another member of their race can find them. If Rokey does indeed have the blood of the Faerie in him, you may stand a chance. However, just because one can find them, does not mean that one will be welcomed. They are surly at the best of times, and have a wicked sense of humor, being especially fond of cruel practical jokes."

"Glaelie," said Rokey, "what else is going to happen to me? Assuming that it's true and all, what other traits should I expect to see?"

"Well, dear boy," Glaelie responded kindly, "since we don't know the truth behind how *you* came to be – *you*, it is really not possible to say with any degree of certainty. However, one *can* speculate that any of the traits which the sidhe possess that humans do not may conceivably, at some point, manifest themselves in you."

"For instance?" asked Stamford.

"Wings, for one thing. All of the sidhe have them in some form."

Rokey quickly tugged off his shirt and turned his back to Flaskamper.

"Anything?" he asked the elf.

Flaskamper examined Rokey's back closely and declared him wing-free.

"What else?" Rokey inquired.

Glaelie pondered for a few moments.

"Well, aside from the wings and eyes," she said slowly, "and the fact that the sidhe are generally smaller, the principal difference is in their inherent magic. You know of course, that your elf friend here has certain magical qualities about him."

"You mean like their good luck," said Rokey.

"Exactly," said Glaelie, "and there are other things as well. But as much intrinsic enchantment as the elven folk possess, it is a mere splash in the pail compared to the magical qualities of the sidhe. As with the elves, these qualities differ among individuals, as does the potency of the magic. Each sidhe man and woman is different, just as each human is unique, possessing different tastes and talents. The only thing one can safely say is that, in general, the enchantments of the Faerie tend to center largely around trickery, and artifice, though that is by no means the extent of their abilities. A Faerie ring can conjure elementals, summon demons, cast a pall..."

Flaskamper abruptly snapped his fingers.

"That's it!" he cried. "Rokey, that's where I'd heard the tune you were humming. It was part of a Faerie ring spell. I studied it years ago in my Cultures and Customs of Firma class."

"Then my memory," said Rokey. "The dance with my mother in the circle. It was a Faerie ring!"

"The sidhe *must* have been the ones who cast this concealment spell on you," said Flaskamper, "don't you think, Glaelie?"

The ghost, however, disagreed.

"The sidhe are part of this mystery, to be sure," she said, "but as to this particular spell of concealment...that is something beyond even their capabilities. Had it been the work of the Faerie, my reveal spell would have banished it in its entirety. I am well versed in their arcana, and the means of countering it. No, there is a much deeper aspect to this enigma yet to be unraveled, mark my words."

For the next mark or two, Glaelie filled the company in on what she knew of the history of the sidhe people. Rokey listened with rapt attention, convinced now that his mother had been a member of this elusive population.

The sidhe, Glaelie explained, was one of the oldest races on Firma, older than humans and even elves. At some point in the distant past, the Faerie had lost the ability to reproduce with one another. How it had come to pass seemed to have been forgotten, even by the Faerie themselves. But the cause, Glaelie explained, had almost certainly been supernatural, because the sidhe were still able to produce offspring with members of other closely related races. Since they had always preferred to live apart from others, they had rarely chosen this option. However, being nearly immortal, they had continued to exist, dwindling slowly, yet inexorably in number until, over the centuries, the population was reduced to the small band that still dwelt in the woods somewhere to the west of Glimmermere.

The account filled Rokey with excitement, and not only at the prospect of finding his mother's people. If the sidhe were nearly immortal, perhaps she was not dead, as he had always believed. Perhaps he could find her again...be reunited.

This thought he kept to himself. He knew what Flaskamper would say. *'Don't build your hopes up, Rokey.'* Well, he wouldn't build them up, but that did not mean he had to abandon them entirely. After the events of these past few weeks, he now believed that anything was possible.

When they had finished discussing the sidhe, Glaelie turned the subject to the thing that had brought them to Glimmermere – the oracles.

"I must admit," said Rokey, "I haven't really given much thought to what I should actually ask the oracle – oracles. How many are there Glaelie, and how do they work?"

"There are two," the ghost answered. "The first is the Whispering Tree. The second is the Reflecting Pool. A petitioner may ask them each a single question. Some ask a different question of each. Others try out the same question on both, in hopes of piecing together a clearer response. Now, the Whispering Tree, as you might have guessed, will whisper its answer to you. The Reflecting Pool will form an image in its waters.

"The thing to remember," she continued, "is that oracles are tricky things. They almost never answer a query directly. In fact, more often than not, the responses they give have no apparent connection with the questions whatsoever. It is usually only later on that the meaning of their advice becomes clear.

"Great," said Flaskamper, "just what we need – more riddles."

"Don't dismiss them out of hand," Glaelie warned. "The oracles' advice, though cryptic, might be of critical importance, especially in a situation as complex as this. Heed and remember what they tell and show you. I promise you, you will be glad of it later."

"Where are the oracles?" asked Fia. "We walked all around the perimeter of the golden curtain. We saw nothing more remarkable than the grass and fruit trees."

"Aye," Glaelie replied with a smile, "that is because they are hidden. Only I have the power to reveal the bridge that leads to their glade. That is why I am here."

"How long have you been here?" Lorq asked her.

"Oh goodness," she laughed, "a long, long time. I was the last guardian of Glimmermere, back when it was a real place, and I was a living person."

"A real place?" Fia asked, confused.

"Aye," said Glaelie. "The Glimmermere you see around you now is merely a ghost, as am I, but many centuries ago, this entire swamp was a lush, green valley, just as you see here within the curtain. Glimmermere was its focal point, visited constantly by pilgrims, kings, wizards and warriors, all keen to partake of the knowledge of the oracles. In this little house lived the guardian, who had been chosen by her predecessor as *she* neared the end of her lifetime. It was considered a supreme honor to be asked to become part of the selection pool, and candidates from all over Firma were chosen."

"And you were the last of them to be appointed?" Stamford asked. "What happened?"

"One year, less than a decade after my appointment, there was a terrible earthquake," she said. "and the entire valley, including Glimmermere was swallowed up by the ground. Hot tar springs bubbled up from the earth, covering everything over. In the blink of an eye, it was all gone – the oracles, the house, even...the guardian. But there was far too much magic in the place for it to stay under the ground for long. Within a few score years, Glimmermere had risen from the dead, myself along with it, and its beauty was preserved within this field of enchantment. So it has been ever since, and hopefully, so shall it always be."

They all sat quietly for a time, taking in the amazing story. Then Glaelie turned to Rokey.

"Now, young man," she said, "it's time that we prepared you to meet the oracles you've come so far to see."

Chapter 19:

Cryptic Counsel

G laelie led Rokey, the others trailing behind, to the rear of Glimmermere's protective enclosure. There appeared to be nothing there but a lush woodland beyond the golden curtain. This they knew to be an illusion. In fact, there was nothing but swamp beyond the curtain, or so they thought. Glaelie raised her hands and recited a short chant.

"Agrum cor visium veritol
Petronum mitgum ent ortheniol"

Abruptly the scene in front of them changed. Instead of a woodland beyond, there now stood a magnificent bridge of rough, grey stone. The bridge was wide on both ends, tapering in the center, and at each corner stood a high turret made of similar stone. The area beneath the bridge, as well as the area on the other side was shrouded in mist, lending a dreamlike quality to the entire scene.

"Now, Rokey," Glaelie said, "the oracles only allow one person at a time in to see them, and the bridge makes sure that the rules are strictly enforced. As you cross over, you'll find that the mist will recede. Don't worry if you haven't quite decided on your question, or questions yet. You may stay there as long as you like. Remember though, only one question per oracle. They don't take kindly to those that try to cheat."

Rokey had no intention of trying to cheat. The last thing he wanted was a thousand year old oracle angry at him.

"Are you ready to go?" she asked him.

"In just a minmark," he said, and walked back to where his friends were standing.

"I want to go with you," said Flaskamper.

"You can't," Rokey told him. "The bridge won't allow it."

"Bugger the bridge!" Flaskamper exclaimed.

Rokey shook his head.

I have to do this alone, Flash," he said, and put his arms around the elf. Flaskamper kissed him good-bye.

"Don't take too long," said Flaskamper. "I'm going to be worrying the whole time."

"I'll be back soon," Rokey said, "I promise."

He said good-bye to each of his other friends, then headed back to where Glaelie awaited him.

"You'll need to leave your sword here," she explained. "The bridge doesn't allow any weapons near the oracles."

Rokey unfastened his sword and placed it on the ground.

"Well," he said, "here we go."

Rokey took a deep breath and proceeded slowly toward the bridge. His stomach was flip-flopping, and he had begun to sweat. As he stepped onto the bridge, he could hear it humming with power. He would definitely *not* want to try to cross while in violation of any of the rules. He reached the midpoint of the bridge, and noticed that the mist had indeed receded. He could see the grass, and a white pathway on the other side. He stopped for a moment and peered over the stone railing. Down below he could hear the rushing of water, but the view was entirely obscured by the heavy mist.

When he reached the end of the bridge, and stepped out onto the white crushed stone path, the mist immediately vanished, and he could see the entire landscape before him. The grass on this side was even thicker and continued on for what appeared to be miles. Rokey knew that much of this was illusion, but from here he could not see the shimmering golden curtain anywhere. The white road ran straight ahead, and was lined on either side by rows of tall royal ash, their velvety, lance-shaped leaves rustling in the warm, steady breeze.

He made his way along the path, enjoying the weather and the scenery. After nearly a mark, the road forked in two. There were no signs, but Rokey was sure that each road led to one of the oracles. He chose the left-hand fork, which took him up and over a small hill. As he crested the hill, he gasped as he caught sight of what could only be the Whispering Tree. It was incredible – an immense fairy willow, dark red in color, with masses of long, flowing branches that arched up and then cascaded back toward the ground like some huge, glorious fountain.

Even from this distance, Rokey could hear the wind rustling through its mighty tresses. After all that they had been through, he was finally here, and in moments would be standing before this magnificent auger, all of its wisdom and power poised to hear his question. As he continued on, he suddenly felt giddy, and more than a little awestruck. The road ran in a wide ring around the Whispering Tree. In several spots, wide marble benches had been placed just outside the white stone ring; places where one could sit and meditate, rehearse one's question, or ponder the answer, Rokey assumed. Before sitting on any of the benches, Rokey made the complete circle, taking in the remarkable willow in all of its splendor. He wanted desperately to walk over and touch it, to see if one could actually feel the power flowing through it. He held off though, not wanting to risk offending whatever entities were responsible for the tree's prophetic qualities.

Finally, Rokey sat on one of the benches and gathered his thoughts. He had already decided what questions he wanted to ask, but now that he was here, he went over them again and again in his mind, just to make certain. Having made the final decision, he next began to ponder the etiquette of such a situation. How did one greet an oracle? Was one expected to make some lengthy entreaty, or simply ask one's question? After rehearsing a few possibilities, Rokey finally settled on the simple, direct approach.

"I greet you, wondrous tree. My name is Rokey, and I have come from far, far away to appeal for your help. I understand that I may ask you one question, and one question only. While there are many which I would have answered, one is uppermost in my mind."

Rokey took a deep breath, and asked the tree his burning question.

"Whispering Tree, please tell me, who was my mother?"

Abruptly, the wind died, and for several moments, there was complete and utter silence. Then the breeze began to gather again. Rokey could feel something in the air, like the charge one felt when a thunderstorm was imminent. This time, when the wind touched the tree's long slender tendrils, he heard more than just the random jostling of the leaves. Now he could pick out the distinct sound of words being formed. He strained to hear, then realized that the words were in a language he didn't even recognize!

"Alright," he said to himself, "Glaelie said that the oracles rarely answer a question directly. Even though I have no idea what it's saying, I need to memorize it. It's surely going to be important later on."

The tree, apparently sensing his need, repeated the strange phrase over and over, until Rokey had successfully committed it to memory. Then the whisper disappeared, reverting once again to the simple but strong rustle of the breeze through the branches. Although Rokey had tried to prepare himself for disappointment, he felt it nevertheless, splashing over him like a pail of cold water. He told himself not to be silly. The information he had been given *was* going to prove valuable. He merely had to exercise some patience. Hah! – easier said than done.

Frustrated though he was, he nevertheless thanked the tree sincerely, and headed back the way he had come, back to the fork in the road. This time he took the right branch, which seemed to slope gradually, but steadily downhill. When the road finally leveled off, it made a sharp turn to the right. The royal ash trees lining the road became an entire grove, with the white stone path cutting straight through it. As he entered the woods, he could hear a loud roar in the distance, like a massive rushing of water. As he continued, the roar grew louder and louder, until he could scarcely hear his own thoughts over the din.

After walking through the trees for half a mark or more, he at last reached the end of the ash grove, and stepped into the open again, only to be confronted with another breathtaking spectacle. Straight ahead was a steep cliff, towering high into the air, and from the top, a huge waterfall gushed over a large promontory, plunging straight down into a lovely, peaceful lagoon. Around the lagoon were trees, bushes and a myriad of flowering plants, all of which were reflected by the shimmering lakelet to form an almost painfully colorful scene. The white, crushed stone road ended, but heavy, flat, sun-bleached rocks formed a pathway through the vegetation around the right side of the pond. Rokey strolled slowly over the warm stones, enjoying the cool mist cast up from the point where the waterfall merged with the lagoon.

When he reached the end of the path nearest the waterfall, he saw that there was a small runoff just beside it, which flowed over the rocks just in front of him into another smaller pool. This pool was utterly still; the stream that fed it tricked in so slowly that not even a ripple crossed its surface. Rokey looked down into this quiet little basin and saw his own reflection, clear as that of a looking glass, staring back at him. This, not the large lagoon, was the true Reflecting Pool, Rokey concluded. This was the one to which he would address his question.

Then his attention wandered back to the shimmering lagoon, and he suddenly felt an overwhelming urge to swim in it, as though the pond itself were beckoning him to jump in. With no hesitation at all, he stripped off his clothes and dove in. The water was cool and instantly refreshing. As he splashed around, he felt fatigue lift from his body, replaced by a tingle of vigor and energy. He swam toward the waterfall and climbed up onto the ledge underneath it, then stood letting the water rush over his naked body, sweeping his cares away.

Besides making love with Flaskamper, this was the most wonderful sensation he had ever felt.

After far too brief a time, Rokey swam back to the edge of the lagoon. He climbed out onto the flat rocks near the quiet Reflecting Pool and lay back for a while, letting the sun dry him off before reluctantly dressing again. He felt whole and renewed, and ready to ask the little pool his second question. He leaned over and stared down at his own long, wet hair, suntanned face and...new, glittering golden eyes! He was distracted by his altered appearance for a few moments, but then gathered his thoughts and addressed the pool.

"I greet you, life-giving waters. My name is Rokey, and I have come from afar in search of your aid. I have asked my question of the Whispering Tree, and now sit ready to pose my second question to you."

Rokey paused to shift his position for a moment, then went on.

"Reflecting Pool, please show me who is behind these attempts on my life?"

The placid little pool suddenly began to shimmer, obscuring his reflection. Rokey could see the image changing, but when the waters grew still once again, he could not believe what he was seeing. The pool pictured a large, vaguely egg-shaped boulder, sitting to the left of a dirt pathway. On the right was a small, undistinguished thicket of melody trees. He waited, wondering if some person, or group of people would wander into the scene. No one did. A boulder, a path, some trees – that was his answer.

Once again, Rokey was crestfallen. He had hoped so fervently that he would be able to glean some kind of clue in the answer to this second question, after learning so little from the first. As he stood, the image faded, and rippled back into the image of his own dejected face.

"I cannot hide my disappointment," he said to the pool, "but I know that you have shown me something that will one day help me to answer my question. For that, I give you my heartfelt thanks."

He turned and made his way back to the white road, turning for one last look at the lovely pastoral scene, then stepped back into the ash grove on his way to rejoin his friends. Physically, he felt wonderful, but his rejuvenating experience under the waterfall was tempered by his sense of discouragement. As he once again reached the fork in the road, however, he heard an amazing thing.

Rokey. Rokey. Rooookey.

Rokey shook his head in astonishment. Was he going mad? Hearing things?

Rokey. Rooookey.

No, he could clearly hear his name, wafting through the gentle breeze. It could only be coming from one place. He turned left and sprinted toward the Whispering Tree.

The tree was still calling to him as he ran down the little hill, but as soon as he arrived, the wind ceased, and with it, the sound of his name. Then, a few moments later, he felt it begin to stir again, and a different message emerged from the Whispering Tree.

"Darkness looms
And Firma falls.
Find the heart
To free us all."

It was over so quickly that Rokey could easily have convinced himself that he'd imagined it. But he had *not* imagined it. The Whispering Tree had given him a message of its own volition, and a dire one indeed. But what could it mean? He couldn't wait to get back and tell the others about this. His earlier disappointment forgotten, he bowed his head to the Whispering Tree and hurried off back the way he had come, the ominous verse still echoing in his head.

*   *   *

Glaelie was astounded by Rokey's story, and made him go over his visit in minute detail. When he finished, she shook her head in awe.

"I don't know what to say," said Glaelie. "I've never heard of such a thing happening, not since the oracles began these many centuries ago. Flaskamper, when I said that your friend was extraordinary, I fear I was making an egregious understatement."

They were all sitting on the grass. Flaskamper sat behind Rokey, his arms wrapped around him. Although he knew in his head that the oracles had posed no danger to his love, he was nevertheless wholeheartedly relieved to see him appear out of the mist and cross back over the bridge.

"It is just further proof of what we've suspected the whole time," said Stamford, "that this all goes far beyond our current situation. Firma as we know it is in some kind of jeopardy, and our boy here is an instrumental part of the means by which it can be saved."

"But it seems so ridiculous," said Rokey. "I mean, yes, it's certainly strange that someone is going to so much trouble to eliminate me, but as to Firma itself – I mean, what's really happening that's so calamitous? A higher crime rate in Duncileer, a marauding creature in the Elfwood forest... Both terrible, yes, but are they really signs that Firma is in danger of being overrun by – by some kind of evil menace?"

"In and of themselves, no," replied Stamford, "but when you put those things together with the findings of Battista and Jamba, and the dark warning from the Whispering Tree and the strange spell which continues to bind you, despite every effort to dispel it...."

He didn't finish his thought. He didn't need to. Everyone got the point.

"It's unfortunate that the clues the oracles gave you were so obscure," said Fia. Glaelie had managed to reactivate her pendant, so she was now beautiful again. "It gives us precious little guidance as to what our next move should be."

"I think our only choice is to head west and try to find the remnants of the sidhe population," said Stamford. "Clearly they are part of this whole web of intrigue, the only part that we stand some chance of tracking down at this point."

Rokey was glad to hear this, for it was exactly what he had wanted to do. If there was any chance at all of finding his mother –

Don't get your hopes up.

He would not get his hopes up, but he did have hope. Surely there was nothing wrong with that, was there?

They all agreed that this should be their next mission, and began making preparations to depart. As the others packed their things, Fia took Lorq to one side.

"Lorq," she said, "you've hardly said three words since we arrived here. You're not still blaming yourself for Pico are you?"

The giant nodded, his eyes tearing up.

But it's not just that," he sniffed. "I know he was bad, but – but I miss him."

"Of course you do," she told him. "He was your friend, at least you thought he was, and it always hurts when we lose a friend. But you mustn't blame yourself for anything, or think that we blame you, because we don't. Do you hear me?"

Lorq nodded, and Fia hoped that she had mollified him some.

"When this whole complicated mess is over, we'll find you another pet, one we can be certain really *is* your friend, alright?"

"I like rabbits," Lorq said with a hopeful smile.

"A rabbit sounds like a fine idea," Fia said. "You keep that in mind when you're sad from now on, and as soon as we're able, we'll see about finding one for you."

The giant smiled, and Fia gave him a hug before returning to her packing.

When they were all ready to go, Glaelie brought them to a section of the curtain in back of an old stone well.

"If you go through here, and continue straight on, you'll find solid ground the entire way, until you're safely through. Just don't try to come back that way, or you'll be extremely disappointed. It's just getting light outside the curtain, and you should reach the western edge of Aldaji by midday."

They all thanked her for her help, and one by one disappeared through the shimmering curtain. Rokey, the last to step through, tarried for a moment with the ghost.

"I don't know why," he said, "but I have the feeling that I shall be seeing you and Glimmermere again."

Glaelie smiled and nodded her head.

"I shall look forward to that day, Master Rokey," she said. Inside though, she wondered just how long it would be before that meeting took place, and how drastically Firma would be changed by that time. Rokey waved to her once more, then turned and vanished through the golden curtain.

Chapter 20:

Capture

"**F**lash, tell me about Stamford," said Rokey.

They were lying in their tent, nestled around one another like mice in a den. Both were tired from lovemaking, but neither was ready to sleep just yet.

Flaskamper ran his fingers up through Rokey's hair and kissed him on the back of the neck.

"What do you want to know about him?" asked the elf.

"Well, what about all those scars he has?" Rokey asked. "Where did they come from? Has he always been a mercenary?"

It was their third night out on the southern flats, and so far everything had gone well. With the spy gone from their midst, no further attacks had occurred. The weather had been cool, but remained dry, which was fortunate for them. During the rainy season, the entire southern flats region became a huge, muddy and virtually impassable mire. In this drier late fall climate, however, the land remained firm and easy to cross.

The scenery, though, was frightfully dull. Mile after mile of nothing but flat, open plains gave them the impression that they were going nowhere, and by the middle of their third day, the company was yearning for any change in their surroundings. Unfortunately, it was not to be. Day three ended as the previous two had, with no appreciable difference in the landscape. Stamford told them not to despair, that by the end of the following day they should at least be able to see the Lower Wilds in the distance. The others were not particularly heartened by this news, though they admitted that it would be some relief to at least have the end in sight.

Now, inside the little tent, Flaskamper stretched, then wrapped his arms back around his love. Had anyone else asked him for Stamford's history, he would have politely told them to go ask Stamford himself, or not so politely to go to blazes if he was in a less obliging mood. However, given the dark man's attitude toward this entire quest, Flaskamper did not think Stamford would mind if he recounted some of his past to Rokey.

"Alright, I'll give you the story on Stamford if you really want me to," said Flaskamper, "but I have to warn you, it's not a pretty one. Once I've told it to you, I guarantee you'll never look at him in the same way again."

"After an intriguing tease like that," said Rokey, "I'm even *more* eager to hear it."

"Well, Stamford was born in the poorest section of the kingdom of Ulgiarrah, which is some days to the north and east of where we are now. His mother died giving birth to him, a heartbreaking event that his father forever blamed *him* for. His older sister, Adella, loved him and took care of him as best she could, but she also grew ill and died when Stamford was only seven. His father had taken to heavy drinking and wanted little to do with Stamford, so from that time on, with no one to look after him, he grew up primarily on the streets, stealing what he needed to survive. By the time he was twelve, he was already a member of a criminal street gang called The Pack, and had been in and out of jail several times. He was a tough, hardened lad, and had learned through many hard lessons not to put his trust in anyone except for himself.

"A couple of years later, the reigning King of Ulgiarrah was toppled by a violent coup. The new king, Sangor, executed the deposed monarch's remaining guardsmen, and pressed many young men, including Stamford, into service to replace them. Amazingly, Stamford actually thrived in this harsh, structured environment. He did so well, in fact, that it wasn't long before he became a member of the king's own Black Guard, a secret police force that used fear and intimidation to stamp down any resistance that might crop up. The Black Guard caused anyone who dared raise his or her voice in opposition to the king to disappear. Many men, and even women were abducted, tortured and killed in the castle's dark dungeons, some of them at Stamford's own hands.

"Over about ten years, Stamford rose to the rank of High Captain. He was one of Sangor's most loyal servants, and one of the most hated and feared men in the kingdom. He became so influential, in fact, that one of the king's chief advisors, feeling threatened by Stamford's position of trust, falsely accused him of plotting against the crown. It was complete bunk but, like most tyrants, the king was fearful and suspicious enough to believe anything, even about one of his most faithful followers. Stamford was found guilty and sent to the salt mines deep in the Hattiar Mountain. He was brutalized there, and forced to work there under horrible conditions with some of the same people he himself had imprisoned. The seven years he spent there in the mines were grim ones, but they gave him time to reflect on some of the wrongs he had done to others during his lifetime. He vowed that if he were ever able to leave the mines, he would work for the rest of his life to try and remedy those wrongs."

Flaskamper paused.

"Are you still awake?" he asked Rokey.

"Of course," said Rokey. "I'm listening."

"Alright, just checking," he said. "I'm really not much of a storyteller."

"No, no," Rokey told him, "you're doing fine. Go on."

Flaskamper leaned down and stole a kiss, then continued.

"One day, there was a terrible cave-in. Many men were killed, but it was a boon for some, who took the opportunity to escape. Stamford was one of the lucky escapees. He went into hiding in Ulgiarrah, and joined a rebel force determined to oust the king, and put him on trial for the crimes he had committed against his subjects. The plot took over two years to organize, but with Stamford's detailed knowledge of the inner workings of the palace, they at last succeeded in toppling Sangor.

A new king was crowned, and it looked for a while as though conditions in Ulgiarrah would improve. But Stamford soon found the new ruler to be as corrupt and despotic as Sangor had been. When the new king offered him a post as captain of a new Black Guard, he refused, and left Ulgiarrah, disgusted and disillusioned. He began to travel throughout Firma, offering his services as a professional mercenary to anyone, so long as he was satisfied with the quality of the person's character. He swore never again to work for the kind of brutal oppressor that seemed to gravitate to the throne of Ulgiarrah. During his travels, he tried to help out those in need as often as he could. He was determined to do everything in his power to make up for his past misdeeds whenever he had the chance. Over time he was joined, one by one, by his three loyal companions –"

"Four loyal companions," said Rokey.

"Of course," said the elf, laughing. "Well that's it really. I gave you the short version, with most of the gore edited out. If you knew all the details, I'm not sure you'd want to face him again."

Rokey sighed.

"Wow. I guess I have no right to complain about the way my life has gone," he said. "Even in my darkest times I have good friends, a new love..."

"Be careful about what you call your darkest times," warned Flaskamper. "Times have an curious way of becoming ever darker."

"I suppose you're right," Rokey agreed. "We have no way of knowing where all this will eventually lead. I still feel somewhat guilty, leading Stamford and the rest of you away from your normal lives, and thrusting you into all this – this chaos."

"Hah!" Flaskamper laughed. "If I've somehow given you the impression that we led anything resembling normal lives prior to making your acquaintance, *chatka*, then I've horribly misled you. Besides, Stamford has always said that he was destined one day to find a quest to which he could devote his life, one that would once and for all allow him to atone for all the transgressions he has committed while a member of Sangor's Black Guard. He believes that your quest is it, Rokey, the one he has waited for."

"Really?" said Rokey. "It means that much to him?"

"Absolutely," Flash replied. "He is convinced that you represent a force of good that will soon be pitted against a great evil, and that in serving your cause he may bring about his own salvation."

Rokey shook his head in wonder.

"It's so strange," he said. "It hadn't really struck me until now, in spite of all we've been through, and all we've discussed, just how significant this whole thing really is. I mean, I guess I've just been trying to convince myself that it can't possibly be true, that I can't possibly be that important."

He clutched at Flaskamper, trembling suddenly with deep emotion.

"Gods, Flash, I'm afraid," he said, tears wetting the elf's bare shoulder. "I'm ashamed of myself for it...but I am."

Flaskamper held him tightly, rocking him gently back and forth.

"You don't have to be ashamed of being afraid," he said softly. "Great Secta, you'd be a fool if you weren't. I'm afraid too, *chatka*; we all are. Just remember, we're all in this together, no matter where it leads."

Rokey ran the back of his hand over Flaskamper's cheek.

"How many times have you saved my life?" Rokey asked him. "I've lost count."

"I told you before, my motives are purely selfish," Flash replied glibly, his hands sliding down to Rokey's buttocks. "Now go to sleep. We've another long day's travel tomorrow."

"I love you," Rokey whispered.

"And I you," Flash answered, "with all my heart."

*   *   *

The next day was sunny once again, and unseasonably warm, so the companions were able to take off their cloaks and enjoy the fair weather. Stamford however, was in a grim mood. He directed everyone's attention to the north, where they could just make out a series of irregularly shaped cliffs.

"Those are the Linonjar stacks," he told them. "We didn't spot them yesterday because of the haze. I didn't think that we would be passing this close to them. I suggest we push due south for a few miles."

"Why?" Flaskamper asked.

"Because right now we may be in Saebrilite country," said Stamford, "and if we are, we're in serious danger."

"Saebrilite country," Rokey repeated. "Wow, is it true what they say about them?"

"Well, depends on what you've heard," said Stamford. "They're a society whose females are giant warriors, and whose men are human sized and subservient.

"Is it true that the women are all samers?" Rokey asked, "and that they take men captive to use as breeders?"

Stamford nodded his head.

"I've heard that they sometimes send raiding parties out to kidnap men to renew their bloodlines," he replied, "those they don't kill outright anyway, but that may be only a campfire story. I've also heard that the Saebrilites don't tolerate any strangers getting too close to their territory. They stay pretty close to home for the most part, allowing only female merchants in occasionally for trade."

"I heard about that whole raiding party business when I was in Tanohar," said Flaskamper. "They say there that the Saebrilite women will come over the mountain range just to the south, and abduct travelers on the outskirts of the kingdom. I always thought that story was just so much dung. Maybe I was wrong."

"It would make sense," said Stamford. "The Hiang Mountains are just behind the stacks. You can just about see one or two of the peaks on the horizon. They're supposed to be impassable, but the Saebrilites may know a way through. If so, that would make Tanohar by far the closest accessible kingdom, though I've heard stories of Saebrilite encounters as far away as Oraque. Since I don't know anyone who has dealt with them personally, there's no way of knowing what's truth and what's legend. One thing I *do* know for sure – I don't want us to be the ones to find out. I suggest we turn south right now."

They turned and began traveling due south. For nearly two marks, they saw nothing except a lone mountain hawk flying high overhead. However, just as they had begun to think they had skirted disaster, they began to hear a rumbling in the distance – the pounding of horses' hooves on the hard clay ground. Soon Rokey spotted them in the distance, his new sidhe eyes picking them out long before the others could see anything except a far-off dust cloud.

"It looks like seven – no, eight of them, coming our way at top speed," Rokey told them. "They look well-armed with both blades and bows."

As the company was on foot, there was no way to outrun them, and no place to hide out on the open flats. Their choices were to fight or surrender. Flaskamper was all for the fight, but Stamford surprised him by shaking his head.

"The Saebrilites would not hesitate to kill us if we were to resist them. Granted, we'd take a few of them with us but, assuming that they mean to take us prisoner, I think we ought to go quietly and live to fight another day. We'll find some means of escape."

"You mean we should just stand here and do nothing?" Flaskamper asked in astonishment.

"Not at all," Stamford replied, "I suggest instead that we employ a little strategy. Fia, *you* are now officially in charge of this troupe. I have a feeling that that will greatly increase our chances of survival. When you deal with them, be friendly but firm. We'll all be sufficiently deferential."

"Do you think they'll buy it?" asked Fia.

Stamford laughed.

"Let's face it, I'm only in charge here as long as you let me be. We're just going to make it official for a while. Don't overdo the toadying, men – that would give us away. I don't think the Saebrilites will find a woman in charge of a band of mercenaries to be an incredible notion, though, because it isn't. I've met one or two in my day. Just remember to keep your tempers in check, whatever happens."

Stamford looked pointedly at Flaskamper during that last remark.

"Alright, alright," said the elf, holding up his hand. "I get the message."

It wasn't long before the Saebrilite riders caught up with them. Rokey studied them in awe. Each of the women was well above an average woman's size, the largest standing nearly as tall as Lorq. Their torsos were completely naked, except for the decorative necklaces that a few of them wore, made from the teeth of some large animal. Four of them were armed with longswords, and the other four with bows and arrows, which they now had trained on him and his companions. All wore skirts made of long, dark leather strips with metal studs on the ends and leather guards covering their shins and forearms. Perched upon the leather-clad forearm of one warrior was a mountain hawk, which Rokey suspected was the one they had spotted earlier, circling above them. The horses they rode were magnificent giants with large, shaggy manes. Their colors varied from white, to grey, to chestnut brown.

Fia stepped forward to face the eight women, raising her hands in a gesture of peace.

"I greet you, sisters," she said confidently. "I am Fia, the leader of this party. I know you to be Saebrilites of the Linonjar Stacks. I apologize if we have trespassed onto your lands. I had thought our route veered far enough to the south to avoid your territory."

One of the Saebrilites, a striking woman with dark red hair, urged her horse forward a step.

"I am Hethra," she said. "We will spare you the indignity of disarming you, but your males must surrender their weapons immediately. Then you must all accompany us back to Braeden's Keep, where our chieftain will decide what consequence your incursion merits. *You* may ride with me if you wish. The males must walk, but may remain unbound, so long as they offer no resistance."

Fia glanced at Stamford, who nodded almost imperceptibly.

"Very well," Fia responded, "though I protest being detained in this way. I have urgent business to the west of here."

"It is not in my power to allow you to continue," Hethra answered shortly, offering her hand to assist Fia. Fia took it and swung up onto the huge horse. She felt like a little child, sitting in front of the giant Saebrilite. Another of the women dismounted and collected the men's weapons in a large sack. When this was done, they all started off north toward the Linonjar Stacks.

The troupe marched along at a brisk pace that the four men found exhausting. Nevertheless they persevered, not wishing to show weakness to the Saebrilites. There was a brief stop for food and water, then they were underway again. During the trip, Stamford noticed that one of the women kept eyeing Lorq. She was a beauty, with raven hair and bright blue eyes. During the rest stop, he brought her to Lorq's attention.

"It looks like she might be interested in you, old buddy," Stamford told the giant. "See if you can flirt with her a little. It might help us later on."

"I don't know how to flirt, Stamford," Lorq told him.

"Look, there's nothing to it. Just smile at her and make eye contact. You don't want to try to talk to her now. That would just attract the attention of the others. We don't want that. Just look at her and smile for now. That shouldn't be too hard. She's pretty easy on the eyes, eh?"

"She's very pretty," said Lorq, "but do you really think she likes me? I thought you said the Saebrilite women were all samers."

"Maybe they're supposed to be," Stamford replied, "but that doesn't necessarily mean that they are. Remember, people don't choose to be what they are. They just are."

"All right, Stamford," said Lorq. "I'll smile at her."

"Good man," said Stamford, thumping him on the back.

Darkness had begun to fall as they reached the Linonjar Stacks. Rokey assumed that they would camp for the night before venturing in, but to his surprise, they kept moving, weaving amongst the strange, jutting cliffs until they had lost all of the remaining light. Rokey, who could still see everything clear as day, wondered if the Saebrilites also had some sort of special night vision. Then, one of the warriors lifted a large hunting horn, and blew a call that echoed throughout the hills. A few moments later, they were met by several more Saebrilite women, on foot and bearing torches, who guided them up a rough path hewn into one of the steep cliffsides. At the top of the stack, they came to a heavily walled fortress of grey stone. It reminded Rokey a little of the stone that made up the bridge in Glimmermere, rough and solid looking.

"Braeden's Keep," said Hethra. "Our home."

In response to their arrival, the heavy iron portcullis was raised, and the group made their way swiftly into the massive enclosure. They rode, men in tow, through the Saebrilite city. In its center was a large amphitheater. In response to Fia's query, Hethra explained that games and contests were an important part of the Saebrilite culture, and that the amphitheater was busy throughout the year. They veered off to the left, to a large stable, and dismounted, turning their tired horses over to the stable hands who came out to meet them. These were all women. There was not a single male in sight anywhere.

Hethra ordered four of her warriors to escort the four men to a holding area.

"Wait a moment," Fia protested. "What are you planning to do with them?"

With everyone now on foot, she was acutely aware of the huge disadvantage they had in this realm of giant women. She wondered whether Stamford's decision had been the right one after all.

"Do not worry about them," said Hethra. "They will be fed and given a comfortable place to sleep. However, they will not be free to roam about. That is not our way."

"And what of me?" Fia asked.

"Our chieftain, Lorinda, will wish to speak with you. If you had been male, we would have taken you all without negotiation, but your being a woman changes things. It may be that we will compensate you in some way for the loss of your males."

"And suppose I do not wish to 'lose' my males?" Fia asked.

"It is unlikely that you will be allowed to keep them," Hethra said. "Your males meet a certain need we have at present. But it is not for me to decide such things. That is for you and Lorinda to discuss."

They walked from the stable back the way they had come. Now Fia noticed an immense statue of a beautiful nude woman directly ahead of them. Her white marble form reflected the light from the torches which burned all around the keep, lending her a warm, lifelike glow. In one of her hands, the woman held a large chalice, in the other – a sword.

"That is Saebril," Hethra told her, "our matron goddess."

"She's lovely," Fia remarked.

"She is indeed," said Hethra proudly. "She embodies those things for which we all strive – the balance of beauty and strength, of hospitality and defense."

"I see," said Fia. "Kidnapping me and imprisoning my men is the Saebrilite idea of hospitality?"

"Our hospitality does not extend to the male gender. In our culture, their function is to serve our purposes. As for you, once you have spoken to Lorinda, you shall no doubt be free to go if you wish. But as long as you remain and cause us no harm, I can assure you that you will be treated as an honored guest, as are all females who visit us."

"But why bring us all the way here?" Fia persisted. "Why not simply let us pass? We were doing you no harm where we were."

Hethra was silent for a moment.

"The needs of the realm," she explained at last, "must always be our primary concern. It would not be my place to say any more than that. Lorinda will explain, or not, as she sees fit. This way."

They approached the door to a large building located just inside the main gate. The guard at the door raised her hand in a salute as they passed. Inside, they proceeded down a short, bare corridor, then made an abrupt left turn. There was a closed door there with a plain wooden bench just outside it. Hethra gestured toward the bench.

"Sit here and wait," she said. "I must go in and make my report first."

Fia sat down as the Saebrilite rapped quickly on the door, then entered. The doors were thick and heavy, so she could hear no voices coming from the other side. A quartermark or so later, the door opened and Hethra motioned Fia inside. She stood and entered a spacious room, sparsely appointed with simple wooden furniture – two desks at right angles to each other and four chairs. The only other feature of the room was a long rack, on which hung a variety of spears, swords, battle axes and other instruments of death.

Lorinda was standing at the window. Upon Fia's entrance, the Saebrilite chieftain turned and studied her closely, probably trying to assess the truth about her claim that she was the leader of this party of men. Fia studied her in return. She was not a beautiful woman, but *was* striking in appearance, with long reddish blonde hair pulled back into a single tight braid, a straight, sloping nose and piercing, blue-grey eyes. At last, the Saebrilite seemed to have reached some conclusion, for she gave a single sharp nod of her head. The expression on her face remained constant – neither welcoming nor hostile.

"I am Lorinda," she said. She did not invite Fia to sit. "I am the present chieftain of Braeden's Keep. I will not keep you long, as you are no doubt weary from your journey, but I see no point in keeping you in suspense of your situation. You and your males were caught on the southern edge of our territory. You claim to have been there unintentionally. Perhaps that is true...perhaps not. It makes no difference. You were captured in our realm and are therefore now subject to its laws. One of those laws is that all males are wards of the realm."

"And what does it mean, exactly, to be a *ward of the realm*?" Fia asked.

"Simply put...it means that they may be used, with or without their consent, for whatever purposes are deemed most useful to us."

"I see," Fia said, trying to remain calm. "Tell me, chieftain, what precisely is the difference between a ward of the realm and a common slave?"

Lorinda regarded her coolly.

"Hethra will show you to quarters," she said, ignoring her question. "You are not a prisoner here, and are free to move about as you choose, so long as you violate none of our laws."

"I would prefer to stay with my men," Fia told her.

Lorinda shrugged.

"As you wish," she said, "but only for tonight. They are in a temporary holding area now. Tomorrow they will join the rest of the male population and be given assignments and corresponding quarters. After that, we shall determine what is just compensation for your hardship."

"There is no just compensation for the enslavement of my friends!" Fia said, her ire rising.

The chieftain smiled tightly, but there was no warmth in it.

"Our cultures differ," she said, "and if we did not have need of your males, I should have been tempted to let your incursion pass. But such is not the case. We are short of workers at present, especially in the mines, and they may also possess traits that make them suitable for fertilization duty."

"Fertilization duty?" Fia cried. "This is outrageous! How can you treat people this way, like – like breeding stock?"

"It is not my intention to waste time attempting to justify our ways to you." Lorinda said sharply. "It would serve no purpose. The males of our population are very well treated, at least, those who remain cooperative. Those chosen for fertilization duty are treated better still. Most consider it a privilege. "

"And what if those chosen do not care to breed with your women?" Fia asked. "What if they do not care to breed with any women at all?"

"A breeder's sexual proclivities are irrelevant," Lorinda explained. "Our women, well, let us say the vast majority of our women, view copulation with males as a distasteful duty, but one that must be done for the continuation of the realm. As to our males, many of them choose to have relationships amongst themselves, whether they are samers by nature or not. So long as it does not interfere with their duties, we do not interfere with these liaisons."

"How generous of you," Fia remarked dryly.

"As I said," the Saebrilite snapped, "we shall discuss your compensation further tomorrow. If you elect to refuse the offer at that time, then that is your prerogative."

"Lorinda," Fia begged, "is there no way that I can appeal to you to let my men go with me in peace? We have done you no harm, and I give you my word, we will never trespass again in your territories. We are on an urgent mission, the outcome of which may affect all of Firma. It is vital that we be allowed to continue. Please – won't you reconsider?"

She saw the chieftain's expression soften ever so slightly, then she breathed out a small sigh. For a moment, Fia had hopes that she might relent. But the woman shook her head.

"Whatever my personal inclinations in the matter might be," she said, "my first duty is to my realm, and my realm right now is needful of males. I am sorry, Fia, but that concludes the matter. Until tomorrow."

Lorinda turned back to the window. Hethra opened the door, and Fia preceded her out. She was *damned* if that concluded the matter, but she knew that no more could be accomplished tonight. They would devise a means of escaping this fortress, however long it may take.

Hethra said nothing as she led Fia to the holding area, where her friends were confined. It was a small building with a single barred window on the right hand side and only one door, guarded by two armed warriors. Hethra ordered one of the guards to open the door, then turned to Fia.

"Are you certain that you want to stay here?" Hethra inquired. "I shall not return until morning, and the guards will not open the door for you should you change your mind."

"I'm certain, thank you," Fia replied.

Hethra turned to leave, but then paused.

"I realize that your inclination will be to attempt to help your friends escape," she said. "I cannot say that I blame you, and were I in your situation, I might well be considering the same thing. However, I must caution you that we would not take such an attempt lightly. It is possible that it would result in your own imprisonment. As for your males...let me just warn you – corporeal punishment is used sparingly in Braeden's Keep, but it is used. I advise you to keep that in mind."

Hethra left. The guard opened the door for Fia to enter. She was surprised to see another door just beyond it.

"You must enter first," the guard explained. "When the outer door has been secured, the inner door will open."

Fia stepped into the tiny anteroom, and the door closed and locked behind her. A moment later, there was a click, and the metal door in front of her slid heavily to the side. The room behind it was large, and dimly lit by several torches that were protected from tampering by heavy iron latticework covers. The room was quiet. The rest of the company was asleep, all curled up on the large straw mats covering the floor. Well, she couldn't blame them. She was exhausted herself, and she had been on horseback the better part of the day. The thought filled her with sorrow, then with anger. She was *not* going to allow this to happen.

"Stamford, Lorq, boys...wake up!" she whispered. "We've got planning to do, and tonight might well be our one and only chance to do it."

Chapter 21:

Long Days

R okey hefted a large chunk of white, powdery stone onto his shoulder and carried it across the cavern floor, about fifty feet, before dumping it, with a grunt, into the large, wooden cart. It was mid-afternoon, and he had been in the mine since early that morning. He was filthy – the thick, white dust mixed with his sweat to form a gritty paste that covered all of his naked torso. From the waist down he wore the thin, muslin pants issued to all the miners at the beginning of the day. At night, they were made to strip naked and wash thoroughly, and were then given their after-work clothes to put on. It was a humiliating process, but Rokey had now grown accustomed to it. It had been two weeks since they were captured by the Saebrilites and brought to Braeden's Keep. It seemed to Rokey like two years, yet he remembered their first night like it was yesterday.

* * *

When Fia had gone off with Hethra, the men had been herded to a small stone building with bars on the one window. The guard unlocked a door, then pulled down a lever that jutted out from the front wall. They saw a second door slide open inside. The guards took their packs from them and ordered them in. The room was large enough, lit dimly with torches, the floor covered with straw mats. A wide clay pot, the purpose of which was obvious, sat in a corner. Then one of the guards stuck her head inside the door.

"We will bring you something to eat," she said. "The door is well-guarded at all times, so escape will be impossible. If you should think of somehow taking a hostage, do not bother. We do not bargain for hostages. I advise you to get some rest. It is likely that your days will be extremely busy from tomorrow on."

She departed and the inner door slid closed. They heard the outer door close and lock also. Stamford went and looked out the window, then they made a closer examination of the room. There was nothing apparent that could assist them in escaping.

"Well," said Flaskamper, "we sure in blazes are in up to our necks this time. We should have fought. I bet we could've taken them."

Stamford bit back an angry retort. Flash had a legitimate point, just one with which he happened to disagree.

"Possibly," he argued, "but I seriously doubt it. Chances are we'd be dead and our quest would be over. Going by what the guard said, they likely mean to use us as laborers. That means we still stand a chance of escape. If Fia handles herself well, she will hopefully remain free, and can help us."

"It's not going to be easy," said Flaskamper. "These women are battle ready all the time. How many of them do you think there are?"

"A keep this size," replied Stamford, "I'd say as many as five, maybe even ten thousand – if it's occupied to capacity. We won't know for sure how many until we get out and about though, or what the ratio of men to women is."

"I wonder how the men are treated here," Rokey wondered.

"We'll find out soon enough," said Stamford.

Soon another guard came with bread, cheese and water for them. Stamford sniffed the water suspiciously, but declared it safe. They ate and drank quietly, none of them able to muster the energy for conversation. It was useless to try and plan an escape, at least not until they saw Fia and could get some more information about their situation. Despite Flaskamper's earlier comment, the elf knew that they had made the right decision. Though frustrated and humiliated, they were still alive. Somehow they would find their way out of this mess.

After supper, Stamford suggested that they take the guard's advice and try to get some sleep.

"We don't know when Fia will return," said Stamford, "and there's no point in just sitting here staring at one another."

They all lay down on the straw mats that covered the floor. The long, fast-paced march caught up with them all then, and they fell almost immediately asleep. A short time later, they were awakened by Fia's urgent whisper.

"Stamford, Lorq, boys...wake up!" she whispered. "We've got planning to do, and tonight might well be our one and only chance to do it."

When they were all awake, she sat down on the floor and they all gathered around her.

"What happened?" Flaskamper asked. "What did you find out?

Fia filled them in on her conversation with Lorinda, as well as Hethra's warning.

"Breed – with them?" said Flaskamper. "I'd rather be buggered by a troll!"

"Well, hopefully we won't have to worry about that right away," said Fia. "What concerns me more immediately is where they'll be assigning you to work. She mentioned a mine – "

"What kind of mine," Stamford asked, his eyes abruptly grew bright and fearful – a look that Rokey had never seen on him before.

"I don't know," Fia said, "Lorinda didn't say."

"Fia, you know I can never go into a mine again," said Stamford.

Of course, Rokey realized, *Stamford's years in the salt mine. They must have left him with a fear of such places.*

"I will *not* let them send you to the mine, Stamford" Fia insisted. "I have already thought it out. Lorinda has offered to compensate me for taking you. I shall insist that my compensation be her promise to keep you from the mine – all of you if I can manage it, but definitely you, Stamford."

The dark man relaxed a bit, but his eyes still held the look of a wild animal, backed into a hole.

"I didn't get much of a chance to look around," said Fia. "It's dark, and I was accompanied all the time. I'm afraid we're going to have to play along as best we can, and keep our eyes and ears open for a means of escape. I've been told that I can remain here as long as I want, so long as I behave. I've been thinking, perhaps I should do more than behave. Perhaps I should let myself be captivated by this Saebrilite lifestyle – "

"You mean so that they begin to trust you," said Rokey.

"Exactly," Fia said. "I'm sure that they won't trust me entirely, but if I appear to embrace their culture, they may relax enough so that I can move a bit more freely. That could be crucial, especially if you four are separated. The more access I have to you all, the better."

"Good point," said Stamford. "I think you're on the right track. Now, is there anything else we can do, any strategy we can focus on in the near term?"

"The four of us should get friendly with as many of the men as we can," Flaskamper suggested, "find out if there are any potential allies among them. There's bound to be some that have contemplated escape. And even those that haven't still know this place inside and out. That information will help us."

"Good boy," said Stamford. "We'll be friendly with everyone, and I mean everyone. Even the guards. No matter how they treat you, you smile back, got it? We don't want to give them any reason to think we're a threat until we have a way out of here."

"Assuming I have access to all of you," said Fia, "one of my jobs will be to disseminate whatever information each of us learns, so that we're all in the loop. I'll try to arrange as many visits with each of you as I can."

"Yes, but don't overdo it," said Stamford. "You want to give them the impression that you're being enticed into their lifestyle. It would seem suspicious if you lost interest in us entirely, but you don't want to seem like you're on a mission either."

"Agreed," said Fia, "I'll try to strike the proper balance."

"I'm sure you'll be brilliant," Stamford said. "Well, I think that's all we can do for right now. Just remember, no piece of information is unimportant. Learn about everything and everyone. Now, we'd better get some rest. As the guard said, we're bound to have a busy day ahead of us tomorrow."

*   *   *

A shout from the guard roused Rokey from his reverie. He went back to loading the cart with more blocks of the heavy white rock, which they had learned was called Saebrilore, that the other crew had earlier chiseled free from the mountain. His mind, however, remained on that first day, and the days that had since passed.

*   *   *

Fia had asked to be taken to Lorinda when the guard brought their breakfast. Apparently she had met with limited success. Stamford was not assigned to the mines, but to the kitchens. Lorq, who was deemed too large for mine work, was given stable duty. Rokey and Flaskamper were not so fortunate. They were taken to the mines, shown the routine, which was relatively simple, and put to work. Though the labor was grueling and dirty, the two boys were at least glad to still be together. They were usually assigned to different sections of the mine, so they seldom saw each other during the day, but they spent the nights together, curled up in one another's arms.

Fia came every two or three days after dinner, filling them in on all she and the others had learned. So far they hadn't found anything that would help them form a plan of escape, but they all kept at it, storing all information away in case something should prove useful later on. She told them that the Saebrilites were still distrustful, but had begun to open up some. As promised, she was treated as an honored guest, and given the run of the keep, though certain sections, like the armory, were always guarded and off limits to any unauthorized persons. However, she had the entire place mapped out, and little by little, was passing the layout on to her friends.

"I don't know when," she told him and Flash one day, "but knowing this is going to prove valuable one of these days."

Meanwhile, he and Flaskamper were getting to know the other men on the mining detail. They were surprised at how many samers there were amongst the general male population, and each of the boys had already been approached numerous times by men with romantic intentions. Though it would no doubt have benefited them to take advantage of some of these opportunities, in the end, they could not bring themselves to consider having sex with anyone else. They would politely explain the situation to would-be lovers and most, though disappointed, were understanding.

Others were not. One day, shortly after they arrived, two of the larger men had grabbed Rokey in the shower room and pushed him up against the wall, intent on raping him. They had assumed that Flaskamper, with his slight build, would be no impediment to them. They were wrong. As the men held Rokey, forcing his legs apart, one of them felt a tap on his shoulder. He turned around and saw the elf, naked and dripping wet, standing in front of him, his eyes burning with fury. A derisive comment was halfway out of the man's mouth when, the next second, he was on the ground, doubled in two from a brutal blow to his midsection. The second man let go of Rokey and rushed at Flaskamper. The elf stood his ground and, at the appropriate moment, sprung into the air, impossibly high for a human, and kicked the man squarely in the face. He grunted, and fell like a stone. Flaskamper took Rokey protectively in his arms, and other men gathered around them. Many of *them* had suffered the same fate at the hands of the two bullies, only no one had been there to rescue them. By the time the guards looked in, they saw nothing out of place except the pair of thwarted ruffians, picking themselves up from the shower room floor; one was cradling his broken, bloody nose. The guards assumed that the two had been fighting one another. When the men pointed Flaskamper out as the culprit, the women took one look at the slender elf and burst out laughing. They then hauled the battered pair roughly away for punishment.

Neither of the boys were bothered after that. In fact, the incident greatly increased their popularity, especially among the more timid males, who came to look upon Flaskamper as something of a hero. They used this to what advantage they could, but were ultimately surprised by how little resentment existed among the males toward the Saebrilite women. Most of them were native born and had few, if any, thoughts of trying to leave; they were actually happy in their situation. After attempting for over a week to ferret out some level of resistance, the two began to realize that, for most of these men, this was the only kind of life they had ever known.

There was at least one exception though, a man named Thanop. He was a burly fellow, with curly graying hair, a patch over his missing right eye and a large scar across his cheek. He had been quick to let them know that he was not a samer, that his wife and three children had been left behind when he was captured by the Saebrilites some twenty years before. Since that time, Thanop had made several attempts to escape, once getting nearly all the way to Tanohar before being recaptured. When Flaskamper had asked him what the consequences of his captures had been, the man had showed them his back, which was covered with long, thin scars.

"They don't use the whip very often," he had told them, "but when they do, they lay on hard."

When Flaskamper had mentioned their interest in escape, Thanop had simply shaken his head.

"I'll give you all the help I can, short of actually going," he said. "In my twenty years here I've never known anyone to escape, nor do I know anyone who has known anyone. It's a lost cause, boys. Trust me, I've found out...the hard way."

Another interesting thing Rokey had learned from Thanop was the nature of the rock that they were mining.

"They call it *Saebrilore*," Thanop said. "It's what makes the Saebrilite women grow big and strong like they are. They grind the stuff up and eat it every day."

"They're not born that way?" Rokey exclaimed. "You mean that anyone can become a Saebrilite?"

"Not exactly," the man explained. "First off, it only works on women. For men, it's no better than salt. The other thing is, you have to start young; no more than five or six. Older than that, it'll give them a kick, but it won't produce a Saebrilite warrior."

"That's amazing," said Rokey. "So Saebrilite women bear normal-sized children."

"That's right," Thanop replied. "They start the girls on the Saebrilore as soon as they're on solid food, but before that, they're just like the boys... just like any other human babies in Firma in fact."

The one encouraging thing they had discovered was that breeding only took place on certain, special occasions. Apparently the right to mate with the man of one's choice was highly prized amongst the Saebrilite women. On these special days, the women participated in games and contests of strength and agility, the winners of which would be allowed their pick of males. One of the men who was often fiercely competed for, a handsome blonde named Yuli, also worked in the mines, and was happy to share what information he could with them.

"They're called Union Festivals," Yuli told them. "It has actually been some time since the last one, so I expect there will be another soon. For the whole day, five hundred women compete in the arena for the right to mate with whatever man they choose. The winners and their prizes then go off alone for three days to conceive a new crop of Saebrilite children. All of the women of Braeden's Keep attend the festival, except for the perimeter guards of course. Even a few of the older men, ones who are no longer considered of mating age, are allowed to come and watch. It is quite a jovial day. They drink lots of wine, even share it with *us*. Granted, some of them do that because they need to be drunk in order to have sex with a man. But don't be fooled by the rhetoric. Many of our women enjoy it. More than would openly admit it. I should know. I'm considered something of a trophy, and have mated with many. And between Union Festivals, there are always plenty of lonely lads to keep me busy."

He winked at them mischievously.

"Doesn't it bother you?" Rokey had asked him, "being...bred, like that?"

Yuli laughed.

"I suppose you *could* look at it like that. Outsiders often do, at least in the beginning. But I was born here. Being a native, it's perfectly natural to me."

*   *   *

The cart was now full. Rokey called to the guard, letting her know that it was ready to be hauled away. The guard called two other men over, who each grabbed one of the front wagon shafts and began to tow it from the cavern. Horses were not used, because they were considered too expensive and valuable for such mundane labor. A few moments later, another empty wagon was brought in, and Rokey began filling that one too.

At the end of the day, the miners all returned to the small shed just at the mouth of the cave where they checked their tools and clothing. Rokey was glad to see Flaskamper, also covered in white muck, emerge from where he had been working, chiseling the stone somewhere deeper in the mountain. He worried when Flash pulled deep mine duty, afraid that one day there might be a cave-in. Others had assured him that there had been no cave-ins in recent memory, but that did little to assuage his fears.

The two boys shared a brief, gritty kiss before they stripped down and headed for the showers. This might have been one of the more pleasant parts of the day were the water not freezing cold much of the time. As it was, they scrubbed the layers of grit and grime off as quickly as they could, then hurried from the room to towel off, dress, and head for the men's dining hall for supper. Like every evening,

Flaskamper took Rokey's hand as they walked. It was one of the little things that Rokey looked forward to as he chiseled, loaded or hauled the backbreaking chunks of Saebrilore all day long.

Two weeks. Two bloody weeks.

He wondered what it would be like in two months...or two years.

Don't, he scolded himself. *Don't think like that. We're going to get out of here soon.*

Flaskamper squeezed his hand, as if sensing his thoughts. The elf had been quieter since their capture, more introspective. In fact it had been Rokey that had been responsible for conducting most of the conversations with the other men there since their arrival. The change was beginning to alarm Rokey. That night, as they lay cuddling in their two beds, which they pushed together each night, he asked Flaskamper about his reticence.

"It's being trapped here, *chatka*," the elf explained, "having no control. I know it bothers you too, but you've managed to make the best of it – to use the time to our advantage. I thought at first that I'd be able to do the same. No problem. Instead, I'm finding it's all I can do to just get through each day. Every morning, I feel as though a hood has been slipped over my head, suffocating and strangling me. Each hour is like an eternity, especially when I'm down there deep in the mines. I can see why Stamford is crazed at the prospect of being sent into one again. If I'd been down as long as he was, I'd be half mad at the prospect too. With me, I don't know where it comes from, but ever since I was little, I've hated feeling trapped. It's one of the reasons I was so eager to leave home. Sometimes even there, I'd have this same feeling, more and more often as I grew older. Not as bad as now. It's never felt this bad before. As it is, the only time I feel truly able to breathe is at night, when I'm here with you. You're my sanity, *chatka*. You're the rock I'm leaning on to get through this."

Rokey kissed him tenderly. Flaskamper responded by pulling Rokey tightly against him. The elf's hands slid down Rokey's back, then down into his shorts, cupping his buttocks, and he begun to kiss him more passionately. Rokey felt self-conscious. There had been little sexual activity between them since their capture. The other men there were accustomed to having sex under the watchful eyes of their roommates, but neither Rokey nor Flaskamper had felt comfortable in that environment. While his lover was apparently beginning to overcome his shyness in this regard, Rokey wasn't sure he could manage it.

"Flash," he whispered, "Flash, we can't. You know there are people watching."

"I don't care," the elf responded. "I need you. Please, Rokey. Please make love with me. I need to so much tonight."

It was a plea so full of longing that Rokey couldn't bring himself to refuse it.

Oh, bugger it, he thought, and shoved Flaskamper onto his back. With a single yank, he slid his lover's shorts off, then quickly shed his own and climbed on top of him.

"If we're going to put on a show," Rokey said, smothering the astonished elf with kisses, "let's give them one worth watching."

Flaskamper was all too happy to cooperate.

*   *   *

That same night, Fia lay on the bed in her quarters, staring up at the ceiling. The moon shone through the window, glinting off the tears that rolled down her cheeks.

For the past two weeks she had racked her brains, trying to think of some way for them to escape. She had explored every bit of the keep, and questioned the women about every facet of their culture, trying to find some weakness that they could exploit in order to gain their freedom. So far though, she had come up empty. The Saebrilites ran a tight operation. They were happy, unified, and disciplined. It was starting to seem hopeless, and Fia's optimism was beginning to crack, at least in the privacy of her own quarters.

Luckily, it seemed as though the others were doing alright, as far as she could tell anyway. Lorq was focusing his attentions on the care of the horses, the boys had one another to help them cope with the conditions in the mines, and Stamford – well, there she wasn't quite as certain. He was putting on a brave face during her visits with him, but she could see the strain this was inflicting on him. His years in the mines of Hattiar had nearly broken him, and though her negotiations had spared him the agony of returning to that specific environment, captivity of any kind was a torture for him. In addition, though Stamford had a healthy respect for women, Fia was quite sure that, for a man of his upbringing, the fact that his captors were female was bound to rub even more salt in the wound. It was not something he would admit to, not even to himself perhaps, but she knew it was there, chipping away at his dignity.

As she lay there, lost in thought, a knock sounded on the door. Surprised, Fia hurried to answer it. Behind the door stood a woman that Fia recognized instantly. She had been a member of the party who had captured them. Stamford had told Fia that the girl had seemed interested in Lorq, and that he had encouraged him to flirt with her, to the extent that the bashful giant could manage anyway. They found out later that her name was Kyzee, and since Lorq had been assigned to the stables, he'd reported that she had visited him there on several occasions. According to Lorq, they had not talked of anything important. She had seemed interested in life outside of Braeden's Keep. The giant had also blushingly admitted that he thought that the Saebrilite girl was indeed sweet on him. She had mentioned an upcoming Union Festival, and had told him of her intention to compete for the rights to be with him. When Fia had explained to him what that entailed, Lorq's eyes had grown wide, and he had turned even redder.

That had been nearly a week ago. Now Fia would swear that this was the young woman standing before her, looking furtive and fearful.

"We have not met," she said when Fia greeted her, "but I must speak with you. My name is Kyzee."

"I know," said Fia. "You have made a friend of Lorq, I believe."

Kyzee's eyes met Fia's, and a hint of a smile touched her lips.

"So he has told you about me," she said.

"Yes," said Fia. "He says that he enjoys your visits very much."

"I, too, enjoy his company," said the Saebrilite, then looked quickly about her. "May I come in? I would as soon not be seen here, for I have something private I wish to discuss with you."

"Then by all means, come in," said Fia, "and tell me what is on your mind."

Kyzee stepped inside and Fia shut the door behind her, then went to the window and drew the curtain.

"There," she said. "Now we shall have some privacy. Please, sit down."

The girl sat on the bed, wringing her hands in distress. Fia gave her a few moments to collect herself.

"I'm not sure how to begin," Kyzee said finally. "I fear that you will think that I am some kind of spy, sent here to worm your intentions out of you, and I have no means by which to prove otherwise. But it is important that I persuade you to trust me."

"Now, now," said Fia, "Why don't you just go ahead and tell me why you've come. I promise to keep an open mind."

Reassured, the Saebrilite launched into her story.

"For some time now," she began, "since the end of childhood really, I have felt – out of place here at Braeden's Keep. I didn't know why at first, just that something did not feel quite right. Other girls my age had already begun to have their first love affairs, beginning the process of finding a life partner. That is the normal course of events for a young Saebrilite woman. But when the time came for me, I had no interest in it. Other girls pursued me, but I wanted none of them. They eventually said of me that I was just conceited, that I considered myself too great a prize for them, but that was not it at all. I simply wanted nothing to do with love and relationships."

Fia listened patiently, her hopes beginning to climb. If Kyzee was going where she suspected she was with this – "

"Go on, dear," said Fia gently.

"But then, when your party was captured, and I set eyes on Lorq... I – I don't know how to describe it. It was as though something inside me...awoke. He was so handsome, and his eyes – his eyes looked so gentle and kind. And later, he smiled at me, and I thought – I thought I would fall off my horse!"

Fia laughed, and Kyzee laughed with her.

"I know that outside of Braeden's Keep, it is common for women to fall in love with men," she continued, "but here, it would be considered wrong...an aberration. While it is true that many of the women actually enjoy the process of mating with the men, more than would ever admit to it, it would be nearly unthinkable for one of them to actually fall in love with a – a *male*. And yet...that seems to be exactly what – what I've done."

Kyzee's large blue eyes were bright with tears. Fia took her by the hand to comfort her.

"You're right," she told the Saebrilite, "throughout the rest of Firma, it is perfectly normal for men and women to fall in love. In fact, in many places now, it doesn't make any difference at all whether you fall in love with a man, a woman or a duck. People are allowed to love whomever they want. Not everywhere yet, but things are steadily progressing. And I was joking about the duck."

Kyzee laughed again.

"It sounds wonderful," she said, "and Lorq tells me so many other extraordinary things when I visit him. It has started me thinking that, well, perhaps I would be better off there, rather than here."

"Kyzee," Fia said slowly, "are you suggesting – "

The Saebrilite nodded.

"I want to help you free Lorq, and your other friends," she said, "on the condition that, when you go, you allow me to go with you."

Chapter 22:

Gambit

T he day of the Union Festival came only two weeks later. Women began to arrive at the arena at sunrise, in order to get the best seats. A small section was reserved for Lorinda and her personal guests, but the rest were open, and whoever was first to arrive got their pick. Food and wine had been prepared the previous day, and would be brought round the aisles throughout the day by males who, for whatever reason, had not been selected to mate. The preliminaries began early, those being young girls, too young to compete for actual mates, but eager to participate in the celebrations. Their athletic competitions filled up the early morning slots. The real action began at mid-morning, after the sounding of the game horn.

Shortly before the horn was to sound, Fia entered the arena and took a seat near one of the exits. She stayed to the rear to avoid being spotted by Lorinda. She was afraid that the Saebrilite chieftain might invite her to sit with her entourage, up front near the field. This would make it nearly impossible for her to slip away when the time came. Other women, a few with men in tow, continued to pour in, until the arena was filled nearly to capacity. Fia wasn't sure how many people this amphitheater was built to hold, but she suspected that Stamford had underestimated the keep's population by perhaps several thousand.

The game horn sounded, and the women and men all took their seats. An older woman carrying a bullhorn walked alone to the center of the field.

"Saebrilites... women, and privileged males," she shouted, "I bid you welcome to our autumn Union Festival." The crowd cheered. "We have a fine group of strong young women today, eager and – one hopes – fertile, competing for the rights to choose from, I must say, an above average crop of accommodating males."

The crowd roared again. The older woman strode from one end of the field to the other, encouraging the applause.

"Five hundred women," she continued. "Two hundred males. Some will leave disappointed, others will go happily, having won their choice of mates, and three days to conceive Braeden's Keeps newest citizens!" More cheers. "But before we begin our contests, let us have a look at the prizes! Bring in the males!"

Amid the roar of the crowd, the men were brought onto the field. All of them were shirtless, and wore clean white muslin pants and leather sandals. It was indeed a fine-looking group. Fia spotted Lorq easily, as he towered above the other men. A moment later, she spotted Stamford, looking embarrassed and humiliated. Flaskamper and Rokey, however, were nowhere to be seen. That was odd. Why wouldn't they be amongst the eligible males? This was not good. Their plan had been formed with the idea that all four of them would be here. Oh well, there was nothing to do now but wait. She would not be able to talk with Kyzee to rework things until after her contest had finished.

After the hoots and hollers of the crowd had died down some, the mistress of ceremonies continued.

"As is the tradition of our Union Festivals," she shouted, "the premier event will be the First Season Challenge. This autumn we have five young women who are participating in our mating contests for the very first time – five lucky young women, who shall have the cream of this festival's crop. The competition is a footrace, the winner of which shall have first choice among all of these fine young males. The second place winner shall have second choice, and on down the line, and while it is certainly an honor to win, I guarantee that none of these girls will be – dissatisfied. Now let us introduce this festival's first timers – Lazia, Kyzee, Mirra, Estrann and Diel!"

The five young women came out to the cheering crowd, bowed, then took their places at the track which ringed the arena. Kyzee had told Fia that this was to be a double lap footrace, and that she felt reasonably confident of winning. While victory was an honor, it was not something for which a girl would normally train hard, since each First Timer invariably wound up with an excellent choice. For Kyzee, however, winning Lorq was crucial to their plans, and thus to her chance at future happiness. She had been training fiercely since they had formulated the plan two weeks previously.

As the women crouched on their marks, Fia saw money changing hands around her. Apparently a few side wagers were also a part of this time-honored tradition. A moment later, the gong sounded and they were off. Mirra was off like a filly, taking an early lead, but with a two-lap race, an early lead was not necessarily an indication of victory. It was important to pace oneself, to avoid tiring at the critical final stretch. Kyzee ran at a steady pace falling behind two more of the girls, but not too far behind. As they rounded the first corner of the oval-shaped track, she was in fourth place. Fia wrung her hands. Although she knew the strategy involved in winning this type of race, she worried nevertheless.

Kyzee caught up to third place as they rounded the first lap. Mirra was still ahead of the pack, but her lead had narrowed. Sure enough, halfway through the second lap, she lost it entirely, dropping all the way back behind Kyzee. Now Lazia and Estrann were battling for first place, with Kyzee still bringing up third. As they came around the final turn, Kyzee poured on the power, but was it too late? Fia clenched her fists and willed the girl's legs to move.

Faster. Faster. Come on Kyzee. You must win this.

At the last possible moment, Kyzee drew forth what looked like a nearly superhuman burst of energy, passing the second place Lazia and flying across the finish line with Estrann at what looked like the exact same time. A cheer came from the crowd, followed by a puzzled murmur. No one could determine exactly who had come first. Fia heard someone say that this would be one for the judges to decide. This was confirmed by the mistress of ceremonies, who came out onto the field and announced that the judges would confer and deliver a verdict momentarily. Fia looked down at Kyzee. She was bent over with fatigue, but when she straightened up, the look on her face reflected the anxiety that Fia herself felt.

The wait was only a matter of minmarks, but it seemed to Fia like an eternity. Nevertheless, it gave her time to think of an alternative plan. Unfortunately, she couldn't convey her notion to Kyzee. She could only hope that, should Estrann win and pick Lorq, the girl would keep her wits about her and choose the one other option that could work for them.

At last the elder woman returned to the field, the five girls trailing behind her. She put Estrann and Kyzee on either side of her, and the other three behind. Then she raised her bullhorn to the crowd.

"The judges have reached a consensus," she shouted. "Though both should be congratulated for a supreme effort, it has been determined that one *did* cross an instant before the other. The winner of this festival's First Season Challenge is – "

Fia held her breath.

"Kyzee!" The mistress held Kyzee's hand in the air, and Fia nearly fainted with relief. Now they could go through with their plan as it had originally been conceived.

The young Saebrilite made a convincing show of looking all of the men over thoroughly, before finally choosing Lorq. The crowd roared and catcalled, joking amongst themselves about his size and the size of – well, other things. When Kyzee and Lorq left the field, Fia stayed to see if any of the other girls chose Stamford. When none of them did, she left her seat and slipped quietly out one of the rear exits. There she found the two of them, waiting at their appointed rendezvous point behind a smaller statue of the goddess Saebril.

"Did you see, Fia?" Kyzee said excitedly. "My heart was in my throat the entire time!"

"As was mine," said Fia. "But you did a superb job, and now we are just where we wanted to be, except for one problem."

"Yes, your other two friends are not part of the contingent of eligible males," Kyzee said anxiously. "What are we to do?"

"Where do you suppose they would be right now?" Fia asked.

"Probably in the large holding area in the northeast corner of the keep," said Kyzee. "That is where they put those who are neither eligible to mate nor to attend or serve. But they won't be expecting any trouble, so there's unlikely to be more than one guard."

"Good. We'll bring her some wine too. That should do the trick," Fia agreed, "but what about the other men? I'm worried that some of the other captured ones will demand to come along, or else the natives will attempt to warn their women."

"I think I can avert either of those situations with a bit of play acting," said Kyzee, but I'll have to go alone to accomplish it."

"Very well," said Fia, "we'll leave that to you. Now, none of the First Season Challengers chose Stamford as we had hoped, so I'll need to return and watch until we determine with whom he winds up. Is the wine ready?"

"Yes," Kyzee said. "I stole the midnight root powder from the apothecary last night and added it to the wine. It should put them to sleep in – oh I should say a quartermark, perhaps a bit more. There's a large skin and a small skin back in my room."

"Good," said Fia. "How long will they be out?"

"It depends on the size of the warrior," Kyzee replied, "but I'd guess at least a mark. I dared not make it too strong for fear of accidentally killing someone."

"That should give us plenty of time," said Fia, "provided things go as expected. Now, you go and wait in your quarters. As soon as I've determined Stamford's destination, I'll come for the small wineskin, you'll begin making the rounds with the large one, then return after the appropriate interval to retrieve the boys. Lorq, you're off to the stables to ready the horses. Do you think you can find ones that Stamford and Flaskamper can handle?"

Lorq nodded.

"There are two that should be easy to handle," said the giant, "even for undersized riders."

"Excellent," said Fia. "Then it's time to move. Stamford and I will meet you all at the stables as soon as possible. Good luck you two."

Fia returned to the arena, and was relieved to see that her seat was still vacant. Now the competition was broken up into age groups, and the oldest women (those between thirty and thirty-five) were participating in a triathlon consisting of archery, pole vaulting and long jumping. There were only forty contestants in this group, the top sixteen of which would be allowed to choose a male. Fia suspected, and hoped, that Stamford would be the type to appeal to this age group the most, as he tended to intimidate younger women, Saebrilites or not.

Luck was not with them though. None of the top sixteen finishers chose Stamford, and the field was set up for the next group of women – the twenty-five to thirty year olds. As the grounds were readied, the mistress of ceremonies explained to the spectators that this was the largest group, three hundred women, one hundred eighty of which would be eliminated, leaving the top hundred twenty to choose. This was to be a pentathlon, consisting of a single lap sprint, a javelin throw, a high jump and an obstacle course, all followed by a grueling four lap endurance race. Fia was immensely relieved to be a spectator and *not* a participant. What bothered her was that, with this many contestants, the entire sequence of events could take marks, and the longer it took them to carry out their escape, the greater the likelihood that they would be found out.

As it turned out, it was not as bad as she had thought, for the events were not held in sequence. Instead, the contestants were split into groups, and the five events were staged concurrently. There was a complex elimination process, which was tallied on a large board. Many in the crowd followed the developments on the board with avid interest, no doubt hoping their wagers would pan out, while others chose to focus on the events themselves. When the finish came, a little over two marks later, one hundred twenty women remained, each holding a number that indicated in what order each had finished. First in line was a beautiful, tall, redheaded woman named Fierell. None of the women around Fia were surprised at this outcome. Apparently Fierell was a ferocious warrior, as well as a fierce competitor. Still sweating from her exertions, Fierell strode over to where the remaining men stood. Fia could see that the men were cowed by her, and all bowed their heads or averted their eyes as she passed.

All, that is, except for Stamford. Though the Saebrilite was over two heads taller than him, the dark man met her stern gaze with a defiance that made Fia smile behind her hand. She was somewhat dismayed, though not at all surprised, when Fierell clapped her hand on Stamford's shoulder, indicating that her selection had been made. As the two of them left the arena, Fia slipped out to follow them.

Fierell's quarters were on the opposite side of the compound from Kyzee's. This was unfortunate, not only because it meant a greater chance of being spotted, but also because Stamford would have to spend more time alone with his would-be *mate* before the drugged wine arrived. *That,* Fia imagined with a pang of melancholy, was not likely to bother Stamford nearly as much as it was bothering her.

Having established the pair's location, Fia hurried to Kyzee's quarters and rapped on the door. Kyzee let her in and quickly handed her the small wineskin. When Fia told her which woman was to be drugged, Kyzee nodded with satisfaction.

"Fierell enjoys her wine, and she's not likely to share it with a male," she explained. "The only drawback is that she's quite large, which means the drug will not keep her out as long. We'll have no time to waste once she falls asleep."

"I need a pen and paper," said Fia.

"On the desk there," Kyzee directed.

"On second thought, you'd better write the note in your own language," said Fia. "If it's written in Common Firmish, she'll be suspicious."

Kyzee took a quill and dipped it into the ink, then paused to think. Finally she settled on just two words.

Congratulations. Enjoy.

Fia examined the note.

"Fierell has many friends," Kyzee explained, "any one of whom might do this sort of thing. She should not even think twice about it."

"Alright then," Fia said, "I'm off to deliver our gift."

"And I to free your other friends and pacify the perimeter guards," said the Saebrilite.

Fia sneaked back across the grounds of the keep. Again she passed unseen, though she was forced to take cover once or twice to avoid running into other freshly paired couples on the way to begin their three day fertility mission. She wasted no time at Fierell's door. She merely set down the wine and the note, knocked sharply and beat a hasty retreat. Her job now was to hide nearby and wait for the drug to take effect. She found a shadowy spot in back of the administrative headquarters with a perfect view of the warrior's door. She saw the door open. Fierell picked up the wineskin, read the note and laughed, then went back inside. She began counting down the time. If Stamford hadn't opened the door within a quartermark, something may have gone wrong.

A quartermark came and went, with no visible activity. Fia began to worry. The contingency plan was for her to get in and help Stamford to overpower the Saebrilite. In that plan, however, lay the very real possibility that an alarm could be raised. She decided to wait a bit longer. Another quartermark passed. Nothing. Then, just as she left her hiding place to try to get a look in the window, the door opened and Stamford peered out. She waved and hurried over to him. Silently, he motioned her in and closed the door.

Inside she saw evidence that a great deal had occurred before Fierell had passed out. The Saebrilite lay naked on her bed, and Stamford's thin muslin breeches did little to hide the fact that he had recently been there with her. Misery stabbed once again at Fia's heart, but this was no time for self-pity. The sands of the mark glass were now falling, and there was not a moment to lose.

*   *   *

Kyzee approached the large holding compound with her large skin of wine and a bag full of wooden cups, chosen because they would each hold enough of the drugged wine to put most any woman in the compound to sleep. As she expected, there was only one guard, an older, grey-haired woman named Mali.

"So, it was you drew the short straw this festival, eh Kyzee?" Mali said.

Kyzee nodded, pouring out a cup of wine. Actually, it had been Lazia that had drawn the short straw determining which of the First Season girls would have the duty of delivering the wine to the guards before claiming her prize. Kyzee had had to make up a reason to trade for the unenvied task, but Lazia had been too happy to be rid of the job to think anything of it.

"My thanks, Kyzee," Mali said, as Kyzee handed her the wine. "I've been parched this past mark.

The older woman was sound asleep against one of the fencing posts well within the quartermark. Kyzee returned and called Rokey and Flaskamper over. When they approached, she put on a stern façade.

"The chieftain wishes to see the two of you," she said to Rokey and Flaskamper. The boys were confused for a moment, but soon realized that this must be part of a contingency plan. Thank the gods for Fia's quick thinking!

Kyzee opened the gate and let the two boys out. As she secured the door again and readied to depart, however, she was surprised when an older male called out and motioned her back to the stockade.

"Yes, what is it?" she demanded, trying not to let her nervousness slip out in her voice.

"Warrior," the man said softly, "I beg you...do not tell the chieftain that Mali has fallen asleep. She is a good woman, and none of us wants to see her in trouble. I promise that none of us will cause any trouble, so please...don't mention it will you?"

Kyzee nearly laughed out loud with relief.

"I will say nothing," she told him firmly, "this time."

"Oh, thank you," he said. "Thank you."

She turned and marched the boys ahead of her until they were out of sight of the enclosure. Then she relaxed and worry played across her face.

"What happened?" she asked them. "Why weren't you on the field with the other eligible males?"

"Apparently there was some question about our breeding potential," Flaskamper replied, "because I'm an elf and Rokey has sidhe traits. Lorq has qualities that they desire, but they weren't sure about us, so we were left out."

She nodded, angry at herself for not having considered that. Then she pointed west across the compound.

"It would be better if I had time to lead you to the stables myself," she said, "but I dare not. I must get this wine to the perimeter guards immediately, lest the other two wake before we can make our way clear. The stables are straight across that way. Be very careful. More and more couples may be about, and if you are spotted, all will be lost."

"Don't worry about us," said Flaskamper, "you just take care of yourself with those perimeter guards."

Kyzee left them and proceeded to the stairway next to the gatehouse. She climbed the steep steps and was met by Ginnan, a seasoned guard captain in her early forties. The younger Saebrilite smiled and showed her the wineskin and cups.

"A little fortification for you and the others," Kyzee said in a conspiratorial tone.

"Well now," said Ginnan, "I was wondering if anyone was going to remember us this time. We are much obliged."

"Not at all," said Kyzee, and turned to leave.

"Wait, wait," said the captain, pulling the stopper out of the skin. "What's your hurry. Why not stay and have a sip with us?"

"Oh I'd love to, really," Kyzee said, "but I've really got to be going."

"You're Kyzee," said Ginnan. "I've heard talk of you. Some of the other girls say you're kind of standoffish. Now that I meet you, I begin to wonder myself."

"I assure you Captain Ginnan, it isn't that at all. It's only that, well, I won the First Season Challenge and, my prize is waiting for me."

She offered the captain a sly look and a wink.

"Ah-ha!" said Ginnan with a chuckle. "Well, my girl, off with you by all means."

"You will see that all of your hard-working women get some of that, won't you captain?" Kyzee asked sweetly.

"Oh, have no fear of that," said the watch captain, "I'll see that they all get their fair share."

Kyzee waved good-bye and swiftly descended the stairs. She then made directly for her own quarters, to watch the activities of the captain and her women. From her window, she watched as each of the perimeter guards took a cup of the wine from Ginnan, then returned to their posts. Some of them were stationed outside of her view, but she could safely estimate the point at which they fell asleep by keeping an eye on those along the front wall. Just as she had hoped, a quartermark later, all of the guards in her field of view were asleep, including captain Ginnan.

Using extreme caution, Kyzee slipped once again from her room and hurried to the stables. There, she was relieved to see the rest of the group gathered, ready to go, except for one problem.

"We'll need our packs," Stamford told her, "and our weapons."

"They are in the command headquarters," said Kyzee. "We can pick them up as we leave. But we must go now."

They mounted the three horses that Lorq had selected, he and Stamford on one, Flaskamper and Rokey on the second, Kyzee and Fia on the third. They left the stable and rode quickly, but quietly, out of the stable, skirting the far western side of the keep where there were no living quarters. When they reached the main gate, Kyzee pointed out the gatehouse where the portcullis mechanism was located.

"It works on a counterweight system," she explained, "so all one has to do is pull the lever and turn the wheel. But if we are to gather your things, we should all go and hide behind the headquarters, lest someone spot those of us waiting."

They rode to the command center, positioning the horses on the south side of the building, so that they were visible neither from the arena nor from most of the living quarters. Kyzee and Stamford went in to retrieve the sack of weapons, as well as the packs.. They could not find them immediately, and worried for a moment that they had been moved elsewhere. Then they came across them in a small closet in the back of the building. The packs were still there with their clothing. The provisions were gone, but Kyzee had managed to stockpile enough over the previous two weeks to get them by. Lorinda had already returned the group's money to Fia. The two of them retrieved everything that remained, including their swords and Flaskamper's bow and quiver from the weapons rack, then left the building, stopping just long enough for everyone to rearm themselves and don their packs before remounting.

The three riders and their passengers made their way slowly but deliberately toward the iron gate. When they reached it, Rokey hopped down and ducked inside the gatehouse. A moment later, the portcullis began to rise with a clang. Fortunately, the noise was muffled by the cheers coming from the arena. Rokey climbed back onto the back of the huge horse and settled down behind Flaskamper. Then they were off, through the open gate towards the steep, narrow, cliffside pathways. Just over a month after they had first entered the foreboding walls of Braeden's Keep, the companions, with the help of the group's newest member, were at last tasting freedom again.

As they began to descend the sloping trail, Rokey took a moment to gaze back at the tall, grey stone walls. As he murmured his silent good-bye, however, his heart suddenly jumped to his throat. Up over the wall came the figure of a Saebrilite warrior. The guard was clearly unsteady on her feet, and her fingers gripped hard at the edge of the wall for support. As Rokey continued to stare in horror, their eyes met for a moment – his filled with fear, hers with rage. Then she turned and began to walk, slowly, but with savage determination, until she reached the object she'd been aiming for – an enormous war horn. This snapped Rokey out of his freeze, and he screamed at them all to get moving... fast. Just as their heads disappeared down over the crest of the stack, they heard the massive horn sound. The race for their lives had begun.

Chapter 23:

Into the Fire

"They're gaining on us!" Rokey shouted to Flaskamper. "There's nothing more we can do!" the elf yelled back. "We're going flat out as it is, and our horses are tiring!"

They had been galloping at a breakneck pace for several marks, hoping that at some point their Saebrilite captors would give up the pursuit and turn back. So far that had not happened. Flaskamper suspected that their pride would not allow it. He assumed that *their* mounts must also be tiring by now, yet strangely, the gap between them was still narrowing. At this rate, they would likely catch up within the next mark.

There *was* hope though. They were coming down out of the hills, and from here they could see, in the distance, the Hiang mountains to the north and another mountain straight ahead. Now with his keen sidhe eyesight, Rokey could see that the two came together ahead to form what looked like a narrow canyon pass. If they could reach it, there was a chance that they could lose their pursuers there. In any case, Flaskamper doubted that the Saebrilites would chase them beyond their own territory, which he believed ended at the mountain ahead. He shouted this opinion over to Kyzee, who confirmed it.

"We call... Shamble Mountain," she called to him. "I've never... there. Supposedly... huge... there..."

"What?" Flaskamper yelled. "I can't hear you!"

"Some kind of... giant... Saebrilites don't... there," she said.

Flaskamper didn't get it all the second time either, but it seemed that she was saying that the mountain was a place that the Saebrilites avoided because of some sort of giant. He swerved over toward Lorq and Stamford's horse, veering as close to it as he could safely get at their current speed.

"Kyzee says danger ahead!" Flash hollered at them. "Saebrilites don't go there. What do you think?"

"Considering what will happen if they catch us," Stamford yelled back, "I can't think what could be worse!"

Flaskamper could actually think of quite a few things, but he agreed that they should forge on anyway. After another brief, shouted conversation with Kyzee and Fia, they all agreed to make for the pass, and hope the Saebrilites would continue to avoid it. The hills were behind them now, and they were back on level ground. This seemed to give the horses a second wind, and they all but flew across the hard, flat countryside. Unfortunately, the Saebrilites also picked up speed, and their lead continued to shrink as they approached the narrow mountain gorge.

They were only minmarks from entering the pass when they heard a voice coming from behind them. Fia recognized it as Hethra, shouting through a megaphone.

"STOP!" Hethra shouted. "DO NOT RIDE INTO THE PASS. THERE IS GREAT DANGER THERE! STOP AND WE WILL NEGOTIATE!"

"Negotiate, my arse!" Fia heard Stamford yell. She could understand how he felt, how all the men must feel, tasting this freedom after a month of servitude. She was beginning to worry, though. Something ahead was bad enough to scare a squad of armed Saebrilite warriors, and they were heading straight for that something. She looked back at their pursuers. The warrior named Hethra was there alongside Lorinda. So, the chieftain herself was leading the pursuit. They were close enough for Fia to see the sweat on their horses, and the eyes of the chieftain, blazing with fury, but something else as well. Concern? Fear? It gave her a moment's pause, but it was too late for discussions now. Shamble Mountain loomed in front of them. They were approaching the pass.

The riders were forced to slow down slightly in order to enter the narrow space between the two mountains. In that time, the Saebrilites drew closer. Moments later, when the gap widened slightly, several of the warriors were able to get around and in front of them. They were caught. The companions all drew their swords, determined to remain free at any cost.

"Don't be fools," said Lorinda. "We outnumber you two to one. Surrender and come with us now, out of this canyon before we attract–"

Before she could finish her sentence, a huge boulder flew from the mountain above and crashed to the ground directly in front of them.

240 Pat Nelson Childs

The horses all reared, throwing the companions and several of the Saebrilite warriors to the ground. Before they had a chance to recover themselves, two more massive rocks flew overhead in rapid succession. One landed just behind them, blocking most of the path. The other hit one of the mounted Saebrilites, knocking her off her horse and crushing her to death instantly.

"What in blazes is going on?" cried Flaskamper.

"This is the territory of the rock behemoths," Lorinda answered. "We must get out of here at once."

But it was too late. One of the beasts was already charging down the mountain. Lorinda hadn't exaggerated calling them behemoths. This one looked to be at least thirty feet tall. It appeared vaguely human, but wore no clothes, and its skin was hard and reddish brown, the same color as the surrounding stone. It had a single large eye in the middle of its forehead and from the corners of its mouth grew two long, sharp tusks.

The creature wasted no time. It grabbed the horse from which Stamford had just been thrown, snapping it's neck with a powerful twist. Then it picked up one of the warriors by the throat, snapping her neck and crushing her windpipe, and threw her dead body aside like a rag doll. The rest of the Saebrilites drew their swords and prepared to fight.

"Whatever our differences," Stamford said to Lorinda, "I suggest we put them aside for the moment."

"Agreed," said the chieftain.

"How do we kill it?" he asked.

"Their skin is like stone," said the Saebrilite, "but there are a few vulnerable spots. The eye is the primary one, but the joints too are vulnerable, as is the inside of the mouth."

"Not much to work with," he remarked.

"That is why we avoid this area," she said.

Stamford looked around. The giant moved quickly, and seemed to be focused solely on their utter destruction. He suspected that, should they lose, they would wind up salt cured as part of these creatures' winter food stores. He quickly relayed Lorinda's information to his companions who were already busy dodging the beast's huge, stomping feet

Flaskamper immediately readied his bow, but he had less than half a quiver of arrows left. He would have to use them sparingly. Flaskamper lined up a shot, but the beast grabbed another warrior, making it impossible for him to shoot without risking her life. It was a pointless caution, however. Within tiks, the Saebrilite was dead, and the giant tossed her carelessly to the ground. The elf quickly let loose a volley of three arrows, hoping to hit creature's eye. However, the beast turned its head, and the arrows bounced harmlessly off its stony hide. His next shot was equally ineffective. Flaskamper cursed. He had only three arrows left, and had done no damage at all.

The Saebrilite warriors were fighting fiercely, hacking at the giant's legs with their longswords, but they were as useless as Flaskamper's arrows. One by one he was picking them up and crushing them like so much soft fruit, and there seemed to be nothing they could do. Then, as the creature reached down for yet another victim, Hethra rushed up, unslinging the huge battle axe from her back. She swung the weapon with all of her might, and neatly cleaved off three of the rock giant's fingers. The beast howled in pain and fury, knocking Hethra down hard as he yanked his hand away. Greenish-grey blood poured from the wound and splashed on the ground all around them. The wounded giant raised his foot high in the air, intent on squashing Hethra, who still lay stunned on the ground. Without a second thought, Stamford dove to the ground next to the Saebrilite, and quickly stood his sword up on the ground just as the giant's food crashed down. The creature's own weight drove the sword straight through its foot. As it reflexively stooped to pull the sword out, Flaskamper leapt forward and up onto the beast's back. He wrapped his legs tightly around the beast's neck and held on for dear life. The giant howled in pain and frustration, swatting at the elf and dancing around on its uninjured foot. Then, when one of the other warriors distracted it with a chop to the leg, Flaskamper drew one of the last three arrows from his quiver and, with a powerful swing of both arms, drove it into the beast's bulging eye. As the arrow entered its brain, the rock giant stiffened, then began to topple. Flaskamper jumped clear at the last moment before it hit the ground, but he landed hard, banging his knee on a rock. The creature lay there twitching uncontrollably for a moment, and then died with a final, rasping sigh.

Rokey went and crouched next to Flaskamper, checking his injured knee. He suspected that it would be all right, though it was already beginning to swell some.

Lorinda seemed equally concerned about Hethra. The chieftain was on the ground, stroking the captain's hair. As Stamford approached, she stood to face him.

"I am in your debt," Lorinda told him. "You risked your own lives to save your enemy. You have great character for males."

"Thanks Chieftain, I think," Stamford answered, smiling.

"There are enough of my warriors still alive to take you and the others into custody, or kill you for your attempt at escape. However, ingratitude is not our way. You are all free to go."

"I appreciate that, Chieftain," said Stamford. "All we ever wanted was to go in peace."

"Then so you shall," said Lorinda.

Five of the Saebrilite warriors were dead. Three more injured, but mobile. Flaskamper was able to stand a short time later, none the worse for wear except for a bit of a limp. He popped a wad of rembis leaves in his mouth and chewed them to relieve the pain, then offered some to the injured Saebrilites. As they were all regrouping, Lorinda took Kyzee aside.

"You are sure this is what you want?" the chieftain asked. "You are aware that once you leave, you will not be allowed to return, not ever."

"Yes Chieftain, I know," Kyzee answered, "and I have thought long and hard on the matter. Though I love my Saebrilite sisters, I have fallen *in* love with a man."

"But are you certain of this?" Lorinda asked. "You are very young still."

"It's true. I *am* young," Kyzee said, "but I know what is in my heart. I know that I love Lorq, and want to be with him, in a place where that love will be accepted. You and I both know that Braeden's Keep is not that place."

Lorinda nodded.

"I wish you the best, sister," she said. "We shall miss you."

"As I shall miss all of you," Kyzee replied.

It was agreed between Stamford and Lorinda that the Saebrilites would see the companions through the pass, until they were safely out of the rock behemoths' territory, after which they would return the three horses they had stolen in order to make their escape. Stamford would have argued for them, but soon they would be passing into the lower wilds, and chances were that the horses would be more of a hindrance than a help. At least, that's what he told himself.

"Come," said Lorinda, "we must be off. More of the creatures may soon arrive. We want to be well away from here when that happens."

They made their way slowly across the winding path, until they had cleared the mountain, and stood on a promontory overlooking a heavily wooded valley. As the companions dismounted, Lorinda pointed out to Stamford the path, which sloped down into the woods. As they talked, Flaskamper put his arm around Rokey and pointed off to the west.

"You see that mountain range way off there in the distance?" he said. "Does it look familiar?"

Rokey shook his head.

"Why," he said, "should it?

"Not from this side, I guess," Flaskamper replied. "It's the Emerald Mountain Range. We've nearly come round full circle."

Rokey's eyes widened. It seemed impossible. He had come so far since leaving those mountains, accomplished so much in some ways, yet so little in others. Now circumstances seemed to be drawing him back towards them again. He shook his head in wonder.

"Of course they're still a long, long way off," said Flash, "and we don't have the slightest idea which direction we'll be heading in a week from now."

"A week," Rokey muttered. "I'm having all I can do just thinking about where today will lead."

Flaskamper laughed.

"You're not the only one," he said.

Before the Saebrilites departed, Lorinda spoke again to Stamford.

"As chieftain of Braeden's Keep," she told him, "I have granted you your freedom in recognition of your selfless act toward one of my guards. But Hethra is more to me than just a guard captain, as I am sure you have guessed. She is also my life partner."

Stamford nodded.

"Therefore, I owe you and the elf a personal debt as well," she continued. "I hope someday to have the opportunity to repay it. I should hate to leave this world with such an obligation outstanding."

"I thank you, Chieftain," said Stamford, "I'll do my best to give you that opportunity one day."

"Farewell, all of you," she said. "I wish you success in your journey."

The Saebrilites left, taking the horses with them. The six companions studied the forest below, trying to decide on which path to take.

"I can see there's a stream that winds most of the way through the wood," said Rokey. "Should we follow that?"

"Well, it's as good a plan as any," said Stamford, "but there's not much of the day left. I see a clearing just down that way." He pointed to a spot a short way northeast of the foot of the promontory. "Why don't we make for that and set up camp for the night. I'm tired, and I just want to relax and enjoy our newly won freedom for a little while. Tomorrow we'll start our search for the illusive Faerie folk."

They followed the path down to the base of the outcropping, then set off northeast toward the clearing. It didn't take them long to reach it, and they had the camp set up well before sundown. As they were finishing up, Lorq approached Flaskamper, looking embarrassed.

"What is it big fellow?" the elf asked. "What's the matter?"

"Flash, I have a problem," said Lorq, shuffling his feet nervously.

"Well, tell me about it. I'll see if I can help you," said Flaskamper.

"It's about Kyzee. I – I don't know how – I want her to – I want her to share my tent," Lorq blurted out at last. "But I don't know how to ask her. I'm afraid, you know, that she'll be insulted.

"Lorq, have you ever had a girlfriend?" Flaskamper asked.

"No," Lorq muttered, putting his head down.

"Oh for pity's sake, Lorq, that's not something you have to be ashamed of," Flaskamper told him. "I only brought it up to point out that neither of you has any experience with this. I'm sure that, as glad as she is to be here now, she's probably just as nervous and uncertain as you are. I think the best thing you can do is just be honest with her. Don't pressure her. Just tell her how you feel. I don't believe she'll think you're a cad for telling her you want to be with her. Women like honesty from men, though they often get precious little of it. Of course, I'm no expert on women, but I really think she'll admire your candor. Then she'll either say 'yes, I'm ready' or 'no, I'm not ready'. You'd obviously be happier with the first answer, but either way you'll be a winner with her."

Lorq grinned and squeezed Flaskamper's shoulder.

"Thanks, Flash," said the giant. "I'm going to go talk to her now."

When Lorq had gone, the elf smiled and rubbed his shoulder.

"That is definitely going to leave a bruise," he muttered.

* * *

The six of them sat around the campfire later that night, talking and joking, glad to be in one another's company again. Fia had managed to alter one of her tunics so that it would fit Kyzee, as the sight of a bare-breasted woman, of any size, would be unacceptable outside of the Saebrilites' territory. Apparently Lorq's talk with Kyzee had gone well, Flaskamper thought, for she sat between his knees, leaning back, with the giant's arms resting comfortably over her shoulders. As it turned out though, they were not going to share a tent, not because Kyzee had refused, but because Fia had. Apparently she was not willing to share a tent with Stamford, a possibility that neither Lorq nor Flaskamper had ever considered. The whole thing had made for an awkward moment or two, but it had blown over quickly. If anything, Rokey remarked to Flaskamper, the new couple seemed somewhat relieved.

"That's because they don't know what they're missing," Flaskamper whispered to him, nibbling his ear. Rokey swatted him. He was happy to see that his love was already acting like his old self again. Hopefully this meant that their captivity had done him no permanent harm.

"It's going to be strange now, making love without an audience," Flash told him.

"You think you'll be able to manage without the onlookers?" Rokey teased.

"Just you remember," said the elf. "no matter who was watching, I was only performing for you."

"What are you two muttering about?" Stamford asked. "On second thought, don't tell me."

It seemed to Rokey that Fia was especially quiet that night. As they were all going to bed, he stole a moment to ask her if anything was wrong.

"What makes you think there's anything wrong, sweetie," she said, smiling warmly at him.

"Well, I haven't known you for very long, it's true," he said, "but I think I know you well enough to be able to spot when there's something amiss. Of course, it's none of my business. I just wanted you to know – I don't know..."

"I *do* know," she said, placing a hand on his cheek, "and it's very sweet that you care about me. As to what is wrong... well," she gave a wistful sigh, "sometimes it *does* help to discuss certain kinds of troubles. But then there are others – others that are just best kept to oneself. Do you understand?"

"I think so," said Rokey. "But – if there's ever anything I can do – "

"But you've already done it, dear," said Fia. "You've reminded me what a splendid friend I have in you, and that alone lightens my heart."

She kissed him on the cheek and stepped into her tent, leaving Rokey to wonder, as he made for his own, what it was that had darkened her heart in the first place.

Chapter 24:

Strange Sights

"You know, this would be a damn sight easier if we knew just what the blazes we were looking for."

This remark came from Stamford as they trudged along the winding stream that snaked through the Lower Wilds. They had started early in the morning, breaking camp and following the stream in search of...well, therein lay the problem. None of them knew exactly *what* they were looking for – a certain clump of trees, a village, a cave. No one knew how the sidhe lived, if they still lived at all, or what they or their dwellings looked like.

Rokey understood Stamford's frustration, for he was feeling it himself. He knew somehow that if the sidhe chose to stay hidden, they would never be able to find them. He was hoping, however, that they might take an interest in him, especially now that his true eyes had been revealed, and show themselves. Also in the back of his mind was a notion that his new eyes may reveal something meant to be invisible to ordinary men. So far, however, neither he nor any of his companions had seen anything but a common wooded valley. The joy of being free again was still fresh in their minds, and it was such a fine, sunny day, no one minded spending it outside in the fresh air.

However, as the end of their first day of searching approached with nothing to show for it, a sense of discouragement began to settle upon them. Rokey tried to maintain his positive attitude. *It simply isn't possible*, he said to himself, *that you have come all this way, through so many obstacles, simply to wander aimlessly in the woods until you finally give up and – and what? Where is there to go from here?* He knew more than he did when he started, but not nearly enough to be able to tackle the problem of who was trying to kill him and why. And what about the two – no, three messages from the oracles? Were they to be of no help to him at all in this search? No. He was not yet ready to accept defeat. They had found nothing today, but tomorrow they would.

Just at the point when they were starting to think about camping for the night, they made a strange discovery. It was Rokey that first noticed it, and at first wondered if he were starting to see things. When he pointed it out to the others, however, they confirmed that it was, indeed, there, though they were also at a loss as to why...and how.

It was a road – a road which began abruptly in the middle of nowhere and ran... well that was the question that was on all of their minds.

"It's practically *begging* us to follow it," said Fia.

"I know," said Stamford. "That's what worries me. It may lead to some kind of trap."

"Well if it is, it's a damn clever one," said Flaskamper, "because there's no way we're *not* going to follow it, right?"

"What do you think, Rokey?" Fia asked

"Well," Rokey answered, "if it *is* a trap set by my enemies, it's a lot more subtle than their other attempts. And Flash is right. We just *have* to find out where it leads. I say we proceed, but with our hands on our swords."

The plain dirt path wound back and forth, allowing them to see very little of what was ahead. It was also heavily shadowed by the trees that grew thickly on either side. Unfortunately, they were only able to follow it a short way before the sun began to sink down below the tree line, and they were forced to begin scouting for a spot to set up camp for the night. As the light faded though, and they rounded the next bend, they were met by yet another astounding sight.

"Well, I'll be damned," said Flaskamper.

"I don't believe it," said Stamford.

"How is it possible?" Fia asked.

On the side of the road in front of them stood an inn. The sign in front identified it as *The Gilded Swine*. It was a large, two-story building that looked like it had simply been plunked down here in the middle of nowhere, very much as the road had suddenly appeared. This made the entire company wary again.

"Is it a trick?" asked Lorq.

"Well, unless we've stumbled upon a settled area that none of us has ever heard of, I'd say most definitely yes," Stamford replied.

"So we should stay clear of it?" Kyzee asked.

"No way," Flaskamper answered. "We've come here to find the sidhe. Maybe we've found them. Who's to say they haven't got themselves an inn, right Rokey?"

"Anything's possible, I guess," said Rokey hesitantly. "But Glaelie said that they didn't care for the company of others, so my first guess would be that this is some sort of a ruse."

"Well, maybe they've changed their ways," said the elf. "We won't know unless we investigate, now will we, right Stamford?"

"As much as it pains me to say it," said the dark man, "I think Flaskamper has a point, someplace other than the top of his head for a change. We're not going to find out anything by avoiding such an obvious temptation. Let's go in, but keep our eyes open."

They entered *The Gilded Swine* cautiously. Inside they found a well-decorated tavern, with colorful rugs on the floors, and finely crafted chandeliers hanging from the ceilings. There were numerous tables of different sizes and shapes, some already occupied by what appeared to be perfectly normal human men and women. Along the back wall was a long bar, lined with stools, three of which were also occupied by men apparently enjoying a late afternoon tankard. From behind the bar came a portly innkeeper, a grisly-haired fellow with a bushy brown beard and coal black eyes. He smiled and held his arms out to the new arrivals.

"Welcome folks, welcome to the Gilded Swine," said the man. "Please sit down. I'll be right with you. The sofa area is empty, and quite comfortable."

The *sofa area* consisted of a long sofa covered with a multi-colored array of cushions, and several padded leather chairs surrounding a round, low table. Kyzee and Lorq took the sofa, the rest settled into the chairs. The innkeeper returned a moment later.

"We make a fine mead here at the Gilded Swine," he told them, "but we've good beer and wine as well. Will you be wanting supper as well?"

"Eh, first we'd like the answers to a couple of questions if you don't mind," said Stamford, "your name for instance?"

The innkeeper grinned pleasantly.

"My name is Morgrum. Pleased to welcome you, sir. I'm not a gossiping man by nature, but I'll be happy to tell you whatever I can."

"Well, Morgrum," Stamford began, "we're all curious as to why this inn is here, on this lonely road in the middle of the forest. I shouldn't think there would be enough traffic to keep such a place in business."

"Oh, I'm afraid you'd be wrong there sir," Morgrum answered, "no offence meant, mind you. But with the township so nearby, we keep quite a few regulars, even during the slower parts of the year."

"Township?" Flaskamper's ears perked up. "What township is that?"

Morgrum gave him a strange look.

"Why the township of Perilee, young sir. Just a few turns down the road. Surely that's where you're headed, or else it's where you've just come from."

"No," Stamford said, shaking his head, "We've just come from – well...the other way. We're strangers to this area, you see."

"Aye, sir, that be plain enough," said Morgrum, "though I'm surprised you didn't hear of Perilee when you passed through Scop's Glen, or did you not stop there at all?"

Stumped, Stamford decided to bluff.

"Er, no..." he said, "no, we didn't stop at all. Not until the sun began to set and we saw your inn. Have you three rooms available?"

"Aye," said the innkeeper. "Nothing fancy mind you, but a warm fire and comfortable beds all the same. I shall need a few minmarks to make them up, though. We've already let the chambermaid go for the season. Can I get you something while you wait?"

"No, that's alright," Stamford told him. "We'll be fine until you get back."

"As you wish, sir," said Morgrum. "I shan't be long."

The innkeeper disappeared through a rear door and headed up a flight of stairs. When he was gone, they huddled together around the table.

"Perilee?" said Flaskamper. "Scop's Glen? Has anyone heard of either of those places?"

"I have," said Fia, "one of them anyway. Scop's Glen is mentioned in an ancient ballad I learned long ago. The song dates back to the time of the First Kings."

"The First Kings?" said Flaskamper, his eyes growing wide, "that's over a thousand years ago. There aren't any townships left in existence that date back that far."

"This is all beginning to sound a bit creepy," said Rokey.

"Listen," said Stamford, "we know that the sidhe date back that far, and further still. I smell their chicanery behind this."

"You could be right," Flaskamper agreed. "I suggest we ask him straight out about the sidhe when he returns... see what he has to say."

"Good idea," said Stamford. "We'll get nowhere by dancing around it."

A short time later, the innkeeper came to the bottom of the steps and motioned them to follow him. He led them to the upstairs hallway, where the doors to three bedrooms had been opened.

"All set, then," said Morgrum. "You are most welcome to come down anytime for supper, or for a drink. There's sure to be folks making merry later on... always are."

The innkeeper turned to leave, but Flaskamper stopped him.

"Just a moment," said the elf. "Don't you want the money for the rooms? I assume you require payment in advance...like everyone else." His eyebrow shot up questioningly.

Morgrum looked flustered for a moment, but then recovered himself.

"Yes, yes, or course. Silly of me. Now let me see...it is the slow time of year after all, so... why don't you just give me whatever you think is fair."

Flaskamper laughed.

"Well, sir," he said, "you're lucky that I'm an honest elf with a policy such as that. For a pleasant place like this, I'm willing to part with all of sixty ducats. How does that strike you?"

"Oh that sounds more than fair, sir" Morgrum said quickly, "in fact, I'll throw in your supper and drinks this evening as well, all for one price. Makes things so much simpler doesn't it?"

This time it was Stamford who stopped Morgrum as he turned to go.

"Tell me, Morgrum," Stamford asked, "do you know anything of a people called the sidhe? They are said to inhabit this area."

The innkeeper's smile twitched a bit, and his eyes took on a slightly glassy quality.

"Why no, sir," he answered flatly. "I've never heard of them. Around these parts you say?"

"Yes," Stamford persisted, "around these parts. Strange, I thought certain you would have heard of them. They are also known as the Faerie. Does that ring any bells?"

"No sir, indeed," said Morgrum, having fully recovered his smile and his demeanor, "no bells at all. I'm afraid that someone must have misinformed you, sir. Now if you'll excuse me, I have some other customers I must attend to. Come on down any time now. I'll be pleased to serve you"

When the innkeeper had gone, they all hurried into the first bedroom and closed the door.

"What do you make of that?" said Flaskamper.

"That he's a terrible liar," said Stamford, "but only because he wasn't expecting that particular question. Even so, it only took him a moment for him to recover himself."

"Sixty ducats," Flaskamper observed, "would scarcely buy you *one* room in the seediest, roadside rat trap, let alone three rooms plus dinner and drinks in a well-kept place like this. This fellow knows nothing of money."

"So, the question is," said Stamford, "just what have we gotten ourselves into?"

"If it's the sidhe trying to trap us in some way," said Rokey, "they're certainly going about it in a strange way."

"Perhaps because trickery *is* their only weapon," said Stamford. "Now Morgrum said there would be others here later. I suggest we mingle and see if we can ingratiate ourselves, especially you, Rokey. You've got the eyes after all. That's bound to have made some impression, even if he didn't show it. Others may be less cautious. We'll have a wash and a rest here, in shifts, and go down later."

"I suggest we also avoid eating or drinking anything offered by them," said Fia. "Poison is the weapon of tricksters."

"Smart thinking," Stamford agreed. "We'll sup on our own provisions before we rest."

They ate a frugal meal, so as not to exhaust their stores, then split up two to a room and slept, one on, one off, to assure no one would sneak up on them. Later, they washed and changed into fresh clothes. They could hear the sound of music and laughter coming from the tavern downstairs, and decided it was time to make an appearance.

"Now remember everyone," said Stamford, "separate and mingle, but keep an eye out for one another. And be delicate with your questions. We don't want to spook them or they'll likely close ranks on us. Order an ale or something to carry around with you, but for pity's sake, don't drink it, even if they pressure you. Lorq and Kyzee, I suggest you stay seated if possible. It will make you look less intimidating. Alright, everybody ready?"

When Rokey and the others emerged through the doorway downstairs, they saw that the atmosphere was merry indeed. Several of the tables had been pushed together to clear a spot in the middle of the room. A trio of musicians was in the front corner of the room, playing a lively tune, and several couples were engaged in a dance that he did not recognize, nor did Flaskamper.

"Nothing I've ever seen," said the elf, "and I'm something of an expert, if I say so myself."

Lorq and Kyzee resumed their places on the sofa, after having procured a drink for show. The others ordered ales and spread out throughout the room. Rokey felt a bit awkward – he had never been comfortable in a group of strangers, but he kept Flaskamper in his sights for reassurance, and bravely soldiered on. The others had no trouble. They were used to chatting up strangers, for it was an important part of their profession.

Over time, Rokey found himself relaxing and having a good time, though he *had* agreed with Flash, who murmured to him at one point that he wished he could be drinking the bloody ale instead of just toting it about. Still, the people were all very friendly and outgoing, and though not one of them confessed to knowing a thing about the sidhe, neither did they seem particularly taken aback by the question. *Forewarned is forearmed*, Rokey thought. The innkeeper had no doubt warned them that they were seeking the Faerie. Either that, he thought, or he and his friends were all crazy and these were just ordinary townsfolk. That could not be, though. Scop's Glen no longer existed. He must not allow himself to be taken in by the atmosphere – an atmosphere, he observed, that was growing increasingly thick. He noticed that a few men were smoking their pipes and, encouraged by that, Stamford and Flaskamper had broken theirs out as well. Rokey wished that someone would open a window, for while the fragrance was pleasant enough, he found it a bit overpowering.

As the night continued, Rokey began to feel rather intoxicated. The music was lulling him into something of a daze, at least he assumed it was the music. At a certain point, he found that he had to sit down. He was starting to feel decidedly inebriated, despite the fact that he had not taken so much as a sip from the tankard he carried. He looked around the room and saw that Flaskamper and Fia had paired off with a young woman and man, who were teaching them the dance that they had seen earlier. Lorq and Kyzee were sitting, his arm around her shoulder, chatting with a small group of townspeople. Stamford – he couldn't see Stamford at the moment, but he was certain the dark man was somewhere nearby.

A young man sat down beside Rokey and introduced himself as Napa. He was a handsome, sturdy lad, rather like Jar had been. *Jar,* he thought, *my first infatuation. It seems like such a long time ago. I was so worried about being a samer then. Now it feels so natural, since I met Flash.* Still, he wondered what it would have been like back then at the monastery. What if it had been Jar, not Barrett, who had asked him to go to the stables that night? *What would Jar's kiss have been like?*

"You're eyes are so beautiful," Napa said softly. "So much like ours."

Rokey barely noticed that he had spoken, for he was now completely lost in his own thoughts. The room swirled about him. He could still hear the music. It sounded more distant now, yet at the same time, closer, as though it were playing for his ears alone. Had the young man gone? No, he was still here, sitting next to him.

Then he was whisked back to the monastery again, to the stables, lying in the hay. Jar was kissing him, passionately, and removing his clothes. Jar kissed his chest, teasing his nipples with his tongue, then his lips moved lower. He felt his breeches sliding off. *Am I dreaming?* It seemed real enough, just a little foggy... foggy? Smoky. Thick, pungent smoke filled the room. Were the stables on fire? No, it was pipe smoke he smelled, some sweet, intoxicating type of kingsleaf. He strained to open his eyes. The smoke was so dense now, he could barely see the room at all. Through watery eyes, he could just see the image of Flaskamper, lying quite near him, naked. He was not alone either. He was with that same young woman, only now she looked different – her eyes looked just like his, and the most beautiful set of butterfly wings had sprung out on her back. They were not dancing. Flaskamper was lying under her, a look of blind ecstasy on his face. They were –

No, it couldn't be! Not Flash. Flash was a samer, like he was. Besides, Flash loved him. He would never do – *what I am doing now with Jar.*

Only, this wasn't Jar. It was the other young man – Napa – pleasuring Rokey, even as he watched Flaskamper cavorting with the Faerie female. His eyes fluttered briefly over the room. He could see others also, in twos, even threes, all writhing together.

What are we doing? This is wrong. The smoke – just like the smoke in Jamba's ritual chamber – it was fogging their minds – clouding their judgment. He tried to struggle, but found that he couldn't move. *Why would you want to move,* said a soothing voice inside his head. *Just lie back. Enjoy this handsome lad's skillful attentions, and then sleep...a long, blissful sleep.*

Finally, he surrendered, worn down by the smoke's soothing enchantment. Soon, powerful waves of pleasure began to surge through him. His hands ran through the boy's thick orange hair, then over the slender, delicate wings that grew from his back. Afterwards, he felt the young man pull gently away. Rokey was exhausted, and could no longer hold his eyes open. Somewhere in the distance, he heard Flaskamper's familiar cry of satisfaction. The sound of it brought on feelings of pain – pain and deep regret. *I'm sorry Flash. I'm so sorry.* Despite all of their precautions, they had been beguiled, had fallen prey to the sidhe, and their dark sense of humor. A tear rolled down his cheek, and Rokey felt his consciousness slipping. The blackness was about to bear him away. He wondered whether or not he would ever return again.

Chapter 25:

Whispers and Wings

"Rokey! Rokey are you up yet?"

Rokey, a bright, handsome lad of ten, awakes and swings his gangly legs over the side of the bed. He yawns, rubbing the sleep from his eyes.

"Rokey, hurry and get dressed. Your father is waiting for you, but he isn't going to wait all morning."

"I'm coming, mother!" Rokey calls, and stumbles to the basin. He washes himself thoroughly, then finds that his towel is gone. He finally dries himself off on his sheet, then searches for his tunic.

"Rokey!," his mother yells, "What's taking you so long?"

He pulls on his shoe and reaches for the other, but it is nowhere in sight. He looks all over the room, even under the bed. It is nowhere to be found. Cursing to himself, he digs through the pile of clothes on the floor, and finally finds the missing footwear. Now fully dressed, he pulls at his bedroom door.

It will not budge. He tugs harder, trying to force it open, but it is stuck fast. His mother calls yet again.

"My door is stuck!" he calls back. "Don't let him go! I'm coming!"

A moment later, he manages to get the stubborn door unstuck and races to the kitchen. His mother is standing at the sink, her back to him, washing the breakfast dishes.

"Where is he?" Rokey asks. "Where's father?"

"He's gone, Rokey," his mother tells him, without turning around. "I told you he wouldn't wait. But maybe if you hurry you can still catch him."

Rokey runs outside, where he sees his father's cart a short way down the road.

"Father!" he hollers. "Father, wait for me!"

He sprints after the cart, as fast as his boyish legs can carry him – running and running, until his sides ache and his breath comes in short gasps. The cart continues to grow smaller and smaller, however, until finally it disappears from view altogether. Heartbroken, Rokey turns and walks back the way he had come, toward home. Instead of his home, though, he finds himself suddenly in the middle of a city, a place that he doesn't recognize. Confused, he wanders the streets, looking for his house. The people he passes all stare at him as though he has grown a second head. It makes him feel embarrassed and afraid.

As he turns down yet another small side street, a large hand reaches out and grabs him. He struggles, but is held fast.

"What are you struggling for, Rokey? I'm not going to hurt you."

Rokey looks up into the eyes of Brother Barrow. Abruptly, he bursts into tears.

"There, there now," says Brother Barrow. "What's the matter now. You can tell me."

Rokey explains to him that he is lost, and is trying to get home to his mother. The brother shakes his head sadly.

"Your mother has been gone for many years, Rokey," he says. "You have no home to go to."

"That's a lie!" Rokey shouts. "My mother is not gone. I just left her a short while ago. She was – doing... dishes and – " his voice breaks.

"You've been dreaming, Rokey," says Brother Barrow. "That's all, son. Just dreaming."

"NO!"

Rokey shakes free of the brother's grip and dashes away. The brother calls after him, but he pays him no heed. He just runs and runs, past the city limits, back into the countryside. Soon he spies his own home, off in the distance. He streaks toward it. When he arrives, he throws open the kitchen door, only to find that his mother is no longer there.

"Mother?" he calls. "Mother, are you here?"

There is no answer, so he goes through the house in search of her. He reaches the door of his parents' bedroom and, hesitantly, pushes it open. His eyes widen at what he sees. His mother is there. She is naked and straddling the man who is lying on his back beneath her. This man is not Rokey's father. He is not even a man – but an elf. He knows him, somehow. Perhaps he is a friend of his father's.

His mother pauses and looks over at Rokey. Her eyes are gold and glittering. He backs up a step, terrified, but his mother just smiles at him.

"Hello, dear," she says. "You're home early."

The elf also looks over at Rokey, shooting him a wide grin. His hands are around his mother's waist. Where does he know him from? Why is he doing that with his mother?

"Now, now, lad," says the elf. "You shouldn't be here. This isn't something you're supposed to see."

The two turn back to their revelry. Abruptly, a huge set of wings springs from his mother's back. They are dripping wet, and as she shakes them, droplets splash onto Rokey's face. He quickly turns away and slams the door behind him. He wants to be alone, but now Abbot Crinshire suddenly appears. He grabs Rokey and drags him outdoors, towards a huge pit. He screams at the abbot to stop, and promises to do whatever he wants.

"You had your chance, Rokey," says Crinshire. "Now it's too late."

Rokey struggles. The pit is huge, like a gaping maw, and it's so deep... so dark. He fights frantically, but the ten-year-old boy is no match for a full-grown man. He lifts him high in the air and casts him headlong into the pit. He screams as he falls – farther and farther down – into the black abyss.

Then, in the darkness, a picture forms in front of him – A picture of a huge Faerie willow. He recognizes it, but why he does not know. He ceases to scream, and there is only silence, and the rushing of the wind around him. Then slowly, the sound of the wind changes. It begins to form itself into words – words that are familiar to him. Over and over, the tree whispers a phrase, and after a few moments, Rokey begins to whisper it too.

*   *   *

Rokey awoke, still muttering the strange phrase, the one he had learned in Glimmermere, from the Whispering Tree. He looked up and saw the sky. It was a clear and sunny day. He was outdoors. His mouth was dry as ash and had a terrible taste in it. He wanted water desperately. A chill gripped him, and he realized that he was stark naked. It was then that the memories came flooding back. The sidhe had managed to drug them after all, and to make them all do – gods, could *he* possibly have been born of a people who could do such things to others for amusement?

He tried to sit up, but found that something was holding him back. He gathered up all his strength and tried again. This time he succeeded, snapping the long vines of grass that had grown over him as he slept. Disgusted, he pulled the spidery tendrils off and chucked them aside; then he had a look around. He was in a clearing. Around him, he could see all of their things strewn everywhere – packs, weapons, clothes. But where were the others? He stood carefully. It was cold. He really needed to put something on to warm him up. He spied his breeches nearby, and his tunic. He quickly retrieved them and put them on. As he was looking around for his boots, he spied them – five grassy mounds. Two were much larger than the other three. He had found his companions – but were they still alive?

He rushed to the nearest mound and began tearing through the grassy foliage. Underneath he found Fia, naked also, and unconscious. He bent down and listened for signs of life, and was finally rewarded with faint sounds of her shallow breathing. He tried to wake her, shouting at her, shaking her – but nothing made her stir. He frantically ran around and freed the others from their entombment. For pity's sake, how long had they all been asleep? Days? Weeks? A century? No, not that long. Their clothes would have rotted away already. As he freed each one, he tried desperately to wake them. He found Flaskamper last. Rokey sat down and held his lover's head tenderly in his lap, sobbing inconsolably. *It's all my fault, he thought bitterly, my stupid quest that brought him here – that brought them all here, to spend eternity buried alive in this miserable place.*

A sudden fury gripped him. The sidhe had done this. He would find them and make them reverse it. There must be a way. What they had done, they could surely also undo. He laid the elf's head gently on the ground and stood, giving the area a closer scrutiny. There was no inn, no road either. It had all been a fabrication. The Faerie were, after all, masters of illusion. The clearing in which he stood seemed to be literally in the middle of nowhere. Thick woods surrounded the circular glade. There were no indicators of any kind to help him plot a course. They did have a compass though. It should still be in Stamford's pack, or somewhere near it. Rokey looked about until he located Stamford's pack. It had been emptied, the contents strewn everywhere. He searched through the long grass, growing more and more panicked as time passed. The sun was getting lower. He would soon know for certain which way was west, but then he would be stuck here, alone in the dark wood. Gods, forget the bloody compass. He needed the tinder kit. He pawed around some more, and did manage to find the tinder kit. Now he must gather some wood and get a fire ready. On his way to the edge of the wood, he found one of their water skins. He yanked off the stopper and took a long drink, after which he felt much better, physically anyway.

By the time the sun went down, he had started the fire, and also gathered much of their gear together. He had wanted to try and dress his friends, but their arms and legs were too stiff for him to move, so he settled for tucking blankets under and around them. He did not know if they felt the cold, but he felt it for them. He wasn't hungry at first, but eventually his stomach also awoke, and at that point he became ravenous. The bread that they were carrying had long since been consumed by mold, another clue as to how long they had been asleep. Some of the cheese was still good, though, and all of the dried meat, so he had his fill. Afterwards he sat, staring into the fire, pondering his next move. How was he ever to find the sidhe if they were unwilling to be found.

A strange phrase sprang suddenly into his mind.

It had been the Whispering Tree's answer to his first question; the one about his mother. He remembered now that he had been dreaming of the tree when he awoke, and of the phrase it had whispered to him. During his imprisonment at Braeden's Keep, he had all but forgotten it. Now it was back, sounding off like a trumpet in his head. Was that because it was now time to use it? And if so, how? If he simply called it out into the forest, would anyone hear him? Would anyone care? Well, it was worth a try. After all, what was the worst thing that could happen? He would look foolish in front of a few squirrels. He stood and walked to the center of the clearing. The moon shone brightly over his head, and the stars twinkled at him encouragingly. He brought his hands up around his mouth and shouted deep into the woods.

"Allaha begas, lei richna duo diegas.
Allaha begas, lei richna duo diegas.
Allaha begas, lei richna duo diegas."

Over and over he screamed the phrase, at the top of his lungs, until his throat had grown raw and his voice hoarse. Then he returned to the fire and sat back down, wondering if his action would draw friend, foe, or worst of all... nothing. He didn't want to sleep for fear that he would once again become like the others, but he must have nodded off for a moment – and that was when *she* appeared.

She was an adorable little thing, small enough to fit in the palm of one's hand, with a gauzy, near-transparent lavender frock that matched her tiny little paper-thin wings. Her hair was a deeper shade of purple, tied up with small ribbons of spun silver. She flitted around Rokey's head for a bit. Instinctively, he tried to swipe her away like an insect, and she retreated, hovering in front of his face, just beyond reach. The glow that she emitted soon woke him. It was many times brighter than that of a firebug. For a moment he thought he was dreaming again. Then, when he realized that he wasn't, it took all of his willpower not to make a grab for her. Calm yourself, he thought. You must calm yourself, or you may lose this chance forever. Marshaling his self-control, he relaxed, smiled even, and addressed her.

"Hello," he said. "My name is Rokey. Did you come to answer my call?"

"So it *was* you," she said. Her voice, too, was miniscule, like the jingle of a little glass bell. "I wasn't sure. You're not one of us, but your eyes –"

"I believe my mother was one of you," he told her. "Thank you...for coming."

"When we hear that call, we are bound to answer it. More would have come, but they're all in Tram Vallai. The king is holding court. My name is Pija. I was on my way there – I'm always late for everything – but then I heard your call of distress. You don't appear to be in much distress though."

"No, it's my friends...there." He pointed to where his friends lay sleeping beneath their blankets. "They're under one of your spells, of the sidhe I mean. Have you any idea how to wake them? It wasn't a funny trick; not funny at all."

A glint of comprehension came over the girl's face.

"Sooo, you're the one," she said, "the one that Morgrum and the others were telling about."

"Morgrum, yes!" said Rokey. "Morgrum was the name of the innkeeper, at least, he pretended to be an innkeeper. Then you know all about it."

"Course I know," said Pija with a broad smile. "All of us know. It was the best bit of fun had round these woods in years and years." She giggled, and Rokey felt like swatting her, but he held his temper in check.

"Pija, how long ago did they – did it happen?" Rokey asked. "How long have we been asleep?"

Pija took her chin in her hand and thought for a moment.

"Let me see," she replied, "not long now. Only twenty, maybe twenty-five days. No more than a moonsround for sure."

"Twenty-five days?" Rokey repeated incredulously. "That's impossible. We would have all frozen to death."

"Nay, you silly thing," she twittered. "The cradle grass protected you, kept you all warm and cozy, just like little babes."

"Well, Pija," Rokey said in a well-measured voice, "everyone has had their fun at our expense. Now I should like to have you tell me, please, how do I go about waking my friends?"

The Faerie girl grew serious, frowning and biting her lower lip.

"Well," she said. "Fun is fun, but it is also protection, is it not? I mean, there are few enough of us left. Strangers bring us nothing but trouble. Such has it always been. Best if others learn to fear the forest, and avoid it."

"I – that is, we did not mean you or your kind any harm," Rokey assured her. "We were only looking for you so that I could ask for your help."

Pija scoffed.

"Now what help could you possibly be needing from my folk?" she asked.

"Just some information," said Rokey. "That's why we've traveled all this way, just for the answers to a few questions."

The girl was silent for a few moments. Rokey left her alone to think. If he lost her now, he was doomed. He had no idea where to begin looking for this – this Tram Vallai. At last she seemed to make up her mind. He was relieved when she smiled at him.

"You're a handsome fellow, for a man, well, half-man," she said, "and you do seem sweet enough."

"Then will you please help me to wake my friends?" he asked, hopefully.

His heart sank as she shook her head.

"It is *not* that I do not want to help you," she said, noting his crestfallen look. "It is that I haven't the power. Your friends are under the spell of the greyblanket. Come to think of it, you were as well. How is it that you happened to wake all on your own, I wonder?"

Before Rokey could answer, she snapped her tiny fingers.

"Of course," she said. "The greyblanket does not affect us, the Faerie I mean. It is the blood of the sidhe in you that caused the spell to wear off. Were it otherwise, you would still be slumbering there with your friends, all bundled in cradle grass."

"Pija," Rokey insisted, "there must be some way of reversing the spell. There just has to be."

"'Tis a very young mind you have, Rokey," Pija observed, "thinking that for every *do* there is an *undo*. It is not always the way of things. Still, if there were a way, King Reighm would surely know of it. The question is, would he help you? His moods can be...unpredictable."

"Take me to him," Rokey pleaded. "I'll convince him to help. If I have to beg on my hands and knees, I will. Please, Pija, will you take me there?"

"I shall take you," she said with a nod, "but you may regret that I did so. I told you, we do not welcome outsiders, half-blood or not. The king may sooner have you staked to a mighill than lend you aid."

"I understand," said Rokey, "but it's the only chance I have of saving my friends."

"Your friends are fortunate to have you as their champion," said the Faerie.

"Oh, Pija," said Rokey, feeling a lump rise in his throat, "if you only knew my story, you would know that it is *I* who am privileged to have *them*."

"Can you fly, Master Rokey?" Pija asked unexpectedly.

"I'm afraid not," he answered.

"Well in that case," she said with a smile, "we shall have ample time on our way to court for you to share your story, and convince me just how privileged you truly are."

*   *   *

Tram Vallai was not in a fixed location. Rather the king's palace floated continuously to and fro throughout the whole of the Lower Wilds, invisible to any who had no business there. When Pija shared this fact with Rokey the next day, he wondered aloud how the king's subjects were ever able to find him. The Faerie laughed.

"The same way a nook sparrow finds its way back to the bogs every spring to mate, I suppose," she answered. "Truthfully, I am not certain how we know... we simply know."

They had been traveling through the woods now for several marks, he on foot, she flying just ahead of him. Rokey had tried to sleep a little the night before, but had been almost completely unsuccessful. The one time he *had* managed to drop off, he was plagued by horrible, disturbing nightmares. At last he'd given up and sat watching the fire, waiting for Pija's return. She hadn't said where she was going when she left, but had promised him that she would return for him at first light. He had feared the whole time that she would not come back, but she had arrived with the dawn, just as she had said she would.

Rokey's next concern had been for his friends. He was not happy with the notion of leaving them there in the clearing unprotected. His new companion had solved that dilemma by casting a simple spell, which had caused the cradle grass to grow back swiftly, covering each of them, just as they had been before.

"Nothing will harm them now," she had assured him, and he had believed her.

As they made their way through the forest, Rokey told Pija something of the circumstances that had brought them to the Lower Wilds in search of her kind. She listened to the tale with fascination, especially the part about his experience with Glaelie and the oracles at Glimmermere. When he finished the story, she remained silent for a while, mulling over his account, Rokey imagined. Then she stopped in midair, so abruptly that he nearly walked into her. She flew around to face him and, to his amazement, began to grow – larger and larger – until at last she stood on the ground before him, her plum-colored eyes level with his. Without a word, she threw her arms around him and kissed him on the cheek. Rokey laughed, more out of surprise than mirth.

"Well, well," he said. "To what do I owe this honor?"

"To the fact that you have suffered through so much pain and hardship," she told him, "yet your heart remains generous and kind. I do not know how much assistance I can render in this quest of yours, but whatever I *can* do, I shall...happily."

As Rokey looked at her, in her human-sized form, he felt the sharp stab of a painful memory – the memory of Flaskamper, blindly coupling with that other Faerie woman. Though he knew that his lover had been under the spell of the smoke, and not in control of his actions, it still hurt him to think back on it. He wondered how Flash was going to feel about it when he awoke.

"What's wrong, Rokey?" Pija asked, her voice concerned. "The saddest look just came over your face."

Rokey tried on a smile, which didn't feel right, but he kept it there nonetheless.

"Just a ghost," he told her. "One of many that I'll need to find a place for, once this is all over and done with."

Rather than return to her smaller size, she chose to continue the journey as she was. Perhaps, Rokey thought, it was her way of lending him comfort. He was grateful, but while the gesture did ease his sense of loneliness somewhat, he was reasonably sure that true comfort was going to be a long time in coming.

Chapter 26:

Tram Vallai

"Where do the sidhe live?"

Rokey and Pija had been traveling through the forest for most of the day now. The sky had become overcast, threatening to rain on them at any time. Fortunately the forest canopy was thick, and it would take a considerable downpour to reach them. He was taking advantage of the time to learn as much about his people as he could. Strange, he was already thinking of them as *his* people. At first, the idea had appalled him, the things that had been done to him and his friends – for amusement. However, the time he had spent with Pija had quickly begun to change his opinion of the Faerie. True, their ways were, in many respects, at odds with what he had been raised to believe was right and just, yet he found Pija so easy and enjoyable to talk to. If she was a typical example of the sidhe–

But was she? She had told him that King Reighm's moods were unpredictable. Perhaps *that* was more typical Faerie behavior. Given what the others had done, it wasn't difficult to believe the worst of them all.

"Well, where we live rather depends," Pija said in answer to his question. "Mainly, we are solitary creatures. Most of us having been alive for millennia are much too set in our ways to be able to abide sharing our quarters, and our lives. However, the rule among the Faerie is that there are no rules, and some of us cohabitate now and again."

"But where?" Rokey persisted. "I've seen no signs of habitation anywhere."

"Ah, well *that* depends on one's size," she answered. "Some of us are tiny enough to dwell in a tulip blossom, or the hollow of a tree. Others live in small caves, or little shacks, often built into the outcropping of a hill. One of the reasons you don't see signs of habitation is because, as I said, we're chiefly solitary folk. There are no villages or towns. We come together only for celebrations which, granted, are numerous, or to deter intruders, as Morgrum and the others did when you and your friends arrived."

Rokey felt a flash of anger again, but he suppressed it, trying to look at it from the sidhe's point of view. They *were* intruders after all. Still, the way they dealt with them – *Enough, you'll get nowhere with the king if you can't control your anger.* Their ways were different. Sex was merely a game to them, just as it is with some humans.

Just as it had once been for Flash.

The vision of his coupling with the Faerie female intruded on his thoughts once again. He had no reason for jealousy, given the circumstances, but it crept in anyway, like the cold creeps into one's bones in the winter. It troubled him, for he had an idea that, though Flash would feel terrible about what he had done, he would not be haunted by it, nor would he feel the same pangs of jealousy that Rokey was now feeling. Flaskamper was a man of the world, experienced in these matters. He could distinguish what was meaningful from what was not. In a way, Rokey envied him that experience, despite what Flash had told him about the emptiness he had felt before – *before you came into his life. You fool. Flaskamper adores you, yet you allow yourself to pout like a child over a thing that was not his fault, a thing to which you yourself succumbed. You must stop this nonsense immediately, else you will prove yourself unworthy of the love he feels for you.*

"Rokey, is something wrong?" Pija asked.

"No, nothing," he told her. "My mind was just wandering."

He could never explain to her the depth of the damage their little game might had caused, and might yet cause. He felt better now that he had berated himself, and had few worries about Flash, but what had the others done, and how were they going to feel about it when they awoke?

Suddenly Pija stopped.

"What is it?" he asked, concerned that they had gotten lost along the way.

"We have arrived," she announced.

"We have?" said Rokey doubtfully.

He looked around him. It looked just like the rest of the forest, thick with trees and brush. Then Pija raised her hands in front of her and spoke the name of their destination.

"Tram Vallai."

Abruptly the scene in front of him transformed, and a vast clearing appeared. In the distance was a castle, more amazing than Rokey could ever have imagined. It looked as though it were formed entirely of white basalt. It had clearly been constructed, yet it had the appearance of having grown right out of the ground. The castle stood on two enormous legs that gently curved impossibly upwards, thirty feet or more, before coming together to form the foundation, on which most of the structure sat. The entire building was actually a group of variously sized turrets, which jutted from the rough-hewn base at odd angles, giving it the look of a crystal formation. Atop the turrets, great clear multi-faceted crystal spires shot high up into the air, catching the sunlight, which had peeked out from behind the clouds, and splitting it into a multitude of rainbows. From where Rokey and Pija stood, a road that looked like liquid gold ran toward the castle, branching in two halfway along. Each fork meandered across the flowering meadowland, and up a different leg of the magnificent structure. From there, he could see that it wound all the way to the very top, where stood the largest turret of all. Its great spire seemed to touch the sky itself.

"Well," Pija said softly, "what do you think of it?"

Rokey couldn't find words to describe it.

"It's – it's...glorious," he whispered simply.

"Yes, it is indeed," Pija agreed. "I still get a bit breathless at the sight of it, though I've looked upon it a hundred thousand times. Shall we go?"

They stepped onto the road. It felt more like water than earth, giving ever so slightly with each step. Though it was now late autumn, the meadow's flora was in full bloom, and they basked in the sweet smell of honeypots, purple bonnets, dragongems and butter lilies. Rokey watched fat fieldhoppers as they leapt nimbly from one tall blade of meadow grass to another, and though he could not see them, he could hear a symphony of fiddlebugs chirping happily from their hiding places. Whatever he had been expecting, it was not this – no, nothing like this. How splendid it must be to live here in such serenity.

At the fork, there stood two beautiful, tall white walnut trees, resplendent with lush green leaves and heavy with the sweet, delicate nuts that they bore. Pija stopped and bowed to each of the trees, then veered off onto the right-hand path. Rokey thought the bow an odd gesture, but as he knew nothing of the sidhe culture, he said nothing about it. They followed the winding path until they reached the right hand leg of the castle's foundation. Here they were faced with what seemed to Rokey like an endless meandering staircase that had been carved right into the stone.

"How high are we going?" Rokey asked.

"All the way, I'm afraid," replied Pija. "The King's Court is in the uppermost tower. As most of the sidhe can fly, it is not so inconvenient as it may seem. Unfortunately –"

"Unfortunately," Rokey finished, "I am only half sidhe, and have no wings."

"I am awfully sorry," she said. "If I were larger, I could fly up and bear you with me. However, this is as large a form as I am capable of assuming, and my wings will not support us both."

"It's alright," he said. "I've just had a months rest. I'm sure I can make it. You go on and fly up. There's no point in us both walking."

Pija wouldn't hear of that, so they both started up the long stairway. It was even steeper and more difficult than it had seemed. At each level, they stopped to catch their breath before continuing on. After what must have been a mark or more, they finally reached the top level. Rokey was surprised to see that, where the door should have been, there was only what appeared to be a gigantic emerald, as tall as he was, set into the wall.

"Do not worry," said Pija, noticing his confusion, "It *is* a door. We have only to walk through it."

She took his hand and led him straight into the huge gem. It felt for a moment as though he were passing through warm pudding, but the next moment, they were inside the King's Court. Though Rokey would not have thought it possible, the interior was even more spectacular than the exterior, but in entirely different ways. In the first place, the room looked ten times larger from the inside than it had from the outside, and though the walls had been solid white from outside, from inside they were transparent, and one could see practically the entire forest. The floor was made of dark green glass, and throughout the room, massive red, purple and green mushrooms seemed to be growing right out of it. These had been shaped, or had grown in the shape of chairs and lounges, most of which were occupied by Faerie males and females. Their clothes were all made of the same shimmering, gauzy material that Pija wore, in every color of the rainbow. It looked as though it were spun from a spider's web. Music was playing, and in the center of the room a dance was in progress. The dancers, Rokey counted eight of them, were fluttering about in circles, carrying long red ribbons, which would form complex loops and whorls as they flew. It all seemed quite intricate, yet they all seemed completely at ease. The rest of the guests were engaged in a variety of activities – watching the dance, eating and drinking. Some were doing things that it embarrassed Rokey to witness, and though he tried to keep the shock from registering on his face, he felt himself flush nonetheless. Pija seemed not to notice, or else was simply being polite. Either way he was grateful.

"The king is there," she told him, pointing to the far end of the room. There he saw King Reighm, sitting in a large red and white mushroom throne. He looked much younger than Rokey had expected, though he knew that the king must be a thousand years old, if not more. *Do the sidhe ever age at all, he wondered, or do they one day simply cease to exist?*

Pija led him forward toward the throne. Suddenly he was very nervous. He worried about how the king would receive him. Could he ever persuade him to awaken his friends? And if not, what was he to do? He realized as they grew closer that he had given very little thought to this during their long walk here, and now that the moment was at hand, he was shamefully unprepared. Well, he had told Pija that he was ready to beg, and damn it, he would if he had to. He would do whatever was asked of him, however degrading or humiliating it might be. Pija bowed when they reached the king, and Rokey did likewise.

"Your Highness," she said, "I have brought you a visitor. He is one of those who came not long ago, the ones that Morgrum – dealt with. Though he, like the rest of his party, were placed under the greyblanket, he has awoken, because he is a half-blooded sidhe. At least, that is what we surmise. His name is Rokey, Sire. I humbly request that you hear him."

The king gazed steadily at Rokey, his face inscrutable. A long moment passed, and Rokey began to fear that he would not even be given the opportunity to speak. Well, by the gods, he was going to make his case, come rain or ruin. His friends, his lover, were all depending on him. He steeled himself, and spoke up.

"You Highness," he began, "as Pija told you, my name is –"

"I know who you are, Rokey," said the king calmly. "I feared that one day you would return."

Rokey was dumbfounded. This was not at all what he had expected.

"Return?" he finally sputtered. "You – you know me?"

"Certainly I know you," said King Reighm. "I have been king of this realm for just over two centuries now, since my mother and father went to ground, and I make it a point to know everything that goes on in my kingdom, especially a case of – well, a case such as yours."

Rokey shook his head, completely baffled. Then the truth began to dawn on him.

"Of course," he said slowly. "Of course you know me. You know me because I was born here."

"Precisely," said the king.

268| Pat Nelson Childs

"In the flash of memory I had, my mother held me as we danced in a circle. That was here. Before I was brought to the Noble Contemplative, I was here."

"Naturally," said Reighm.

Rokey couldn't believe that he was just now putting this part of it together. The sidhe were all but immortal. Fifteen years seemed like an eternity to him, but to them it had been but the blink of an eye. Did that mean – could it mean that his mother...

"Your Majesty," Rokey said, his voice quivering, "is my mother still alive?"

Instead of answering, the king abruptly stood.

"Come with me," he said. Pija, kindly wait for us here."

He turned right, and Rokey followed him to a large round rug not far from his throne. The king indicated that he should stand on it with him, which he did. A moment later, it began to descend, sinking down into the floor. Rokey looked around and saw that they were being lowered into another small room. When the rug reached the level of the floor in this other room, it stopped, and the two of them stepped off. The rug immediately began to rise again. Rokey asked if it were magic or some mechanical device. The king informed him that it was a little of both.

In this room, the walls were not transparent. It was furnished with only four mushroom chairs, and a tapestry depicting some great battle hanging on one of the walls. King Reighm seated himself in one of the chairs and invited Rokey to do the same. He waved a finger in the air and a little bell tinkled. In a moment, a Faerie male flew in carrying a tray with two tulip glasses on it. The king took one and, upon his invitation, Rokey took the other. The attendant then withdrew. Rokey eyed the glass suspiciously.

"Fear not," said the king. "It is only cherry wine. Believe me, I mean you no harm."

Rokey sipped some of the wine, which was wonderfully sweet and refreshing, then realized to his deep shame that, with all the thought about his mother, he had momentarily forgotten his friends.

"Your Highness," he said, "before we discuss me, I entreat you to aid my friends. As Pija said, we were all put under what you call the greyblanket. I awoke, but they are still trapped in that horrible sleep. I beg you to help me wake them as well. They do not mean you any harm. They merely accompanied me on this quest to help me find you to – to help me discover some answers. Please, Your Highness, please set them free."

"Ah yes, of course," said the king. "You must forgive Morgrum his little prank, Rokey. It is his responsibility to see that outsiders do not tread too close to our realm. Had he known who you were, things would have been handled...differently."

King Reighm folded his hands and closed his eyes. Several moments later, the rug began to descend again, carrying a somewhat older male, with bright yellow eyes, slightly protruding front teeth, and the wings and ears of a bat. When the rug touched the floor, he bowed.

"This is Fernspire, my chief magician," said Reighm.

"I thought that all sidhe were magicians," said Rokey.

The king smiled.

"It is true that the sidhe are all magical, by our nature," he said. "But to be *magical* is not to be a *magician.* A magician studies for many years to master spells, potions and other forms of arcana. I myself wouldn't have the faintest idea how to awaken your companions, though my own innate magic is quite strong. The whole business is really somewhat more complicated, but that will do for now. The point is that Fernspire here will know, that is, if anyone does. What say you Fernspire? Surely there is a way to lift the greyblanket. Has anyone ever done it before?"

"The answers are *yes,* and *no,*" said Fernspire, his teeth causing him to lisp slightly. "Yes, there is a potion to lift the greyblanket, and no, I do not believe it has ever been attempted before."

"Well, then," said the king, "how do you know it works?"

"I do not know for certain, Sire," said the magician, "but as I have yet to concoct a potion that has not performed as intended, I believe I can predict success with some considerable certainty."

"Well said, Fernspire," said the king. "No false modesty about you, to be sure. How soon can you have the potion ready?"

"I shall have it for you in the morning, Highness," said Fernspire.

"Very good, then. That will be all."

Fernspire bowed, and then the rug began to rise once again. When Fernspire was completely gone from view, the king returned his attention to Rokey.

"There, you heard him," he said. "Tomorrow morning you will have the means to awaken your friends. But I cannot give them leave to linger here in the forest. You, even as a half-blood, are still one of us, and are therefore always welcome. But the others are not, however dear to you they may be. As soon as they are revived and recovered, you are to take them out of here. Is that understood?"

"Yes, I understand," said Rokey, nearly choking with emotion. "Thank you, Your Highness. Thank you so much."

"All thanks are premature until the potion actually works," said Reighm, "but I've never had a reason to doubt Fernspire, and I see no reason to do so now. Meanwhile, we have some things to talk about, you and I. I don't know how much you know already –"

"Nothing, Sire," said Rokey. "Nothing at all. I had only a fragment of a memory when I began my quest. Then when I arrived at Glimmermere –"

Rokey told the king about Glaelie's reveal spell, and about his subsequent visit with the oracles. The king listened closely, his eyes widening slightly at the news of the Whispering Tree's second message. When he finished his story, King Reighm sat back in his chair.

"I am going to tell you the entire story," he told Rokey, "but I warn you now, it will *not* answer all of your questions. There are still details about which I myself am still ignorant, though before I go to ground, I too would very much like to know the entire account. If what you tell me is true, it is a tale well worth hearing in full. The part that I have to relay goes as follows.

"About....hmm, how old are you now?" asked the king.

"Nearly eighteen," Rokey replied.

"Very well," said the king. "A little over eighteen years ago, a man entered the Lower Wilds. He was a young, handsome fellow, not unlike yourself, but a few years your senior. It wasn't long before news of his presence reached Morgrum, and he dispatched a small team of Faerie guardians to observe him. One of those guardians was your mother.

"When they found the man, they discovered that he was badly injured and had fallen unconscious. It was apparent that if they did not step in and render some type of assistance, he would most certainly die. Now I do not wish to give the impression that we are an unfeeling people, though it may seem that way occasionally. Those who do not share our history cannot begin to understand the reasons behind our actions. After some careful consideration, the consensus was leaning toward doing nothing and letting nature take its course. That is, until your mother stepped in, and persuaded Morgrum and the others to change their minds... to help the man survive. I think that she had already begun to fall in love with him a little, though she had barely set eyes upon him. It *does* happen sometimes between humans and Faerie, though it is an extremely rare occurrence. In any case, the decision was made to bring the man here to Tram Vallai, where he could not only be cared for, but also guarded. I think it may have also been in Morgrum's mind that bringing him here would place the onus of the final decision upon me. I would not blame him if that were true. I myself found the choice to be a difficult one, and have questioned it more than once over these past eighteen years."

For a few moments, the king sat quietly, seemingly lost in thought. Finally, he collected himself.

"Where was I?" the king continued. "Oh yes, the man was brought here, and his wounds treated. Slowly, he began to recover. It was obvious from the moment he awoke that he had not come to the Lower Wilds to seek us out. He had merely been attempting to escape from some deadly enemy, though he would tell us nothing about those from whom he'd been running, nor why they meant him harm. He was a gentle and polite fellow, grateful to us for our assistance, but very reticent. It was apparent to me that some great burden was troubling him, one that he felt he could not share, that is, except with one other."

"My mother?" Rokey guessed. King Reighm nodded.

"They spent a great deal of time together. I warned her that it would only lead to heartbreak, but she was headstrong, and ignored my advice. Before long, she admitted to me that she was carrying his child. While the news distressed me, I also found it exciting. There had not been a child born here amongst the sidhe for centuries, so once the shock had worn off, everyone was delighted, myself included. But at the same time I feared that the secret from which the man was trying to hide would eventually catch up with him, bringing danger here to the denizens of my realm. He apparently shared my concern, for a month before you were due to arrive, he departed, suddenly and without warning. He left a note for your mother, which said only – *You understand what must be done.* I know this because she showed it to me before she burned it. I asked her what it meant, but she would not explain. It was then I realized that he had shared with her whatever burden had been upon him."

The king drained his glass and rang his invisible bell again. The attendant returned, this time wheeling a cart laden with fruit, cheese, bread, meat and more wine. The king continued his tale as they ate and drank together.

"The following month, you were born," said the king, "and for a time your mother, indeed all of us, forgot about the dark circumstances that had haunted your father. Humans experience joy at the birth of a child, yet for them it is a common event. Imagine the joy *we* felt when *you* arrived, the first baby to be in our midst in so many hundred years. The celebrations went on non-stop for weeks, until we had thoroughly exhausted ourselves." Reighm laughed and shook his head. "It was a grand time."

"And my father..." said Rokey, "did you ever see him again?"

The king's smile dimmed slightly, and his eyes became sad.

"I was hoping that you would not ask me," he said, "for I would not have volunteered this information had you not. The truth is, I never saw your father again...alive. He was found just after you were born, on the outskirts of the forest. His would-be murderers had apparently caught up with him at last. I never told your mother. Her heart had already been broken when he left; I could see no point in adding to her pain."

Rokey found that he was weeping – mourning the father he had never met. He had never really realized until this moment how strong his hope had always been that he would one day find him alive. Now that that hope was gone, he felt a deep emptiness inside, as though a part of him had suddenly been stolen away.

"The – the brothers told me that I came to them when I was two," said Rokey. "Was I here the whole time before that?"

"Yes," replied the king. "You were with us for just over two years. We hardly had time to get used to your being here, before you were gone again."

"Why did my mother bring me to the Brotherhood?" Rokey asked.

"Because she didn't believe you would be safe here," the king answered. "I don't know precisely what it was that she feared; she would never tell me. But I knew something was odd, even odder than the pairing of a human and a sidhe. And how did I know? You told me that the ghost of Glimmermere's spell transformed your eyes from human to sidhe. What you do not know is that the eyes you now have are the eyes you were born with. For the first few days of your life, you looked exactly like one of us – minus a set of wings. Then suddenly one morning, your mother looked into your cradle and discovered that your eyes had taken human form. It came as a great shock to the rest of us, but she did not seem at all surprised. In fact, it appeared to me as though she had been expecting it to happen. After that, she grew more and more nervous about your continued presence here. All she would confide in me is that she had good reason to fear for your life, and always would so long as you remained with us. Finally, she could bear it no longer. We knew, of course, that the Noble Contemplative was nearby in the Emerald Mountains. Your mother came to the conclusion that since you now looked like an ordinary human, that would be the safest place for you, hidden among the other orphans at the monastery. One night she bundled you up and left, telling no one but me where she was going. She was gone for only three days. Few even realized that she had gone. When she returned, she told everyone that you had died, and from the way that she grieved for you, no one had any difficulty believing it. She was never the same afterwards. The light was forever gone from her eyes."

"Your Highness," Rokey said, his voice just barely above a whisper, "what happened to her? You speak of her as though she were dead, and yet, I get the impression that there is more to it than just that. Tell me, please, what became of her?"

"You are perceptive, just as your mother was. To answer your question, I must explain to you something else about the sidhe. You see, Rokey, it is not our way to die, as humans do. We are primordial creatures, all but immortal. But while we do not age perceptibly, we do grow old, and weary. When that happens, we perform a ritual that we call *going to ground*. It means that we permanently undergo a transformation to another, simpler form, usually a tree. You must have seen the two white walnut trees growing where the road forks?"

Rokey nodded.

"Those are my mother and father, Rokey. They went to ground together, just over two hundred years ago. They have flourished ever since, but without the cares and tribulations of life as we know it."

So that's the reason Pija bowed to the two trees, Rokey thought. The former king and queen certainly merited that courtesy.

"I think you can guess what I am going to tell you next," said the king.

"My mother has also gone – gone to ground?" Rokey rasped.

The king nodded.

"Yes she did," Reighm said gently, "just a few moonsrounds after she brought you to live with the brothers. She was very young to have made such a choice, and I did attempt to dissuade her, but the ultimate decision belongs to each Faerie citizen. Even as king, I had no power to stop her."

The king leaned forward to place his hand on Rokey's shoulder. Rokey was, for the moment, oblivious to him. He had begun to sob openly, his face buried in his hands. His two fondest hopes had vanished in the space of a mark. His father was dead, and his mother, though not dead in the human sense of the word, may just as well be. He would never be able to speak with her, to feel her arms around him. They would not be able to walk together in the meadow, just the two of them, or dance again in the Faerie ring, as they had done when he was a baby. More importantly, she would not know how he loved her, how he had loved her for all these years, and that he forgave her for giving him up, for doing what she thought was best for him. After a few minmarks, he realized that he had fallen to pieces in front of the king. He hastily apologized, but the king told him to think nothing of it.

"I know how you must feel," said the king. "I know that it must seem to you that your mother is dead to you. We do not feel that way about those that have gone to ground, but I cannot expect you to understand that, being unaccustomed to such an alternative."

"Where is she?" Rokey asked. "Can I see her?"

"It is dark now," King Reighm replied, "and you need rest. First thing in the morning, I will take you to her myself."

Chapter 27:

Reunions

Rokey fully expected to be sick at any moment. He never thought that he had a fear of heights, but at the moment, he was nearly scared out of his wits. He was sitting on a perilously thin strand of rope, which was tied around the waists of the Faerie King and his new friend, Pija. They were flying high above the treetops of the Lower Wilds. When Pija had first suggested that they use this method to transport Rokey to the site where his mother had gone to ground, he hadn't liked it very much. But now that they had been airborne for nearly a quartermark, he liked it even less. On the bright side, the king had assured him that the trip would take no longer than a halfmark – so they were halfway there.

He had barely slept a wink the night before. For one thing, his mind couldn't let go of all the things he had learned. Also, he desperately missed Flaskamper. He felt guilty sleeping in his soft mushroom bed while Flash and the others lay outside on the cold ground. Of course, they couldn't feel it, but he felt wrong about it nonetheless. He was relieved when Pija had come to his room at sunrise to collect him.

His two winged bearers hit some sort of wind pocket and dipped abruptly. Rokey's stomach lurched again, and he had all he could do to keep down the redberry pastry he had eaten for breakfast. One more swoop like that and he would wind up imprisoned for vomiting on the king.

Finally they began to descend, plunging toward the ground all too quickly for Rokey's comfort. At the last moment they slowed, however, giving him the opportunity to get his feet under him before he was deposited once again on solid ground, shaken but still in one piece. It took him a few moments to get used to gravity again. When he had adjusted, he looked around, trying to get his bearings.

"The clearing we want is just ahead," said the king. "It is on top of a small hill. It was your mother's favorite spot in the forest, a place that she used to come to reflect." He chuckled. "That is not a thing the Faerie are renowned for, despite our centuries of accumulated wisdom."

They pressed forward, up a shallow embankment, and when they reached the top, the king stopped.

"The clearing is just through these trees, Rokey," he said. "Perhaps you would prefer to go in alone."

"Thank you, Your Highness," Rokey replied. "You are very considerate."

He started in, but stopped.

"Is she – will she....be aware of me, at all?" Rokey asked.

The king sighed.

"Now that is the big question, isn't it?" the king replied. "It is one that we have much pondered over and debated throughout the centuries. The truth is, no one knows for certain, but if you want my opinion, I think a spark of the being that once was must surely remain. It may be that I believe this simply because it pleases me to think that something of my own mother and father are still here with me. But it is how I feel, nonetheless."

"How will I know which one is my mother?" Rokey asked.

King Reighm smiled broadly.

"You will know, Rokey," he said. "Trust me, you will know."

Rokey held his breath as though he were about to plunge into the sea, then walked through the trees and into the clearing. At first he saw nothing out of the ordinary. It was just a small, oval-shaped glade, the ground softened by a bed of evergreen needles. The branches stretched up and out overhead, blocking most of the sun, so he found himself growing quite chilly. Then, just as he began to feel a twinge of discouragement creeping in, he saw her.

She was beautiful – a tall golden ash, illuminated by a single bright shaft of sunlight that had pierced the canopy. He knew that it must be her, for there were no others like it in the vicinity – none in the entire forest as far as he had seen. Her long white trunk was smooth and slender; her top, resplendent with thousands of fiery golden leaves. Amid the darker walnuts, oaks and evergreens, she shone like a beacon.

Rokey simply stood and stared at her for a long time, taking in all of her exquisite beauty. If the form one took upon going to ground was in any way indicative of how one appeared in life, then his mother must have been breathtaking. Or perhaps it was more an indication of one's inner beauty. Either way, it was no wonder that his father had fallen in love, despite all of his troubles. At last, he approached her. It was an awkward moment for him. Could she really be aware of his presence – aware of anything at all? He proceeded forward until he stood directly in front of her. *Well,* he thought, *if she is aware of you, she shall be frightfully disappointed if you travel all this way and don't speak to her. And if she isn't, well, no one is here to see you talking to a tree, right?*

"Hello, Mother," he began hesitantly. "It's me, Rokey. I know you probably don't recognize me. I was so young when you – when you were forced to – I won't say it. I don't want to make you feel bad, but I want you to know that I don't hate you for it. I admit, there were times at the Brotherhood, when I was sad or lonely, when I did get very angry with you. But that was before – before I knew why you did what you did. I know now that you were only trying to protect me. I still don't know from what yet, or whom, but I'm going to find out. You see, I've made some wonderful friends in the last few months. They've been right beside me throughout my entire journey, helping me to figure things out. And Mother, I've fallen in love. He's – it's a he. I hope you don't mind. It wasn't my idea to be a samer. I just...I just turned out that way. I can't believe you'd mind, though. Your culture seems willing to accept most anything. Apparently it's also perfectly acceptable in many other parts of Firma. Guess I was the last one to find that out. Anyway, his name is Flaskamper. He's an elf, and something of a devil too. But I love him so much, Mother, it make my insides hurt just thinking about him. He and the others are asleep nearby. Today I shall go and wake them. I miss them all terribly, but especially Flash. When I see him again I'm going to – well I suppose there are some things a boy should *not* share with his mother." Rokey grinned mischievously, but then grew serious again. "I've thought of you so many times over the years, made so many wishes, and imaginary plans of things we would do together one day. I think it's something all children who've lost their parents do. I knew lots of other boys at the monastery who used to talk about their parents as if they might walk through the gate at any moment and take them on a picnic. I suppose I was like that too sometimes."

Tears began to flow down Rokey's cheeks. He told his mother more about himself, about growing up in the Brotherhood, and the tragedy that had resulted in his expulsion. He told her about their journey, about how he had met Flaskamper and the others, and all of the adventures they had had on their quest so far.

"Now I'm finally here," he said, wrapping his arms around the tree's delicate trunk, "and I want to believe that you can hear me. I *have* to believe it, because I need for you to know how much – how much I love you, how horribly I've missed you all these years, and how happy I am to have finally found you. I feel that there is so much still for me to do, so much I have yet to discover. But even if I fail utterly in the rest of my quest, at least I have discovered who you were – who you are, and that you loved me so much – so much that you were willing to let me go."

Rokey sank down to the soft forest floor and cried. He could not tell if the tears were of joy, or sorrow, or simply relief. A breeze stirred through the clearing, rustling his mother's lovely golden leaves. For a moment he stopped to listen, half-hoping that perhaps she, too, might whisper a message to him. But the only sound was the gentle sweep of the wind through the branches. He would simply have to believe; believe because, as the king had said, it pleased him to think that something of her remained. At last, Rokey stood and said good-bye, with the promise that he would return to visit her as soon and as often as possible. He took one of the golden leaves that had fallen to the ground beneath her and tucked it into his pocket. Then he turned and left the little clearing, and his mother, to rejoin Pija and the king.

They said nothing to one another on the journey home. Rokey's head was so full he scarcely had a chance to feel ill, and before he knew it, they were touching down again directly in front of Tram Vallai. Fernspire was waiting for them, holding a small, blue bottle in his hand. The king took it from him and they spoke for a moment, before the magician flew off back into the castle.

"Here is the potion, Rokey," said the king, "as promised. Fernspire's instructions are to simply place a drop or two between their lips. They should then wake within a mark."

"Thank you, Your Highness." Rokey said with emotion. "Thank you for everything."

"No thanks are necessary," the king told him. "and you are welcome to visit us anytime. Despite your human blood, you are one of us. Pija, I trust, will see you safely back to your friends."

The king turned and made to fly off, but Rokey abruptly stopped him.

"Your Majesty," he said, "in all that has happened, I forgot even to ask – what was her name?"

King Reighm smiled warmly at Rokey.

"Her name," he replied, "was Adeylia."

With that, he too flew off toward the high castle turret, leaving Rokey and Pija alone.

Adeylia, Rokey thought, *even a beautiful name.*

The two set off back out into the forest, and Rokey was sorry to see the magnificent castle – along with the entire meadow – shimmer and vanish behind them, as though it had never existed. He was poor company for Pija on the trip back. His thoughts preoccupied him completely, switching alternately between the visit with his mother

278| Pat Nelson Childs

and his impending reunion with Flaskamper and his friends. He was so torn with conflicted emotions, he scarcely knew from one moment to the next whether he would laugh or cry. He did at one point come around enough to apologize for his unsociable behavior, to which Pija replied that unsociable behavior was a hallmark of the Faerie culture, and that he shouldn't worry about it.

It was late in the afternoon when they reached the campsite. Rokey was relieved to see that nothing had been disturbed, especially his slumbering companions.

"Well Rokey," Pija said, "I know that you're eager to revive your companions, so I'll say good-bye now."

"Oh, Pija, don't go," said Rokey. "I want you to stay and meet my friends, I mean, my other friends."

Pija smiled and wrinkled her nose at him.

"It's kind of you," she said, "really it is, but I wouldn't feel quite right about it somehow. We Faerie are quirky that way. But don't you fear. I shall keep my eye on you until I know that the potion works."

Rokey stepped closer and gave her a hug.

"Thank you for all that you've done for me, and for my friends," he told her. "I can't imagine what I would have done if you hadn't come to my rescue."

"You would have found another way," she replied. "You're a resourceful boy. It's the sidhe blood in you."

She giggled, and then suddenly had reverted to her smaller form again, and was fluttering just in front of his face.

"Good luck to you Rokey," she said. "I hope that we'll meet again one of these days."

She flew away, back into the forest, and Rokey waved her good-bye. He had grown to like her a great deal in their two days together, and would definitely miss her.

Rokey wasted no time in once again freeing his friends from the cradle grass that covered them, and administering the required dose of potion from the little blue bottle. Flaskamper received the last two drops, and Rokey plunked himself down beside him, so as to be there the moment he awoke. After what seemed to be an eternity, he heard the group begin to stir. It was actually Lorq that sat up first, yawning and stretching. It took him a moment to realize where he was, and that he was completely naked. Rokey had thoughtfully laid out clothes for each of them, and he called over to Lorq that he need only look behind him to find suitable attire. Lorq grabbed it gratefully. The others began waking just moments later. Finally, he heard a moan come from his lover's lips.

"Flash," said Rokey eagerly, "Flash, are you awake?"

"I must be," the elf muttered. "If I were dead, I wouldn't feel so horrible."

"I've got clothes for you right here," Rokey told him.

Flaskamper sat up, rubbing his sore head.

"Why the devils am I – oh gods, the tavern!" he said, suddenly wide awake. "Those bastards got us with some kind of – "

"Smoke," Rokey finished for him, "magical smoke."

"Then it *was* all real," he groaned. "Those things I did – oh great gods, Rokey, I'm so sorry. You must hate me now."

Rokey leaned over and wrapped his arms around Flaskamper, holding him tightly.

"No sweetheart. I don't hate you. I love you more than life. You couldn't help yourself, anymore than any of us could. Remember, I'm just as guilty as you are, which is to say that neither of us is guilty at all."

"If I ever get my hands on the vermin that did this – " Flaskamper began, rising shakily to his feet.

"Flash," Rokey broke in, "I've already met them, well, not the ones who actually did this to us, but some of the Faerie, even the king – King Reighm."

The others had dressed quietly and gathered around him and Flaskamper. Rokey hadn't seen exactly what each of them had done that night in the tavern, under the smoke's influence, but he knew what had happened to him – and to Flash. What the Faerie had thought of as amusement was as good as rape as far as he was concerned. Having been treated so graciously by King Reighm, he was willing to forgive and – well, forgive anyway. He wasn't at all sure about the others.

"You say you've already met them?" said Stamford.

"Yes," Rokey answered. "I'll explain it all to you in a little while. Right now the sun is getting ready to set, and we need to finish making camp and gather some more wood for the fire before dark. It's grown a fair bit colder since you – since we fell asleep."

"Just how long have we been asleep?" asked Flaskamper.

"From what the Faerie told me," Rokey replied, "I'd say just about a month."

"A month!" cried the elf. "Shite! We're slaves for one bloody month, then toadstools for another. What else can we look forward to, I wonder?"

"You know better than to ask," said Stamford groggily.

They made camp and got the fire going. Flaskamper had neither the arrows nor the strength to hunt, so they made due with what remaining provisions they could scrape up. Over their sparse meal, Rokey filled them in on everything that had transpired after he had awoken. They all listened with great interest. Afterwards, Flaskamper pulled Rokey close to him.

"You're a real champion, *chatka*," he said. "You saved us all again."

"Well, Pija had a lot to do with it," Rokey said, "as did King Reighm."

"Well, given that it was *his* people who – who did what they did with us," said Stamford, staring at the fire, "I'm sure you'll understand why I, for one, am not exactly overflowing with gratitude and warm, fuzzy feelings about them."

"I do," said Rokey. "Believe me, I do. I won't expect you to forgive them for those horrible things they did. *I* was only able to because of the help they gave me, but I'll still not be able to forget it – not ever."

"How do you feel now, Rokey," Fia asked, steering the conversation away from the painful topic, "now that you've found out all these things and – and had a chance to visit with...your mother?"

Rokey was silent for a moment as he tried to put all of his feelings into words.

"It's hard to explain," he said at last. "In a way I feel like I've gained part of myself back, while at the same time another part has gone missing. I – I never realized until after last night and this morning just how much of a fantasy I had built around my mother and father, and around the hope that one day I would find them, and we would be a family again. That's the part of me that's gone now. It's been replaced with the reality; my father is dead, and my mother has gone to ground. We'll never be a family again. We never were a family. And yet – it's all right. I can live with that reality, however much of a disappointment it is because – because I know now how much they loved each other, and me." He shook his head. "As I said, it's hard to explain."

"I think you've explained it very well," said Fia. "It's amazing, to wake up and find that so much has changed."

"It certainly is," Stamford agreed. "I suppose what we need to figure out now is, where do we go from here?"

* * *

Rokey and Flaskamper lay tangled in each other's arms, sweaty and sated. Each of them had gone to great lengths to prove to the other that there were no ill feelings about their drug-induced transgressions. Outside it had gone bitter cold, and a harsh wind was rumbling the tent, but inside they were warm and cozy together.

"How do you think everyone else will handle – you know, what happened?" Rokey asked his lover.

"Well, I spoke to Lorq earlier when we went off to water the bushes," said Flaskamper. "I actually only caught parts of what he said – did you ever hear a giant peeing? No, I suppose not. Well trust me, it's like standing next to the falls at Crooked River."

He cupped his hands and roared into them, imitating the sound of rushing water. Rokey began to laugh, which started Flaskamper going. They held onto one another, both giggling hysterically, until their sides ached. Finally, they got sufficient control of themselves for Flaskamper to continue what he'd started to say.

"Anyway," the elf continued, "Lorq told me that the two of them...ah, consummated their relationship in a little different way than they had hoped. He talked to her about it as they set up camp and they've decided to just put it behind them and start off afresh – forget all about it as best they can. I think they'll do fine, provided of course they don't discover at some point that she's carrying a little Lorq around. Be tough to just forget about *that*. As for Stamford and Fia...I don't know. Neither of them made any mention of their experiences. If I have an opportune moment with either of them, I'll see if they feel like spilling. If not, well, then I guess we should just leave it be."

"Sounds good to me," Rokey replied, wearily, adding, "I wish I could leave it *all* be, Flash. I'm so tired. And it seems the more I learn, the worse things look.

"Go to sleep, *chatka*," said Flaskamper, "You've had a long couple of days."

"Aren't you going to sleep?" asked Rokey.

"Eventually," the elf replied. "I am exhausted, but after spending the past month asleep, I'm a little wary about dropping off again."

As it happened, Flaskamper fell asleep sooner than he expected. When the next morning came, they broke camp and proceeded due west, which they estimated would be the fastest way out of the Lower Wilds. They had not been able to reach a sound conclusion the previous night as to what exactly should be done next. They decided to try to pick up the old merchant road once they left the forest, which, if Stamford's memory of the old maps he had seen was correct, should curve north toward Riversedge, and, eventually, back to Duncileer. It had been decided that, in the absence of a solid plan of action, the city would be the safest place for Rokey to be. From there, they could figure out their next move.

They did not quite make it clear of the woods that day, and were forced to spend one more night beneath the trees. Nothing disturbed them, though, and the following day they reached the western edge of the Lower Wilds. Luck was with them, for the old merchant road ran straight along the wood at their point of exit. They followed it as it wound in a mostly westward direction for the better part of the day. They met no one whatsoever, not even a field hare. As the afternoon stretched on, they came to a fork in the road. One path continued westward. The other curved north, the way they had planned on heading. The group had just stepped onto the northerly fork when suddenly Rokey stopped in his tracks and stared, wide-eyed, off to their left.

"What is it, Rokey?" said Flaskamper. "What's wrong?"

"Flash," Rokey said, his voice in an awed whisper, "look at the other pathway from here."

"I'm looking," said the elf. "What am I supposed to be seeing?"

"Look at the big boulder there just to the left of the path," Rokey replied. "and to the right, that small copse of melody trees. You see?"

"Of course I see it," said Flaskamper, "but what does it mean?"

"Don't you remember?" Rokey asked, "I told you about the vision I saw in the Reflecting Pool – of a path with a big, egg-shaped rock to the left and – "

"And a small copse of melody trees off to the right!" Flaskamper finished for him. "Rokey is this it? Is this the place you saw?"

Rokey nodded vigorously.

"I'd swear to it," he said. "It looks just like the picture in the pool. It's the answer from the second oracle, to the question about who is behind the attempts on my life. The answer lies in that direction, not this one. I'm sure of it."

"But Rokey," said Stamford, "that way leads to the eastern pass of the Emerald Mountains...back to where you started from."

"I know it seems strange," Rokey said, "and I don't know what it means. Perhaps there's something at the Noble Contemplative – some clue as to why my mother brought me there. I'm positive that Abbott Tomasso was going to tell me what he knew about my parents the night he died. Perhaps the story is written somewhere, in a journal maybe. I don't know, but I know that the answer lies there, and that's the way I've got to go."

He turned and started slowly down the other road.

"Well, as the old ballads say," said Flaskamper, "*where goest thou, my love...* and so on..."

The elf shrugged his shoulders in resignation and followed Rokey. The others all agreed, and joined them on the westward path. Their commitment to stay together, whatever the dangers might be, had not diminished. They all smiled as they glanced at one another, then started onward, plunging once again into the great unknown.

Part Three

Chapter 28:

Surprise Guest

Stamford woke up in a cold sweat, a scream of terror on his lips. For a brief instant, he thought he was back in the Hattiar salt mines. It was cold and damp, and utterly black. After taking a moment to organize his thoughts, however, he realized that he was safe in his tent, in the company of his friends. He could hear Lorq sleeping next to him. The giant's slow steady breathing helped him to calm his racing heart. Lorq wasn't awake, which meant that he hadn't actually screamed. The dark man breathed a sigh of relief. The last thing he wanted was to upset his friends with his silly nightmares.

Silly maybe, but frightening… yes, frightening indeed.

He pulled on his clothes and stepped outside. The sky was black with clouds and it had begun to snow. He thought about going back to retrieve his cloak, but decided not to for fear that he would wake Lorq. Outside he found Fia on watch, bundled in her own cloak, tending the fire. He strolled over and sat down beside her. She glanced over at him.

"What's the matter," she asked, "can't sleep?"

He nodded, but did not elaborate. She could see that he was not in the mood for idle chat, so she left him to his thoughts. If he chose to confide in her, he would. For a time, they sat together just staring into the fire. Then Stamford spoke quietly.

"The nightmares have returned," he said.

Fia let this sink in. It had been over a year since Stamford's horrible nightmares had stopped. She wondered what had happened to bring them back again.

"The same kind?" she asked.

Again, he nodded. In his nightmares, he was always portrayed as one who brought death to the innocent. Usually he was dressed in the robes and helmet of the Black Guard of Ulgiarrah, brandishing the traditional long, curved sword, chopping down women, or young children. Their blood would always splatter him, sticking like tree sap, until he was covered from head to toe. He would try rinsing it off – would scrub and scrub, but no amount of washing would remove it. Then the dream would change, and the ghosts of those he had killed would return to take their revenge, rising up from the ground around where he slept. As their lifeless eyes stared and their cold hands reached for him, he would scream... sometimes his screams would be real, but not this time. This time he had not roused anyone around him, thank the gods. The last thing he needed was a lot of attention and worry. He wasn't even sure why he had told Fia except – except that it seemed like the right thing to do.

"What's your explanation for their return?" she now asked.

"I haven't any," he replied. "I had none the entire time we were in the custody of the Saebrilites. One would think that if they were going to return, that would have been the time. Instead, they begin again during a relatively quiet part of our journey. It makes little sense to me."

If Stamford had believed in precognition, he might take this sudden resurgence of night terrors as a warning of some kind. He did not though, at least, as far as his own life was concerned. That was not to say that he put no stock in intuition. His, he would swear, had saved his life on more than one occasion. Perhaps these nightmares were merely accompanying the feeling that had begun to steal over him these past two days – the feeling that they were nearing the mouth of the dragon, and that the time of his greatest opportunity would soon be at hand.

By dawn when they broke camp, there was already over two inches of snow on the ground, and the skies looked as though it might continue throughout the day. Rokey and Flaskamper romped happily, pelting each other with snowballs and wrestling around like bear cubs throughout the day. It lightened Stamford's heart a bit to see the elf so content. He hoped that the two of them would see each other through all the trials that were sure to follow. Flaskamper was the closest thing he would ever have to a son. Funny, that, since in actual years the elf was nearly as old as he. Of course, elves lived much longer and matured much more slowly than humans, so in that sense, he was closer to Rokey's age, and that is how Stamford thought of him.

Lorq too seemed happy with his new mate. Though neither of them spoke all that much, they walked side by side, occasionally smiling at some joke they had shared. The Saebrilite had no clothes suitable for this cold weather, so she was dressed in one of Lorq's outfits. It was too large for her, which made her look strangely childlike and vulnerable, as vulnerable as a Saebrilite could look anyhow.

And Fia – Fia had been strangely quiet since Rokey had roused them all from their slumber. He knew that he should probably try to draw her out, find out what, if anything was troubling her. He did not know what she had undergone while under the spell of the sidhe magic, but he strongly suspected that it was her first experience of a sexual nature. He wondered if perhaps it had had some profound affect on her. He was ill equipped for such a delicate operation, however. For all that he and Fia had been through together, she was still, in many ways, a mystery to him. While he felt comfortable sharing his darkest secrets with her, he would not know how to even begin trying to elicit hers, or what he would be able to do with them even if he could.

Face it, Stamford, he thought, *somewhat sadly, though you now use your skills for good instead of evil, they have not changed. All you know is how to hack, slash and burn – to save lives by taking lives. In all other areas, you are all but powerless.*

The snowfall continued until it was just over ankle-deep, then stopped. As the day was drawing to a close, the clouds vanished, and the sun made a short appearance just before it began to dip down towards the mountains. The six chose a clear spot just off the path and began to set up camp once again. Rokey estimated that they were well within another day's hike of the monastery, which was a relief because their supplies were getting very low. He was both excited and anxious at the thought of returning to the Noble Contemplative. So much had come to pass since he had left, and yet, when he thought back on his last days there, the pain seemed as fresh as if it had happened yesterday. And how would they treat his return? Would they make any effort to help him at all?

As all these thoughts floated through his head, he heard a crackling in the woods. He stood up from where he had been bent over tying off his tent and listened, tuning his newly heightened senses to the surrounding brush. He had almost convinced himself that he had imagined the noise, when he heard it again. There was something out there, something larger than a bird or a rodent. He honed in on the spot from which he thought the noises had come. Yes, there was someone – something hiding there. Slowly and casually, he walked over to where Flaskamper was working on the fire and whispered into his ear. The elf nodded and went to tap Stamford on the shoulder. A whisper and a nod later, they separated.

"I need more firewood," Flaskamper said aloud and plunged into the woods just below the point that Rokey had described to him. Stamford made a wide circle around the opposite way, sliding his sword noiselessly from its sheath. Quietly the two sneaked around behind their quarry. Then, at some unspoken signal between them, they pounced. For a few moments, both of them disappeared into the brush. All Rokey could see were the bushes quivering and cracking. At last, Flash and Stamford stood up, holding a figure between them. Rokey instantly recognized the reddish brown robe of a brother, but he could not identify him, for the hood was covering his face. The man struggled for a short time, but then gave up and simply hung there, held up by his two captors. They dragged him from the woods and shoved him forward into their campsite. The hooded figure stumbled and fell at Rokey's feet, where he lay cowering. Rokey knelt down next to the trembling figure, and gently pushed back the cowl of his robe. He gasped in astonishment as a familiar face emerged, bloody and beaten, but still recognizable.

"Ely!" Rokey cried. "Ely, by the gods, what has happened to you?"

The man slowly lifted his swollen face toward the voice. He peered cautiously at the person in front of him, and his eyes slowly lit up with recognition.

"Rokey...." he croaked. "Rokey, is that really you?"

He tried to stand up. Rokey stood up with him, then caught him as he fell again.

"Yes, Ely, it's me," Rokey said. "It's me. Come on, let's lay you down and have a look at where you're hurt."

"Rokey, Rokey it's you." Ely began to sob.

"Flash, love, can you give me a hand?" Rokey asked. The elf hurried to support the young man's other side, and together they helped him into their tent. Rokey quickly unrolled his blankets, and they gently lowered him down. Flaskamper went to fetch their medical supplies while Rokey stripped off his torn, bloody robe. He was surprised to find that Ely was naked underneath. He had never known his friend to go without the traditional muslin undershorts. Another part to this mystery. He checked him over and, finding no serious wounds, covered him with more blankets. Flaskamper returned with his small medicine bag. Rokey dug out some rembis leaves tore them into small pieces.

"Ely," said Rokey. "Ely, listen to me. I'm going to put these rembis leaves in your mouth. I want you to chew them up and swallow them, all right? They taste a bit nasty, but they'll make you feel much better. Do you hear me?"

After a moment, Ely nodded his head and Rokey tucked the torn leaves into his friend's mouth. Ely winced a bit, either in pain or from the taste, but chewed and swallowed them dutifully. Rokey then held his head up and gave him a drink from his water skin. Almost as soon as the young man finished drinking, he fell fast asleep. Rokey stood and motioned for Flaskamper to follow him outside. Fia was there waiting.

"Who is it, Rokey?" she asked. Is he badly hurt?"

"It's Ely," Rokey replied. "He was my best friend and roommate at the monastery. He looks like he's been badly beaten. I found no large cuts or stabs on him, but I'm no healer. Could you take a look at him please? He ate some rembis leaves and drank a little water, then fell asleep."

"I'll take a look," Fia promised. "You two had better get the fire started and heat me up some water."

Rokey and Flaskamper started the fire and put a small pot of water on it to boil. Fia came out a short while later and steeped a mixture of the rembis leaves and white lannow root in it to make a tisane for him.

"He's awake again," she told them, "and he wants to see you Rokey. Go in and make him drink this, then tell him to get some more sleep. I've put a salve on the worst of the cuts and bruises. That should take down the swelling. What he needs now is a good night's rest."

"I'll make sure he gets it," Rokey said. "Don't worry."

Rokey lit a candle then took it, and the tea, to the tent. Flaskamper followed him and stopped him as soon as they were out of earshot from Fia.

"Listen," said the elf, "I don't want to sound like a miserable prig or anything. I mean, I know your friend needs rest and all, but the sooner we find out what he's doing here and how he got in that condition, the sooner we can figure out what needs to be done, you know what I mean? Don't push, but if he's up to it, see if you can get him to spill."

Rokey sighed.

"You're right," he said. "I'll see what he's able to tell me."

Flaskamper put his hand on Rokey's shoulder.

"Are you alright, *chatka*?" asked Flaskamper. "This has got to be quite a shock for you."

Rokey gave a dry chuckle.

"What would really shock me is if shocking things were to *stop* happening. I'm alright, love, thanks."

They shared a quick kiss, and then Rokey ducked inside the tent.

Ely's eyes were closed. Rokey sat down on the ground next to him. By the light of the candle, Ely's handsome face looked even more pale and battered. It hurt Rokey to see him this way. As he sat studying his injuries, Ely's eyes fluttered open. He managed a weak smile.

"I hoped that I would see you again someday," Ely told him, "but to be honest, I didn't really expect it, and certainly not so soon."

"I was sorry that I couldn't stay long enough to say good-bye in person," said Rokey, "but they wouldn't allow it."

"I understand," he said. "I read your note at least a hundred times. I just couldn't believe that they expelled you. It wasn't your fault what happened."

"Well," said Rokey, "I've moved on from that. I've made friends, traveled all over the land, fallen in love –"

"Let me guess," Ely quipped, "The pretty boy that helped you bring me in?"

"Pretty *elf*." Rokey corrected him with a smile. "Yes. His name is Flaskamper. He's the greatest."

"I hope he makes you happy, brother," said Ely. "I mean that."

"I know you do," Rokey replied. "Here, drink this tisane. Fia says it will help you heal."

"Fia is the beautiful girl?" Ely asked. Rokey nodded. "I'd drink the scum off a mud puddle for her." Ely's laugh turned into a cough. He sipped the hot brew and made a face.

"A mud puddle might be the better option," he said.

"Just drink it," said Rokey. "Ely, what in the world happened to you, anyway?"

His friend took another gulp of the tisane and looked up at Rokey, his eyes held pain and misery, something Rokey had never seen in his friend before.

"Rokey," he said, "you're not going to believe me when I tell you."

Rokey shook his head.

"Ely," he replied, "after the things that have happened to me in the last few months, there is precious little that I wouldn't believe. Relax, and tell me your story, then I'll tell you mine."

Ely studied his friend for a moment, then patted his hand.

"You've changed," Ely said, "I can tell. You're not the same tearful lad that left the Brotherhood three months ago. I can't wait to hear your tale."

"I asked you first," said Rokey, smiling.

"All right," said Ely, "I'll give you the whole thing."

Chapter 29:

Ely's Story

"**I** guess to really give you the whole picture," said Ely, "I have to go all the way back to when you left. Well, not all the way back, but very shortly thereafter. Abbot Crinshire's first official duty may have been to expel you, but it certainly wasn't his last. He made some big changes around the monastery. First, he ordered the gates shut and locked and posted brothers there day and night to guard them. Everyone coming or going had to check in and out with them. During the day, we could come and go as we pleased, but from dusk until dawn, no one was allowed in or out without the abbot's approval. Everybody grumbled, myself included. It put one devil of a crimp in my social life, and just when I'd begun a very mutually satisfying dalliance with Manda, the miller's daughter. But Crinshire didn't budge an inch. Another funny thing he did, he moved our preparatory years up. Instead of being sent up in the spring, I was told that I'd be starting immediately, along with everyone else in our class. Now that didn't strike me as a bad thing, mind you, but it drove the teachers crazy because the prior year's group was still in training. Crinshire reworked it all – the whole bloody curriculum. He started holding one-on-one sessions with the brothers. None of them knew what for, and none that had gone to one would spill what they were all about. It had all of the brothers on edge I can tell you.

"Anyhow, I started in on my preparatory year and the very first thing I learned will knock your sandals off, Rokey. You know how we all are taught that the Brotherhood has no magic, or magical teachings? Well, it's all hogswallow. The brothers have magic coming out of their arses. Some more than others, granted, but they're all schooled in it. I only got the very beginnings of instruction, but it seems that one of the missions of the Brotherhood is to use their magical skills to help maintain what they call the Age of Harmony. That's what they call the era we live in now, with all the kingdoms bound together with treaties of cooperation and trade, the language of Common Firmish – all except Ulgiarrah, that is. I don't know the story behind it, but that kingdom, for some reason or other, is excluded. Anyhow, it turns out that a big chunk of a boy's preparatory year is spent schooling him in basic magic, acquainting him with the Patron Spirits and testing his potential for the higher arcana. And the novitiate knows nothing whatsoever about it! Can you believe that shite?"

"Patron spirits?" Rokey asked. He was getting lost.

"Yeah, that's part of it. I only got the basics of the basics, but from what I was told, humans can't do their own magic. Sorcerers and necromancers and such all have either spirits or demons (depending on whether they do white or black magic) to help it along. That's all I know about it really."

Rokey shook his head. He was starting to form a notion – a notion that disturbed him deeply. Ely paused to sip more of Fia's concoction, then continued.

"So," said Ely, "I've started my prep year, which means I've got my brown robe and been moved into the brothers' quarters. Things seem normal enough at first, considering the fact that Crinshire's turned the place into a bloody prison. But before long, I start to hear talk among the brothers. They're much less tight lipped when there's no novices about. So the brothers are grumbling a bit, about the abbot, about changes in the magical rites and the spirit invocations. I didn't really give it much thought at the time to be quite honest, but now that I look back on it, I should have been a lot more suspicious of the goings on there. But you know how it is there, Rokey. I figured I had enough to do trying to sort myself out without sticking my nose into a lot of babble about things that didn't concern me. Ha! I found out before too long just how wrong I was about that.

"Anyhow, not to get ahead of myself here – about three weeks into my studies, our friend Brother Neesuch pulls me aside one day and says to me 'Ely, you've always been a bright, ambitious lad. How would you like a chance to get into a special program, to move up the ladder a bit quicker than the rest?' Well, I thought maybe he was just blowing a little smoke in my arse to get a tumble out of me, so I made it clear to him which side of the fence I was on. He laughed and told me no, this was on the level. I'd be studying with a special group of students taught by a special group of brothers. All I had to do was go through a special ritual first, swear to be loyal to the group and all, and I'd be in. Well, being the dumb, trusting shite that I am, I said 'sure, that sounds great. Sign me up!' So he hauls me over to Brother Dalfore, the abbot's personal assistant – sorry Rokey, I forgot for a moment. I don't imagine you'll ever forget *him* will you, bein' as he's the one that set you up for the fall, so to speak. I'm so stupid sometimes."

"It's alright, Ely," said Rokey. "Go on with your story."

"Alright," said Ely, wincing in pain as he shifted positions. "Where was I? Oh yes, Dalfore leaves me in the hall while he talks to Neesuch. They spent quite a bit of time in Dalfore's office, then Neesuch comes out and tells me it's all taken care of. He's to start preparing me for *The Ritual* right away. I still wasn't entirely convinced that this ritual didn't involve my bum in some way, but I went along with it, and it turned out to be the real deal, as far as it went. Brother Hebret, Brother Levinton and Brother Calron all congratulated me, and told me that I'd be studying with them just after the ritual was done with. I was very excited, thinking of all the doors that were suddenly opening for me. I imagined myself with a posh diplomatic post somewhere, swimming naked with eager young dilettantes in some far-off palace bathhouse. I let it all go straight to my head, Rokey, just like a bloody pikefish with a shiny lure dangling in front of it. I snapped it up and they reeled me right in."

Ely paused for a moment, wrestling with his emotions. Rokey wanted to put his arms around him and comfort him, but he wasn't entirely certain Ely would find it comforting. Besides, after recent events, he didn't want to do anything that might give Flaskamper the wrong impression. He settled for placing a hand on his friend's shoulder.

"Do you need a break?" Rokey asked. "We can pick this up later, after you've had a rest."

Ely shook his head.

"No," he said, "I want to get it all out. I'll rest afterwards, while you tell me about your adventures."

"Well, alright then," said Rokey, "but don't feel you have to continue for my sake. If you get tired, please, stop and rest yourself."

"I will," said his friend, "I promise."

Ely took a moment to collect his thoughts.

"Anyhow," he continued when he'd gotten the thread, "Neesuch prepared me for this *Ritual of Rebirth*. I was never told exactly what was going to be said, just that I would be saying 'I do' and 'I swear' a lot. Brother Neesuch told me that much of the ritual was archaic and in some dead language, but remained in place because of tradition. The whole idea seemed a bit creepy to me, but I only had all of three weeks magic training. I figured, *what do I know about this stuff?* So I just soaked it all in thinking I would be truly glad when it was over and I could start my special studies program.

"Finally the big night arrived. At moonrise, Neesuch came for me and took me to the administrative building. I thought to myself that the ritual must be going to take place in the banquet room, or maybe in Dalfore's office. I walked in through the main doors and my jaw nearly dropped to the floor. The big stone door was wide open! When Neesuch urged me to go on, I nearly pissed myself with excitement. I was going into that super secret room – the one that we spent all of our childhood years wondering and making up stories about. I have to admit, my knees were shaking a bit when I walked in, and with good reason. The inside of the room was painted blood red, I mean floor, walls, ceiling, the whole bloody place, pardon the pun. Torches were burning in sconces all along the wall, giving the whole place a gloomy, shadowy feel. It's not a very big room, just long and narrow. Six other brothers were there, besides Neesuch, all in black robes. *Black.* Can you believe it Rokey? Have you ever seen a black robe before at the Brotherhood? I hadn't either, and it gave me the creeps even more. I couldn't tell which brothers were there on account of their cowls being up. One of them had this strange mask on though. It sort of looked like a clown that had gone to the bad. I can't really describe it better than that. I figured that was probably the Abbot, but then he spoke, telling me to approach the altar, and I knew it wasn't Crinshire. I'd know his mewl anywhere.

"Anyhow, to the right as you walk in, there's this big stone altar. Brother Clown was standing there behind it, holding this big old dusty book. The rest of them were lined up along either side of the wall. Neesuch put on his own black robe and joined the line-up, then the clown started reading from the book. Well, just as Neesuch had told me, most of the rites were in a language I'd never even heard before. Once in a while, he'd break back into common tongue and ask me to say 'I do' or 'this I avow' or something similar, just like I'd been told. But then it got weird, or weirder I should say. In front of the altar there's this big copper tub and an amphora. One of the brothers from each side came over to me and they started stripping off my clothes. That wasn't something Neesuch had told me was going to happen, and it gave me pause for a moment, but I thought, *oh well, I've gone this far.* So I went along. They stripped me bare-arsed and stood me in the copper tub. Then Brother Clown read some more gibberish, and lifted up the amphora and poured it out all over me. That's when I really started to get scared, because the amphora was filled with mucking blood! Now I'm standing there in this copper tub dripping with fresh blood. The stench of it nearly gagged me. Then, quick as a wink, the clown picks up this big knife, made from some kind of black, sharpened stone, and he tells me to hold out my hand.

"That's when I'd had enough Rokey. I mean, I'm not the brightest burning candle in the chandelier, but I know that you don't shed blood over something unless you know exactly what it's all about. I stepped out of the tub and started to back toward the door. The brothers started in after me, so I grabbed my robe off the floor and ran like a demon. Brother Clown stayed behind, but I heard him yell at the others to catch me and bring me back. I had a bit of a head start though, and I sprinted down the corridor and out the main doors before they'd even left the back room. I ran over to the bathhouse, took a fast plunge to wash that nasty, stinking blood off, then I put on my robe and went and hid under the porch of the Academics building. From there I saw the brothers scrambling around looking for me, only now there were more of them. I heard Brother Neesuch and another talking just above me.

'You should have prepared him better,' the other brother says.

'I didn't want to scare him off,' Neesuch answers. 'But that's exactly what happened. I assumed he was dumb and ambitious enough to endure anything for a chance to get ahead of the pack. I was mistaken.'

'The High Lord won't be happy about this,' the other brother tells him.

'I know,' says Neesuch. 'But if we get him back and initiate him quickly, the consequences may not be so great. He won't initiate willingly now, of course, but he'll still be useful nonetheless.'

"I hunkered down and waited, wet and shivering, hoping they would give up after a while. Later on that night, things seemed to quiet down. By then I had decided that since I didn't know how many brothers were on the side of the *initiated,* or even who the other six in the room were, I had better just try making a run for it out the back gate. It was locked now, but not guarded, or so I thought, so I sneaked out of my hiding place and scampered out back, quick as a rabbit. As it turned out, I wasn't so smart as I thought. There were two brothers lying in wait for me, Oland and Mirabaur. You know them Rokey."

Rokey did indeed. They were two of the Brotherhood's largest and strongest. Neither of them were teachers. They were strictly part of the monastery's defense force, friendly enough to talk to, but Rokey would not want to take either of them on in unarmed combat, let alone both of them.

"The two of them jumped me, but I slid out of their grip and gave Oland a swift kick to the kidneys. Well, that just made him mad. Anyhow, to get to the meat of the matter, I got away up over the gate, but not before those two bison had beaten the stuffing out of me. I got in a few good licks myself, but I definitely got the worst of it, and I was damned lucky to have gotten out. I hauled myself down the path as fast as I could, and got a good distance away from the monastery. But just when I stopped to rest a bit, I heard them coming after me. Not just those two. There were others as well. I had to keep going. I ran as much as I could, walked when I couldn't, all night long, until I got here. Just as the sun was starting to rise, I stumbled off into those bushes and collapsed. I guess I must have passed out from exhaustion and pain. I had just woke up, and was still a little dazed, when your friends grabbed me. I fought because I thought they were brothers. Good thing it wasn't because, as you could see, I didn't have much fight left in me.

"Anyway, that's the whole story, Rokey. I don't know what to make of it, but it looks like some foul element is rotting the Brotherhood from the inside out, and I'm not sure what can be done to stop it at this point."

Ely lay back onto the pillow, his strength exhausted.

"You should get some rest now," said Rokey. "I can come back later."

"Oh no you don't, chum," Ely told him. "You're not going anywhere until you tell me everything that's happened to you since you left. I promise to lay here an' rest quiet whilst I listen."

Rokey smiled.

"As you wish, Your Majesty," said Rokey. "My story begins the very first night after I left..."

Rokey filled Ely in on all his adventures. To his credit, the young man remained awake for the entire tale. It wasn't until Rokey had finished that he finally dropped off to sleep. Rokey then crept out of the tent and joined his companions by the fire. Now he recounted for *them* the story he had just heard from his friend.

"Well I'll be damned," said Flaskamper, shaking his head when Rokey had finished. "Well, I suppose it has already occurred to you that the source of all your troubles may just be right here where you started from. Either that or it's one devil of a coincidence."

"I agree," said Rokey. "It's too much of a coincidence. There has to be some connection with what's happening here and what's been happening to me. The question I still need answered is *why me*? In a strange way, I'm glad we've found all this out about the Brotherhood. It makes it just that much more likely that I'll be able to learn something here."

"Maybe so," said Stamford. "But it's also a great deal more dangerous than we'd imagined. It's damned lucky we ran into your friend, Rokey. Otherwise we would have walked right into their hands. Now at least we have the advantage. *We* know about *them*, but *they* don't know about *us*... not yet anyway. We must figure out a way to use that to our advantage."

"I can't help but find just a touch of dark humor in the immense irony of this situation," said Flaskamper, "I mean, given that we've traveled to three of the four corners of Firma trying to find out who your enemy is."

"But what we still don't know," Stamford observed, "is who these people are. I don't mean individually, though that will definitely factor into our plans; I mean whom they represent. Who is behind this coup that's going on in the Brotherhood? What is their objective? And are they connected with the other sinister happenings throughout the rest of Firma? We cannot simply assume that it's all connected, tempting as that may be. We need more information."

"What we need is a spy," said Flaskamper. "One of us needs to get in there and find out what it is they're up to."

"Not a bad notion," said Stamford.

"But how would we infiltrate them?" Fia asked.

"Dressed as a brother of course," said the elf.

Rokey shook his head.

"An unfamiliar brother would arouse suspicion," said Rokey. "But there's another possibility."

Rokey stood and went quietly into his tent. He emerged a few moments later, carrying his old blue robe. He came back and held the robe out to them.

"I thought you burned that," Flaskamper exclaimed.

Rokey shook his head.

"I couldn't do it," he replied. "Anyway, as I was saying, an unfamiliar brother would arouse suspicion, but an unfamiliar *novice*, well, that's not unusual at all. New novices are coming in all the time, and it wouldn't seem at all odd to a brother if he didn't recognize one. The only one to avoid would be Brother Dalfore. He processes all the new novices, so he would know each one by sight."

"Well, that's settled then," said Flaskamper. "The question now is how and when to slip me in there."

"You?" said Rokey. "Flash, no."

"Well, love, it has to be either me or Stamford," said the elf, "and of the two of us, I'm the one with the necessary stealth skills."

"You're right," said Rokey. "It was a dumb idea in the first place. It's much too dangerous for anyone to try and sneak in there. Let's just forget the whole thing. Excuse me, I need to take a walk."

Rokey left the campfire abruptly and began walking down the narrow road. It was dark, but the moon was out, glistening off the accumulated snow. Flaskamper caught up with him a moment later.

"Rokey, come on," he said. "You know it's the only way. We have to find out what's going on in the Brotherhood. It may not be too late to do something about it."

"Flash, I'm not going to let you walk into that kind of danger," Rokey said stubbornly. "What if you're caught? I'd never forgive myself if anything were to happen to you. So, no. I want nothing more to do with it."

Flaskamper came around and cut him off, taking him gently by the shoulders.

"Rokey," he said calmly, "if you just think about it, without letting your emotions cloud your judgment, you'll see that there's no other way...and no other person. We have to get into the monastery and learn their plans, so we can stop them, if possible. And *I'm* the only man, that is, elf for the job. It's not that I'm particularly thrilled about the idea. I may be brave, but I'm not stupid. I know it's a risky prospect. But *chatka*, you know there's more to this than just *our* troubles. Stamford says we can't be certain that this is connected with the other things happening around Firma. But I'll tell you this right now... *I'm* certain. I'm also certain that we're going to be very sorry if we stand by and do nothing to stop this – this... movement, coup, whatever you want to call it. So I'm going to do this, because I have to. Not just for us, but also for my family...and my people. Your help would make me a lot safer in there, but with or without it, I'm going to try and find a way in. So please... think it over, won't you love?"

Flaskamper turned to leave him alone, but Rokey took him by the arm.

"I don't need to think about it," said Rokey, emotion cracking his voice. "I would never let you go into danger without giving you all the support I could. You know that don't you?"

Flaskamper nodded, and took Rokey in his arms.

"It's going to be alright," said Flash. "Because you're going to tell me everything I need to know before I go in there. You're going to keep me safe."

Rokey wiped his eyes.

"Gods, Flash," he said, "is there ever going to be a time when we're not in danger, when we can just relax and enjoy one another's company without worrying whether or not it will be the last time?"

Flaskamper kissed him, then ran his fingers through Rokey's long, black hair.

I hope so, lover," said the elf. "I truly hope so."

Chapter 30:

Subterfuge

Rokey paced back and forth, his brow knit into a frown of concentration. Flaskamper sat patiently on a log and waited. Suddenly, Rokey spun around to face him.

"Alright," he said, "you meet a brother in the colonnade, and he asks you what class you're supposed to be in. What do you say?"

"I tell him to get stuffed and mind his own business," Flaskamper replied with a grin.

Rokey sighed and shook his head, unamused.

"Flash, come on, be serious," he said. "This stuff is important."

"If I'm going east, I tell him I'm on my way to my riding period," said Flaskamper, rolling his eyes skyward. "If I'm heading west, it's my free period and I'm heading to the bathhouse for a wash. I know it's important Rokey, but we've been over all this stuff a hundred times these past three days. I know the place inside and out. I've got the jargon down. What more is there for me to do, besides get in there?"

"You're not ready yet," said Rokey, turning away.

Flaskamper stood up and walked up behind Rokey, wrapping his arms around him tightly. The elf rested his chin on his lover's shoulder.

"You know that I *am*, Rokey," he said. "I'm as ready as I'm ever going to be. It's *you* that's not ready."

He spun Rokey around to face him.

"Look, I understand," Flaskamper told him. "If our roles were reversed, I'd be killing myself trying to think of ways to slow you down too, if not stop you altogether. Sending someone you love into danger has got to be the hardest thing in the world. But *chatka*, it has to be done. And the sooner I go in, the sooner I can come out again."

"Or the sooner you can get yourself killed," said Rokey.

"I won't get myself killed," said Flaskamper. "If there's any sign of trouble, I'll haul my shapely arse out of there before you can blink twice. I promise. I don't want to be a hero."

Rokey gazed into his beautiful green eyes, love and concern both showing plainly on his face.

"You already are a hero," Rokey told him. "I just don't want you to become a dead one."

"It's not going to happen," said Flaskamper. "I'm well prepared for all contingencies."

"I know you are," said Rokey. "and there's nothing more I can teach you that will be of any further help. If we *must* go through with this, then now is the time."

That night, at a point when the moon had skirted behind the clouds, Flaskamper scaled the monastery's eastern wall, dressed in Rokey's blue novice robe. The trees outside overhung the stone edifice there, making the climb easy, on one side at least. Once atop the wall, things were trickier. There was no way down but to jump. Even for an elf, this was quite a feat. If he landed wrong, he could easily fracture an ankle. That would end their plans in a hurry. Flaskamper walked a short ways around the top of the wall, to the southeast corner. There he found a small bit of luck in the form of what looked like an old mulch pile covered with snow. It only came to about two or three feet off the ground – not much, but *some* help at least. The elf sat down on the wall just above the mulch pile and lowered himself slowly down until he was hanging by his fingers. Then with a quick prayer to the moon goddess, he let go. The mulch was both deeper and softer than he thought, and he sank down nearly to his knees. Fortunately it was dry rather than fresh, so his fall was broken without getting him too dirty. Flaskamper extricated himself easily, then went about covering the traces of his entry, in case a guard should pass this way. After that, he headed immediately for the stables. Rokey had told him that this would be the safest place for him to hide during the night, especially now that, according to Ely, the abbot had made midnight trysts there considerably more difficult.

"Be careful just the same though," Rokey told him. "Apparently I was not the only samer in the Brotherhood, so not everyone's plans may have been foiled by locking the girls out."

There were no lovers in the stables that night, only horses, who greeted the elf with indifferent snorts. Flaskamper climbed up into the hayloft and found an out-of-the-way corner. There, he removed the blue robe, under which he wore a dark tunic and breeches. These he would wear while sneaking about at night. On his back he had strapped his bow, the few crude arrows he had made and a pouch with some paper and writing charcoal. Tonight's mission would simply be to practice, to familiarize himself with the place, then shoot an *arrived safe* message back over to their prearranged spot on the other side of the eastern wall, where Rokey would arrive to pick it up just after dawn. Flaskamper tucked the novice robe under the hay and made his way silently back down the wooden ladder. *Just a quick look round tonight, he told himself. You've got to be rested and sharp tomorrow, if you're to be a proper novice.* He chuckled to himself as he stepped out into the darkness.

* * *

Rokey dusted the snow off a tree stump and sat down to open Flaskamper's message. It was the second day since the elf had infiltrated the monastery. Yesterday's message had simply said I'm here! Rokey sincerely hoped that today's note would not be so short on details. He untied the scroll and unrolled the two sheets of paper. The charcoal writing, though a bit smudged, was still perfectly legible.

Chatka,

There were no problems today. Two brothers and several novices asked me about myself. You were right, they were surprised to see an elf among the novitiate, but they bought the story of my joining to escape my overbearing father and an older brother who always outshined me. Lesson one when making up a lie: always stick as close to the truth as possible. A couple of the novices who are interested in elf culture tapped me to have dinner with them and talk about it. It was all fine. I didn't slip up once. You'd have been very proud of me.

I'm already proud of you, Rokey thought, smiling, then continued to read.

It isn't difficult to get them to talk about the changes in the Brotherhood since the new abbot took over. Ely wasn't the only boy who had his romance nipped in the bud. It has gotten even worse since he escaped. Now the gates are locked day and night, and everyone needs permission from the abbot's office to leave the premises. It has several of the novices up in arms, talking about leaving the order. I haven't heard anything from the brothers themselves, but I can't imagine they're any too happy about it either, at least the ones who aren't already initiated. As to that, it is not apparent to me whether or not a brother has already turned. Perhaps if I had known any of them beforehand I could tell, but it isn't something a stranger can immediately detect, even one looking out for such a change. I'll keep my ears open though. Perhaps the novices will give me a clue. Tonight on my rounds, I sneaked over to the brothers' quarters to have a listen at the windows, but they are all shut fast because it's been so bloody cold. If only it were summer! I also had a peek at the administrative building, but it was all locked-up tight. I guess there's nothing more for me to do now but go to bed.

Until tomorrow, lover.

P.S. I know how all these randy brothers feel. Being locked in here without you is making more than my heart ache!

Rokey read the note twice before carefully rolling it up, so as not to smudge it more, and tucking it into his pocket. Then he stood and headed back to camp. They had moved their campsite closer to the monastery, but not too close for fear of being discovered, so it was still a considerable hike. It gave Rokey far too much time alone to worry about all the things that could go wrong with this plan of theirs, and to wonder why in the world he had ever agreed to it in the first place.

The others were anxious to read Flaskamper's message when he reached the campsite. Now wishing that Flash had not written that embarrassing last line, he handed it over to Stamford, who read it soberly, then handed it to Fia.

"Sounds like he's doing very well...in most respects," he said. Rokey blushed. He should have known that Stamford would not pass up the opportunity to tease him.

"Ignore Stamford, Rokey," Fia said kindly. "It's just Flaskamper's way of saying how much he misses you."

Rokey gave her a grateful smile, but Fia could see the pain behind it. This was certainly much harder on him than it was on Flaskamper, so far anyway.

"Aw, c'mon, Rokey. You know I'm only teasing," said Stamford, with uncharacteristic contrition. He, too, was aware of the strain that the boy was under. He was feeling some of it himself. He and Flaskamper had faced many hazards together, but never before had Stamford been in the position of sitting idly by while his friend walked into danger. It irked him no end.

When everyone had read the note, Rokey carefully replaced it in his pocket and went to visit Ely. His friend was still recovering from the beating he had been given, though he was thoroughly enjoying being nursed back to health by Fia. Rokey had not told him Fia's secret. It was not his place to do so, and he could see no reason why it should matter anyway. Ely was awake, sipping on stew made from one of Flaskamper's stew bricks. It was one of the few things they had left to eat. Rokey and Stamford planned to go hunting that day, hoping to catch a partridge, or a winter hare to supplement what little food they had.

"Did word come from your friend?" Ely asked.

"Yes," said Rokey, and pulled the note out for Ely to read.

"Ha! He has my sense of humor," Ely laughed and handed back the papers.

"Yes, he does," said Rokey. "He reminds me of you in many ways, in fact. I had never really thought about it before, but now you're back, it's obvious to me."

"You realize that that's very flattering to me," Ely said. "Though I'm sure that wasn't your intention."

"Great gods, no!" Rokey exclaimed. "Why should I wish to further inflate your ego?"

"Seriously though, Rokey," Ely said, "You're happy with this fellow?"

"Very," Rokey replied, "though we've had precious little time to be happy since we met. We've never been more than a few marks from some perilous confrontation."

"Ah, but I suspect you've made the utmost of those few marks," Ely said mischievously. "Listen, I've always wanted to know this about samers. How do you decide which one's the driver and which one's the...the ah – "

"Horse?" Rokey volunteered.

"Aw, c'mon, you know what I mean," Ely laughed.

"Ely, anyone but you would get punched in the nose for that question," said Rokey.

"I know, but I'm your best friend, so you can tell me, right?" Ely responded shamelessly.

"NO!" Rokey cried, blushing. "Now shut up about it."

"Alright, alright," said Ely, grinning broadly. "Keep me in the dark if you must. Look, I'm sorry if I embarrassed you. I'm really glad for you, my friend. If anyone deserved to find happiness after the rotten way you were treated... ah, well, there's some explanation for that now at least. We now know that something foul was already afoot behind the monastery walls. Hopefully your friend can get to the bottom of some of it so that we can find some strategy for fighting it."

"Above all, I hope to find where *I* fit into it all," said Rokey. "Finding my mother was a wonderful thing, but in truth, the whole experience with the sidhe has raised more questions than it has answered. If I can't find some clue about my father's secret within the Brotherhood, I shall be at a dead end. I have no other leads to follow."

"There has to be something there," Ely reassured him. "The oracle sent you here in response to your question, right? You thought it meant that there was a clue here as to who was behind all of your troubles. Now you know, or let us say, strongly suspect, that the person himself is here. If that *is* true, then the answers will surely lie with him."

"Undoubtedly," Rokey replied. "The question is, will he, or *they*, be willing to share those answers with me? I have no means of forcing him, or them, even if we should prevail, which is by no means assured."

"Have faith, chum" Ely told him. "We'll get it all worked out. I know we will."

"I hope so, Ely," Rokey answered. "With all my heart, I hope you're right."

*　*　*

Chatka,

Had a close call today. I was on my way across the compound and only avoided running into Dalfore by a kitten's whisker. I saw him coming a mere moment before he saw me and changed course. It wasn't very subtle, but he clearly had something on his mind, for he didn't even notice me. I overheard two brothers today making reference to a meeting of some sort tomorrow night in the 'Ritual Room'. I assume that is the room in the administration building where they took Ely. The meeting is at moonrise. I plan to try and sneak into the building and see if I can pick up anything useful. I know, I know...it's dangerous, but I'm not getting any closer to finding out what this is all about by talking to the other novices, and the brothers aren't likely to talk candidly in front of me. I'll let you know how it comes out tomorrow. Nothing much else to report, I'm afraid. Things are all buttoned up here at night now, so I can't get in and snoop around anywhere. But it's not all bad. I'm getting quite chummy with one of the horses. Don't worry though, we're just friends.

Until tomorrow, lover. I miss you bushels.

*　*　*

Flaskamper stood crouched behind one of the pillars of the colonnade, watching as two brothers entered the Administration Building. He had counted twenty-eight of them, so far. He wondered if this relatively small number constituted the portion of the Brotherhood who had been willingly initiated. If so, it was a good sign. He could only hope that the unwilling contingent was similarly small.

These last two were obviously late arrivals. When he was relatively sure that no others were coming, the elf crept from his hiding place, dashed across the road and up the stone steps to the building's large double doors. He peered cautiously through the window. At the far end of the hall, he could see that the large stone door Rokey had described was ajar. Red light spilled out into the corridor. Taking a deep breath, he slowly pulled open one of the doors. Its creak sounded loud as a wolf's howl to him, but it caused no stirrings in the room beyond. When the opening was just wide enough, he squeezed in, then slowly eased the door shut again. Now he would have to be quick. He was completely exposed here in the open. Quickly but quietly, he hurried down the hall until he reached the open door of the kitchen. He ducked in and stood silently for a moment to assess what he could hear. The answer was...nothing. He would have to risk getting closer.

One careful step at a time, he crept closer to the stone door. As he neared the opening, he could hear someone speaking. Another step, and the speaker's words became clear.

"...has been working toward the voluntary initiation of nearly a dozen more brothers into the Order of the Bone. Based on past successes, we can fully expect to realize half of these potential initiates within the next several days. Those who refuse, of course, will join the ranks of our masses who, though initially reluctant to participate in our great movement, nevertheless now serve a vital role in our operations. Now we will hear status reports from each of our recruiters. Brother Alban..."

Flaskamper *felt* rather than heard the presence behind him. As he began to turn, something struck him hard on the side of the head. He immediately saw stars and sunk down the floor.

"Gods, Rokey, I'm sorry," he thought, and then the world went black.

* * *

Rokey frowned down at Flaskamper's message. There was nothing about it that he could pinpoint as being wrong, but he had a strange feeling about it nonetheless. He looked down at the note again.

Chatka,

I learned a great deal last night, too much to tell you about in a note. Please meet me at the east gate at moonrise tonight. I'll tell you everything then, and there's someone I want you to talk with. Come alone, please. I don't want to scare him.

The beginning was the same as all of his other letters, as was the handwriting. He had no reason whatsoever to doubt that it had come from him. Still.... he pocketed the note and dashed back to camp. He would get Stamford and the others' thoughts on this.

When he arrived, he handed the dark man the message wordlessly. Stamford read it and looked up at Rokey.

"It smells," he said.

Rokey nodded.

"I get the same impression," he told him. "I just don't know why."

"Intuition," said Stamford. "Learn to trust it. You'll have to go, of course, in case it's real, but you won't be going alone."

"Alright," Rokey agreed.

"If it's not real," said Fia, "it means they have him. I'm sure I'm not telling you anything that hasn't already occurred to you, Rokey."

Rokey gave a curt nod. He did not trust himself to speak about it just yet.

Ely, who had come out of the tent in time to hear most of the conversation, came over and hugged Rokey.

"Don't worry, brother," he said. "If they've got him, we'll get him back."

"If they haven't killed him already," said Rokey, in a voice thick with emotion.

"They won't have killed him," Ely insisted. "He's useful to them. Whoever they are, they're not stupid, and in this case, that's to our advantage."

"Junior's right, Rokey," said Stamford. "If he's been captured, they'll keep him around until they know everything he knows. Before that, we'll have him back."

Rokey wanted to believe them. Better still, he wanted to believe that the message had been genuine, and that tomorrow night, he would see his love again. However, the sick feeling in his stomach that had come when he first read the note stayed with him all through the day.

At moonrise, Rokey approached the east gate. Behind him, in the woods, Stamford crouched, watching, ready to come to his aid if necessary. The gate was open, but Rokey wasn't about to go inside.

"Flash," he called softly. "Flash are you there?"

A figure in a blue robe stepped out of the shadows, but his cowl was up, so Rokey couldn't see his face. Rokey stepped back a step.

"Flash, if that's you," he said nervously, "show me your face."

He stood waiting, poised to run. The figure stepped forward and pulled back his hood.

"Of course it's me," said Flaskamper. "Whom did you expect?"

Rokey heaved a huge sigh of relief.

"Oh, thank the gods," he said. "It thought it was a trick. I thought they'd taken you."

"You poor thing," said Flaskamper, holding out his arms. Rokey stepped into them eagerly, hugging the elf tightly. But immediately something felt wrong. There was no warmth in this embrace...no love. Before he could pull back, though, something was put in front of his face. It smelled strong and – and...sweet. The whole world began to spin, and he felt himself collapse. The arms around him held him fast. The arms of his lover, but it couldn't be – it just couldn't. Hurt and confusion were the last things he felt, before he felt nothing at all.

From his vantage point behind the tree, Stamford saw Rokey walk into Flaskamper's arms. A moment later, he seemed to slump, overcome by emotion, no doubt. Then, all of a sudden, he saw a figure in a dark robe streak across the opening, and the gate slammed abruptly shut.

"Shite!" Stamford cursed and rushed toward the gate. He reached it only tiks later, but it was already locked fast, and Flaskamper, Rokey and the shadowy figure had all disappeared. Cursing the whole way, Stamford ran back to the campsite to gather the others. He wasn't sure what had just happened, but it looked for all the world like his best friend had just betrayed his own lover and helped to capture him. He knew there was an explanation behind it. Clearly Flaskamper had been drugged, or put under some spell, but it was damn disturbing nonetheless.

There was nothing to do now but take the monastery by force. Now that their enemy had Rokey, they would not keep him alive for long, not after having put so much effort into the boy's destruction. As for Flaskamper...it was a trick, it *had* to have been. Flaskamper would never have willingly betrayed Rokey. For all he knew, they had already killed him – substituted some sort of changeling.

Tears sprung into his eyes. He had failed, but he *would* make it up to them, whatever the cost. His friends would be rescued, or else avenged - avenged with all the cold fury a former Ulgiarrahan Black Guardsman could muster. With the camp looming just ahead of him, Stamford began to shout.

Chapter 31:

Combustion

"Let me in brothers. I must see the abbot immediately."

The guards at the main gate blinked at the dark-robed figure outside. It was difficult to make him out clearly in the pale, pre-dawn light.

"Who is it then?" said one of the guards. "Identify yourself."

The man outside stepped to the gate and threw his hood back.

"Can you not see?" he said. "It is I, brother Ely. I must have in at once."

"Ely?" the other guard stepped forward and peered out at him suspiciously. "We heard you had left the order for good."

"It was a ruse, brother," said Ely without hesitation. "I had a special mission to fulfill on behalf of the abbot. I have now completed it and am overdue to report to him. Kindly let me in so that I may do so. Otherwise there's sure to be trouble for someone."

"Trouble," the first guard grumbled, wrestling with his keys. "Seems to be plenty of that to go round these days." He turned the key in the lock and swung the gate open.

"Alright, in with you then," he said gruffly.

Ely entered and stepped quickly to the side. The guards turned to him in surprise, A moment later, the giant and the Saebrilite rushed at the open gate, Lorq swinging his iron-tipped staff; Kyzee brandishing her huge greatsword in one hand, a feat which greatly impressed Stamford, who followed closely behind with Fia. The guards fell back in terror at first, but then shouted an alarm. Soon a dozen reinforcements had joined them, and the fight was on. The companions had agreed during their hasty strategy conference that, since they could not be certain which brothers had been turned already, they would not kill them with abandon. This made the fighting much more difficult for them. Stamford had argued that since it was their own carelessness and complacency that had resulted in their infiltration by evil forces, they deserved no special treatment, but Fia's compassion had tempered the battle plan somewhat, and at last they had agreed to attempt first to wound, and only to kill as a last resort. Stamford acquiesced, but warned that what they saved in conscience, they would likely pay out in blood.

Stamford overheard one brother send another to relieve Oland and Mirabaur at the rear gate and send them forward.

Oland and Mirabaur...the two who nearly killed young Ely.

Well, thought Stamford, *at least my conscience will not be troubled when I lop off those two heads.*

He surgically slashed one brother's hamstring, relishing the prospect of some unfettered combat. Somewhere in the back of his mind, a voice that sounded suspiciously like Fia's chided him for his bloodlust, but Stamford willed it silent. If his friends were already dead, then let the blood of these dogs spill until the ground was stained crimson. If not, then the less time spent dancing about with them, the more likely they were to be able to effect a rescue. He conked another robed opponent on the head, knocking him senseless.

Oh do hurry forth, Oland and Mirabaur, he thought, his teeth bared in a wolf-like snarl, *the sword of vengeance awaits you.*

*   *   *

Rokey awoke and rose, unsteadily, to his feet. It took a moment for the fog in his head to clear, and for his eyes to adjust to his surroundings. Only then did he realize that he was locked in a large iron cage. The room he was in was dark, lit by only a handful of torches ensconced on the walls – walls that were *not* painted red. So this was *not* the ritual room where Ely had been brought. He peered out through the bars and saw a male figure on the other side of the room. Chains held his arms above his head, suspending him so high by the wrists that his feet barely touched the ground. The figure was shirtless, and even in this poor light, Rokey could see that his pale yellow body had been battered and bruised.

Great gods, Flash, Rokey thought, his heart aching in empathy, *what have they been doing to you?* Then another thought: *Was it really you who met me at the gate?*

"Flash," Rokey called out in a loud whisper. "Flash, wake up, love. It's Rokey, honey. Wake up... can you?"

The elf groaned and his head lolled back and forth, then one eye opened. The other was swollen shut.

"Rokey," Flaskamper rasped. "Rokey....so....sorry."

"You don't have to be sorry, dearest," Rokey reassured him. "Not at all."

"Made me drink...and put – put a spell on me," Flaskamper struggled to form the necessary words to communicate. "Had no control. I wrote...letter...lured you here."

Tears began to flow from his inflamed eyes. Rokey clutched the bars of his cage in fury, not at his lover, but at the monsters who had done this to him.

"Don't cry, Flash," said Rokey gently. "Don't cry, love. It's not your fault. It's not."

At that moment, Rokey became aware that another had entered the room. He could barely make out the robed figure at the far end of the irregularly shaped chamber, a few paces beyond where Flaskamper was chained.

"Touching," a familiar voice came from beneath the cowl. "So, our wayward novice has found love out there in the cold, cruel world. How wonderful for the two of you. More's the pity that you neither shall be long with us to enjoy it."

"Crinshire," Rokey spat the name in disgust, "you cur."

"Tsk, tsk, tsk," the abbot clucked. "How quickly they lose their respect. But then, you made no secret of your disapproval of me, even before, when I held your very life in my hands. One *might* say that showed integrity. But now...I would say it is more akin to foolishness, wouldn't you?"

Rokey was about to hurl another invective, but bit it back and made his best attempt at sounding conciliatory.

"Alright... *Abbot* Crinshire," he said. "You have *me* now, the one you want. You have no need of Flaskamper anymore. Why not let him go? For that, I *would* give you the utmost respect. For that," he admitted truthfully, "I would give you anything."

"What a shame," he answered, shaking his head. "Had I known that earlier, before the bolu I sent to spy on you was destroyed, I might have done things differently – sparing myself considerable... pain."

The abbot moved forward a few paces, until he stood next to Flaskamper, who seemed to have fallen unconscious again.

"But," said Crinshire, "that was not the way it happened. Instead, you and your gang of riffraff somehow managed to thwart my every attempt at you, making me look, I'm afraid, rather a fool in the process. That cost me, young pup. It cost me dearly."

"Then take your revenge on *me*," Rokey pleaded, "But not on him. Please, please let him – "

"I WILL NOT!" shouted the abbot, pounding his fist against the wall. Flaskamper groaned, then went silent again.

"I will not," he repeated, somewhat more calmly, "because you wish it so. Because if I did, then no matter what I did to *you*, you would always have the satisfaction of knowing that at least your lover was safe and sound...that he would live on. I cannot have that, no, not after the pain you have caused me."

"What pain?" Rokey asked. "What pain have I caused you, other than the embarrassment of having failed to kill me a few times?"

"What pain?" the abbot whispered, his voice high and icy. "The pain that came when my superiors had to be told, time after time, that I was unsuccessful in completing my assigned task, a task which, though seemingly trivial to me was, in fact, of the utmost urgency to them."

"Superiors?" Rokey asked, confused. "But you are the abbot. *You* are the one in charge."

"I am in charge of the Noble Contemplative, witless boy," snarled Crinshire. "I refer to the *other* order to which I belong, the one that is even now in the process of taking over the Brotherhood – The Order of the Bone. I am but a loyal servant to he who heads the order in this part of Firma. Sadly, I have been a disappointment to him."

"No more, Crinshire," intoned another familiar voice. "You disappoint us no more."

Rokey's jaw literally dropped as he entered the room. Crinshire made a sweeping bow to the burly, red-haired man – Rokey's teacher and mentor, brother Barrow.

"You did, at last, achieve your objective," he told the abbot. "You merely required a little nudge along the way in order for you to muster the necessary...drive to succeed." He turned to Rokey. "Unfortunately for you, lad, that *nudge* has left the abbot here with a burning desire to take his revenge upon you. Why don't you show him, Crinshire – give him an idea of how...seriously we take such matters."

Abbot Crinshire pulled back the hood of his robe, and Rokey gasped in horror. The entire left side of his face had been badly burned, leaving it hideously disfigured. His left eye was gone, not merely blinded, but missing completely. Rokey's stomach turned over, and he had all he could do not to vomit. An icy chill crept up his back.

Great Gods, Rokey thought with a shiver, *if this is what they do to their own people –*

He fought off the rising panic. It would do him no good. He must keep his wits about him if he had any hope of saving Flaskamper.

"Brother Barrow," Rokey said, choosing his words with care, "I know, at least, I think, that you once felt some fondness for me – "

"Oh yes, Rokey," Barrow replied, his tone light, even friendly. "I liked you a great deal. In fact, I still do. But the needs of the Order must come first. One cannot allow personal feelings to interfere, not with all the vital work ahead of us. I, too, have superiors, whose chastisements can also be...stern. Their orders must be obeyed without fail."

"Then at least tell me why!" Rokey cried. "Why me? What is so bloody important about *me* that so many should be moved to want me dead – to *need* me dead?"

Brother Barrow frowned and shook his head. For a moment, Rokey feared he would refuse to tell him anything. Then the brother seemed to come to a decision, for he raised his head and smiled.

"Why not," he said. "I've promised Crinshire to leave your ultimate fates to him, a small token to soften the blow of his earlier reprimand. But I *do* like you, and for that reason, I shall tell you what I know of the matter. Let us call it your 'last request'. I do not know all of the details, for they were not given to me, but I do know some, and those I will share with you."

"I hope it's a long story," said Rokey, using the black humor to offset his blinding fear. The brother chuckled.

"I shall try and stretch it out as best I can."

* * *

Blood was running freely into Stamford's right eye, momentarily blinding it, but he had no time to wipe it clear. He was barely keeping up with the two brothers' fierce attack. He parried one's blow, spun and parried the other's. He felt foolish now, having wished these two upon himself, for each was nearly as good as he was. Together –

He leapt aside as Oland, or Mirabaur, he wasn't sure which was which, swung his bastard sword down in a wide, fast arc, nearly succeeding in cleaving him in two.

Shite, I must eliminate one of them, or I am beaten.

After a few desperate moments of thought, he settled on a plan. It was a dirty trick, but this was no gentlemen's duel. He dove at the brother in front of him, hacking and slashing with all the speed and power he could muster. The sudden ferocity of the attack drove the man backwards several paces, also taking the one behind by surprise. Stamford carefully calculated the precise moment. He would only have one chance at this maneuver.

Now.

He made to lift his sword for another downward blow to the front, but at the last tik, shifted it in his hand and swung it downward, twisting sideways in the direction of the blade. His sword caught the other man, who was running to catch them, plunging it straight into his gut. Stamford continued to spin sideways, using his momentum to withdraw his bloody sword. Now he was standing to the side of the two brothers, who were facing one another. The sword of the one that had been facing Stamford nearly connected with the other man, but he managed to check the blow at the last tik. It mattered little though. The other man was mortally wounded, holding his stomach, trying in vain to staunch the blood that poured from his belly. A moment later, he fell to the ground, and the first man's attention returned to Stamford.

Now I have a fair chance, thought Stamford. *Come for me, you bastard.*

*   *   *

Brother Barrow paced back and forth in front of Rokey's cage, careful not to get too close.

"It started all the way back when I returned from my assignment abroad," he began. "You remember, Rokey? You were only, what, ten years old then? And I had been gone since, well since before you came to the Brotherhood. While I was away, I came to know members of the Order of the Bone, who were able to persuade me to join them in their movement."

"What is the Order of the Bone?" Rokey asked.

"Ah," Barrow replied, "well, that is another story. One for which I'm afraid our time is too short. If I thought you could be persuaded – " He shook his head. "No, it is not possible. The necromancers have made it very clear. But, I get ahead of myself. Of the Order of the Bone, I shall only say that our presence is growing throughout the land, and when we have finished growing, and accomplished our objectives, Firma will be a very different place indeed."

The brother's eyes began to shine with a kind of adoration and awe.

"Oh, Rokey, my boy..." he said softly, "if only I could have been given the chance to win you over. You've seen only the darker aspects of the Order, but there is more to it than that – so much more."

He shook his head, coming out of his brief reverie.

"But to return to the facts that pertain to you... upon my return, I began working slowly on the conversion of the Brotherhood. The plan was expected to take years, for we wanted as many willing converts as we could manage. But there was one that I needed right away."

"Brother Dalfore," Rokey muttered.

"Yes!" the brother said, clapping his hands. "You have such a quick mind, Rokey. I have always admired that about you. Yes, indeed, I needed Brother Dalfore so that I could see that Bone Order members were admitted to the Brotherhood, and that promotions and assignments were manipulated in ways that benefited the Order. I had no time to persuade him to join willingly, I'm afraid – a shame really. He would have possibly made a fine sector chief.

"You tamper with their minds," Rokey surmised, "alter them somehow so that they follow you. That's what you did to Flash to make him..."

Barrow nodded.

"Right again," he said. "You're doing quite well. Unfortunately, the potion and spell – it is a two-part process – the potion and spell only work for a short time on elves. We've tried it on one or two before with the same result. For a few marks, they're as compliant as lambs, but then the effect wears off, and the elves are totally immune to it thereafter. That is, sadly, why we are unable to keep your friend alive and in our service. Otherwise, I assure you we would, despite my wish to reward Crinshire."

"How kind of you," Rokey said.

"Oh not at all," said Barrow, either oblivious to or else deliberately ignoring the sarcasm. "We should love to be able to recruit elves into the Order. They'd be no end of help to us. As it is, we shall probably have to eliminate Elfwood entirely, with the exception of any willing recruits we might succeed in gathering. But that is, thankfully, not my decision to make. Anyway, I'm digressing again. Where was I?"

"Coming to where I fit into all of this," Rokey reminded him.

"Yes, yes of course," said the brother. "Well, after Dalfore, the next targets were the higher magicians, those who made their life's work the study of the magical tomes in the library. Having left while still a novice, you would not have seen that section. Its access is restricted to brothers only. The reason we wanted them first was because there are certain humans on which the spell and potion will not work at all. By means of some complicated magic, it is possible to learn, with great certainty, whom the process will properly affect and whom it will not. As the initiation ritual is complex and requires the time and energies of at least one willing member of the Order, it is to our advantage to have this information in advance."

Brother Barrow paused, glanced back at Crinshire, who was wringing his hands impatiently, then continued the story.

"I don't know how the screening process works exactly...something to do with aura shine and spiritual resonance. Nothing I understand. I'm only a swordsman. But when our necromancers – that is the name, I am told, for a magician who practices the *dark arts* – when they screened you, they saw something that intrigued them. Don't ask me what it was, because I haven't the foggiest, but it interested them enough to begin carefully observing you, studying you, trying to pinpoint where the strange – whatever it was – was coming from. And it was during that process that the omens began to appear...signs, portends, however you wish to refer to them. I'd have thought it all hogswallow a few years ago, but I've learned a great deal since then, and I now take them quite seriously."

"And these omens," asked Rokey, "what were they saying about me?"

"Well, that you were a threat, dear boy," Barrow exclaimed, "a dire threat to the Order itself, if you can believe that. I couldn't when I first heard it. Neither could they. They checked again and again, but it always kept coming up the same way. Allowed to continue unopposed, you would eventually constitute a serious impediment to us all, to everything we've been working so hard to accomplish. Once those higher up the ladder became convinced, it took them some considerable time to settle on what to do with you. I know you won't believe me, Rokey, but none of us has any wish to harm the innocent, if it is at all possible to avoid it. Even when they were absolutely certain, there was no great glee in the prospect of snuffing out an eleven-year-old boy. Seeing no immediacy in the threat, they waited, hoping to learn more about this risk you would pose, lest there be others about who represented a similar danger. Plus, we had few members within the Noble Contemplative at the time, and no willing initiates save for myself. It would not suit our plans for a quiet, gradual takeover to have a boy suddenly go missing, or wind up dead. So we waited, and we watched as you grew into a fine and, in all apparent respects, harmless young man. I continued my quiet recruitment, garnering more than twenty willing members for the Order of the Bone, and an even greater number of those less than willing. It is all but impossible for an outsider to tell which are which. But then, something else happened...something that brought the matter of your future urgently back to the forefront."

Despite their dire predicament, Rokey was thoroughly enthralled by the story. He had, after all, fought his way all across Firma and back to hear it. He felt a pang of guilt, but simply could not help himself. Besides, what purpose did it serve to not hear the story? To the contrary, the longer Brother Barrow kept talking, the greater the chance that Rokey would be able to find some way out of this predicament.

"What happened?" Rokey asked.

"We discovered the location of the femur," said Barrow, "the last of the sacred bones, save the skull."

"What does that mean?" Rokey inquired, confused.

The brother shook his head.

"It is far too complicated to explain," he said. "All you need know is that it was a momentous occurrence, which moved our cause forward by great leaps. And as our cause moved forward, the signs began to scream your name again. Not literally, of course, but the necromancers saw greater urgency now in whatever threat it was you were to pose. A decision was made. Crinshire had been brought in a few years back, and we knew his ambition was to be abbot. We offered that prize to him on condition that he find a way to get rid of you that would not attract undue attention to us, for we were still not quite ready as yet to make our move here. As it turned out, the plan he came up with *was* quite ingenious."

"You arranged for me to be put in charge of old abbot Tomasso," said Rokey, but then shook his head. "But in order to know what would happen, you would have had to..."

A lump formed in Rokey's throat as the horrible truth dawned on him at last. His face grew pale, and his stomach churned violently again.

"Gods – oh, gods. Ooooh gods, no," he groaned. "You murdered the abbot that night." Rokey leaned against the bars for support, but his knees would not hold him, and he sunk down to the floor of the cage. "You arranged for the servant to be absent, and when I went to make the tea..."

"Yesss," he heard Crinshire hiss from across the room. "I did it myself. When you went to the kitchen, to brew the tea, I sneaked into Tomasso's room – what is now *my* room..."

Trembling, Rokey covered his ears, but he could still hear Abbot Crinshire's voice as he spewed forth his horrific confession.

"It was almost too easy. I simply grabbed his feet and pulled on them, until his head was under the water. He had not the strength to shake free of my grip, though he thrashed about like a carp in a fishbasket. In a few moments, it was all over. I would soon be abbot, and you would soon be sent away in disgrace. After that, it was only a matter of arranging for you to be dispatched at some isolated spot along the road."

"Ah, but that is where your plans began to go awry, Crinshire," said Barrow, in the light, teasing tone that Rokey now knew completely belied his true nature. Crinshire had also found that out, and it gave Rokey a grim sense of satisfaction to know that all of his narrow escapes had been the reason for this loathsome man's terrible punishment.

"Well, Rokey," said Brother Barrow, "That about brings us up to date. You know more than we do about what happened to you after your departure. I'm afraid I must leave the abbot to his workings now, though I will be just outside the door. The High Lord of the Order still doesn't quite trust our friend here with such a prize as you, so I am ordered to remain at hand. But I shan't watch. Truth be told, I haven't Crinshire's zeal for this sort of thing."

"But – but...wait!" Rokey cried as Barrow made to depart.

"Something else?" the brother asked.

"Everything else!" Rokey demanded. "Everything about why – why me? What's the big secret about me? In what way do I represent a danger to your order? You've given me no answers at all!"

Barrow gave him a pitying look.

"I'm afraid I don't have those answers to give you, Rokey," he said. "I simply don't know. If those above me know, they have not as yet chosen to share the information with me. I know it is not what you wish to hear, but I have no reason to lie to you. I've given you all that I have, and that is all the necromancers had as well. Identifying and removing the menace was the focus of their task. The whys...they simply weren't important to them. Good-bye Rokey. I *am* truly sorry."

The brother departed, shutting the door, and in the terrible silence that followed, he heard the cold, angry hiss of the abbot's voice.

"Pay attention, boy," he said. "This is something you really must see."

* * *

The battle outside continued. Stamford had thought that the resistance would be fierce, but ultimately minimal. He had been correct on the first point, but mistaken on the second. Already he and the others had incapacitated half a dozen brothers, and been forced to kill two or three more, including Stamford's other challenger, Oland, or else Mirabaur. They were both dead now, whichever one was which. Yet they were still no closer to being able to break away and look for Rokey and Flaskamper. Each of their opponents was an excellent swordsman, and he and his friends were all tiring. For the first time since he had made the decision to accept this quest as his own, he was having real doubts about its outcome.

He glanced away from his present opponent, a young blonde man with more enthusiasm than adeptness, and quickly assessed the situation. Fia was locked in combat with a man twice her size. Though he was far stronger, she was using her size and superior agility to her full advantage. Lorq and Kyzee were holding their own, each battling three opponents simultaneously. And Ely – poor Ely; He had not yet fully recovered from the beating he had received, and his foe looked to have the better of him. When he finished with this one, he would have to –

It happened then. He had looked away – been distracted for just a tik too long. He missed a parry, and felt the young man's sword bite into him, slicing through his tunic and into his abdomen. His reaction was more from surprise than from pain. He could hardly believe it, and at the hand of this youngster...

Gods, no, he thought. *Not now. Please, not now. Not before my mission is complete. I must do more – I must redeem...myself.*

The blood flowed through his hands, spilled out onto the ground.

I guessed that the ground would be crimson, but I did not think that any of the blood would be mine. Your arrogance has undone you Stamford, and now your chance is gone.

The dark man fell to his knees. His opponent had already left him for dead, rushing off to join the group that was fighting with Lorq. The sounds of battle grew dimmer and dimmer in his ears, and in the distance, he thought he could hear music – the sound of a reed flute, trilling softly as the ground came up to meet him.

*   *   *

The abbot was thoroughly enjoying himself, tormenting Rokey, dragging out the inevitable.

"I've so longed for this moment," he said gleefully. "So many times, I've awakened in the night, in agony from the scars of my punishment. To alleviate the pain, I would think of *your* pain – the pain that one day I would see in those pretty brown...but no, they are gold now. I'm sure there is an interesting story behind that, but no matter. There will be such pain in them soon, and I will have the satisfaction of knowing that it was *I* who put it there."

Rokey had tried desperately to think of a way out, or, at least a way for him to free his lover. But there *was* no way; no way at all.

Crinshire picked up a pail of water and, whirling abruptly, threw the contents on Flaskamper. The elf gasped and came awake.

"What's happening?" he said, dazed and disoriented. "Where am I? *Chatka?*"

"Flash, I'm here!" Rokey called.

The abbot approached Flaskamper. Chained as he was, with his hands over his head, he was completely helpless. Rokey's knuckles whitened as he gripped the bars of his cage.

"Watch this, lover boy," Crinshire called cheerfully to Rokey. "Watch this!"

With one hand he grabbed Flaskamper's forehead, slamming it backwards against the wall. Then with the other hand, in one fluid motion, he grabbed a dagger from his belt and drew it across the elf's slender throat. The abbot cackled as blood began to spurt from the wound.

"Let's see it, lover!" Crinshire shrieked. "Let me see the pain in those pretty eyes!"

Now Rokey screamed. The world collapsed around him like a snow-laden tent, and he could see nothing in front of him but the life's blood pouring from Flaskamper's neck. The entire room seemed to grow red with it. Then, from somewhere in the distance, he thought he heard the sound of pounding hooves, of a thousand horses galloping at full stride. The din of it was deafening, and his eardrums felt as though they might burst.

Let me see the pain in those pretty eyes!

There was more than pain there, though. More than anger. From the deepest recesses of his soul bubbled a white-hot fury, which overwhelmed all of his senses. Rokey could feel himself losing control. It was as though his body was being taken over, and all he could do was stand helplessly by and allow it. The pressure continued to build. Some aspect of him was growing, trying to break free of – of what?

And then, the world exploded. The cage that held Rokey flew apart, into a thousand pieces – a thousand projectiles hurtling across the room. The scene slowed, just long enough for Rokey to send out a mental shield to protect Flash from the flying metal. Then the combustion resumed in full force. A large, flat, metal chunk from the shattered cage caught Crinshire, shearing the top of his head cleanly off. The abbot was dead before he struck the floor.

The boiling fury continued. The door burst open, and Brother Barrow rushed into the room. He took one look at the carnage in front of him and cried out in terror. Then he tried to run; to Rokey though, he was barely moving at all. He stretched out his mind and seized the panic-stricken brother, turning him slowly around – forcing him to face the wrath that he had wrought. Whatever Barrow saw, it caused him to open his mouth again to scream, only this time, no sound emerged. The great, strapping man lost all control of his bodily functions, soiling himself like a frightened animal.

"P-p-p-please," was all Brother Barrow managed to utter, his voice nothing but a wisp in the wind.

Then Rokey could see the man's mind in front of him, a jumbled mass of confusion and fear.

"Don't," he heard a small voice cry from far, far away. "Don't do it."

The sound of the pounding hooves returned, though, drowning out the little voice, and the river of rage overflowed again, pouring its molten contents into Brother Barrow's already addled brain. The man produced one last scream before the light in his eyes was forever extinguished.

Rokey felt nothing. He let the body of Brother Barrow fall, like a rag doll, to the floor. For a moment, there was absolute silence. Then a new explosion came – an explosion of grief hit Rokey so hard that he fell to his knees. He forced himself back up and across the room, to the far wall. With just the ghost of a thought, Flaskamper's chains fell open, and the elf came tumbling forward. Rokey caught him gently and took him up in his arms. He heard what he thought was the wail of a banshee, but soon realized that it was only his own cries of grief. The agony was so strong, that he was sure that the force of it would tear him to pieces. And he welcomed that. His love was gone; he wanted to be gone as well.

Then slowly, amid the chaos, a new sound began to creep into his consciousness.

ka-thump.

It was so faint as to be barely audible at all, yet it carried above all the other madness swirling in his head.

ka- thump.

It was only an occasional drumbeat. Not the strong, steady rhythm that would give one any hope, any hope at all that life could remain there. But along with that faint, irregular beat, the little voice returned, the one that had been drowned out by the storms of anger and grief.

With the power to destroy, it said, *comes the power to heal.*

"What?" he asked out loud, not quite grasping what had been said.

With the power to destroy, comes the power –

"– TO HEAL!" Rokey shouted at the top of his lungs.

He laid Flaskamper's lifeless body carefully onto the floor. Gingerly, as though he were handling a butterfly's wing, he placed his hand over his lover's ravaged, bloody throat, and focused every fiber of his being on that single thought.

HEAL!

He felt a new energy now. Whereas before, the power had been red and scorching, now the flow felt like a cool blue river. Just as Rokey had been able to see the havoc he had wreaked in Brother Barrow's mind, so too could he see the cut in Flaskamper's neck closing, the blood vessels and muscles reconnecting, until it was fully healed. Other than a thin, white scar, it was as though the elf had never been wounded at all.

There was more to do, though. Flaskamper had lost much of his life's blood, and he was no longer breathing. Rokey concentrated again, picturing the cool breath of air that flew in through the open windows in the springtime. He guided it into the elf's still chest, making it rise and fall. Again and again he sent the air in, until Flaskamper finally took a breath on his own...then another. The random, intermittent drumbeat that had first drawn Rokey's attention was steady now – weak, but steady. With time, and care, he would recover.

Rokey had just time to breathe a sigh of relief, before yet another strange sensation overtook him. It felt as though he were shrinking – collapsing down into himself. Intense, near-mortal fatigue flooded through his body. He tried to stand up and walk, but made it only a step or two before he crumpled into a heap.

"I did it," he thought as he blacked out. "Even if I'm dying...Flash will live."

Chapter 32:

Wreckage and Revival

Flaskamper awoke as he was being loaded onto a litter by two brothers. He tried to sit up, but his head spun and he sank back down. He had never felt so weak in his entire life. One of the brothers stepped away and returned a moment later, accompanied by an angel.

"Fia." His lips formed the words, but no sound came out.

Fia smiled at him, but there was so much pain behind her eyes that he immediately grew alarmed.

"Rokey."

"He'll be alright," she told him, after reading Rokey's name on his lips. "He's unconscious. I don't know what happened to him, or to – to the other two men who were in that room with you. But Brother Pilarus, he's the Master healer, he says that he thinks Rokey will probably come out of it eventually, though he could give us no ideas as to when."

Fia paused. She was hesitating, he could tell. He mouthed for her to spill.

"Flaskamper," she said. "Flash...it's Stamford, honey."

Tears started to spill down her cheeks. A look of panic spread across his face. She saw the question in his eyes.

"Not yet," she answered. "But his wound is beyond anything the healer can repair. I was just with him when the –" her voice broke " – when the brother came to tell me you were awake."

Flaskamper tried to get up, but had no strength at all in his muscles. He struck the ground in frustration. Fia quickly signaled for two of the brothers.

"Please, take him to see Stamford," she instructed them. "I'll let you talk to him privately," she told the elf. "I'll join you both after a little bit."

The brothers lifted the litter and bore their charge away. It was only now that he noticed that he was no longer in the underground room, the one in which he had been chained. He remembered so little. It seemed to him that his throat – and now, he could not speak. What in the name of the gods had happened down there?

As they passed into another room, Flaskamper caught sight of Lorq and Kyzee. They had both received wounds, and someone, the healer he supposed, had bandaged them up. Lorq was wrapped in Kyzee's arms, sobbing inconsolably. The Saebrilite held him gently, an empty look on her face.

Grief, he thought, *grief and shock. Goddess Secta, please do not let me be too late.*

He was not too late. Stamford was still alive. The brothers set him down next to the litter on which the dark man had been made as comfortable as possible. With every ounce of strength he could gather, Flaskamper righted himself, so that he could look at his best friend. Stamford had been stripped of his tunic, and his abdomen completely bandaged. The dressing was soaked with blood, though; it was obvious that the wound was a mortal one. Flaskamper thought of the owl's eye, still somewhere among his possessions, but then remembered his mother's instructions; the eye could swap only life energies, not physical wounds. Even if he *could* find the thing in time, it would be of no use.

Stamford's face was covered in sweat. Straining to reach, the elf picked up a small towel from the floor next to him and passed it over the dark man's brow. At the touch of the cloth on his head, his eyes fluttered open. For a moment they were empty and sightless, but then they focused on Flaskamper, and Stamford smiled.

"I'm...glad you...made it," he said haltingly. "They thought...the worst...for a moment there."

Flaskamper gestured to his throat, furious that he could not speak. Stamford gave a chuckle that turned into a wet, heavy cough.

"What a treat," he said when he had recovered himself. "I get to talk...to you...and you can't...talk back...for once."

For some reason, the little jibe broke Flaskamper's heart more than anything else could have. His body began to shake silently, and tears poured from his swollen eyes.

"Hey...hey," said Stamford. "Cut that out...now. I need to tell you...something, and there's not...much time."

The elf fought to recover himself, wiping the tears from his eyes and forcing his body to stop trembling. When Stamford was satisfied that Flash was sufficiently composed, he reached out for his hand.

"I just wanted...to say," he continued, "how glad I am...that you have...your family back. See...I've always thought of you...as a son, Flash. And I know...what losing you...would do...to me."

Stamford was struggling. The flute was trilling louder now, its master just around the corner, waiting patiently for him. But he must finish first. He had been given time to speak to Lorq, and to Fia. He must finish what he wanted to tell Flash.

"Fia... told me," he pressed on, "they think... that Rokey's.... going... to be alright. I *know* that he is. I can... feel it... here." He put a hand to his heart. "I've fulfilled... my quest... helping him get... this far, but his – his own quest... still has... a long way... to go. Stay with him, Flash. Help... him... to help... Firma. Promise me you will... son."

Flaskamper nodded his solemn promise, and Stamford smiled and squeezed his hand. Then, suddenly, in that next instant, he was gone. The elf dissolved into tears once again; from his throat, sharp, ragged sobs tore, just loud enough to bring Fia and Lorq running. Fia sat and Lorq knelt, and together they wept, until there were no tears left to cry.

*   *   *

Rokey awoke three days later, and also grieved for Stamford. He would often wonder, in the months and years that followed, what the dark man might have said to him had he also been there at the end. From Flaskamper's account of his final words to him, it seemed clear that he had understood some things that were still a complete mystery to Rokey. When he visited him in the temple mausoleum, where Stamford's body would lay until spring came again, Rokey thanked him for all he had done, and asked him, if it wouldn't be too much trouble, to keep watch over them all as their quest continued.

"I could sure use the guidance," he said with a tearful smile.

Fia explained to him what had been done to rescue them, and how things outside had abruptly changed after a tremendous noise had sounded somewhere deep in the ground. They now assumed that it had come from the room in which he and Flaskamper were being held. A few moments later, many of the brothers had suddenly stopped fighting and simply stood in the middle of the commons, groggy, as though they had just awakened from a long sleep. The rest were easily subdued or killed. It was only then, after the battle, that they had discovered the gravely wounded Stamford, and later still that they found the secret chamber under the ritual room. He and Flaskamper had been lying there, unconscious, in the midst of what could only be described as a scene of utter devastation.

For his part, Rokey had no memory of anything that had taken place after he saw the Abbot slash Flaskamper's throat. Master magicians from the Brotherhood surmised that from within Rokey had risen some tremendous force, which had totally seized control of him, destroyed his enemies and, somehow, healed Flaskamper's mortal wound. There remained, however, no trace of that power now. Only his golden sidhe eyes gave any indication that he was anything but an ordinary human boy. The nightmares and flashes of memory would not begin for some months yet.

The Brotherhood had been severely compromised. A substantial number of its finest minds had been drawn willingly to darkness by the persuasive arguments and charm of Brother Barrow. Many of them had fought the company to the death that day in the yard. Those that lived were shipped away to Duncileer, to be tried under the Treaty of Common Justice, which the monastery held with the city. The Noble Contemplative was in no shape to mete out justice of its own at the moment. Ely jumped to the administrative forefront as soon as he had taken his vows, helping the remaining elders to set up a restoration council, and recall brothers from far afield to help make the Brotherhood whole again. Nevertheless, it would take years to rebuild it to what it had once been. Until that time, it remained vulnerable.

Two weeks later, when all had sufficiently recovered their strength, the friends prepared to leave the monastery, and the Emerald Mountains. Their destinations this time, however, were not the same. Fia had decided to continue on to Respite, the place where the four of them had been headed when they'd first encountered Rokey. With gold from both Flaskamper and the Brotherhood, she had the means to afford a good, long rest. She also had the letter from the mayor of Riversedge, which she expected would later secure her a fine position in Respite's royal court. Her good-byes were quick ones, for her nerves and emotions were still raw from Stamford's death. Though Rokey knew they would miss her, and she them, he sensed that, right now, they only served as a painful reminder of the loss she had suffered, which was deeper than any of them could have imagined.

Lorq and Kyzee were traveling to Duncileer, where they planned to marry. Flaskamper had had an even more difficult time saying good-bye to the giant than he had to Fia. The two of them took a long walk together, in spite of the fact that it was now freezing cold outside. Rokey did not ask what they had discussed, and Flash, this one time, did not offer to tell him. That was all right though; some experiences were for friends alone to share. Lorq and Kyzee had pledged to the both of them that they would come at a moment's notice if and when they were needed again. Rokey was glad of this pledge, for he knew that his quest was not over, and that nothing could rival a pair of good friends at your back.

They said their farewells at the four corners crossing, where the giant and the Saebrilite headed north, and Rokey and Flaskamper went east, beginning a long journey that would take them through Riversedge and Tanohar. Eventually, they would join up with an elf squadron led by Flaskamper's brother, Alrontin. The brothers had arranged, via messenger hawks, to meet at an appointed place and time and to travel all together back to Elfwood. There had been no question of where the boys would go. Flaskamper knew his family needed him, and Rokey's next move, whatever it turned out to be, could just as easily be accomplished from there. Besides, Rokey teased, the Elfwood palace had the most comfortable beds in all of Firma. Flaskamper responded that it would be even nicer, now that they'd be sharing one. The two stopped in the middle of the road and shared a kiss, each from under his long heavy cloak. They had a cold, hard road ahead, but Rokey was filled with warmth and joy, for Flaskamper was with him still. Only the faintest white line along his beloved's neck remained, to serve as a constant reminder to him of what he had so nearly lost.

Epilogue

T he High Lord listened with great interest to the report from his underling, one of his personal spies, who had just come all the way across Firma from the Emerald Mountains. When the young man finished his story, he sagged visibly, obviously exhausted from his long journey. The High Lord wasn't quite finished with him though.

"You're quite certain the part about the Faerie is accurate?" he asked.

"Yes, my lord," said the lad. "I saw his eyes meself. Gold as a sunrise they was. And the story I got straight from the horse's mouth, or near enough. I listened in when brother Ely gave an account to what's left of the brotherhood's high council – an accurate enough account I should think, sir."

"Indeed. Well done, Clement," the High Lord responded. "Go now and get a good meal and some rest."

The young man bowed and exited the room, leaving the High Lord to ponder the astounding story he had just heard.

I should never have trusted Barrow and that fool Crinshire with such an important task, he thought. *Still, it may be just as well, given this new information...*

He stood and went to the window. From here, on a clear day, one could see far past Harrow Yawn, all the way to Vanquadi Mountain, far to the south. Today, however, the weather was dark and overcast, and the distant mountains were obscured by thick, gray clouds. He could see only the lands of Moribar now, the Wormspine mountain range, on which the castle sat, and the forest of Gloomsveldt. He

Printed in the United States
106728LV00001B/51/A